Talk of the Ton

Eloisa James

Julia London

Rebecca Hagan Lee

Jacqueline Navin

JOVE BOOKS, NEW YORK

THE BERKLEY PUBLISHING GROUP
Published by the Penguin Group
Penguin Group (USA) Inc.
375 Hudson Street, New York, New York 10014, USA
Penguin Group (Canada), 10 Alcorn Avenue, Toronto, Ontario M4V 3B2, Canada
(a division of Pearson Penguin Canada Inc.)
Penguin Books Ltd., 80 Strand, London WC2R 0RL, England
Penguin Group Ireland, 25 St. Stephen's Green, Dublin 2, Ireland (a division of Penguin Books Ltd.)
Penguin Group (Australia), 250 Camberwell Road, Camberwell, Victoria 3124, Australia
(a division of Pearson Australia Group Pty. Ltd.)
Penguin Books India Pvt. Ltd., 11 Community Centre, Panchsheel Park, New Delhi—110 017, India
Penguin Group (NZ), Cnr. Airborne and Rosedale Roads, Albany, Auckland 1310, New Zealand
(a division of Pearson New Zealand Ltd.)
Penguin Books (South Africa) (Pty.) Ltd., 24 Sturdee Avenue, Rosebank, Johannesburg 2196, South Africa

Penguin Books Ltd., Registered Offices: 80 Strand, London WC2R 0RL, England

TALK OF THE TON

A Jove Book / published by arrangement with the authors

ISBN: 0-7394-5331-9

JOVE®
Jove Books are published by The Berkley Publishing Group,
a division of Penguin Group (USA) Inc.,
375 Hudson Street, New York, New York 10014.
JOVE is a registered trademark of Penguin Group (USA) Inc.
The "J" design is a trademark belonging to Penguin Group (USA) Inc.

PRINTED IN THE UNITED STATES OF AMERICA

Contents

A Proper Englishwoman

Eloisa James

Chapter One

*In Which a Quote from Shakespeare
Insults the Stodgy and Horrifies the Staid*

March 15, 1817

Lady Cecilia Petworth to her sister, the Countess of Bredelbane

Dearest Sister,

I take my pen in hand although it is almost dawn, because I know you will be most distressed when the news of this evening's entertainment at Sandleford House reaches you. Kerr has made quite a spectacle of himself, and although there's nothing new in that (as we've said of your godson before, he gives new definition to the term rakehell), last night his debauchery reached new heights. To the horror of all, he escorted a French *très-coquette* to Lady Sandleford's ball. Making mischief as usual, Lord Dressel strolled up to the couple and asked Kerr if he'd set a date to marry his fiancée. Kerr merely tightened his arm around his bird of paradise (for, not to mince words, she was no better) and drawled the most excruciating vulgarity:

something like *not until she has my baby in her belly and my ring on her finger.* Lady Sandleford was naturally quite insulted by such unseemly behavior under her roof, and I'm certain that the story is traveling like wildfire . . . one must be grateful that Kerr's mother has gone to her rest. I shall write again tomorrow but, dearest, I think the time has come to put your foot down and cause your benighted godson to marry that poor girl—what is her name? It's too late at night for an old head like mine. I shall write again in the morn.

Yours in all affection,
Cecilia, Lady Petworth

March 16, 1817

The Countess of Bredelbane to her godson, Gilbert Baring-Gould, Earl of Kerr

Kerr,

I have received a distressing communication from my sister regarding your behavior—or should I say, the lack of it—while attending Lady Sandleford's ball. What needs have you, pray, to leave your usual haunts and attend the assemblies of my friends? Of course poor Cecilia didn't recognize the provenance of your disgusting reply to Dressel; Shakespeare was never in her line. The least you could have done was to reverse the quotation and put the bit around the ring before the question of the baby. Your fiancée will no doubt be horrified to find that her ability to get with child (and that without your knowledge) is on the lips of every Londoner. I demand you make haste to the country and marry Emma immediately, preferably with a special license. I shall expect to hear that you have left for St. Albans by tomorrow at the latest.

Yours with all proper esteem,
Countess of Bredelbane

March 16, 1817

Mrs. Broughton to The Hon. Emma Loudan, St. Albans,
Hertfordshire

Dear Miss Loudan,

I am not convinced that you will remember me, since we had only the slightest of acquaintances at Miss Proudfoot's School for Ladies. My maiden name was Laneham. I write you from the deep reverence I feel toward you and indeed, all my fellow students at Miss Proudfoot's School. The Earl of Kerr spoke of you in such a fashion last evening that I had difficulty restraining myself. To be precise, he said that he would not marry you, implying that you were with child. I know that this information will come as a great shock, given the unpleasant implication as regards your reputation. I hasten to tell you that no one believed it in the least. If our positions were reversed, and I as isolated from the town as you have been, I should wish to be told of his disgraceful comment.

In hopes that you are not angered by my communication,
Mrs. Broughton

March 16, 1817

The Countess of Bredelbane to the Earl of Kerr

Kerr,

As regards my note earlier this morning, I have now had missives from Mrs. Witter and Lady Horne. Lady Horne informs me that you exemplify the depraved appetite of this vicious age. Picture my dismay on hearing my godson described thusly. How long has it been since you even visited St. Albans? I know that you have had a difficult time since Walter's death, but your brother would not wish you to lose all sense of decency. Next week at the latest I shall expect to hear of your nuptials.

The Countess & etc.

March 17, 1817

The Earl of Kerr to the Countess of Bredelbane

My dear, dearest Godmama,

    I can't take myself to the country today and marry my provincial paragon; I have an appointment to look at a horse. And a fencing match to attend as well. She will have to wait. Granted, I haven't seen Miss Loudan for some time, but she seemed clear-headed enough when I last found myself in St. Albans. She won't think twice of these rumors of my degeneracy, should they make their way to her.

    Affectionately yours,
    Gil

March 17, 1817

Lady Dyott to her cousin, The Hon. Emma Loudan, St. Albans, Hertfordshire

Dearest Emma,

    This will be a quick note, as Dyott awaits me. We're off to Tattersall's to find a pony for Garret who is quite a bruising rider at age five, and does us proud. You know how much I hate bibble-babble, but I'm told Kerr informed a roomful that you are too old to bear a child; I merely wished to reassure you that I was all of forty-one when Garret was born, and since you are half that age, breeding is not a concern. I only have to think of your sporting nature, and I have no concern for your future. Thank God you didn't marry Kerr already, because he's nothing more than a job horse, and you deserve a high-stepper. Do come to London, and we'll find you a proper spouse.

    Much love,
    Your cousin Mary, Lady Dyott

March 18, 1817

The Countess of Bredelbane to the Earl of Kerr

The news of your appalling jest has spread throughout the town. I have no doubt but that Emma has heard every loathsome detail. Can you not consider your duty, which is clearly to provide an heir to the estate without delay?

The Countess & etc.

March 18, 1817

Gilbert Baring-Gould, Earl of Kerr, to the Countess of Bredelbane

Dearest Godmama,

I'll marry Miss Loudan someday, but not this week. And certainly not due to a jest on my part, if admittedly in poor taste. Don't you think that the *ton* has become alarmingly illiterate, given that no one seems to recognize a Shakespeare play? I shouldn't worry about the question of an heir; I've heard that country air is remarkably healthy. I can turn out five or six little Kerrs in the next decade.

Yours with affection,

Gil

March 19, 1817

Lady Flaskell to her sister, The Hon. Emma Loudan

Dearest,

I was suffering from a stomach upset and so missed the initial flurry of news about Kerr. Darling, I'm so sorry! But we must move quickly, Emma, given that your betrothal obviously must be terminated. You are all of twenty-four now, and fiancés, especially those with a hefty fortune and title, do not grow on trees. You have been immured in the country so long that you have no idea what it is like here. Women are considered decayed at two and twenty. You must come to London at once and find a husband. I shall arrive tomorrow and expect to find you packed.

    With love,
    Your sister Bethany Lynn

March 19, 1817

The Earl of Kerr to Mademoiselle Benoit

Madeline, *ma cherie,*

    While I naturally adore you and kiss your feet in pure admiration, it would not be prudent for me to accompany you to the opera tonight. The Puritans are out in force. In fact, I am very much afraid that I shall have to forgo the pleasure of your company in the future. Please accept this ruby as the smallest hint of my regard for you. *Tu seras toujours dan mon cœur même si tu ne seras pas toujours avec moi.*
    Kerr

March 19, 1817

The Countess of Bredelbane to the Earl of Kerr

Kerr:

    I can't force you to abide honorably by the vows that your father made on your behalf. I take your behavior much amiss though, and I say that to you seriously. I shall write Emma myself and try to soothe her feelings. I've no doubt but that she's hearing the same as I: that you intend to marry some rubbishing

Frenchwoman with putative claims to being a lady. Do so, Kerr, and you will never darken my door again.

The Countess of Bredalbane

March 20, 1817

Gilbert Baring-Gould, Earl of Kerr, to the Countess of Bredalbane

Tsk, tsk, dearest Godmama.

You who know your Shakespeare so well should avoid clichés about darkened doors and such like. When my sainted godfather was alive, did he object to your sharp tongue? I go about my business with a rejoicing heart, knowing that you will soothe Miss Loudan's troubled brow. You needn't worry about Mademoiselle Benoit. While I shall always find a French accent *irrésistible,* I concede that the country charmer is my fate. I also know that you, my sainted godmother, would never wish for me, her beloved godson, to be unhappy, so you will forgive me if I cease to think about marriage this very moment.

Yours & Etc.

Gil

Chapter Two

March 21, 1817

The Countess of Bredelbane to Gilbert Baring-Gould, Earl of Kerr

Kerr:

You were always an impudent child; I shall never forget how you made me laugh when you first arrived in my house, and your parents gone but a month. Still, there is an edge to your jests that gives me concern. How dare you speak of being unhappy to marry Emma? The poor girl will surely have need of valor, given that your foolish quotation has gone so terribly awry. I am surprised that she has not yet terminated your engagement. Expect me tomorrow after nuncheon.

Yours & etc.

The Countess

.   .   .

15 St. James's Place, London

"You are the shame of your sex," Lord Lockwood said, stretching out his long legs and regarding his boots with pleasure. "You make far too much of yourself, and have strayed into dissolute habits, and now your doom is upon you. I am inordinantly happy to see it happen."

"Don't be so intolerably smug," his companion retorted. "Your reputation is as low as mine has ever been. 'Twas *you* who thought it'd be a good idea to bring Madeline and her friend to Sandleford's house. I said it'd be a boring affair."

"It wasn't boring after you made such an ass of yourself quoting the bard," Lockwood pointed out. "Would you put on a shirt, if you please? It turns my stomach to look at your shoulders. You're muscled like a barge man, Kerr. Grotesquely unfashionable, I might add."

"The boxing does it," the earl replied, unperturbed. He was seated at his writing desk, wearing only black pantaloons. "At any rate, I didn't ask you here. I've a mountain of correspondence to get through, and I'm expecting my secretary any moment."

"I'll take myself off. Were you foolish enough to invest in Hensing's canal scheme?"

"No. It sounded intriguing, but the man's a fool."

"I suppose that's why your estate keeps growing, while my living shrinks," Lockwood said. "But don't you think there's a chance he'll make a go of it?"

"Unlikely," Kerr stated, not even looking up as his pen scratched over a leaf of stationery.

But Lockwood paused at the door to the chamber and turned back, driven by insatiable curiosity. Kerr had finished sanding his letter and was reaching for a new sheet of foolscap. "So, are you going to marry, then? To be specific, are you going to marry Madeline Benoit, as all London appears to believe?"

Kerr narrowed his eyes. "You think less of me than I deserve."

They'd been friends since Oxford, and yet Lockwood flinched slightly at the expression in Kerr's eyes. "I merely thought—"

"I heard about your bet in White's. You'll lose that money, as you'll lose any blunt you put into Hensing's canal. I shall fulfill my obligations to Miss Loudan," Kerr said, turning back to his sheet as if he had no further interest in the conversation.

A grin spread across Lockwood's face. Kerr looked up and frowned. "What are you smirking about?"

"You just made up for Hensing's canal. I placed a bet in White's that you'd marry Mademoiselle Benoit, but that was only to give Etherege enough courage to take my bet on the other side . . . that you would honor your betrothal."

"Etherege must have thought you were drunk," Kerr observed. "Why the hell would you bet one way in White's and place the opposite bet with him?"

"I gather he didn't notice that the bet in White's was for a shilling or two. He put a good four hundred pounds on your propensity to marry the mademoiselle, thinking I was too castaway to remember my own opinion."

Kerr snorted. "Meet me at Miss Bridget's tonight?"

Miss Bridget was a Frenchwoman who ran a house that was not precisely one of ill repute but damn near close, to Lockwood's mind. "I see that your taste for Frenchwomen is much like the English taste for food: predicated on quantity rather than quality," he remarked.

Kerr smiled faintly. "I thought it would amuse the *ton* to

see me with a woman other than Madeline. We'll take one of Miss Bridget's young friends to the opera."

Lockwood laughed. "That'll put the cat amongst the pigeons."

Kerr turned back to his papers. "Quite."

Chapter Three

March 22, 1817

Mrs. Broughton to The Hon. Emma Loudan, St. Albans, Hertfordshire

Dear Miss Loudan,

Thank you so much for your gracious response to my letter; to be sure, I trembled before I took pen in hand. I should most dislike to be thought a gossipmonger, or some such, and yet I have every sympathy with your difficult position. I consider it my honor—if not my pleasure—to offer you such tidbits of news as might interest you. I hasten, then, to reassure you that it is no longer believed that the Earl of Kerr intends to marry Mademoiselle Benoit. Last night he and some friends made an appearance at the Royal Opera House accompanied by a group of young Frenchwomen. Everyone noted that Kerr paid particular attention to one of them, and since she cannot be considered a possibility for matrimony, the consensus is that your fiancé has a propensity for women of Gallic origin. This is a most unseemly topic, and I feel reprehensible for even bringing it to the attention of an unmarried lady. But my loyalty to Miss Proudfoot's School rises above manners.

Yours with all esteem,

Mrs. Broughton

Emma Loudan, daughter of Viscount Howitt, was painstakingly painting bees, one after another. *Bees,* she thought to herself, *are profoundly uninspiring insects: after one has painted one round yellow body and then another, one has learned all there is to know about bee painting.* But there was no relief in sight: Titania and Bottom both mentioned bees in *A Midsummer Night's Dream,* and Mr. Tey had decided that bees must swarm over every backdrop, and never mind that the audience would think the insects were flying marigolds. Emma sighed and dipped her brush into yellow paint.

She was just putting a finishing touch on one of three beehives when the door opened.

"Lady Flaskell," announced the butler, Wilson.

Emma put down her brush just in time as Bethany hurdled herself across the room and threw her arms around Emma. "Careful!" she said, laughing. "You'll get painted."

"It's quite all right. I'm wearing nothing but rags for the trip."

Emma put her little sister at arm's length and glanced from the saffron-colored flying ribbons on her glorious little bonnet to the tips of her silk slippers. "Rags are looking better every moment," she observed, untying her voluminous apron.

Bethany's eyes narrowed at the sight. "Your gown *must* have been created by Madame Maisonnat!" she cried. "The

Duchess of Silverton was wearing just the same costume in sage green, only last week. Everyone was talking about it. How on earth did you obtain that gown here, in the depths of the country, and without coming to town?"

"I have my means," Emma said, tucking a stray strand of hair behind her ear.

"What means are those?" Bethany demanded. "I could beg, plead, and cry at Madame's door, and I'm quite certain that she would fulfill her other orders before mine."

Emma glanced down at her morning gown. It was designed *à la militaire,* in amber-colored poplin with garnet buttons marching down the bodice. It followed her curves to a T and made her feel like an extremely feminine brigadier general. She smiled at her little sister. "It's not a dark secret. Madame knows my measurements, and she simply sends me those gowns that she thinks would interest me."

"Before anyone else?" Bethany said, her eyes narrowed.

Emma grinned. "I also pay her approximately twice the customary price, for her trouble. I must dress well in order to keep up my spirits here in the country."

"Piffle! You could join me in London any moment you pleased. Mama's death was well over a year ago now. The truth is that you like being immured in St. Albans, Emma." Bethany walked over to the stage set, with its fresh paint and clusters of bees. "How can you prefer to sit about in the county and paint? Are those insects?"

"Bees. Obviously."

"Proving my point absolutely. Painting insects while dressed in Madame Maisonnat's latest creation! You've lost your wits."

Put that way, Emma could see what she meant. "I like painting sets," she said.

"That's irrelevant," Bethany said. "For once, you must take me seriously, Emma. You are in trouble." She took a deep breath, her chest swelling impressively. "You are in danger of becoming an unmarried woman!"

"I've been an unmarried woman for four and twenty years," Emma noted, opening the door. "Shall we retire to the morning room and have some tea? You must be fatigued after your journey."

Bethany trotted through the door and down the hall, talking all the way and paying no attention to the presence of the family butler and two footmen. She finished up as she entered the morning room: "The point is that *unmarried women* are dreadfully out of fashion. If they ever were in fashion at all."

"Wilson, will you bring us a tea tray?" Emma asked the butler.

"Immediately, Miss Loudan," he said, bowing his way out of the morning room.

"You really mustn't speak like that in front of Wilson," Emma said, settling herself next to the fire. "When he is upset, he falls prey to stomachaches."

Bethany plumped herself into the settee and turned her reticule upside down. "I cut a piece from a gossip column that you must read . . . ah! Here it is!" She waved a bit of newspaper in the air. "From *La Belle Monde,* and it says quite firmly that there is nothing more fatal to a woman than the lack of a husband. Listen to this: *'Though they are the very ornament of their sex, they will await invitations that do not arrive. When they are invited to an occasion, one sees them flock to the side of the ballroom, like crows made dismal by rain.'* How awful, Emma! You do *not* look well in black."

Emma was beginning to feel nettled. "I have a prospective husband," she said coolly. "Simply because Kerr hasn't yet presented himself to undergo the rite of matrimony doesn't mean that he won't do so in the near future.

And besides, I firmly reject the implications of that piece of drivel. I could find another husband in five minutes, if I wished."

"How long has it been since Kerr visited you?" Bethany demanded.

Emma hesitated.

Bethany answered for her. "He was coming last Christmas—No! It was *two* Christmases ago, but then he traveled the Continent after his brother died. And before that—" She stopped, trying to remember.

"It's been three years," Emma said, feeling a mild astonishment at the fact. She was so comfortable living as she was that she tended to forget her fiancé's existence. "I was so glad not to hear from him during Mama's illness, since I had no wish to leave her, that I haven't taken close account. But he has been in mourning for his brother, you know."

"Mourning!" Bethany shrieked. "From all accounts, he took himself to Paris and enjoyed himself there so much that he had to fight at least two duels with outraged husbands. And the only reason he wasn't challenged much more often was because he's so skilled with the short sword. He told the Prince of Wales, in front of a large group, that he had drunk so much wine every night that he wouldn't remember if he had had an affair with the Empress Josephine herself."

Emma laughed. "A formidable amount of wine must have been called for to reach such a state."

Bethany scowled at her. "A disgrace! That man is a disgrace! *You* are a disgrace to let him behave thus! He hasn't even come here to apologize for those remarks of last week, has he? The churlishness of it! Obviously Kerr already sees you as a dismal crow on the side of the ballroom."

"The truth is, Bethany, we hardly know each other. I doubt we've met more than three times. Well, four, if you count his brother's funeral. Perhaps the man resents his father's actions in kitting him up with an infant bride."

Bethany snorted. "He shouldn't be such a fool. It's an excellent match, with nothing against it but his own lackluster character and your placid acceptance of his neglect."

Emma felt her temper rising. "And just what do you propose that I should have done? I spent three years nursing Mama, as you well know. When she died, should I have rushed to London and tracked the man down like an errant child who has missed his supper?"

"Of course," Bethany said. "Women must needs think of matrimony, because men have no inclination to it. What possible incentive has the man to bring himself to the altar? He doesn't need your inheritance, he clearly feels no need for an heir, and he's fully occupied by flirting with every woman with a French lisp and a glad eye!"

"Distasteful," Emma said, pressing her lips together.

"All men are distasteful by nature," Bethany said with a wave of her hand. "Women are only distasteful if they wither into old age without a husband at their side."

"Marriage has made you unaccountably vulgar," Emma observed.

Bethany raised her chin. "It's my duty as your sister to call a spade a spade. I mean to speak to Father as well."

Emma laughed shortly. "Good luck with that. He's recently discovered that a flightless bird has been observed in the Galāpagos Islands. I believe it's a cassowary, or cassolary, or some such. He has hardly surfaced from his study in days, except for breakfast."

Her little sister chewed her lip for a second. Then she said, "We can't bicker over this, Emma. It's too important."

"I'm not worried about marriage. I have always had

faith that Kerr would fulfill the terms of our engagement. I don't know him well, but I would swear that he is an honorable man. In fact, I would guess that he is trying to drive me into terminating the arrangement as a sort of honorable escape."

"Whether Kerr would eventually announce his intention to marry is irrelevant. His rudeness necessitates that you find a new spouse. You cannot marry a man who speaks of you in such terms and without even a hint of apology!"

Emma could see that her little sister was fairly pulsating with anxiety. "I shall not become an old maid," she said cheerfully. "I'm not beyond my last prayers yet, you know." She smiled over her teacup. "If you're looking for an appealing display of modesty here, my dear, you won't find it. I have avoided London from disinclination, never due to fear of the competition."

"Well, I know *that*," Bethany said, eyeing her sister. Emma didn't look decayed, by any interpretation of the word. No crow ever had copper-colored hair swept into an elegant knot from which a few curls tumbled onto creamy shoulders. Even a little sister could see her eyes had an erotic tilt to them. "You're too beautiful and funny to become an ape leader."

"As I said, I'm not worried," Emma said with a trace of impatience. "I'm disappointed that Kerr has made himself *persona non grata,* but if it's a challenge to find a husband at my age, all the better! I've never been one to shrink from a contest, have I?"

"More the opposite," Bethany said, thinking of how her elder sister loved to set herself a challenge, whether it was painting theatrical scenery (unheard of amongst gentlewomen), or winning archery matches. "I just want you to marry well, come to London, and have some children," she said. Her hand fluttered to her stomach.

Emma's eyes narrowed. Was her little sister looking rather plumper than usual? Bethany *plump,* even though she would never even touch a dessert because plumpness was not in fashion?

"Bethany!" she cried, jumping up. "Darling, are you carrying a child?"

Her little sister blushed. "Well, perhaps . . ."

But even as a five-year-old in the nursery, Bethany had always displayed an alarming tenacity. It was only a moment or two later that she observed that the future arrival of her child was precisely the reason that her sister must marry immediately.

"I need you in London," she said.

Emma looked at her narrowly. There was a hint of fear in her sister's voice. "All right," she said briskly. "I shall come to London and pick out a husband for myself. I doubt it will take a great deal of time. It's a pity, because Kerr rather suited me. He left me alone, he's handsome enough, and I like what I read of his speeches in Parliament. He seems intelligent."

"You couldn't," Bethany said with a shudder. "After he said such an appalling thing about you!"

"You mean that I'm too old to bear a child?" Emma inquired.

"That wasn't it. It was worse! I couldn't even tell you."

Emma fixed her with an elder sister's glare. "Tell me."

"He said that he wouldn't take you as wife until you had his baby in your belly and his ring on your finger."

There was a moment of silence.

"I shouldn't have told you," Bethany added morosely. "One is *not* supposed to discuss babies or bellies with unmarried ladies."

"Don't be a ninny," her sister said absently. "Mrs. Morrison in the village had her baby last week, by the way."

"Oh, were you there? Is it a lovely babe?"

"Just like his father, if without the beard, but rather adorable nonetheless. Of course I was there. Dr. Placket arrived a half hour late, as usual, and stinking of gin. Do you really mean that Kerr said *precisely* that sentence, Bethany?"

"Or thereabouts."

Emma laughed. "I said he was intelligent, didn't I? Well-read it seems, as well."

"Who cares for his brains? He's intolerably rude to speak of you in such a fashion."

"The man was quoting Shakespeare," Emma said. "I can't remember the exact quotation, but the line is from *All's Well That Ends Well.* A perfectly loathsome specimen of manhood, the Comte de Rousillon, announces that he won't accept his wife until she has the ring from his finger and his child to boot."

"I never liked Shakespeare. The plays are so long and invariably lurid."

"Don't be such a philistine, darling," Emma said with amusement.

"Why do you have that look about you?" Bethany demanded.

"I'm thinking. . . . Don't you suppose that Kerr's parents sent Father a ring at some point in the betrothal negotiations?"

"Negotiations?" Bethany repeated. "You mean, back when you were five years old?"

"Precisely."

"Well, I can tell you that John's family never sent me a ring. The only ring I received was the one he gave me when we married."

"It seems to me that there was talk of a ring," Emma said, puzzling over it. "I shall have to root Father out of his study and ask him."

"Why does it matter?" Bethany asked. "You may have the ring, but you still don't have the baby. And you can't—" She caught sight of her sister's face. "Oh, Emma, you can't!"

"He's challenged me," Emma said with a grin, a diabolical, mischievous, laughing grin. "He's thrown down the gauntlet, Bethany. You heard it yourself!"

"No, he didn't mean that!"

"You said that I need to marry quickly."

"But not—"

"And you said that I should have gone to London and forced him to marry me."

"Yes but, Emma, I didn't—"

"But darling, I'm just going to obey your express desires. I shall go up to London and force the man to marry me. I'll go on my own terms—or rather, on *his*. Where is my Shakespeare?"

Chapter Four

March 22, 1817

Lady Dyott to Miss Loudan, St. Albans, Hertfordshire

Dear Emma,

We bought the pony, and two other horses that caught Dyott's fancy. I'm writing to urge you to come to London; no one is talking of Kerr's impudent remarks anymore, and the season is well in force. The only subject on everyone's lips is Lord Cavendish's masquerade ball that he holds at Burlington House. Dyott and I attend as Caesar and his wife. I understand that Caesar's wife was quite unexceptionable, although I have demanded that my gown cover rather more of my figure than was apparently common in the period. By all accounts Rome is warmer than London. I know you will likely stay with your sister, but we can mount you on a very nice mare. She has a good mouth and beautiful hocks.

A touchy disposition, alas, but I never saw a mare that you couldn't handle.

Yours,

Your cousin Mary, Lady Dyott

The Countess of Bredalbane was never one to stand on ceremony. When Gil walked into her house at age twelve, orphaned, starched outwardly, and inwardly crumpled, she took one look at him and said, "Thank God, you're not too young for backgammon. I loathe children." And so, while his younger brother Walter was taken to the nursery and deposited with a nursemaid, Gil found himself seated at a backgammon board and sharing his store of jokes, those about gluttons, and scholars, and even the one about the priest and the dairymaid. The countess liked them all, except for a joke about a shrew and a sheep. Her eyes flashed, and she told him to avoid offense, and then told him a bawdy jest about a gentleman and his wife's jewelry box, not a word of which he understood. But he laughed and laughed and felt quite comforted.

Almost twenty years later, her hair was just as black as ever and her eyes just as fierce as the moment when he strayed into that joke about a shrew. She paused in the doorway. "The time has come, Kerr!"

"It's lovely to see you, too," he said, crossing the room to kiss her cheek.

"I'm serious," she said, pushing past him and his kiss to sit in her favorite upright chair beside the window. She never cared about the fact that sunlight cast harsh light on her wrinkles; she loved seeing who passed the house too much for such nonsense. "You must marry Emma, and directly. You've made a fool of yourself—and worse, of her—with your foolish quotations. And just what were you up to at the opera, pray?"

"Accompanying a lovely young lady," he said mildly. "May I offer you a glass of ratafia?"

"What's the o'clock?" she demanded.

"Two in the afternoon."

"I'll have a brandy," she said. "I never drink before nuncheon, you know, but one might have a sustainer now and then."

He motioned to Cooper. Of course, his butler had had the brandy poured from the moment his godmother entered the room.

Suddenly she thumped her stick. "No flummering me with your pretty manners, Kerr. You've always had the gift for sweet talk. But this is serious."

"I know it," he acknowledged, sitting down. "I don't mean to tease you. I've sent a letter to my man of affairs, informing him of my upcoming nuptials. I do want to assure you that I never meant to duck my responsibility to Miss Loudan. At first, I didn't wish to pressure her, given her mother's prolonged illness, and then somehow the time slipped away after Walter died. I can't go to St. Albans this week—"

"A horse is no excuse!" she interrupted.

"We're bringing the vote on the *Habeas Corpus* Act to the House this week. Since I sponsored the move to revoke its suspension, I need to stay for the hearing."

"Ah," she said begrudgingly. "I suppose that's a better excuse than some. So why did you offer me all that Spanish coin about your horse and your tailor and the rest?"

"Because I greatly dislike having my affairs curtailed or arranged due to gossip circulating through the group of foolish people that passes for the *ton*," he said, and there was steel in his voice.

"That's the way of the world," she said, but she looked into her glass rather than at him. "At any rate, there's nothing about *habeas corpus* that requires you to make a fool of yourself with French prostitutes."

"If you refer to my escort at the opera, Marie is not a prostitute," Gil said, a little half smile playing on his lips. "She's a generous woman, that's all."

The countess snorted.

"I thought she'd distract people's attention from the rumor that I might marry Mademoiselle Benoit," he noted.

"Well, it did that. Now everyone's wondering which member of the French nation you'll bring to the Cavendish masquerade."

"What costume shall you wear?" he enquired, changing the subject.

Her eyes snapped at him. "I'm going as Cleopatra," she said. "And I'll thank you to go alone, Kerr. I've no wish to see you escort yet another light-heeled Frenchwoman and make me hesitate to open my correspondence in the morning. You'll come alone, and the following day you'll go to St. Albans and marry Emma, *if* she'll still have you."

"Her refusal is, of course, always a possibility."

"Don't look so damned hopeful about it!" his godmother snapped.

Chapter Five

Bethany Lynn was beside herself with anxiety. Her elder sister had, by all appearances, utterly lost her mind, and nothing Bethany said seemed to convince her otherwise. "Kerr will never believe you're French!" she said desperately. "Everyone says that he did nothing but drink and seduce women when he was in Paris. He's an *expert* on the subject of Frenchwomen."

"Of course I can fool the man," Emma answered, clearly unperturbed. "I shall pretend I'm with Mama. She never spoke a word of English in the last two years of her life; there were times when I felt I was forgetting my native tongue."

"You don't look in the least French."

"Sometimes I feel as if I understand men better than you, for all that you're married," Emma said. "My expectation is that if I throw on a French accent, babble a few phrases, and appear happy to see him, my true nationality will not matter. I'll make him believe that we first met in Paris."

"He'll never believe that," Bethany insisted.

"You just said that Kerr admits to being so routinely drunk that he could have had a clandestine encounter with the Empress Josephine without remembering. What's more, I know the name his intimates call him. I'll use it to prove our acquaintance."

"What is it?" Bethany asked.

"Gil. His godmother, the Countess of Bredelbane, wrote me with that bit of information. She writes quite regularly, trying to make up for her godson's neglect."

"I'm not convinced," Bethany said stubbornly.

"From what I've heard in the village," Emma answered, knowing that she was about to shock her little sister, "if one wishes to seduce a man, there are only two tools that matter: alcohol and a scanty gown. Most of the stories I hear have to do with either a drunken man or a naked woman. Or both."

"Who is telling you such things?" Bethany demanded. "You'd think the village women would have more respect for the delicacy of a young lady."

Emma snorted. "And if I was so delicate, who would help birth the village babies?"

Bethany scowled. "You know what I mean."

"The point is that if I can't get Kerr to drink himself into a fever of lust, I'll simply unclothe myself, and that will do it. By all accounts, a man cannot resist the sight of the undressed female form. Wouldn't you agree?"

Suddenly Bethany had a little smile on her lips that made Emma feel a sudden stab of envy. Her little sister's betrothal dated back to her fifth birthday, just as did Emma's, but Bethany's future husband, John, appeared on their doorstep after Bethany's sixteenth birthday, took one good look at his bride's brandy-colored curls and blue eyes, and promptly began begging for an early ceremony. That was in sharp contrast to her own betrothed, who had driven out to St. Albans to formalize the betrothal once he was of age, stopped by casually a few times if he happened to be hunting in the district, and hadn't been seen at all for the past three years.

"You should probably leave your hair down," Bethany said, beginning to get into the spirit of the thing. "And show lots of bosom."

"I can do that," Emma said, pulling pins from her dark red hair. It fell to the middle of her back.

"Frenchwomen always wear *maquillage*," her sister pointed out. "You would laugh to see how many ladies in London paint a red circle on their cheek and think it gives them the air of a French *comtesse*."

"I already use *maquillage*," Emma said.

Bethany peered at her. "Oh. You've darkened your lashes."

"And my eyebrows."

"You're locked away in the country, and you wear the very best gowns and face paints. And yet you look—well, you look absolutely delicious, Emma. Why?"

"I feel better when I am properly dressed. But I do think you're right. I've been without an audience."

"This is absurd!" Bethany said, reversing herself. "Kerr will recognize you. Be serious, Emma! He may not have visited in a few years, but he's seen you on at least five or six occasions, and one does tend to examine the face of one's future bride rather closely."

"He won't recognize me with a mask on," Emma said, grinning at Bethany.

"A mask? You mean Vauxhall?"

"No. I was thinking of Lord Cavendish's masquerade ball."

"Oh!" Bethany said with a gasp of excitement. "What a brilliant thought, Emma! I have an invitation."

"A masquerade will be an excellent arena for our first meeting in years," Emma said. "I'll wear that Elizabethan gown and mask that belonged to Great-Aunt Gertrude. Do you remember it?"

"She was our great-*great* aunt," Bethany remarked. "Of course I do! Remember how angry Father was when I tried it on and trailed about in the dust? He said the jewels on it were worth as much as my dowry."

"A few years ago I had it cleaned and stored properly in a wardrobe," Emma said. "It was far too beautiful to leave as a supper for moths in the attic. It will make a perfect disguise. I'll go as an Elizabethan lady, and wear the mask that accompanies the dress. It covers most of my face, so I'll be unrecognizable."

Her sister was still biting her lip. Emma sighed. "You haven't changed an iota from when you were seven years old, Bethany. Have a little faith in me!"

"That's just *it,*" Bethany said. "You haven't changed either, Emma. You're playing to win, above all. But you may not wish to win, if you think about it. Marriage is too important to turn into a game."

"You give the evening—and marriage—too much importance," Emma retorted. "I'd just as soon marry Kerr as any other Londoner. He's handsome, wealthy, and titled. More importantly, if I find that I don't like him on closer examination, I'll call my carriage and be away. He will never know that he was assessed and found wanting. I'll simply write him a note annulling our betrothal, come to London, and find a husband more to my taste."

Bethany gave up. "I shall be waiting in the carriage. If

anyone shows a sign of recognizing you, you must leave immediately."

"No, no, we must do the thing properly," Emma said. "I'll take a room at Grillon's Hotel as a French widow. That way no one could connect the two of us."

"Go to the ball in a hackney, from a hotel!" Bethany gasped. "Absolutely not! You would be ruined if anyone found out. You will take a room at a hotel over my dead body!"

"I'll allow you to drive me to the ball," Emma said soothingly.

But Bethany was not fooled. The smile on her sister's face was that of someone who had never lost a challenge yet and had no intention of losing this one. She was alive with joy. There was nothing Emma enjoyed so much as a challenge: the higher the stakes, the better.

"No hotel," Bethany added, trying to sound firm.

"Of course not," Emma replied.

Chapter Six

One Week Later

The carriage rocked over the cobblestones on its way to Burlington House, where Cavendish was holding his masquerade ball.

"What if someone recognizes you?" Bethany moaned. She was indulging in an agony of second thoughts.

"No one will recognize me," Emma said patiently. "I haven't been to London in almost five years, since before Mama grew ill. And I never properly debuted, you remember. Just think of it as a game of charades, nothing more."

The sparkle of passing lights reflected in the gleam of Emma's jeweled dress. She was sitting opposite Bethany, facing backward since her dress took up the entire seat. It laced up the front and then cut wide over her breasts, flaring into sleeves whose brocade flowers were picked out in jewels.

Bethany gasped. "We forgot to discuss—to discuss—"

Emma raised an eyebrow.

"The baby!" her sister sputtered.

"Oh that," Emma shrugged. "I certainly understand the mechanics. And given Kerr's reputation, he should have no questions in that area."

"But the mechanics—" Bethany moaned, her alarm clearly growing.

Luckily, the carriage was slowing down; Emma judged she had better hop out before her little sister tried to issue a veto on the evening. "Deficient though I may be in experience," she said, "the trifling embarrassment of allowing my fiancé to do the necessary will not overset me. It must be done at some time, must it not?"

Bethany seemed to be having trouble catching her breath.

Emma sighed. "Unless I have been gravely misled, the act is nothing to which one should attach undue sentiment. Although I have no particular feelings about where this event takes place, I should prefer a location other than the carriage. In fact, I shall insist that I, as a representative of the French nation, should not be deflowered in a carriage."

Bethany gulped.

"I suppose that you did the thing properly, in a dark room under the covers," Emma said kindly. "But you know that I've never had a grain of proper sentiment about me, Bethany. I have no particular feelings for Kerr. But I do think that it will be an excellent thing for our marriage if he discovers that he has, in essence, been *'hoist with his own petard.'*"

"Is that Shakespeare?" Bethany asked dubiously.

"I have to win the challenge," Emma explained, "because

otherwise Kerr will see no particular reason not to continue in his indifferent ways. I think it best to take him in hand before we marry."

"Oh, Emma, I wish I'd never told you Kerr's comment! John would not approve of this evening," Bethany moaned.

Emma laughed. "Of course your husband wouldn't approve, darling. He's a sweet, thoughtful man who is a perfect match for you."

"That's not the point. Kerr isn't sweet nor thoughtful!"

Emma waved her hand to silence her. "Neither am I, darling. Neither am I."

Bethany looked up at her sister and bit her lip. Truly, Emma didn't look sweet nor thoughtful either. She looked dangerous, her eyes glinting wickedly over her mask, her gown's tight lacing enhancing her breasts. "I'll be waiting in the carriage for you."

Emma grinned. "You needn't wait, love." She descended from the carriage and then peeked back in. "I've taken a room at Grillon's Hotel, and my maid is already waiting for me there."

They probably heard Bethany's shriek in the next county. But Emma just waved good-bye and adjusted her mask.

The competition had begun.

Chapter Seven

The footmen who had been set to guard the door of the Cavendish ball were having a difficult time of it. They'd had to turn away at least a score of people who had no invitations, and more recently, five whose invitations were obviously fraudulent. One could tell from the very way they walked that the invitations wouldn't prove to be genuine, James thought to himself. They didn't have that air of command.

Not like the prime article getting out of the carriage now: tall and slender, but with a bosom that made his mouth water. She had buckets of red hair, all curled and looped down her back, and the contrast between all that red hair and the white gleam of her plump breasts made James's knees feel weak. He hardly glanced at her card, so mesmerized was he by the faint smile in her green eyes as they regarded him over the edge of her mask.

"Here you are, my lady," he said, breathlessly handing back the invitation, even though they'd been expressly told to keep them so that no one could hand them out the back window to a friend.

"*Merci beaucoup,*" she murmured, and the shiver went straight down James's legs. She was a Frenchwoman, she was. And if all Frenchwomen were like this, the world would be a better place.

The ballroom was brilliant with a shifting mass of bright silks, swaying feathers, and the glint of gems. Off in the corner, a small orchestra was making a valiant effort, but people were far too excited to dance. The whole ballroom was filled with Marie Antoinettes and Julius Caesars, screaming with delight when they glimpsed each other and darting across the room to press powdered cheek to powdered cheek.

Emma felt a pure stab of excitement. It had been too long since she went to a ball. Painting sets for Mr. Tey was fascinating in its own way. But painting was a lonely skill and offered none of the heart-thumping pleasure of a masquerade. She drifted through the crowd. People parted before her, drawing back, their voices drifting toward her: "*Who's that . . . really?*" "*It can't be . . . darling, I've never seen her before. . . .*" And then: quite clearly: "*Those are real diamonds; she's no governess.*"

She felt a peck of annoyance at herself. She *should* have come to London so she would know who all these people were. There was no doubt that she would recognize Kerr, but not his friends. A gentleman was standing just to one side, gaping at her as though she had fallen straight from the sky. She dropped her eyelashes, slowly, and then looked at him again. He had such a mindless expression that she felt certain he would be a friend of Kerr's.

It appeared the young lord was called Duffer, a thoroughly appropriate name. He almost stumbled over his own boots in his haste to kiss her hand. And a second later he took Emma into the gaming rooms, where he last saw Kerr.

Kerr was seated at a table playing *vingt-et-un,* his head bent to the side, studying his cards. Emma paused for a moment, letting Duffer's hand slip from her arm. Her future husband (*if* she decided to give him the honor) was remarkably good looking: tall and dark, with a gypsy face and slanted eyes. He wasn't wearing a costume, just a stark black coat and a carelessly tied scarf, but he looked better than all the peacocks he was sitting among.

"Kerr!" Lockwood hissed at him. "Wake up, man. There's a woman behind you!"

The last thing Gil wanted was trouble with women. Tomorrow he was going to St. Albans, and . . .

He looked. She was trouble. Trouble in all the ways he most liked.

"My lord," the woman said huskily. "You are playing with such devotion that you haven't noticed me."

"I'm afraid that I'm at a disadvantage," Gil said, rising and bowing. "I am Gilbert Baring-Gould, the Earl of Kerr."

"Mais, monsieur," she cried, drawing back, her voice breaking slightly, "Darling Gil, you haven't forgotten me, have you?"

Gil blinked. Surely he hadn't—

"Oh, but you *have* forgotten me," she said, her voice dipping into a husky lament. *"Hélas,* gentlemen—"

She cast a brilliant smile around the circle. "This is why we Frenchwomen consider you Englishmen so very dangerous."

"Dangerous?" Gil said. He was almost certain he'd never met her before. Except perhaps there was just the faintest hint of something familiar about her. "Absent-minded, perhaps, but not dangerous."

"You admit it," she said, pouting.

Lockwood was clearly anxious to assuage her disappointment. He stepped forward and kissed her hand. "Ah, mademoiselle," he said softly, "my heart is French, I assure you. I could never forget the merest press of your fingertips."

"Do you tell me, sir," she said, in the most ravishing lisp, "that you Englishmen are not all as unmannerly as Lord Kerr? For I do believe that he has quite forgotten our acquaintance."

Gil was torn between amusement, disbelief, and just the faintest—faintest—hint of embarrassment. Could he truly have forgotten such an exquisite bit of womanhood? "You must help my decrepit English memory," he said. "When was that encounter, mademoiselle?"

She pouted. "That shows the worst of your memory," she said, "for I am no mademoiselle, but Madame de Custine. And *you,* sir, were so kind as to—" She stopped and gave him a smile that told the entire room just how kind he had been. *Damn that French brandy,* Gil thought to himself. There was nothing to do for it but accept the scandal: his godmother would hear of this within five minutes. "I gather I was kind enough on that forgotten occasion that *you* remember *me,* my dear Madame de Custine," he said, kissing her hand again. "I consider that quite generous."

Her eyes were glinting at him above her mask. The very curl of her mouth surprised Gil. How did he ever drink enough brandy to forget her? "Consider it a tribute to your skills, my lord," she said, and the innuendo in her voice was unmistakable. Lockwood stepped back and picked up his cards. The man next to Lockwood turned and whispered to a friend.

Gil sighed inwardly and threw down his cards. An ace and a king fell onto the table. Actually, his godmother would know within three minutes.

"Gentlemen," he said, "I must beg your leave to make my apologies to this lady."

Chapter Eight

"Would you say," Gil asked, staring down at the glorious bit of womanhood who had sought him out, "that you might have embroidered a bit on our acquaintance?"

"Pas de tout."

"I just thought that you might have taken poetic license," he said, steering her toward the windows leading to the garden. "Cast a romantic tone over an encounter of the most pedestrian nature . . . Did I help you into a carriage, perhaps?"

Emma gave a little gurgle of laughter. The pleasure of being French had gone to her head. She felt tipsy with a sense of power, exuberant with her own lies. She pitched her voice to a purring reproach. "How can you say such a thing, Lord Kerr? I vow that you came close to breaking my heart!"

They passed through the doorway, Emma's wide, brocade skirts sweeping the door panels. Why on earth hadn't she come to London before? Why hadn't she known how much pure fun it was to hunt for a man, to cut him from the pack, just like one of Farmer Ben's sheepdogs might do with a prize ram?

"But I don't mean to scold you," she said, breaking off a sprig of jasmine. It smelled dizzily sweet.

He didn't answer, simply walked at her side, the lightest touch on her elbow leading her farther into the gardens.

He wouldn't try to take her virginity in the gardens, would he? Well, of course, he had no idea that she was a virgin, and Emma had the distinct impression that he would never know, if he were sufficiently drunk.

The garden was alive with shadowy figures, laughing and stepping in and out of patches of moonlight: Harlequin in his spangled costume brushed by a fairy whose right wing trailed to the ground. There was Homer or perhaps Zeus: at any rate, a man who thought to ape the gods or Greeks.

They settled primly onto a bench, and Emma put away thoughts of intimacies in the garden. Of course Kerr had no such idea in mind. He would take her to his house before something of that nature happened. She felt an inner tremble of excitement at the very thought.

"So, madame . . . I am sorry," he said, turning to her. "I have quite forgotten your name again."

"You may call me Emelie." Somehow her smiles didn't seem quite as potent when thrown in his direction. The young lord she'd collared inside looked faint at each movement of her lips, but Kerr's face didn't change an iota.

"Ah," he said sleekly, "Emelie."

"It was my grandmother's. A charming name," Emma said.

"Moi, j'y avais penser toujours la meme chose," he said. *"Comment pourrais-je oublier votre nom, quand votre visage si comme une fleur y apparaitre ensemble?"*

For a second Emma panicked. But she spoke French like a native. She only needed to keep her head. He was talking flummery, asking how he could have forgotten her name since she had the face of a flower. *"Le mystère du recollection d'un homme: qui peut savoir pourquoi ils oublient les choses les plus importantes?"* she said. That was good: men *did* seem to forget what they should most remember. And then, as quickly as she possibly could: *"Se souvenir d'une femme, c'est à moi: je trouve que ce soit impossible d'oublier meme les details de notre rendezvous nocturnale."* That was good, too: if she *had* spent a night with Kerr, she definitely wouldn't forget the smallest detail.

There was a liquid promise in his smile that made her feel light-headed. "You're speaking too rapidly for my poor skills, Mademoiselle Emelie—"

"Madame de Custine," she said, *"if* you don't wish to address me as Emelie." If he had the faintest idea that she was not a widow, her whole masquerade would be for naught.

"I do feel I should apologize for the dastardly event of forgetting our original meeting," he said silkily. "Where did you say that we met?"

"It's inconsequential," she said softly. "I know you likely forgot, as it was years ago . . . but I could never erase you from my mind. Never." She leaned forward so that he could look into her cleavage, except he seemed fascinated by her eyes instead.

"You couldn't?" he asked.

"Now I'm to marry a worthy burgher—a merchant, as you call them here in England." Oops, she had almost let her accent slip there. It was something about the spicy smell of his skin. She drew back a little.

"I wish you the very best in your forthcoming matrimony," he said.

"Of course," she purred. "But marriage is such a serious

endeavor ... pleasant, altogether necessary, and yet sti-
fling. I know, since I was married to my beloved Pierre until his much lamented death."

"Ah," he said.

Emma rushed on before he could ask any questions she
might not be able to answer. "At any rate, it's been years
since we—since we—but it was in Paris, monsieur."

"Paris," he said, and his tone hardened. A crease suddenly appeared between his brows, and Emma relaxed.
There was something different in the air between them
now: a smell of possibility. Bethany had been right about
his dissolute behavior, then.

"Paris," she said, the words soft in her mouth. "You
probably don't remember, my lord. I'm afraid you had
sampled a bit too much brandy that evening."

"Undoubtedly," he said, his voice hard.

"But I could never forget ..." Emma couldn't believe
how much husky longing she poured into her own voice.
Perhaps she should have run away and joined a traveling
theater troupe! "When I saw you across the room this evening, it seemed a gift from the gods."

"Well," he said, "I suppose that I should be grateful that
I apparently behaved in an acceptable manner, even while
a drunken sot."

"I am to marry my wealthy burgher in a week," Emma
said. "I am only in London to choose my wedding clothes.
'Twas a mere accident that I happened to be at the masquerade."

"Ah."

She bent over and ran a finger down his cheek. Small
prickles tingled her finger. "I wish you to do me a favor,
my lord."

"Of course." But his voice was courteous, detached. The

mention of Paris had convinced him that they had once met, but it had also iced him over somehow.

"You see, my lord, I do believe you owe me a favor."

"Indeed?" his voice was positively chilly.

"Certainly." Her finger slipped to his lips. His bottom lip was plump, sullen, beautiful. "I am to make the good marriage. My mother, bless her sainted memory, would be joyous. And yet I would like one more experience . . . just one . . . before I lapse into a life of rectitude."

His eyes narrowed. "Could you possibly mean what I think you mean?"

Emma kept her voice low and sultry. "I certainly hope so."

And then she held her breath.

Chapter Nine

Self-loathing is an ugly thing to display before a beautiful woman. Gil forced himself to drain every bit of that emotion from his voice before he spoke. "I'm afraid that I was not myself during my stay in Paris," he said carefully.

Her eyes met his. "I understand that you were having difficulties," she said. "I believe that you were mourning the loss of your brother."

Damn. He couldn't believe that he had babbled of Walter, spoken of Walter's death to this woman. How could he? And since he had spoken to her on such an intimate subject, how could he not remember their encounter?

Her eyes were sympathetic. He made himself gather the shreds of his self-esteem and bury the pain that was Walter down deep in his heart, where he tried not to look anymore. There was no point to that pain, and no end to it. He understood little, but he did understand that.

"I must have bored you to tears," he said lightly.

"Pas de tout," she said. Her hand touched his and sent small shivers of sensation across his hand. "Never that." Her eyes caught his, and she looked away.

For the first time, he took a hard look at her. He'd been amused and faintly bored by her arrival in the card room; the only reason he accompanied her to the garden was because he held another winning hand, and cards had lost their interest. Slim, winged eyebrows rose above her jeweled mask. Her hair was thick, like rumpled silk, and the dark red of a garnet, with the same hints of mysterious depths. A man could hide his face there and not miss the light of the sun. Her eyes were sultry, curious, intelligent . . . looking at him in a way that made him feel unsettled. Had it been so long since a woman looked at him with genuine desire rather than calculated interest?

Since his stay in Paris, he had brought no woman to his house, nor did he accompany them to their abode. He visited Madame Bridget, but only for the pleasure of chattering in French. He played with fire, but dropped the women at their doors, untouched. Sometimes, he wondered if he'd been eunuched by that orgy of grief.

Her forehead was high, an aristocrat's delicate white brow. It was a pity that she was marrying a wealthy burgher. Not a pity, he corrected himself. A joy. She'll have five children and forget the extravagances of her youth.

For she was young, he could see that. Another wave of self-loathing almost caught him on the hip: apparently he had been so sotted on a Parisian night that he ravished a young lady.

Then he caught her eyes again. Well, perhaps she wasn't *that* much a lady. Ladies rarely had such a fascinated gleam in their eyes, at least not Englishwomen. Leave that to a Frenchwoman.

Her fingers were playing on his wrist, as if she couldn't stop touching him. One thing he'd learned in his misbegotten life was that you have to forgive yourself. For being the only one in your family left standing. For not being there to catch Walter as he fell from the carriage.

For ravishing a young woman. Because, apparently, he had conducted himself so well that she wanted a repeat.

And he, as he sometimes had to remind himself, was a gentlemen.

Gentlemen never disappoint ladies.

One moment Emma was sitting on the bench, gazing with some satisfaction into her future husband's eyes, and the next she was on her feet, heading back into the ballroom. Something had changed between them.

He was so much bigger than she, although she was a tall woman. His hand was on her shoulder, and though it was gentle, it made her quake inside. One could only suppose that he had made up his mind to grant her request.

There had been a flash of such pain in his eyes when she mentioned his brother that her stomach clenched at the sight of it. And yet when she glanced sideways at him now, all she could see on his face was a kind of raffish enjoyment.

He slowed as they neared the open doors of the ballroom, looked down at her, and there wasn't a trace of grief in those eyes. They looked wicked, like a promise in the moonlight, like the end of all the great love stories rolled up in one. And that smile on his lips ought to be outlawed. For the first time she really believed Bethany. This man *had* cut a swath through Paris. It seemed likely that not a Frenchwoman in Paris resisted him.

"I gather," he said, ignoring the curious faces that turned toward them, "that you wish me to do you a favor."

"If you would be so kind," she replied, keeping her eyes on his so that they didn't drift to his lips. Was this *her,* wondering how he would taste? She'd never thought of such a thing before. For a moment she felt a sense of vertigo, as if the old Emma who painted bees in her studio had been replaced by a lascivious Frenchwoman, licking her lips at the sight of Kerr.

Well, he was her husband.

Almost.

"Would you like to dance?" he asked.

She blinked, confused. Wasn't he going to sweep her into his carriage and have his way with her? Frankly, she wouldn't even mind the carriage. True, Bethany had said that carriages were not appropriate, but—

"Yes, of course," she managed and took his arm. But she had forgotten that new dances had come into fashion since the days when she and Bethany had a dancing master, and she hesitated at the edge of the floor.

"A waltz," he said to her. "New, German, and quite fast. Allow me." He put a hand around her waist and pulled her close.

She gasped.

"It's a three-step rhythm," he said to her, laughing at her confusion.

Around them was the swish of satin and silk as milkmaids and queens turned in the arms of kings and clowns. She put her hand on his shoulder, and they stepped into the gaily colored throng.

His hand guided her, and after a moment she learned the pace.

"That's it," he whispered into her ear. "Frenchwomen are always fast learners."

Suddenly daring raced through her again, turning her veins to fire. The mask on her face hid the normal Emma,

turning her into another woman, a bolder, more courageous version of herself. "I believe that you must be beginning to remember me, my lord. Those were your very
words on an earlier occasion."

Wonder of wonders, he didn't freeze but smiled back at
her. His hand strengthened at her back and pulled her
closer. Shivers crept up Emma's legs and made her feel
weak in the knees. She licked her lips and felt even weaker
when she saw his slow smile.

"Would you like to take a short drive, Madame de Custine?"

"Emelie," she said. "And yes, that would be quite pleasant." Pleasant wasn't quite the word, not for the sense she
had that the pounding of her heart could be heard by the
whole room.

They began to make their way through the crowded
floor, Kerr brushing off the greetings of his friends. From
the glances that followed them, Emma could say without
hesitation that she would receive at least four letters tomorrow detailing her fiancé's contemptible behavior.

From the corner of her eye she saw her cousin Mary and
quickly turned her head the other way. Her mask may have
served as an adequate guard against Kerr's recognition of
her, but one good look from her cousin, and the masquerade would be ruined.

He was steering her with a mere touch of her elbow.
One jerk of his head, and a footman appeared with her
pelisse, and Kerr threw it over her shoulders. His fingers
lingered for a moment, and a potent whiff of her own perfume drifted to her nose. *That's why women wear perfume,*
she thought suddenly. *For their own pleasure.*

"Have you always had a fondness for Englishmen?"
Kerr asked.

"Of course not," Emma said. "Most Englishmen are so

unattractive: pasty white, with that yellow hair that one knows will sneak away in the night, leave the man naked as a billiard ball within a few years."

She walked ahead, and Gil followed. He was thinking hard. Clearly, Madame de Custine had been in Paris when he was there, and she had somehow found herself in the way of his marauding, drunken self. And if she now wished to have a final *affaire* before she married her worthy burgher, who was he to complain? "Before your comment, I saw no particular reason to celebrate my dark hair," he told her.

She pursed her lips and then gave him a slow, raking glance, from the top of his hair to his boots. Gil almost laughed. There was nothing more enjoyable than a French-woman in passionate pursuit of an hour's entertainment.

"Indeed," she said finally, "Your hair is gratifyingly dark. In fact, I took you for a Frenchman until I heard of your success with the women of France."

"Ouch!" Gil said, laughing. After all, he was to marry, too. Perhaps this French lady would be his last fling before he settled into a dutiful matrimony. He helped her into the carriage and then seated himself opposite her. "I am entirely . . . at your service, madam."

"In that case," she said with perfect aplomb, "I am staying at Grillon's and I would be very grateful if you would accompany me to the hotel."

His eyebrows rose. Little Emelie was remarkably accomplished at the business of making an assignation. For a moment he had a flash of sympathy for her worthy burgher. Her eyes were shining with excitement above her mask. She had lovely eyes, with a wicked fringe of lash that curled at the corners of her eyes, giving her an entrancing coquettishness. Truly, how could he have forgotten this woman?

He pushed away the thought. Two bottles of brandy a night have a way of doing that to a person; and when one is trying above all to forget that one's little brother just died, other things tend to get forgotten at the same time. "Would you care to remove your mask?" he asked.

"Oh, I think not," she said. Her voice sounded like sin, joyous sin. She leaned forward and put a small, gloved hand on his knee. A bolt of pure lust shot to his groin. "I think it would be most amusing this way, if you'll forgive me, Kerr. After all, you don't remember my face from our last encounter, and I should hate to cause either of us embarrassment should we meet again. I am marrying an Englishman, after all."

"You called me Gil at the masquerade. And I am quite certain that I shall forget your face once more, if you ask me to do so."

"You will forgive my lack of confidence," she said, and the rich glow of laughter in her voice was more tantalizing than her hand, which still rested on his knee. "I should like to wear my mask."

"There is more than one way to befog my memory," he said. And then, eyes fixed on hers, he reached up and turned down the small oil lamp that hung at his side. His side of the carriage was instantly cast into shadow, leaving only the light from the small lamp on her side burning. Its glow cast gold on the deep red of her hair, caught brilliance from the diamonds at her ears, turned the deep velvet of her pelisse to shining bronze.

She glanced at her own lamp. Then slowly, carefully, she began to pull off her right glove, finger by finger. "May I attend to your lamp?" he asked, rather horrified to find that his voice had darkened to a growl. There was something unbearably erotic about watching her slowly, so slowly, remove one glove.

She chuckled. She was not the sort of woman who giggled, he noted to himself. Finally, she curled back her glove to reveal a hand as beautifully shaped as her mouth. "One should never tend to oil lamps while wearing gloves," she said, turning down the wick. "It presents a hazard."

The light flickered, cast one last ray of light over the cream of her neck, and went out. Now the carriage was lit only by the flickers of light that came from below the tied-down curtains as they rumbled through London.

He sat for a moment in the dark, every sense aware of her movements. She was taking off her left glove unless he was mistaken.

"I shall not make love to you in this carriage," he said suddenly.

Her laughter was so suggestive that it almost destroyed his control and sent him leaping to her seat. "*Mon dieu,* what a respectable man you are sober," she said. "In Paris, you were *sans cérémonie.*"

"I can only regret my loss of memory," he said, meaning it. "May I hold your gloves for you?" he asked, leaning forward.

"Of course," she said, dropping the gloves unerringly into his hand.

"Do you see in the dark, like a cat?"

"No. But I am accustomed to it, since I have spent some time in the wings of a theater. Theaters don't light the rear, or it will be visible to the audience."

"You're a professional actress?"

Actresses had a reputation for being nothing more than prostitutes, although Emma could have argued the point. Five years of painting sets for Mr. Tey had taught her, if from a distance, that actors and actresses arrived at their ethical lapses in as many ways as other people.

"No, I am not," she said, undoing the clasp at her throat and allowing the thick velvet of her pelisse to fall from her shoulders.

"May I?" His voice had darkened to a husky rasp that made her heart beat faster in her chest. She handed her pelisse to him.

"Then why on earth have you spent time in a theater?"

"I paint drop scenes, the scenes that mark the changing of an act."

"You paint drop scenes," he said, sounding utterly stunned.

"Exactly. I painted one for an amateur performance, a few years ago, and fell into doing more as a favor to the local theater. That's how I met my devoted fiancé," she added, remembering his supposed existence.

"Ah yes," he said, "the worthy burgher, the man whom you marry next week."

"Precisely." Wasn't he going to kiss her? They passed a house with torches burning all the way to the roadway, and the carriage flashed with light for a moment, just long enough so that she caught sight of his brooding eyes.

"How long did you stay drunk in Paris?" she asked impulsively.

He stared across at her, but there was no light in the carriage now, and she couldn't read his face. He must have taken off his gloves, because he picked up her right hand and began caressing it, large fingers slipping around hers. Her stomach felt a liquid jolt of heat.

"Six months," he said, just when the silence had stretched so long that she had to babble of something. "I was drunk for six months. And I gather it was on one of my most oblivious evenings that I met you, *ma chère.*"

But Emma didn't want to talk of that nonexistent meeting. "And the drinking was due to your brother's death?"

He leaned forward and put her hand against his lips. The touch of his kiss to her fingertips made the warmth in her belly burst into flame. She suppressed a gasp. She had to appear experienced, not cast astray by as simple a thing as his touch.

"Walter died in October over a year ago," he said, sitting back again and winding her fingers between his large ones. "He died in a carriage, while up at Oxford. Forgive me if I already told you the details when I saw you last. He was in his third year, and they were larking about—"

He stopped, and his fingers tightened on hers.

"What happened?" she asked, although she knew well enough. She'd been at the funeral, of course. She had pressed his mourning glove with her mourning glove, and murmured something through her black veil, put on for the brother-in-law who would never be her brother-in-law. At the funeral Gil's eyes had been dead, black, expressionless; she could remember the look in them to this day. And the next thing they'd heard, he'd gone to Paris.

"He was drinking," Gil said flatly. "There's nothing unusual about drinking, of course. In some ways, the course of a university career is synonymous with a soak in a brandy bottle. But a man who's been drinking doesn't have good control of the reins. Nor yet of his balance. And Walter fell from the carriage, that's all. Dropped the ribbons, fell out as his carriage swept around a corner."

"I'm sorry," she said softly.

"They say that he didn't suffer."

"I suppose . . . Does that help?"

"Not much."

She leaned forward then and took his hands, both of them, in hers. The carriage was trundling down a long, dark lane, and so she couldn't see anything at all. She let her fingers wander over his hands, over the calluses on his fingers, probably from holding reins.

"So I gather you were trying to get drunk enough to fall out of a carriage?"

There was a moment of silence, and she felt a drop of fear. Had she gone too far? But he gave a bark of laughter. "Something like that, I suppose."

She lengthened her fingers, stretched them over the broad backs of his hands. "And did you succeed?"

"Obviously not."

She waited. The carriage lurched, rounding a corner.

"I fell out of a number of *beds,*" he said finally. "Drunk, blind, trying to find my way to a chamber pot. A kind of death. But one always wakes up, more's the pity."

"So I've heard," she said. She turned his hands over and began caressing his palms, trying to ignore the fact that her fingers were trembling. "I fell out of a carriage once."

He went still; she more sensed than saw it. "What happened?"

"I was eight years old, and trundling along to the village in the old pony cart, driven by an ancient—but quite sober—groom. He didn't know that I was leaning over the side, trying to pull sprays of wild roses into the carriage. He went around the corner just as I grasped a particularly beautiful spray."

There was a little chuckle in his voice. "I believe I hear the echo of pain in your voice."

"Straight into the rosebush," she said mournfully. "I have a scar across my right eyebrow that is still visible."

One hand slipped from hers and traced the shape of her eyebrow. "Beautiful," he said, and the husky roll in his voice made her bite her lip. "Your brows fly above your eyes in a particularly fetching fashion. I saw no break, and I feel nothing now."

"I color them," Emma said briskly, trying to quell the butterflies in her stomach.

His hands slipped to her shoulders and her waist and

then, all of a sudden, he gathered her up, and a moment later she was seated on his lap.

"I gather you grew up in England."

"Actually, we have pony carts in France," she said, hastening to put her French accent back in place.

His face was so close to hers. Perhaps he would kiss her. Emma felt a wave of excitement so acute that she felt almost faint.

"What made you stop trying to fall out of carriages?" she asked quickly, just as his mouth was moving toward hers. He didn't stop though, just brushed her lips with his. Involuntarily, one of her hands came up and curled around his neck. It was a strong neck, muscled and firm.

"I couldn't do it." He said it almost into her mouth. "I could never let the reins go and simply fly into space. Walter had an exuberance that I never had. He drank with enthusiasm and rode with abandon. I'm conservative. I tried to teach him to be less reckless—" He shrugged.

Emma was hoping that he couldn't feel her heart beating against her ribs. He had a beautiful mouth: curved, a little sad, delicious, firm. . . . Holding her breath, she took a finger and rubbed it over his lips.

"Will you take off your mask now?" he asked, his voice velvet dark in her ear.

She reached up to untie it and instantly realized the advantage of having her arms at the back of her head. The motion pushed her breasts against his chest. It felt delicious, dangerous. She stilled, untying the laces of her mask slowly, hardly breathing. She could just see his eyes, shadow pools of black in the darkness, sliding over her skin like a hot lick of brandy.

A second later, his hand slid down her throat to the curve of her breast. She gasped. She'd noticed his fingers were calloused but hadn't imagined that they would weave a spell on her skin. They swept over the top of her bosom and slipped beneath the ornate gold cloth of her bodice.

His eyes held hers, not letting her look down and see what he was doing, where he was rubbing with his thumb, because he—he—

"What costume *are* you wearing?" he asked silkily.

"What?" she gasped.

"Are you Cleopatra, all in gold?" he asked. "But no, this is no Roman tunic." Her eyes widened. His hand was clasping her breast now, pushing her bodice down, almost— almost touching—

"Perhaps you were Venus?" he whispered, his lips tracing a line down her cheek.

Emma couldn't answer; she was simply, absolutely silenced for the first time in her life.

"I believe you must have been Queen Elizabeth." His lips were on hers now. He asked silently, and she parted her lips, having heard of such a thing but never imagined having the inclination herself. Besides, hadn't her governess said that husbands don't kiss in such a manner? Of course! He thought she was a French hussy, and so he dared to kiss her in this fashion.

Emma opened her mouth a little wider, and he came to her. Something like that should have been disgusting, but it just—wasn't. He tasted like . . . like . . . She didn't know. Like a man, one could only think. He was tasting her, too, now, and then his hand stilled on her breast.

Her heart was thudding against her ribs. She felt as if she were a bird, caught between the warmth of his hands and the seduction of his mouth, unable to move or to speak. Gil had a hand behind her head now, angling her so that he could ravage her mouth, take her as he would, and all she could do was—

Her mind was racing. She should do something, or he might get bored and stop. And she didn't want him to stop, did she?

He pulled away. His hand left an unwelcome coolness in its wake, and a small sound broke from her lips. Disappointment? Passion?

"I cannot fulfill your request," he said.

"What?" Emma said, scarcely hearing him through the pounding of her heart in her ears.

He picked her up and, with gentle precision, put her back on the opposite seat. "I cannot make love to you in this carriage, or elsewhere, madame. You must forgive me."

Chapter Ten

Emma opened her mouth, but no words emerged.

"Your request," he said, watching her. "Your one request before you marry the wealthy burgher."

For a moment she stared at him blankly and then the truth—or lack of it—seeped back into her mind. "Why not?"

"It wouldn't be right," he said.

Emma felt a shot of pure rage. This man, who by all accounts had slept with so many Frenchwomen that he likely murmured *je t'aime* in his sleep, was daring to become moralistic at this late date?

"After what we shared?" she said, and there was a generous dollop of warning in her tone, just in case he thought she was a pretty little French miss to be bedded and forgotten. Now she thought of it, he had treated Emelie in a horrendous fashion.

If Emelie had really existed, of course.

He was staring at her lips and seemed to have lost track of the conversation, so Emma drew in her lower lip and then slowly pushed it out again, just to remind him how soft that lip felt against his.

"Think of Paris," she said, her voice softer and as close to sirenlike as possible.

"Thinking of Paris has never done me the least bit of good," he said. "Since I can't remember the half of it."

"How could you have forgotten *me*?" There was genuine indignation in her tone. After all, he *had* forgotten her, off in St. Albans. Just because he'd never seen as much of her as he supposedly saw of Emelie, it was still a desertion.

"I waited for you," she said, pitching her voice low and shaky, and lowering her eyelashes the way Bethany did when she was squabbling with her husband.

"You did?" he asked, unhelpfully. "That's very flattering."

"Foolish, more like," she snapped.

"Well, but you must have married quickly thereafter. . . . Or was I helping you commit adultery?"

"My Pierre was decrepit by the time we met," she said. "The poor, poor man was good for nothing but lying in bed."

"By all accounts, Pierre and I had a lot in common," he observed.

"Not in the most important aspects," she said. She leaned toward him and as boldly as any bird of paradise, slid her tongue along the plumpness of his lower lip. After all, didn't he say that Frenchwomen learned quickly? She had a half claim to French nationality.

She heard his breathing hitch, but he didn't say anything.

So she leaned even closer and put her hand on his knees. She could feel muscles there, strong and sleek under her hand, begging her to run her hand higher, to—

He pulled away so fast that she nearly lost her balance and fell into the well of the carriage.

"I debased myself too many times in Paris, *ma petite*," he said, and there was something implacable in his tone that told her that she had just lost the battle. "No matter how tempting you are, I will not do so again."

"Who could have known that you had turned into a saint?" she asked, an edge to her voice. "By all accounts, you have been universally kind to women of my nationality."

"My kindness is exhausted," he said.

She believed him, that was the worst of it.

"I haven't slept with a woman since I took my drunken self onto a boat coming across the Channel," he said, lifting her chin so that their eyes met in the near darkness. "If I were to sleep with another Frenchwoman, Emelie, it would be you."

She opened her mouth, and he stopped it with a fierce kiss.

"But I don't do that anymore," he said one swooning moment later. "I don't drink, either, in case you're thinking of getting me drunk."

"Do you intend to give up the pleasures of the bed forever?" Emma asked with some curiosity.

"What do you mean?"

"Well, let's see. You sound like a monk. . . ." She paused and let the silence dangle for a moment. "Or a eunuch."

"Emelie! You're shocking me. And you a young lady of good breeding."

"Oh no," she said. "If I was a young lady of good breeding, how would Paris have ever happened?"

"I wonder about that myself," he said a little grimly.

"And it *did*," she continued blithely. "So you needn't worry about sullying my reputation."

"I'm not," he said. "I'm worried about *my* reputation."

"That's not fair!" Emma cried, with all the strength of her disappointment. If she went home without winning the challenge—even if he didn't know it was a challenge—then she would have to cancel their betrothal. There was no way about it other than that. And she didn't—

She stopped that thought and steadied her voice. "I do believe that we are in agreement that you owe me a favor, *monsieur.*"

He looked at her hard for a moment. The smile curling his lips made her squirm in her seat. Then he suddenly thrust open the trap in the roof and shouted something up at his coachman. Emma couldn't hear it.

"What did you say?" she demanded.

"I'm going to fulfill my favor," he said, settling back in the corner and crossing his arms over his chest. He couldn't have made it any plainer that dalliance was no longer on his mind.

Emma narrowed her eyes. She had a most uncomfortable warmth between her legs, and a squirming feeling all over her body, and her heart was still pounding.

"Since I cannot, alas, fulfill your first request," he said, as politely as if he were unable to serve her a cup of hot tea, "I shall do my best to make your brief stay here in England a pleasant one. I shall show you a place that will be of great interest to you."

The only place of interest that occurred to Emma was his house—nay, his bedchamber—but that seemed unlikely to be their destination.

She settled back into her corner. But she wasn't going to wrap her arms over her chest and allow him to bask in his morality. Oh no. She may be a beginner at this seduction business, but she had a feeling that she was a natural learner. So she leaned her head back, as if she were exhausted, closed her eyes, and thought about the way he kissed her, and the way his hand had settled on her breast.

A little breathy sound came from her lips. She threw an

arm over her head and grabbed the curtain, as if to steady herself when the carriage swayed. The bodice on her dress strained to drop below her nipple. The sensation was unbearably exciting and made her shift in her seat. She didn't open her eyes. Either he was looking at her, or he wasn't.

Instead, she concentrated on remembering his kiss. He had run his tongue right into her mouth. If she hadn't heard gossip about such things, she never would have believed it. Of course, she knew about the mating act. But she'd never . . . really . . . in fact, it was rather the same, wasn't it? When Gil's tongue ran along her lips, she opened them as if he was the sweetest piece of sugar candy she'd ever been offered. And he tasted so good, the kind of good that made her heart thud against her ribs even to think of it. She squirmed a little in her seat. Because if kissing *was* like the act of consummating a marriage . . . The very thought made her feel strange.

She was tired of holding on to the curtain, so she dropped her arm and sat up, running her hands through her hair. It was lovely to have her hair swirling around her shoulders. Normally, her maid pinned it on top of her head with so many pins that she found them strewn all over the studio. It felt better this way, like silk rushing past her fingers. If—if she and Gil were ever—she made that breathy little sound again before she could even finish the thought about where he might like to feel her hair.

She was so curious that she had to look. So she popped open her eyes.

Gil was still leaning back in the corner of the carriage. But he didn't look so all-fired moralistic and pleased with his smug little self now. No.

I knew I was a natural at this, Emma thought to herself.

She let a smile curl on her mouth that said. *I know exactly what you wish you were doing to me, you monk,* and then said aloud, "Do tell me where we're going, Lord Kerr. I find it utterly distracting not to know my destination."

"I expect you do," he growled, but then, to her disappointment, he leaned back and closed his eyes. "Since you've had a nice nap, though, I must beg your indulgence while I do the same."

Emma grinned at his supposedly slumbering face. He was a worthy opponent, this fiancé of hers. He just didn't yet understand that she never gave up.

She tied her mask back on while he pretended to sleep. She was feeling optimistic again.

When one's opponent doesn't understand the importance of a contest, it's mere kindness to allow him time to rethink his strategy.

Chapter Eleven

Two minutes later the carriage swayed to a halt, and a foot-man opened the door.

"Where are we?" she asked, taking Gil's hand as she stepped down, and allowing him to wrap her in her pelisse once more.

"In the alley behind Hyde Park Theatre," he said.

"Oh! Are they having a performance tonight?"

"Not tonight. But——" He was knocking on the door with his walking stick. "I expect we can enter, and . . . hello, Je-remy!"

A sturdy man with a walnut-colored head and small round eyes opened the door and peered out. "Who's that? Oh, me lordship." He pulled open the door and stepped back. "Would you like to look around, then?" He showed no curiosity; perhaps Gil took women to the darkened theater on a regular basis. "You'd better take my lantern; I'm having a bit of a sleep, and the dark won't injure me none."

Gil took the lantern in one hand and held his other out for Emma. She allowed him to draw her past Jeremy's strong smell of onions, and up a narrow flight of stairs. Behind them, Jeremy flopped into a seat in the stairwell, leaned back against the wall, and lapsed instantly back into snores.

"Do you come here often?" she asked.

"All the time," he said. "I am a shareholder in the theater. We are just preparing for the opening of *A Midsummer Night's Dream*. I thought you might like to see the sets. They're up already."

"Oh, I should, yes," Emma said.

The familiar smell of dust and greasepaint greeted them as Gil opened the door at the top of the stairs. At the far end of a narrow corridor, a curtain lifted slightly, disturbed by their arrival. A moment later, Gil held aside that curtain, and they emerged onto stage left.

"Just a moment," he said. He walked over to the wall. For a second she saw a flare from a burning twist of paper, and a moment later light broke like the striking of daybreak itself.

"Oh!" Emma cried, startled. "Gaslight in the theater! I've never heard of such a thing."

"We've had it for only a few months," Gil said. "Does that theater of yours use rollers for your drop scenes?" he enquired.

"Of course!" she said. "The rollers are much better than the flats. Before Mr. Tey installed them, I had to cut my scenes in half, which I loathed. You could always see the line down the middle."

"This is a drop scene, of course," Gil said, gesturing at the canvas already in place at stage back. "A man called

Samuel Grieve painted this set of the woods in *A Midsummer Night's Dream.*"

The flat depicted a dreamy, dusky forest, tall trees reaching upwards and a few leaning comfortably to one side or the other. The ground was covered with small purple flowers.

"It's lovely," Emma said, walking over to examine it. Mr. Grieve had painted the flowers out of proportion so that they would look like a hazy, blended mass to the audience.

"I'll bet your theater isn't using *this* yet," Gil said.

He walked across the stage and lit a small lamp, and then pulled forth a rigid side flat. It glided forward smoothly, presumably on a groove set in the wooden floor. It seemed to be nothing more than a large wooden frame, across which was stretched an expanse of colored silk, albeit in a lovely shade of rosy pink.

"What does one do with that?" Emma asked.

"It pivots," Gil expained. "See?"

He gave it a little push. The piece pivoted smoothly, and suddenly she saw that looking at the woodland scene *through* the colored silk was entirely a different experience. The light fell on the silk first, which threw a rosy glow on the woods, picking out small flecks of gold leaf paint embedded amongst the leaves.

"Oh, Gil, how lovely!"

He grinned at her, standing in the middle of the stage with his hands on his hips.

"Is this how you got those calluses on your hands?" she asked.

"What?"

"Working with the sets?"

"No. Painting sets is not gentleman's work, and I find it surprising that you are allowed to paint sets. Of course, you *are* a widow, but even so, theater folk are notoriously immoral. Do you not worry about your reputation?"

"I paint sets and scenery in the privacy of my own home, and my participation is known only by a few," Emma said. "But I regret your rather provincial ideas of actors and actresses."

Gil walked idly across the stage and stood between the pink transparency and the woodland scene. "You see?" he said. "The fairies will dance and play behind the transparencies."

Emma blinked. Through the pink silk, the muscled frame of her fiancé suddenly looked mysterious and seductive, winsome as a fairy king.

"Are you Oberon, then?" she asked, laughing.

"I could be," he said. "I wasn't wearing a costume at the masquerade." He reached down and snatched a wreath of flowers from a bench. "I do believe this is Titania's wreath— tsk, tsk, left about onstage—but 'twill do." He struck a pose. *"Tarry, rash wanton: am not I thy lord?"*

Emma felt a wicked, Queen Titania smile curl her lips. She tossed her hair back and walked a turn, letting her hips take on a seductive lilt. *"Then must I be your lady,"* she said, throwing Gil a glance over her shoulder. She could feel her jeweled mask glittering on her face, turning her into a fairy queen indeed. She took a turn or two just so he could enjoy the swaying of her hips, shaking her hair free so that it floated in the air, the way a queen of the fairies would wear it. The back flat's gold flecks of paint glittered in the corner of her vision, as if a small tribe of fairy servants sparkled in the trees, awaiting her every command.

She glanced over at her Oberon. He seemed to be enjoying her bosom.

"You should accuse me of adultery next," he said

huskily. "Titania accuses Oberon of having a mistress, a warrior love."

Emma shook her head. "That must be anther Titania. *My* husband will never have a mistress."

He began to walk toward her, all slow and easy but with purpose. Pure exuberation raced up and down her limbs.

"And just how do you intend to stop Oberon from his seductive habits?"

But Emma had just realized that there were more side flats, stretched with different silks, waiting to emerge. She pulled at one, and it slid smoothly along its groove onto the stage. Gil's large arm reached over her head and pulled the flat all the way, then spun it on its pivot so that gold silk cast its radiance on the fairy forest. The gold flecks looked closer now, dancing free of the trees.

"It fools the eye," Emma said, awed. "They look like fairy lights."

Her Oberon knew his Shakespeare. *"Didn't thou not lead Theseus through the glimmering night,"* he asked, bending his head and brushing his lips across hers, *"from Perigenia, whom he ravished?"*

Ravished. Emma suddenly discovered she loved that word. She let her neck fall back as he kissed her. His mouth came to her cheek and her chin, leaving small fiery trails in his wake. Her mind fogged, and her arms wound around his neck, when suddenly she remembered her next line:

"These are the forgeries of jealousy!" she said, breaking free and dancing across the stage in a swirl of skirts. She glanced back over her shoulder and gave him the smoldering glance of a fairy queen bent on scolding her mate. On scolding and *ravishing* her mate.

He laughed. "You don't seem to know your Shakespeare as well as one might hope from a well-brought-up young lady. That line does not follow."

"Ah, but I'm not a lady," she pointed out, feeling that they had already covered that ground. Just to prove it, she kicked off one of her silk slippers. It curved into the air, a jewel flashing as it went, and disappeared onto stage left.

"I suppose I can carry you back to the carriage," Gil said with mock despair.

Emma kicked her other shoe into the air. This one thumped against one of the sets and set it trembling.

Then she danced behind the rosy transparent silk. "Are these easy to turn?" she asked.

"Of course," he said. "The boys who play the fairies love to make them twirl."

"I see why," Emma said, awed by the cleverness of it. For with a pull of her fingers, the stretched silk whirled on its pivot, and rosy gleams danced around the room, flashing over Gil's dark hair, on his lean cheeks and high cheekbones, on that wickedly seductive lower lip of his.

He swept the hair out of his eyes as she watched.

"You're quite beautiful," she said, startled to hear the huskiness of her own voice.

"Do you say that as a queen, or as Emelie?" he asked, smiling.

"A woman would walk a mile for a touch of that nether lip," she said dreamily.

"Tsk, tsk," he said, and there was laughter in his voice. "You're mixing your plays. *Othello,* and in such a sad context."

"Titania would never travel even a yard for the touch of a man's lip," she said, pushing the pink silk flat sideways so that it turned just enough to make a barrier between the two of them.

"Perhaps not," he said, amused, and then she saw the words die in his mouth. For she had pulled up her hand-brocaded skirt and was holding one leg out as she slowly,

slowly unrolled her silk stocking. It was a lovely stocking, of the softest gossamer silk.

He made a strangled growl in his throat. She pulled off the stocking, pointed her toes, and took a moment to admire her leg. She had always thought that her legs were most attractive.

Emma peeked at Gil. Clearly, he thought so, too. She gave him a secret little smile.

"Emelie!" he said, "Stop what you are doing. This is nonsense."

In answer, she reached under all her petticoats and slipped her second stocking from its garter. A moment later, that stocking slipped past a slender, pointed toe, and she tossed it over her shoulder.

"I insist that you do not disrobe yourself on the stage," he said, but Emma ignored him. It was good for a man to know straight off that there were times when he might—*might*—be obeyed, and there were others when he should understand his place.

"I shan't," she said, casting him a sparkling, mischievous glance. "I'm overheated."

"Overheated!"

It was the work of a moment to unlace her tight bodice and push it off her shoulders, slipping her wide sleeves down her arms. He made another sound, like a beast in the darkness, when her bodice fell to the ground. Of course, she shouldn't be the one to say so, but her breasts looked rather magnificent. Her little corset was the kind that aimed to levitate, rather than confine, and she had neglected to wear pantalettes. . . . It was a delicious and strange experience.

She shook her hair free again; it swirled around her shoulders with a touch like *fire*. A slow blaze eddied in her belly. "Lord Kerr," she called, "I cannot remove my skirts without some help. This gown is constructed in two parts, as you can see."

She looked up, and Gil was leaning against the pink silk screen, laughing silently. She blinked at him. He wasn't supposed to be laughing at her. He was supposed to be transfixed with lust, driven to the extremities of his self-control, turned to a satyr. Or something akin to it.

"Have I told you that I begin to feel more and more sympathy for that worthy burgher, your future husband?" he asked.

Emma started trying to pull her skirts around to the front so that she could undo all those little buttons herself. Since Gil wasn't inebriated—and apparently he would never be inebriated again—she was going to have to rely on large expanses of naked female flesh to drive him into a more amenable frame of mind.

Just as she began to unfasten the tiny buttons that held up her skirts, Gil apparently figured out her intent.

There was a distinct note of warning in his voice now. "I must ask you again. Please do not disrobe yourself on the stage of the Hyde Park Theatre."

"Why not?" she asked. "Naturally I had hoped we would be at Grillon's. I am partial to starched sheets, but a woman must be prepared for unexpected pleasures when they occur."

There was something about the set of his jaw that made her think that possibly the village women had underestimated the strength of will of an earl when they talked of naked women. But she'd gone too far to stop now. She unfastened the last button, and the heavy, bejeweled skirts fell to the ground with a swish, taking her petticoats with them.

Now she was wearing nothing more than her little boned corset, the clever bit of undergarment that pressed her stomach in while pushing her breasts up. She raised her head slowly to look at him, feeling her hair slide down her naked back.

His eyes were black, half lidded, his jaw still set. He leaned there as if she were a circus exhibit that he'd happened upon, a naked woman on the stage, yet another Frenchwoman amongst the hundreds. It wasn't going to work. She should reach right down and pick up those heavy skirts and pull them on so that she didn't have to meet his uninterested eyes again. This was profoundly embarrassing. This was beyond humiliation.

But she was a woman with Tudor bloodlines in her, and a fierce enough character that she'd never allowed herself to feel dismal over the neglect of her betrothed. She was *Emma.* She painted stage sets. She had exquisite clothing. She could pick up one of those besotted, fish-lipped boys back at the masquerade and marry him in about twelve minutes, whether she had twenty-four years or thirty-four years.

The tightness in her chest eased a little. After all, the theater was warm, and the light of the gas lamps was flattering. She was a naked Queen Titania, that was all.

Still, disappointment was biting in her heart, welling up with resentment. Perhaps he was eunuched. Perhaps those six months in Paris had worn the man out.

She looked back at Gil again. His eyes were scowling, and his jaw set so tightly that he looked like a night watchman waiting for a thief to descend a ladder. But—but—

"Damn it all," he growled, and his voice was black with . . . rage? Resentment? Something else?

She gave him a smile. It wasn't one of her full-lipped, passionate, I'm-a-Frenchwoman smiles. It was a smile with a bit of joy in it, an invitation, a secret, a laugh.

"Damn it," he repeated.

"You swear a great deal," she observed, crossing her legs as she stood and pretending to poke at the ground with her toes. She wasn't used to being naked, after all. Of course, she wasn't *really* naked. She had her corset and her mask. But she was painfully aware of the red curls showing just under the scalloped bottom of her corset.

"I am a conservative man," he said. "A sober man."

"I haven't offered you a brandy."

"I didn't mean it in that sense. I don't veer around corners, with my reins flying in the wind. I don't gamble my fortune on the throw of the dice. I don't—" The words apparently strangled in his throat.

Emma raised one leg slightly, meditatively, looking at the way the light cast through pink silk made her skin look even creamier. But when she looked at him, he wasn't staring at the rosy shadows cast by the dancing silk, but at the curls between her legs.

"Ah well," she said, sliding back into her French accent as if she'd never dropped it at all. "It is the way of the world, no? I shall have to find someone else to have my last *affaire* with before I marry the burgher."

"Someone else?" he said.

"Well, of course," she said, turning away from him and bending down to pick up her bodice. It was so heavy that she remained bent for a moment, trying to find the sleeves before she pulled it from the floor.

And then she felt the heavy, warm curve of a body tucking itself around the curve of hers. For a moment she froze. Gil was dressed, and the feeling of his linen shirt against her back, the rougher wool of his breeches against her bottom . . .

Her heart started to thud an uneven rhythm, as if a horse had broken from its traces and was veering into the woods.

Large hands swept through her hair, tossing it up and over her head so that it fell to the floor. His body stayed immobile, keeping her tucked in his curve, trapped by his weight, his body, the feel of him.

"You're a conservative gentleman," she pointed out, with just the smallest quaver in her voice.

He pushed forward slightly against her bottom, and she almost toppled to the ground, struck by a wave of weakness in her knees.

"Even conservative men lose their minds sometimes," he growled in her ear. His fingers had stopped running through her hair, and they were wandering more dangerously now, sliding sweetly down her neck, drawing her upright as they slid to her bosom, pulling her slender, naked body back against his clothed self.

For a moment she thought what they must look like from the other side of the screen, blurred by the rosy silk with her white against his black clothing, her slenderness against his muscle, her sweep of red hair against his wild fall of gypsy hair.

It seemed the village women were right about naked women after all; it merely took a gentleman a bit longer to give up the shreds of his control.

The breath caught in her throat as Gil cupped a hand around her breast, brushing her nipple, making her teeth suddenly snap shut so that she didn't moan aloud.

"Say it," he commanded. He had her arched against him now, one hand on her breast, the other sliding over her corset, teasing the bottom edge, sinking lower. His lips ravaged her neck, and her lips parted again as his thumb brushed over her nipple, making her wiggle against him, unknowing, uncertain, but—

"Say—" she gasped. "What should I say?"

"Make that sound again, the one you just made, the one you made in the carriage when you tried to seduce me."

She gasped, trying to get air into her lungs. That hand was inching closer, down, surely he couldn't mean to—

His finger sank into her sweetness at the same moment his thumb took that rough pass over her breast again. She didn't make a breathy, sensual sound, but a squeal.

She didn't care. She didn't care. Her head fell back against his shoulder, and she let him do as he will, holding her in place with his hands, his lips caressing her cheeks, the corner of her mouth, the curve of her throat, while his hands worked their magic. She hardly noticed when he nudged her legs apart, when his hands took on a harder, surer rhythm, when it became clear that he wasn't entirely inebriated during his months in Paris. He had apparently learned some important things.

"Of course," he whispered in her ear, "I would never do something like this to an English lady born and bred. But you *are* a Frenchwoman. I learned in Paris that French-women are terribly demanding."

"Yes," she gasped.

His thumb twisted and rubbed again.

"A properly raised Englishwoman would never allow something so depraved to be done to her," he said, his voice wicked.

He didn't have to emphasize that fact quite so much, Emma thought dimly. But what he was doing was making her squirm back against him, gasping, pleading for some-thing that he could—

"I could tell that you are Parisian in a moment. Why if I touched an English lady like this—" He rubbed a thumb over her nipple and then squeezed it. "She would scream with pure indignation."

Emma wasn't paying any attention to his foolishness anymore. Instead she just arched into his hand and let those sounds fly from her throat right up into the rafters, that is, until his hand stopped.

That was a mistake on his part. Something had been about to happen, something quite unprecedented. It had felt like a firestorm building and flying higher with every—

"What the hell are you doing?" she demanded, in good old-fashioned Anglo-Saxon English.

His voice seemed a bit thicker, too, not that it appeased her any. "I thought you might be embarrassed," he said. "To be standing up and all."

She wrenched free of him and turned around, hands on her hips, eyes narrowed, suddenly reminded that this was her future husband, and he needed to be taught a few lessons before she took his ring and his baby and all the rest of it.

Her corset was feeling far too tight, so she took a moment and collected her thoughts while she untied the bow on top. He was watching her as closely as a man could, so she took her time unlacing, massaging her poor breasts while she did it. No one could know how hard it was for them to stay jutting up in the air like that for hours, made into an exhibit for every goggle-eyed man for miles around. Finally she tightened the strings on her mask, which made her breasts rise into the air in a pleasing fashion.

Then when she thought he'd had enough punishment— and she did notice that he seemed to be breathing quite hard—she turned away from him and bent down to scoop up her pelisse. She heard the scrape of his foot on the boards and straightened, saying imperiously, "Don't move!"

He stopped, his eyes sending little sparks in her direction.

Emma was a lady born and bred, and so she took her time lying down and arranging her limbs on her bronze pelisse, making sure that her hair showed to its best advantage.

"Now," she said, looking back up at the man who stood above her. "Allow me to point out that I am a French-woman."

There was a twitch at the corner of his mouth.

"We are slow to anger but fierce when indignant," she told him. "In fact, we may be the fiercest race of people alive on the earth. And since everyone knows that females are fiercer by far than males, it stands to reason that *I,* as a woman and representative of my nationality, am someone to be feared."

He had his arms folded over his chest, and he was grinning, but she wasn't stupid. He was vibrating like a string of a violin.

"I'll thank you to extinguish all these lights," she said. "I believe I shall remove my mask."

He did so. The only light he left was the very dim glow of Jeremy's lantern, set far off in the corner and certainly not lending enough illumination so that Gil would recognize her, if indeed, he remembered his fiancée's features at all. Emma pulled off the heavy, jeweled mask and put it to the side. She could hardly see Gil; he was just a tall, shadowy form, but she could *feel* him: feel his desire reaching toward her, with all the inevitability of a spark hitting dry leaves.

"I'll grant that you are slow to learn, given *your* nationality," she told that dark gypsy shape of her future husband severely, "but the time has come for you to mend your ways."

"Hmmm," was all he said, but he seemed to be moving toward her right on course and as if he couldn't help himself, so she let him take his time.

It didn't take him more than a second to bring her back to that all-important moment, which just goes to show that the man did indeed learn something over in Paris.

And this time, he didn't stop.

Her body danced to the tune of his fingers, as if she were a puppet on his strings. She gasped, cried out, reached for him. . . .

When she pulled herself back together, she was still lying on her own velvet pelisse, staring up at the dusty rafters far above them. Gil was on his knees over her. And every inch of her body was quivering, as if a forest fire had rushed over her, left her scorched and yet unconsumed, burned and yet desirous.

She took a deep breath and focused on his face. There had to be more to this. In fact, she knew there was more to it. He'd taken off his shirt, but he was still mostly clothed. And even if he was looking at her with naked longing in his eyes, and his hand was shaping her breast in a way that made her press up, in his palm—even so, there was something about him that signaled that he thought he'd won.

Won?

She hadn't even started to fight.

Slowly, so she didn't startle him and make him dash back for his shirt and the security of all his vows about not sleeping with women, especially, she was beginning to think, Frenchwomen, she reached out her toes and her arms, and stretched. His eyes were liquid black, watching the arch of her body.

"I gather," she said, "you are still determined to pay me no favors."

"Those favors should be reserved for the man you marry." But his hand was on her breast again, shaping it.

She curled into his palm, making that sound in her throat, the one he liked and the one that seemed to come naturally every time he touched her. Then she nodded, quite as if she understood and didn't think he was feebleminded which, frankly, she was starting to take as a serious possibility.

"In that case, I would suggest that a gentlemen must allow a lady to reciprocate. Not the *favor,* since you are disinclined to grant my wishes. But . . ." She caught his eye and held it, "a reciprocation."

He frowned. "What—"

She pulled her legs to the side and pushed at his shoulder gently, and he finally collapsed on his back, smiling a little crooked smile. For all she knew of the male anatomy (mostly gathered at the births of male babies), she could see from the rise in his pantaloons that there was a miraculous transformation that happened between age one hour and age thirty-two.

But he was like a partridge in the wild: if she startled him, he'd fly away. So she knelt to his side, quite as if she didn't even notice the way his pantaloons were straining, and ran her hands through his hair. His hair was wild, coarser than hers. It sprang back against her fingers and smelled of woodsmoke and some sort of male soap, strong and not perfumed.

He wasn't protesting, so she let her fingers do the thinking for her.

His forehead was high, the forehead of a thinking man, a man who knew Shakespeare, the Parliament, and the way not to fall out of a moving carriage. And how to make a woman fall in love with him, in all of one evening. His nose was a narrow aristocratic triumph, a nose handed down from the Elizabethans. His mouth . . . well, his mouth had everything in it. A sardonic laugh, and one of joy. That plump bottom lip knew grief and—unless she was truly mistaken, and Emma had made a practice never to be mistaken—was longing to kiss her breasts.

Men liked kissing a woman's breasts, for all that Gil had so far only run his hands over her. She edged up closer to him and thought about offering him a breast, but rethought it. For one thought, it felt dismally maternal. For another, his black eyes were so steady and clear that she couldn't quite find the courage. And for the final thing, it just didn't sound right. Perhaps she'd misunderstood when village women talked of men supping at their breast, for all they were babes in arms.

She moved back and let her hands run from his lean cheeks to the strong cords of his neck, down to the ridged muscles on his chest. Were all men so muscled? His nipples were flat against his skin, and his mouth opened slightly as she touched them, although he made no sound.

It would be nice to hear *him* make a sound in his throat. Not looking at his eyes, she ran her fingers over his chest again, but he was silent, just waiting.

His pantaloons fastened themselves at the waist, but she wasn't certain he would allow her to disrobe him. It wouldn't suit his Puritan tendencies, that was certain.

She bent over him, and her hair fell forward, creating a little curtain around their faces. Then she licked his bottom lip again. A woman could spend her life tracing that line, feeling the quake low in her stomach at the curve of it, the softness of his lip, the strength of it.

A huge hand came to the back of her head and pulled her mouth down to his, and in that moment she let her right hand slide from his lean stomach onto the front of his pantaloons. For a moment he went rigid, his mouth warm on hers, *in* hers, and her fingers curled around him as if of their own volition, and then he groaned into her mouth, a queer, hoarse sound that made her sink from her knees so that she was lying on top of his body, boneless, sinking into him.

His mouth was ravaging her, her hand trapped between their bodies, between the softness of her skin and the fabric of his pantaloons.

And then Emma threw away the idea of winning the challenge. If Gil would just kiss her for another moment, kiss her for another five minutes, let her hand rest on top of that part of him that pushed into her palm, demanding something that she knew little of, but was all too eager to discover . . .

It was the first time that she had entirely dismissed the thought of winning the challenge. Who cared about the challenge? The only thing that mattered was that he was rocking up against her, pushing her legs apart, his knees going where—his hands touching . . .

Then he growled something at her.

He said it again. "I give *up*."

She closed her eyes, but she heard him all right. In an instant, she began wrestling with the two little rows of buttons on his pantaloons. But a gentleman's tight evening pantaloons don't slide off his legs without help.

He gave a bark of laughter and rolled to his feet. She lay there, looking up at him, knowing she was all white skin and a spread of red hair. He was watching, so she did exactly what she wanted to do, which was move her thighs apart, just a little. Just enough so that her cheeks flooded red at the same time the burning heat in her belly flared.

He tossed his trousers to the side, followed by his smalls. His legs were golden dark in the dim light from Jeremy's lantern, ridged with muscle and dusted with hair. And then, higher—the color grew in her cheeks but she didn't look away.

She was pretending to be a widow, but she wasn't going to pretend to be less interested than she was.

He came to his knees beside her, but instead of throwing himself on her as she half expected, he cupped her face in his hands. "You're to marry that worthy burgher of yours within a fortnight, do you hear?" he told her fiercely.

She nodded, eyes on his, wondering at the way that love could just rise up and grip you in the heart so fiercely it would never let you go. Those sloe-shaped eyes of his, that lock of hair on his forehead, those lean cheeks . . . "I shall," she whispered. And, in her heart: *I'm going to marry you within a fortnight.*

"Good," he said, as if they'd settled something. "In that case, I give up. I'll pay you that favor. I'm sorry I ever forgot you, that I ever got drunk in Paris, that I ever—"

She wasn't really listening. He had a hand on her bottom, and he slid her legs open, and then—and then he came to her.

It hurt, and it didn't hurt.

Her blood sang and thundered at the same time.

Her eyes closed, and yet she felt she could see through every pore.

He slid in, a little way, and made that hoarse sound in his throat, except perhaps it was she who made it, and then he didn't move again, so she went where her body wanted to go and arched up, against him, training him, teaching him, keeping him close and mindful and *hers.*

He was a good learner, for an Englishman.

Of course, she was French, and Frenchwomen are the fastest learners of all.

Chapter Twelve

They left through the front door. Gil left Jeremy's unlit lantern where he could find it in the morning.

Neither one of them seemed to feel like talking. Emma's throat was tight with something: tears? She rarely cried and only for a very good reason, so that couldn't be it. Come to think of it, the last time she'd really cried had been at her mother's funeral.

Her bejeweled Elizabethan dress felt frowsy now, and unbearably heavy. She couldn't wait to enter her bedchamber in Grillon's and collapse in a bed and try very hard not to think about the evening.

She'd won. Her father had Gil's ring safely stowed away, and she had done her part of the business, and that was that.

Gil was sobriety itself, handing her into the carriage as if she were made of glass. He said good-bye to her there, a sweet little farewell buss on the lips. "I would hope," he said, "you consider my debt repaid, Madame Emelie?"

What could she say? That the debt he had now incurred would take a lifetime to repay?

"Of course," she said and gave him a little kiss of her own. "You're free and clear, my lord."

"Gil," he said. But after that, they didn't say anything to each other.

When she involuntarily winced, climbing down the carriage step, he insisted on scooping her up and carrying her right up the steps of Gillon's. Emma thanked God for her mask; this story was going to be all over London before the morning gossip columns even appeared. It had to be three in the morning, and yet those who'd come to London expressly for the masquerade were just beginning to drift to their beds. They were gathered in small clusters amongst the exquisite pillars of the entryway.

The manager, Mr. Fredwell, saw them coming and hurried toward her. "Madame de Custine!" he cried, taking in the situation at a glance. "You must have injured your ankle."

"Indeed she has," Gil said coolly. "I believe it would be best for madame if you had two footmen carry her in a chair to her chambers."

There was a little rustle of voices, as of wind passing through the poplars. Apparently the Earl of Kerr wasn't going to sweep this mysterious Frenchwoman up to her chamber in his own arms, thereby guaranteeing that she would appear in every gossip column printed on the morrow.

Instead, and to everyone's disappointment, he deposited her in a chair, nodded to Mr. Fredwell, and left without further ado, striding down the steps as if he hadn't whisked her out of the ballroom, sparking a hundred rumors and a thousand delicious speculations.

Emma swallowed hard and didn't let herself worry about the fact that her future husband was the type of man who bedded a beautiful Frenchwoman, told her to marry her fiancé promptly, and then left without a word of farewell. After all, Gil was what he was.

And she loved him, more's the pity for her.

Her spirits rose a bit when the footmen left and her own maid came clucking toward her. "Oh, miss, what did happen to you? Twisted your ankle, did you?"

Emma fashioned herself a graceful limp and allowed herself to be placed in a steaming bath scented with rose, given a tisane, and put to bed in starched sheets, as if she were an invalid.

Her chamber looked over the great inner courtyard of Grillon's. Slowly the sound of tinkling laughter and voices died away, and yet she lay wide awake in her beautifully ironed nightgown, tied at the neck with a blue ribbon, and stared at the stars. Her room opened to a small wrought-iron balcony, along the lines of that onto which Juliet wandered.

The stars were far away, small and cold and quite unlike the twinkling bits of gold flake that still danced at the corner of her vision. She tried to imagine using transparent stretches of silk to revolutionize Mr. Tey's stages, but she dropped the idea without even trying. She didn't want to paint scenery flats any longer. And it wasn't only because Grieve's set had been so much better than hers.

For some reason, it felt as if *she'd* taken Gil's virginity, which was absurd. Absurd. Then why did she feel this dragging sadness?

Clouds kept drifting across the full moon, looking like

boats, frigates, and ships making their way over to France, and all those enchanting, irresistible Frenchwomen.

At last she fell asleep, not even realizing that her cheeks were wet.

Chapter Thirteen

The next day Emma went back to St. Albans and waited for Gil to contact her. A day passed. Another day. Bethany sent a scolding letter, and a former school friend wrote, describing Gil's scandalous behavior at the Cavendish masquerade. By all accounts, he left the ball with a Frenchwoman. Emma smiled to herself. Another day passed.

On the third day, Emma received a letter from her cousin. It seemed that Kerr had danced all night long, the previous night, with the wife of a French *envoy,* and there was talk of a duel. That letter struck like a blow from the dark.

Suddenly Emma realized that she hadn't really thought that Gil would be so dazzled by Madame de Custine that he wouldn't realize who she was, eventually. She hadn't truly believed that her future husband was the sort of man who slept with a beautiful Frenchwoman and never asked for her forwarding address.

But it seemed that Gil was precisely that sort of man.

As the days passed, the Earl of Kerr was as uncommunicative as he'd been for the previous three years. So finally Emma spoke to her father, who focused on his daughter just long enough to agree that perhaps the betrothal had been a mistake.

Kerr responded by return post to her request that their engagement be terminated. Most likely he had been hoping for just such a letter. After all, the man had devoted himself to outraging his fiancée's sensibilities. Her mail was flooded with letters describing a flaxen-haired beauty in his carriage at Hyde Park; the color her hair notwithstanding, no one had the slightest hesitation in asserting the woman's nationality.

As for her, Emma had come to understanding that in winning, one can lose as well. She didn't want Gil on the terms that he had flung forth as a challenge. What's more, the whole baby-in-one's-belly thing must take more than one night, as she'd discovered in the last two weeks. She didn't want Gil on the terms of marriage that her father had established, either. It had never been about winning, although she hadn't understood that at first.

Now she had a new plan.

She has going to dissolve their engagement, and then she was going to London, like Queen Titania, and she was going to choose her mate.

And if he was an earl, with the initials GB-G, that would, of course, be serendipity.

She wrote back and told the earl that she saw absolutely no purpose to their meeting in person. In fact, she was occupied on the day he proposed to visit St. Albans and would rather that the business was taken care of by their respective men of business. To that end, she enclosed the name of her father's solicitor, Mr. Prindle, with all best wishes & etc.

But he was a stubborn man, this Earl of Kerr. Although he agreed with her that it was best for everyone if their betrothal be dissolved since it was initially set up, he pointed out rather unnecessarily, with the agreement of neither of them, he still felt that duty required that they effect this delicate business in person.

"I shall attend you tomorrow, Tuesday, at four in the afternoon," he finished.

Emma stared at his handwriting. Her heart panged with love and desire. That was the worst of it: she found herself lying in bed at night, wrung tight as a spring by memories of their evening together. And yet he, by all accounts, had had so many of such nights in his life that he had forgotten the half of them.

She couldn't seem to forget even the slightest detail, try though she might. She practiced her archery. Her arm brushed her chest as she pulled back the bow, and the pang of lust at the thought of Gil's mouth went straight down her spine. She took a bath and rubbed rose-scented oil on her legs, and that simple, innocent action, which she had completed every day since her birth, was no longer simple. Nor innocent.

He'd changed her. Yet he hadn't been changed at all, and the knowledge of it was bitter as ashes in her mouth.

It didn't change her conviction though.

She would dissolve their false betrothal, come to London as herself, and make him beg at her feet for those same indulgences that Frenchwomen gave to him with such generosity. She ordered a dozen more gowns from Madame Maisonnat on the strength of her conviction.

The next morning, she didn't even feel nervous. *This* was not the game. The game would start when she moved herself to London, to her sister's house, in one week. *This* was merely the prelude.

Her maid wound her hair into a circle of braids and pulled a few curls loose to bob at her ears. Emma's fingers were absolutely steady as she put discreet emeralds at her ears and buttoned the small buttons on one of Madame Maisonnat's military-inspired gowns. She was a general in a campaign of great importance.

Finally she looked at herself in the mirror. Of course, he might recognize her. She had not worn a mask in the darkness of the carriage, nor again in the darkness of the theater. But she didn't think he would. She was forming the impression that the Earl of Kerr was a man who drifted from woman to woman, not examining them very closely. After all, he accepted her tale of Emelie.

No, he probably wouldn't recognize her. Context was important, and the great charm of Madame Maisonnat's gown had nothing to do with an exuberant show of bosom. This was not the dress of a sparkling, glittering Frenchwoman, but that of a steady, responsible Englishwoman, prepared to dissolve her betrothal with an offer of guarded friendship and an acknowledgment of mutual disinclination to commit matrimony based on their fathers' wishes.

He was waiting in her sitting room when she entered, so she gestured to the butler to close the doors without announcing her. He stood by the window overlooking the long sweep of the lawn to the apple orchard. For a moment she just feasted on the line of his thigh, the hair curling at his neck, the impatient click of his crop against his boots.

He was very dear to her. Surprisingly so, she had to acknowledge.

"Lord Kerr," she said coolly, holding out her hand as she came toward him, "it is indeed a pleasure to see you."

He turned around. Her heart stopped. But—nothing happened.

He showed no signs of recognizing Emelie. Instead, he

bowed and took her hand, raising it to his lips as politely as if she were a matron of long acquaintance. "I can only apologize for my overly prolonged absence, Miss Loudan."

She inclined her head with just the right amount of steady, impersonal acceptance. "Won't you sit down, my lord?" She walked over to a settee, but rather than sitting in the chair that she indicated with a wave of her hand, he sat down just beside her. Every atom in her body sprang to life at his scent, at his closeness, at the dearness of him.

"So you would like to annul our engagement?" he enquired.

She pushed away the black flood of disappointment in her heart as firmly as she could. She could think about that later. She knew her beloved's shortcomings when it came to remembering his amorous adventures; there could be nothing new in the idea that she was no more novel than any other woman.

She nodded. "I think it would be best." She opened her reticule and took out the elaborate ring that his father had sent her father as a sign of their agreement. He opened his hand without hesitation, and she dropped it onto his palm. She didn't trust herself to touch his fingers, even in passing.

"I must say, I am grateful," he said. "I wished to tell you this in person, Miss Loudan. Although as a man of honor, I would never have ended our betrothal, I do wish to marry another. I have lost my heart, foolish though that sounds. And so I am grateful for your decision."

"We should never have suited," she said quickly, because a black wave was threatening to pull her under and send her crying from the room. "Child betrothals are a relic of the past."

"True," he said, smiling genially. "Of course, the Elizabethans liked such things and found them useful."

"Quite."

"I am inordinantly fond of Elizabethan customs," he said, obviously making conversation to cover the awkward fact that they, who had been betrothed to each other for years, had nothing to say.

"Indeed," Emma murmured, wondering where her father was. He had promised that he would come into the room and soothe the whole process. Of course, he had probably decided to reread some article on the diet of baboons and quite forgotten that Kerr was coming.

"Almost as much as I love the customs of the French," he said.

Emma's brows pulled together. This was a bit much! Not only did he make a laughingstock of himself and her all over London, with his Gallic obsessions, but he dared to throw it in her face.

"I have heard as much," she said stiffly.

"So, you truly wish to dissolve our betrothal?" he said.

"Even more so now that I hear you wish to marry," she noted, her voice still chill.

"She is a darling," he said pensively. "I do wish that the two of you could meet. I feel as if we have known each other for years, you and I, although we have infrequently met."

She ground her teeth and thought cruel thoughts about her father. "Quite so," she said.

"Will you be coming to London?"

"Naturally," she said. "I shall come for the remainder of the season." If he were a man of any conscience at all, he would know that his discarded fiancée would be desperate to find another husband. Except that at four and twenty she was decayed beyond all hope, as Bethany had said.

"I shall introduce you," he said with perfect sangfroid. "She is French; I'm afraid that I have a weakness for women of the Gallic persuasion."

"So I have heard," Emma said, choking back a wish to

strangle the man. She rose from the settee, thinking of nothing but escape. He rose as well, naturally.

"I'm afraid that I have a very busy morning ahead of me, Lord Kerr." She sank into a curtsy. "If you will excuse me . . ."

"But I want to tell you more about her," he said, and she accidentally met his eye for the first time since he entered the room.

What she saw there made her stand as if she were rooted to the carpet.

"She's exquisite, like all Frenchwomen."

"Of course," Emma whispered.

He was walking toward her, and she knew that devil, wicked, laughing look on his face. She knew it, oh, how she knew it.

"She wears her hair down on occasion. And she's as good at playing the queen as the courtesan, if you follow me."

She nodded.

"But of course I shouldn't speak so to an innocent English maiden, should I? Should I, Emelie?"

Surely that was joy in her heart. It was a new feeling, and so potent she couldn't be sure. "Did you—when did you know?" she whispered.

"Did you never think that I heard of your scene painting?"

Her eyes widened. "You knew before—before we went to Hyde Park Theatre?"

"There was something about you that I recognized, that made me uneasy and yet made me want to laugh." He was standing just before her now, and somehow he'd trapped both her hands and had them at his mouth. "And then you suddenly told me that you painted flats. Darling, you are the only woman in all England who does such a thing. How could you think that I would not know it?"

"It's not at all well-known," Emma objected. "Not a single audience member knows that I painted Mr. Tey's flats."

"Have you forgotten my godmother, the Countess of Bredelbane?"

"Oh," Emma said, remembering all the letters exchanged between the countess and herself over the years.

"She has pursued a relentless campaign to put the two of us before an altar." He was pressing kisses into her palms, and her knees were weak again. "So, darling—" His eyes searched her face. "Am I to gather that you have not succeeded in quite all of my demands?"

Pink crept into her cheeks, and she shook her head. He was sliding something over her finger, a heavy, elaborate ring that once belonged to his forefathers.

"I should like the chance to try again," he said simply.

The smile was almost painful, she felt it so deeply.

"Again. Again and again, Emma. Somehow I fell in love with you. With everything about you."

"Not with Emelie?" she asked, letting him pull her close and closer still.

He shook his head. "'Twas Emma who put on the masquerade, and Emma who paints, and Emma who ravished me as Queen Titania, and Emma who ravishes me as herself."

He gave her a fierce kiss.

"And it was Emma, damn it, who took such an unaccountably long time to contact me. I thought I'd die during these two weeks, Emma. I was afraid that I'd disappointed you, and you had decided to find a new husband."

"I'm sorry," she whispered, tracing that line of his lip with an unsteady finger.

"Don't ever do that again!"

"Do what?" She'd lost track of the conversation.

"Stay away from me. Ever."

"*You* stayed away from me," she pointed out. "If you knew, why didn't you come here the next morning? Why did you dance with a Frenchwoman?"

He looked down at her with his small, crooked smile. "I wanted a bit of revenge. For your calling in the favor. I found it hard, you see, to admit that I had lost the challenge. But I was about to come to you when you finally wrote me."

There was just one thing, one small question that she had to ask: "So you won't wish to return to France someday?"

He pressed a kiss on each of her eyelids. "I'm done trying to throw myself from Walter's carriage. I loved him, and I love you. And I'll love that babe once we have him or her. I have the fiercest wish to hang onto the reins, Emma."

"I love you," she whispered into his neck. *"Je t'adore."*

"In English, Emma. In solid, old-fashioned, Anglo-Saxon English, I love you."

A Note About
Scene Painters and Sisters

As a female scene painter, Emma would have been quite unusual for the 1800s, although not utterly improbable, as women were employed in many areas of the stage by this period. I made Emma a scene painter because my imagination was caught by the description of Philip de Loutherbourg's sets for Drury Lane, created in the 1770s. One of de Loutherbourg's innovations was to stretch colored silks on side scenes that served as transparent shades, casting a brilliant color on the backdrop. As soon as I read this detail (thanks to my brilliant research assistant, Franzeca Drouin), I imagined the scene between Emma and Gil: a proud Titania challenging—and conquering—her wayward Oberon. The description of the fairy woods is purely my invention, although the performance of *A Midsummer Night's Dream* was certainly probable. In the season 1811–1812, for example, there were eight Shakespeare revivals staged at Covent Garden theater alone.

One final note: Emma's sister Bethany Lynn is a real person, blessed with a passionate and loving husband who wrote me a note out of the blue, telling me of his wife's birthday and his wish to give her a particularly interesting birthday present. So . . .

Happy Birthday, Bethany Lynn!

The Vicar's Widow

Julia London

Chapter One

London, 1816

On the chilly December night that Darien, Lord Montgomery, hosted a holiday soiree in honor of his sister's recent nuptials, some happy culprit seasoned the cranberry punch with an entire bottle of gin.

The crime was established quite early when the offending bottle was found, sans contents, beneath the sideboard where the punch was being served. Or rather, *had* been served, as it had proven to be a popular refreshment.

Any and all would acknowledge that it wasn't entirely unusual for a little sauce to be covertly added to the punches at lively affairs in Mayfair's finest homes—particularly when the invitation list included some of the *ton*'s most notorious revelers—but it was unusual for the *ton*'s least-likely revelers to be in attendance, and on this night, the results of mixing those two crowds with a little gin proved to be . . . well, interesting.

Particularly for Montgomery. Not that he'd been among the revelers to have overindulged in the punch (more was the pity), but because he'd been occupied with tending to the comfort of his nearly one hundred guests, as well as ensuring that his good friend, Lord Frederick (otherwise known as Freddie), did not scandalize *every* young lady beneath the mistletoe as he seemed bent on doing.

In light of that, it was an ironic twist that Darien himself would be the one to do the scandalizing.

In hindsight, he could not begin to describe how it might have all happened, other than to note that he did indeed own a reputation for being something of a notorious bachelor. His favorite activity, after all, was women—flirting, seducing, making love—followed closely by hunting and equestrian sports. He was not, in his own estimation, the sort of chap to pass up an opportunity to gaze at a young lady's décolletage or take a kiss . . . or more, were the lady so inclined.

But *that* evening, he had enough to do just playing host.

All right, then, to be fair—he had indeed made a trip or two to one of half a dozen sprigs of mistletoe he had hanging about the grand salon of the old Montgomery mansion on Audley Street, both times hoping to catch the vicar's wife below it.

Oh yes, he'd certainly noticed the vicar's young wife, along with every other man in attendance. How could he not? She was lovely. She had a glow about her, the sort of complexion one associated with the good health of country folk. With her pretty green eyes and reddish blond hair, she was quite remarkably pretty, especially when compared to the pale-skinned debutantes who stocked the streets and parlors of London.

But the most remarkable thing about the vicar's wife was her vivacious smile. When she spoke, her eyes sparkled with enthusiasm. When she smiled, it seemed as if her entire body and those around her were illuminated with the brilliance of it. That smile was the one thing that compelled Darien to attend Sunday services each week, and not, as he had professed, the vicar's rousing sermons.

And Darien imagined that lovely smile was what caused the good vicar, Richard Becket, to return last spring from his annual trek home to Bishop's Castle in Shropshire, quite unexpectedly, with a wife. Darien would have been sorely tempted to do the same, had he been in the vicar's shoes.

This December night, she arrived dressed in a deep green velvet gown that was the exact color of her eyes, and Darien could not seem to keep from looking at her. As the evening wore on, and the guests grew livelier (thanks to their gin-soaked libations), her smile seemed to grow brighter, warmer, and on more than one occasion, it seemed to be aimed directly at him.

But Darien lost track of her altogether when Lady Ramblecourt had a nasty encounter with a chair, after which, having observed that fiasco, what with the wailing and whatnot, the natives began to root about for more of the punch. Darien's butler, Kiefer, was nowhere to be seen, so Darien hastened to the wine cellar to bring up more gin, lest he have a mutiny on his hands.

He was quite pleasantly surprised to find Mrs. Becket on the lower floor, propped up against one side of the stone wall that formed the narrow corridor leading to the cellar stairs, fanning herself. She glanced up when he landed on the last step and smiled prettily.

"Oh, my Lord Montgomery!" she demurred, her gloved hands fluttering near her face. "I pray you will forgive me, but I found it necessary to seek a cool and quiet place for a time."

She did seem rather flushed. "You are more than welcome to any inch of my house, madam," he said sincerely, clasping his hands behind his back. "Or my orangery, or my livery. Whatever you desire, you may have, Mrs. Becket."

She laughed lightly and pushed a loose strand of that glorious red-gold hair that hung across her eye. "How gallant! You are too kind," she said, and closed her eyes.

"Are you quite all right, Mrs. Becket?"

She opened one eye. "Do I seem unwell?" she asked, wincing a bit. "I'm afraid I might have drunk too much of your delicious punch."

"Quite the contrary, actually. You seem, at least to these eyes, rather well indeed," he said, and let his gaze casually peruse the shapely length of her. "In fact," he added, lifting his gaze languidly, "there has been many a Sunday morning that I looked at you and thought that perhaps I was gazing upon one of God's angels, you look so well." He smiled provocatively.

Mrs. Becket opened the other eye and lowered her head, gazing up at him through long lashes with a suspicious smile. "My husband has warned me about men like you, sir," she said pleasantly. "In fact, he's warned me several times of you in particular."

"Has he indeed?" Darien asked, cheerfully surprised that a man like Becket would have discerned the subtle smiles and greetings Darien had freely bestowed on his young wife. "And what has he warned you?"

Now she lifted her chin and filled the corridor with a soft, warm laugh. "That a rogue, by any other name, should smile as sweet, but is still a rogue."

Darien couldn't help his appreciative laugh. He took a step closer and asked low, "A philosopher, is he? And what does the good vicar say about beauty, Mrs. Becket? Does he quote Petrarch?"

"Petrarch?"

"An Italian philosopher, long dead and buried," Darien said and casually reached out, tucked the loose strand of Mrs. Becket's hair that had once more slipped over her eye behind her ear. His finger grazed the plump curve of her ear, and he lingered beneath her crystal earring, toying with it. "Petrarch said that rarely do great beauty and great virtue dwell together."

Mrs. Becket lifted one brow, then smiled fully, touched the strand of hair he had pushed behind her ear. "Mr. Petrarch sounds a rather jaded man. But I'm hardly certain if you mean to imply that perhaps I am a great beauty, my lord? Or possess great virtue? In either case, I should hardly know if I am to be insulted or pleased."

"I am certain you are in firm possession of both," he said with a slight bow, but he smiled a little crookedly. "I can see the great beauty. And I trust the great virtue."

Mrs. Becket laughed low and pressed her gloved palm to her cheek. "My, it seems rather warm, even down here, does it not, my lord?"

"Quite," he said. "I was just to the cellar to bring up a bottle of gin. Perhaps you might help me select. I am certain you will find the cellar much cooler."

She glanced at the stairs leading to the cellar, then at him. "Ah, but that would be less than virtuous to accompany you to the cellar, would it not?"

"Absolutely," he readily agreed. "But then again, there's little harm in being slightly less virtuous in exchange for comfort." He winked, held out his arm to her.

She looked again at the cellar stairs, and after a moment, nodded resolutely and pushed away from the wall. "You will find that I possess great virtue above the cellar, and in the cellar," she said with a bob of her head, and put her hand on his arm.

"What a pity," Darien said congenially, and led her to the top of the stairs. Next to the stairs was a small alcove from where he picked up a candle, lit it from one of the wall sconces, and turned toward Mrs. Becket. Still smiling, he took her hand in his and led the way down into the wine cellar.

At least he'd been truthful about the cellar; it was cooler the deeper they walked in between the shelves of wine and fine liquors.

"It's delightfully cooler here," Mrs. Becket said. "I am feeling quite renewed."

"Ah," he said, finding the shelf with the gin. "Here we are." He put aside the candle and picked up a bottle to inspect it. Mrs. Becket peered over his shoulder. He turned toward her, the bottle in hand, and smiled at her sparkling green eyes. "Rather a good year for gin, I think."

"I wouldn't know, personally," she said with mock superiority, "other than to say the addition of gin to a cranberry punch is most delicious."

"I'm glad you found it to your liking," he said. "It was quite unintentional." And as he moved to put the bottle back and find another, he heard the scurrying feet of a rodent.

Mrs. Becket shrieked at the sound of it and lurched into his chest, grabbing his lapel in one hand. Darien grasped her firmly by the arms before they toppled into the shelving. "A mouse," he said soothingly. "A little mouse as frightened of you as you are of it, I assure you. No doubt the tiny devil has already returned to his den."

"A mouse," she echoed and closed her eyes a moment as she sought her breath. But she did not let go his lapel. When she opened her eyes again, she was looking at his mouth. Her lips parted softly with a sigh of relief, and she drew a ragged breath.

In the dim golden light of that single candle, Darien saw the rosy skin of her cheeks, the smooth column of her neck, the rise of her bosom, and a look in her eyes that he felt deep to the very depth of himself. In a moment of madness, without thought, without so much as a breath, he let go her arm, put his hand around her waist, and pulled her tightly to him at the same time he put his lips to hers.

She did not resist him; her hand loosened on his lapel and slid up to his neck, to his jaw. Reverently, he kissed her, sinking into a vague feeling of remorse for having done it at all. But she wore the scent of gardenias in her hair and on her neck, and the scent filled him with an almighty lust. Remorse was swallowed whole by desire spreading through him.

His hand tightened at her waist; he touched his tongue to hers, and she easily opened to him. He had an image of her body opening much like that, and his desire got the best of him. He kissed her madly, his tongue in her mouth, his teeth on her lips, his hand drifting to the swell of her lovely bum, grasping it and holding her against him.

Her hand sank into his hair, the other clinging tightly to his shoulder, fingers digging through fabric to bone, her desire as stark as his. His cock grew hard between them, and he pressed it against her. Mrs. Becket responded by moving seductively against him, her pelvis sliding against his, her breasts pressed to his chest. It was a wild kiss, full of illicit pleasure, hot and full of longing and anticipation.

But then suddenly, she jerked away, pushed his hands from her body, and stepped back. Her eyes blazed with passion and fear and a host of other things Darien could not identify. She dragged the back of her hand across her mouth, then pressed it against her bosom, over her heart.

"Oh my God," she whispered, staring at him. "Oh dear God, what have I done?"

"Mrs. Becket," he said, reaching for her, but it was too late. She'd already turned on her heel and fled the dark cellar. He could hear the click of her heels against the stairs as she fought her way up to the surface.

Darien stood there until he could no longer hear the sound of her shoes.

He'd just kissed the vicar's wife. A bloody rotten bounder, that's what he was. *Idiot.*

With a sigh, he straightened his clothing, adjusted his trousers, and ran his fingers through his hair. When he was convinced he had returned quite to normal, he picked up a bottle of gin and his candle, and strode from the cellar.

He did not see Mrs. Becket again that night. Nor was she in church the following Sunday.

And every Sunday after that, she pretended not to see him. But Darien saw her. He did not press his case, but he saw her, for he could not take his eyes from her.

A few months later, in a tragic collision of his horse and a rogue carriage, her husband, the vicar, was thrown off Blackfriar's Bridge to the murky Thames below.

His body was not recovered for several days.

Chapter Two

London, 1819

For the first time in the little more than two years since Richard had died, Kate Becket finally gave in to her father's urging and put away her widow's weeds. She donned a new gold walking gown trimmed in green around the hem and sleeves. Standing in her bedroom in the little guest house on the vicar's property—where she and her father had been permitted to live since her husband's death—Kate looked at herself in the full-length mirror and smiled. Gold was a much more becoming color for her than black.

She'd been reluctant to discard her widow's weeds and had worn them longer than the customary two years. It seemed as if taking them off made her disloyal to Richard's memory somehow, as if she was anxious to be rid of his ghost. Nothing could be further from the truth—she had loved Richard, had been devastated by his tragic death, and had truly and deeply mourned him.

But when spring came, she had awakened one morning with the surprisingly resolute feeling that it was time to move past her husband's memory and live her life again.

Today, when she made her weekly call to the elderly and infirm members of the congregation with their fruit baskets, she'd be wearing her new gold gown and matching pelisse and bonnet. It had cost a fortune for a woman on a widow's pension, but it made her feel pretty, and the good Lord knew she had not felt pretty in a very long time.

It was well worth the expense.

An hour later, with her father trailing behind her pushing the small cart of fruit baskets, Kate made her first call to the positively ancient Mrs. Biddlesly, who defied the universe by living past her eightieth year. Mrs. Biddlesly instantly declared her dislike of fruit and pushed the basket aside (although Kate knew she'd eat every last bite once she'd gone), then peered at Kate through rheumy eyes and demanded to know what had happened to her mourning clothes.

"My husband has been gone two years, Mrs. Biddlesly."

"My husband died thirty-four years ago," the old woman said, shaking a crooked finger at Kate, "and to this day I mourn him!"

That she did, in the same black bombazine she wore every day.

"I mourn my husband, too, Mrs. Biddlesly, and I always shall," Kate assured her with a smile. "But life must go on. Don't you agree?"

"*Bah!*" Mrs. Biddlesly said and eyed an apple in the basket. "Rotten stuff, that fruit. Don't bring fruit again!"

Kate assured her she wouldn't, and moved to the door,

smiling at the equally ancient footman who moved to open it for her.

"Ho there, where do you think you are going?" Mrs. Biddlesly shrieked. "I've not said you might go!"

With a look toward heaven, Kate turned round. A full half hour later, she managed to escape, having endured the cataloguing of all Mrs. Biddlesly's physical ailments—in precise detail, thank you.

Kate's father was leaning against his little cart as she bounced down the stairs.

"A list of complaints again, eh?"

"Indeed," Kate said with a laugh. "And she's added quite a few more since last week."

With a snort, her father rolled his eyes. "Don't know why you bother at all, Kate. She's an ungrateful old bat."

"Ah, she is that. But I can't help but do so, Papa—no one else will bother with her," Kate said and adjusted her bonnet. "Well then! Shall we call on Mr. Heather?"

With another shake of his head, her father grabbed the cart handle. He looked up, over Kate's shoulder, and nodded to something behind her as she took another basket from the cart. "Looks as if you'll have an escort again this week."

Kate turned around—and almost collided with Lord Montgomery. Again. Another happy coincidence. In fact, she quickly calculated it was the eighth happy coincidence in as many weeks.

"Beg your pardon, Mrs. Becket. I must have startled you," he said with a mischievous smile.

"Not at all, my lord!" A ridiculously large, unguarded grin split her face.

He glanced over her shoulder at her father and touched the brim of his hat. "Good day, Mr. Crowley. Fine day for a walkabout, eh?"

"Aye, it is, as fine a day as the past Wednesday's walka-bout, and the one before it," Papa snorted. "You go on ahead, Kate," he said, ducking beneath the wide brim of his hat as he busied himself with the rearranging of the baskets in his little cart. "I've a bit of tidying up to do here, and you'd not want to keep Mr. Heather waiting for his victuals."

"Thank you, Papa." She stole a glimpse of Montgomery. "Mr. Heather is undoubtedly pacing the floor, wondering what could be keeping us. He's rather the nervous sort."

"You are so good to engage in such charitable works, Mrs. Becket, and how diligent you are about it!" Montgomery exclaimed. "There are others who are not as gener-ous with either their time or their spirit, myself chief among them."

"Indeed? I naturally assumed you were calling on them yourself, sir. Whatever else might bring you to this street each Wednesday?" she asked with a sly smile.

He chuckled boyishly, took the basket from her hand, and walked beside her as she started down the street. "You give me too much credit. My motives are far more nefari-ous than charitable endeavors, I freely admit."

"Nefarious?" She laughed. "Lord Montgomery, how you tease me! I'd wager you've not a wicked bone in your body!"

He gave her a look that suggested she knew better than that, leaned slightly toward her, and said low, "You'd be quite wrong, madam, were you to wager. I've more than one wicked bone in this body."

That sent a heat straight up her spine, and Kate swal-lowed. There were few persons who could confound her, but Montgomery happened to be the king.

"Ah, look here! I've offended you," he said cheerfully.

Offended was not exactly the word she'd use, and she laughed. "Offended? Never! Titillated is more accurate," she said, and unthinkingly stole a glimpse of her father over her shoulder. He was keeping quite a distance behind her and Lord Montgomery. She slid her gaze to his lordship again; his two thick brows had risen quite up to his hat.

"I'll have you know that the gentleman in me is aghast at having titillated. But the man in me is rather intrigued by it."

She believed him—his eyes were glittering with the intrigue, and she could feel the spark of it herself, all the way to her toes.

"I find I rather enjoy titillating beautiful young widows."

And this young widow enjoyed being titillated—in fact, she was so caught up in the state of titillation that she had not noticed they had come to a crossing point. Montgomery casually caught her elbow, held it firmly as he looked one way and then the other, and propelled her across the street.

"I have misjudged you, then," Kate said airily, thoroughly enjoying his possessive hand on her arm. "You *are* a wicked man if you enjoy titillating widows."

"Ah, Mrs. Becket, I give you my word that I am indeed quite wicked when the situation warrants." They had reached the other side of the street, yet he held fast to her elbow and looked her in the eye. "And I give you my word that I would endeavor to be as wicked as you'd like, given the slightest opportunity."

The fire in her was now burning quite out of control, her mind racing with deliciously dark thoughts of just how wicked this handsome man might be with her. As the heat rose to her cheeks, she laughed. "If I didn't know you to be a gentleman of the highest caliber, my lord, I would believe you are trying to seduce me."

He cocked a brow as his gaze boldly swept the length of her. "What's a man to do then," he muttered, "when a widow puts away her weeds and presents herself so pleasingly?" he asked, slowly lifting his gaze to hers again. "A lovelier woman I've not seen, Mrs. Becket. You are the stuff of men's dreams," he said, as his gaze dipped to her bosom. "A prettier gown I've not seen . . . or perhaps it is the woman who makes the gown so delightful."

Kate laughed at his blatant attempted to seduce her. "You are a rake!" she cried happily and pulled her elbow free of his hand. "I am now quite convinced that the rumors of your . . . *skill* . . . with the ladies of the *ton* must be well deserved."

"My reputation is indeed well deserved!" he said with mock indignation. "But I would toss all others aside for the mere pleasure of your company, I assure you."

Now Kate laughed roundly, tossing her head back with delight. "Honestly, my Lord Montgomery!" she declared. "How silly you are! I am hardly one of the many naive young debutantes who seek your attention, and I daresay I cannot be drawn into your charms with false flattery!"

"Ah!" he cried, bringing a hand to his heart. "I am mortally wounded, Mrs. Becket, for how could one gaze upon a face as lovely as yours and offer anything but the sincerest and warmest esteem?"

"Have you considered the theater?" Kate asked flippantly as she continued up the street. "I should think you'd make a fine dramatic actor!"

Montgomery easily fell into step with her. "I have considered nothing but my heart, and how I long for you to hold it, Mrs. Becket," he said, grinning. "But alas, you think me a rogue, a *roué,* when I only seek the favor of your smile."

"Come now, my lord. Is that all you seek?" she asked, watching him coyly from the corner of her eye.

He sighed with exaggerated frustration. Kate smiled at his square jaw, his thick lashes, the full lips she remembered so keenly. It was almost as if that illicit kiss had happened only yesterday, the very same kiss that had burned in her memory these last two and a half years, making her sick with guilt and heady with imagination.

"There you are, you've caught me red-handed," he said, shaking his head, and smiling down at her as they reached Mr. Heather's stoop. "I should never be content with a mere smile, no matter how beautiful it is. I'd want more. I'd want *all*."

The look in his eyes was scorching, and Kate slowly drew a breath, awkwardly took the basket of fruit from his hand, and held it tightly against her chest. He was smiling, but his eyes . . . there was something else in his eyes, something that made her believe he spoke true.

Thankfully, the sound of her father's cart rattling up behind them snapped her out her trance. "I beg your pardon sir, but Mr. Heather will be wanting his fruit. Please excuse me." She curtsied and stepped away from him.

With a grin that made her heart sink, Montgomery stepped back, swept his hat off a head of thick gold hair, and bowed with a flourish. "I shall indeed leave you to your good works, knowing that I may now go to my grave a happy man, for having titillated the fair Widow Becket." With that, he straightened, put the hat back on his head. His eyes were full of mirth again; the deep-water look had gone.

"Ah, a *roué*, indeed!" Kate said and laughed as she reluctantly put one foot on the steps leading to Mr. Heather's door. "I pity the poor young ladies who will be titillated by you and fall prey to your wicked ways, sir."

"Pity them? Or envy them?" he asked with a subtle wink.

"You're incorrigible!"

"Thank you! I am endeavoring very hard to be."

Kate laughed as her father rolled to a mere crawl to

keep from joining their private conversation. "Thank you for walking with me, sir. Good day!" she said cheerfully.

Montgomery chuckled and touched his hand to the brim of his hat. "Good day, Mrs. Becket," he said, and turned smartly to her father. "Good day to you, Mr. Crowley."

"My lord."

With a jaunty wave, Lord Montgomery started back the direction he'd come, striding long and whistling a cheerful little tune.

Kate was still swimming in a pool of desire, and with a smile that would not possibly fade, she walked up the steps to knock on Mr. Heather's door.

He adored her. He wanted her for his very own, and no one else would do.

As Darien walked down that street, he thought that now she had at last divested herself of those wretched widow's weeds (and hadn't she looked exceedingly lovely today in that brilliant gold?), he could feel his desire more keenly— it could not be avoided or evaded.

How he had come to this state of wanting, he could not really say. For years, he'd been content to be the man about town, flirting with debutantes, engaging in trysts with ladies who'd married money rather than husbands, and frequenting the gentlemen's clubs where all sorts of lecherous games might be arranged. He had enjoyed his reputation of being a wealthy, incorrigible bachelor.

But then his sister Anne had married, and Darien found himself thinking about life.

The more he thought on it, the more he began to realize how weary he was growing of the *ton's* clubs and salons, how the sameness of elite society was weighing on him. Nothing ever seemed to change—the endless round of parties and routs, the endless talk of who was having an adulterous affair with whom, or who was just out, or who had gained a fortune, and who had lost one.

Darien crossed the street, his stride determined. He wanted more.

He had, in the last two or three years, since passing the age of thirty, begun to feel a persistent urge to settle down with a woman, to start a family. Anne seemed quite happy with the state of matrimony and was already expecting her second child. Darien wanted what Anne had, that happiness that comes without thought or effort, that just seems to naturally occur when one's heart is held by another.

Unfortunately, he was not very impressed with the current crop of debutantes and other marriageable women of the *ton*. As a group, they were uninteresting. They seemed to know nothing of the world outside their salons, and worse, did not seem to care.

But Kate Becket . . . now there was a woman who had snatched his imagination and run away with it from almost the moment she had first appeared in Mayfair. She was very pretty and her ripe figure far more attractive to him than the slender and pale debutantes. She was articulate and possessed an uncommon wit. Their banter and exchanges at Sunday services and on the street never failed to intrigue him. He would invariably walk away from those encounters with the intense feeling that there was a living, breathing woman full of passion beneath all that black bombazine, and the man in him ached to touch her.

Certainly that long-ago Christmas kiss had fanned his imagination on that front—he'd never been able to forget it, and many was the night he'd lain in bed, reliving it, feeling her body in his arms, pressed against him, her lips, softly yielding, beneath his.

But while Kate Becket might have suffered a lapse in

judgment that night, aided by a gin-soaked punch, she was not, as a whole, the sort of woman to be drawn in by the usual, empty flirtations men used to seduce. On the contrary, she was far too clever for it. She had pegged him a *roué,* and a *roué* he was—he'd not deny it. But a *roué,* a rake, could be reformed, could direct all of his attentions on the one woman he might love.

That meant, of course, that Darien would have to redouble his efforts to woo her, for she was a tough nut—too resilient to his usual charms, and frankly, deserving of something far better than a mere smile and a crook of the finger.

Fortunately, Darien thought, as he strode down the street to his waiting carriage, he relished the challenge.

Chapter Three

Emily Forsythe, who had just turned eighteen years of age, was now officially out by virtue of having been presented at court and having made her debut at a magnificent debutante's ball just one month ago. Now that the coming out was over, she could turn her attention to marriage.

One bright Sunday morning, she wrote the names of the three men whom she would consider marrying, in order of preference: Lord Montgomery (a bit long in the tooth at two and thirty, but at forty thousand pounds a year, she didn't mind); Lord Bastian (hardly as old as her, and rather undisciplined, but at thirty thousand pounds a year, worth the effort); and Lord Dillingham (perfectly suited to her in terms of age and temperament, but rumor had it that after some disastrous investment, he now had only twenty thousand pounds a year).

Emily studied the names. She intended to have an offer

from one of them by the peak of the season, preferably at the Charity Auction Ball, an affair Lady Southbridge hosted each year to benefit the local orphanage. Emily had a lovely fantasy of being offered for in front of hundreds of the *ton*'s most elite members. She'd be wearing her court dress, of course, but with new gloves and slippers, and when the lucky gentleman made the offer, a round of applause and cheering would go up, and perhaps her friends would toss flowers from their hair to her feet as Montgomery (or Bastian or Dillingham) swept her in his arms in a mad moment of public affection.

With that happy image playing in her mind's eye, Emily put aside her pen and drew on her Sunday gloves, found her reticule, and marched out of her room to join her family for church services and the spring social immediately following. She was not the sort to ever miss an opportunity to further her cause, and as two of the gentlemen in question regularly attended church, she counted it as one of her better opportunities.

When they arrived at the church, Emily's parents and older brother took some time to greet the many friends and neighbors who had gathered on the church steps this brilliant spring morning. As Emily impatiently waited for her parents, her eyes scanned the crowd; she spotted Montgomery off to one side, speaking with the last vicar's widow.

Interesting. Mrs. Becket had put away her widow's weeds and was wearing a blue brocade gown that Emily thought conspicuously bright for Sunday services. The widow was laughing at something Montgomery said, her eyes crinkled appealingly at the corners. Emily instantly urged her father in that direction, hoping for the chance to converse with Montgomery, but her father was engaged in a lively conversation with Lord Frederick and would not be budged. Emily could do nothing but stand by dutifully.

But she could watch intently as Montgomery leaned his head close to the widow and said something that made the woman blush. *Blush!* Imagine it, a widow blushing like a girl! It was, in Emily's opinion, unseemly.

When at last it came time to enter the church, the Forsythe family filed in and occupied the third pew to the right of the pulpit, as was their custom. On the second row to the left of the pulpit, Lord Montgomery had joined his sister and her husband, as was his custom. Emily liked this arrangement—she could watch him in the course of the services. Typically, she alternated between Montgomery and Dillingham, who sat directly before her, but Dillingham was in the country this weekend, and Bastian, alas, was apparently a sinner, for he did not attend services with any regularity. That would, of course, change if Emily accepted his offer.

As the services started, she settled in, one eye trained on Montgomery, the other on the vicar, naturally, lest anyone think she wasn't completely attentive. But her attention to the vicar soon waned as it became apparent to her that Montgomery was not listening to him, either. She couldn't be *completely* certain, but she thought he was watching the widow Becket, who was seated off to one side with her father.

But *why* would he be watching her?

Emily mulled that one over. It wasn't as if Widow Becket was any sort of match for a viscount! Her beginnings were humble, as Emily understood them, and she was living in the guest house on the vicar's small estate. Not only that, she was *old*. Granted, not so old that she required a cane or any such thing, but too old to be contemplating marriage again.

Yet at the conclusion of the insufferably long service, Emily was positively convinced that Montgomery had gazed at Mrs. Becket the entire service. Well, *mostly* convinced—she supposed it was possible that he'd been gazing at the cross above her head, divining some sort of inspiration.

Nevertheless, the possibility troubled her.

At last, the congregation filed out the church and tromped around through the courtyard, across the cemetery, to the old stables converted to meeting rooms where the spring social would be held. Emily escaped her parents, and her brother, who wandered off to join other young men that Emily had no use for, and made her way to sit beside Miss Tabitha Townsend, who, like her, had come out just this season. Emily and Tabitha had known each other since they were girls.

"Have you received an invitation to the May Day Ball?" Tabitha asked breathlessly once the two young women had exchanged pleasantries.

A ridiculous question. Of *course* she'd been invited. "Of course."

"What do you intend to wear?" Tabitha asked anxiously.

"I've a new yellow silk set aside for just that occasion." Emily had managed to convince her father she needed a new gown for every event of the season.

"*Ooh,* how lovely."

Tabitha sighed so longingly that Emily gathered her pale blue gown would be making its third appearance this season. The Townsends were not as wealthy as the Forsythes, which everyone knew, but Tabitha proceeded to launch into a rather lengthy tale of her latest trip to the modiste, and how, in a tragic turn of events, her new silk gown would not be ready for the May Day Ball.

Emily lost interest and began to look around at the congregation milling about, her eyes trained for Montgomery.

He was easy to spot—a head taller than most, his handsome face radiated a warmhearted smile as he spoke with fat old Lady Vandergast.

Emily *would* speak to him today. Determined, she glanced down to straighten the buttons of her gloves as Tabitha droned on. But when she glanced up again, she frowned—Widow Becket was standing very near Montgomery. Again.

"What do you think?" Tabitha asked.

"I beg your pardon?" Emily asked, dragging her gaze away from Montgomery.

"About the shoes. Should I wear the silver, to match the reticule? Or the blue, to match the gown?"

"The silver. Contrasts are all the rage," Emily said instantly. "By the bye, have you noticed that the Widow Becket has come out of her weeds?"

Tabitha looked to where Emily indicated and exclaimed happily, "Aha, she has indeed. Has it been as long as two years since the poor vicar's death?"

"Just, actually," Emily said. "I wonder if she intends to stay on in London, or trot back to Wales or wherever it is she comes from."

"Oh no, I should think she'd stay," Tabitha said instantly and with some authority. "Mrs. Becket is engaged in a charitable endeavor benefiting the Hospital for the Infirm, as is my mother. Mother told me that Mrs. Becket and her father have been granted the right to stay on at the vicar's guest house for as long as she liked. Mrs. Becket said likely she would, as there is so much more she might do with her charity work in London than in Shropshire."

Emily narrowed her eyes and glared at Tabitha. "Are you quite certain?"

Tabitha shrugged weakly. "Fairly certain, yes." She

turned away from Emily's intent gaze and looked at the widow again. "She was a *Methodist,* you know," she suddenly whispered.

Emily gasped.

Tabitha nodded fiercely. "Mother says that our departed vicar found her in a Methodist church in the country and fell quite in love with her. So inspired was he by his love that he convinced her to join the Church of England and come to London." She paused there and sighed dreamily. "Isn't it romantic? He saved her from the Methodists! My cousin Alice had something very similar happen," she added, and launched into yet another excruciatingly boring tale having something to do with more country people.

Romantic it was not, Emily thought. How *dare* Widow Becket, a *Methodist* of all things, insert herself into the *ton*? She thought to stay on in London so that she might carry on indecently, as she was this very moment? Preying on marriageable men and taking the attention from debutantes? Emily glowered across the crowd at Montgomery, who was still speaking to Widow Becket, standing entirely too close to the woman and smiling in a way that made Emily fume. He was bestowing an indecorous smile on a *vicar's widow,* and worse, his lordship clearly held the woman in some esteem!

As for *her,* Widow Becket was looking up at him and laughing in that perfectly adorable way she had of laughing. It was enough to compel Emily to her feet.

"Wh-where are you going?" Tabitha cried, not quite finished with the recitation of her cousin's romance.

"I beg your pardon, but I had forgotten that my mother bade me to sit with her."

"Oh," Tabitha uttered, obviously bewildered.

"Good day!" Emily said smartly and marched off before Tabitha could reply.

She made her way through the crowd, dutifully stopping to pay her respects where necessary, and finally reaching the other side of the gathering where Montgomery was deep in conversation with Widow Becket. Decorum be damned, Emily marched up to the couple and forced a bright smile to her face.

"Good afternoon, Mrs. Becket. My lord," she said, curtsying.

Both of them started a bit at her intrusion. Mrs. Becket instantly smiled and grasped Emily's hand. "Good afternoon, Miss Forsythe! My, how lovely you look today! Positively radiant—it must be the effects of having a successful debut," she gushed.

"I suppose so. Thank you," Emily said stiffly, and turned a smile to Lord Montgomery.

"Miss Forsythe, how do you do?" he asked, perfectly polite.

"Very well, indeed, my lord," she said, and faltered. How to rid Montgomery of the widow now? As it was, the two of them were looking at her expectantly, as if they waited for her to announce something hugely important. "Will you be attending the May Day Ball, my lord?" she suddenly blurted.

Montgomery arched a brow in surprise above his smile. "The May Day Ball? Why, I had not thought of it, Miss Forsythe," he said, glancing at Mrs. Becket. "I can't say I've even been invited."

"Of course you have!" Emily insisted. "Everyone has been invited!" She caught herself there and glanced at Widow Becket—well, not *everyone* had been invited. "I do mean, of course, everyone in the *ton*."

Whatever she thought Mrs. Becket's reaction would be, she had not thought she'd laugh.

"No need to explain, Miss Forsythe. His lordship and I

were just speaking of the many events this season holds," she said and shifted her gaze to his lordship, her smile going very soft for a moment.

"What of them?" Emily asked.

"Beg your pardon?" Widow Becket asked, seeming a little distracted.

"There are many of them for debutantes," Lord Montgomery helpfully clarified.

"Yes," the widow said, turning her smile to Emily again. "How fortuitous you have so many places to dance on your first year out!"

"I suppose that is true," Emily admitted, and clasped her gloved hands tightly together, looked at the stone floor for a moment, wondering why the widow wouldn't take her *leave*? A few awkward moments passed. It seemed to Emily to take forever before Widow Becket at last seemed to understand she was intruding.

"Ah . . ." the widow said.

Emily quickly glanced up; Widow Becket smiled very brightly at Emily. "I think I've monopolized his lordship quite long enough—"

"But you haven't at all," he said instantly.

"I should see if the vicar needs me," she said, stepping back. "Good day, my lord. Good day, Miss Forsythe."

"Good day, Mrs. Becket," Emily called out.

Much to her annoyance, Montgomery's gaze followed the retreating widow.

"And how did you find the service?" Emily demanded.

Montgomery dragged his gaze to her again. "The service? Inspiring, as always. Aha, there are your parents, Miss Forsythe. Shall I take you to them?"

There was no graceful way to answer that but to say yes, was there? Disappointed, Emily nodded, put her hand on the arm he offered, and let him lead her to where her mother and father were sitting, acutely aware that her opportunity was slipping away from her with each step. Before it slipped completely away, as they neared her parents, she blurted boldly, "I hope I shall see you at the May Day Ball," and lifted her gaze to him.

Montgomery glanced down at her. "What a lovely compliment. Thank you." He looked up to her parents. "Mr. and Mrs. Forsythe, how do you do?" he said, lifting Emily's hand from his arm.

He exchanged pleasantries with them, wished Emily a good day, and walked on, into the crowd.

Emily watched him go, a little bewildered. She'd had it from her very own brother that if a woman paid particular attention to a man, he would reciprocate that attention. Montgomery didn't reciprocate. He'd scarcely noticed her at all because he was too intent on Widow Becket. It was disgraceful to a man of his stature.

For the remainder of that luncheon, Emily could not tear her gaze from Montgomery, counting the times he looked for Widow Becket. Eight in all.

That afternoon, when they had returned home from that insufferable affair, Emily plotted her revenge on a woman who had the least right of all the women in London to the admiring looks of one of the most eligible bachelors among the *ton,* a bachelor who, but for some divine intervention, had suddenly become the only man she'd consider marrying.

Widow Becket should enjoy her flirtation now, Emily thought, because she was determined to bring it to a crashing end.

Chapter Four

Emily Forsythe put her carefully devised plan into existence the very next week, when she offered to accompany her mother to the weekly meeting of the Ladies Auxiliary, where the ladies were planning for the Charity Auction Ball.

Her mother was both very surprised and pleased. "Emily!" she said, squeezing her daughter's shoulders. "How good of you to think of someone other than yourself!" Emily shrugged sheepishly, accepted the offer to wear her mother's best bonnet in honor, as she happily put it, of Emily's first step toward benevolence.

The meeting place was an assembly of rooms connected to the church. Only two ladies were present when Emily and her mother arrived. Emily put aside the basket of apples they had brought.

"My daughter joins us today!" her mother announced

proudly, and the two ladies exclaimed gleefully at that. Emily smiled and clasped her hands behind her back as she wandered deeper into the room.

She heard a bit of a clatter and turned toward a door at the opposite end of the room as Widow Becket came through it with a tea service. Her gold-red hair was pulled back and knotted at the nape of her neck, and she wore a heavy canvas apron over her drab brown day gown. "Miss Forsythe!" she called happily as she carried the heavy tea service to the table and set it down. "What a pleasure to have you join us!"

Emily gave her a demure nod.

"My daughter is taking her first steps toward charity," her mother exclaimed for at least the tenth time that day, and beamed at Emily.

"Well! We are very pleased to have you," Widow Becket averred, and reached out, touched Emily's arm.

Emily immediately stiffened; Widow Becket seemed to feel that she did and withdrew her hand, pushed a strand of hair behind her ear, and with a small, self-conscious smile, busied herself with the tea service. "The vicar has sent tea for our meeting this morning," she announced to them all. "He avows it is the finest tea yet to reach England's shores."

The ladies tittered at that; Widow Becket wiped her hands on her apron. "I've some biscuits in the oven. I'll just fetch them—"

"May I help you, Mrs. Becket?" Emily quickly interjected, trying very hard to ignore her mother's proud smile.

The widow glanced up from the tea service, eyed her suspiciously. But in the next moment, she said, "I should appreciate all the help that is offered." She flashed another warm smile—one that made Emily shiver. "Come, Miss Forsythe, and I will show you our kitchen."

Emily put her hand into the widow's and walked stiffly

beside her through the door and down a long row of stairs
into the church's kitchen. Emily had not known before today that the church even had a kitchen, but as Widow
Becket explained, upon seeing her look of confusion, the
very large churches usually had one tucked away to assist
in such activities as charities and wedding breakfasts and
so forth.

Widow Becket walked to the oven and pulled it open,
and with a thick towel, she removed a tin of biscuits and
put them on the wooden table that stretched almost the entire length of the kitchen. She returned to the oven and removed a second tin and placed it beside the first. With an
iron spatula, she began to remove the biscuits from the tin
and put them on the table to cool, and smilingly gestured
for Emily to do the same with the first tin.

"Have you ever been to the Malthorpe Orphanage?"
Widow Becket asked as they worked.

"No, mu'um."

"We thought to pay a call after we finish our work here.
I think you will find the children delightful."

Emily had not given any thought at all to what they actually might *do* at this meeting, and really, it hardly mattered
at the moment, as she was deeply racking her mind for a
way to broach the subject she so desperately wanted to
broach. "Where do the children come from?" she asked
idly, more in an attempt to hide the fact that her mind was
elsewhere.

"I'm not entirely certain," Widow Becket said thoughtfully. "Some of them have lost their parents. Others are
wards of the church . . ." Her hand stilled; she looked up,
as if she was seeing something far away. "I suppose their
mothers have chosen a life not suitable for children," she
said softly and resumed her work with the biscuits. "They

are women who must, for whatever reason, indulge in the most ignoble of human conduct."

Upon hearing that, Emily inadvertently broke a biscuit in two. *"Ah,"* she said, nodding slowly. "You mean the sort of woman Lord Montgomery consorts with."

Her remark certainly had the desired effect; Widow Becket's head snapped up, and she looked at her in astonishment. "I beg your pardon?"

Emily quickly lowered her gaze and continued to carefully slide the biscuits from her tin onto the wooden table. "I don't mean to be uncouth, Mrs. Becket, truly I don't. But . . ." She let her voice trail away, a trick she had learned from her mother, who often left the most important part of her speech dangling when she wanted her husband's full attention.

"But?" Mrs. Becket asked.

Emily looked up and winced as if she were pained by something so vile. "It's *true.* I daresay I had the misfortune one night, returning from the theater with my cousin, of seeing him on the street in their company. And once, I overheard my father speaking with a gentleman friend," she said, lowering her voice to a coarse whisper, "and he said that Lord Montgomery would do well to keep his lady friends in the alleys where they belonged."

Something flit across Widow Becket's face, but then . . . nothing.

Once again, she surprised Emily—she did not seem the least bit offended. She did not gasp, did not make any sound at all, but went on shoveling biscuits onto the wooden table as if she'd not heard a word Emily had said. In fact, Emily worried that perhaps she *hadn't* heard her, and leaned forward, peering up into her face. "You do understand me, Mrs. Becket?"

"Of course I do, Miss Forsythe," she said, and smiled as she walked past Emily to put her tin away.

Was it possible the widow did not understand the implications of what she'd just said? "I suppose that's why his lordship has the awful reputation of being a *roué*," Emily mused aloud. "It's said in all the drawing rooms, you know."

"No, I wasn't aware," Widow Becket said pleasantly, as if they were discussing the weather. "There now," she continued, arranging two of the biscuits just so. "I shall return in a quarter of an hour and they should be quite cool to the touch. Shall we go help the ladies with the charity baskets?"

Bewildered by Widow Becket's reaction—or lack of it—Emily nodded and followed her out.

She did not have another opportunity to reassure herself that Mrs. Becket understood Lord Montgomery's dark reputation but consoled herself with the knowledge that what little she had said most certainly dampened Widow Becket's enthusiasm for him. After all, how could she possibly continue to esteem him, her being a vicar's widow and he being a bloody rake, for God's sake?

All right, then, the part about the ladies and the alleys had been completely fabricated, but everyone in town knew that Lord Montgomery was no stranger to the pleasures of female flesh. And now, the saintly Widow Becket knew it, too.

Still . . . to be doubly sure that Widow Becket was completely out of the picture, Emily begged her leave of paying a call to the orphanage, much to her mother's obvious disappointment, and instead paid a call to Lady Southbridge.

Lady Southbridge was a grand dame of the *ton*. It was said—at least by Emily's father—that if there was anything worth knowing about a person, Lady Southbridge knew it and would repeat it to one hundred of her dearest friends. Emily certainly hoped that was true.

Lady Southbridge was pleasantly surprised to see Emily when the butler showed her to his lady's drawing room. The large old woman was lounging on a day couch, two little dogs at her feet.

"Miss Forsythe!" she cried happily as Emily curtsied before her. "Forsythe has turned you out quite well, hasn't he? Turn round, turn round, and let me have a look at you."

Emily did as she was told, and when she had completed her rotation, she smiled sweetly at Lady Southbridge and dropped another curtsy.

"Oh *my,* you're a lovely one, dear. So come," she said, patting the seat of the chair next to her. "Come and tell me all about your coming out. Have you received any offers?"

"None," Emily said.

"Dunn?" Lady Southbridge squealed.

Emily's eyes flew wide open—Lord Dunn, the positively ancient old man? "No!" she said instantly. "No, no, I beg your pardon, I said *none.*"

"Well then, you must not mumble, Miss Forsythe, for I distinctly heard you say *Dunn.*"

Emily blinked several times. "Forgive me," she muttered.

"Oh, of course, of course," she said, clearly disappointed that Emily's answer was *not* Dunn. But she quickly recovered. "Oh there now, you mustn't be unhappy, Miss Forsythe! It's quite early yet! Why, in my day, a gentleman did not *dare* offer for a young lady before the Charity Auction Ball! It makes a young man seem far too eager if he offers before then."

"Really?" Emily asked, perking up.

"Oh, indeed!" Lady Southbridge cried, and with two hands, patted her enormous chest. One of the little dogs scampered up the hill that was her and happily licked her face. "The Charity Auction Ball is still *the* venue for the most important offers," Lady Southbridge continued, giggling at her little dog as she took him in her arms and crushed him to her. "So, my dear, what brings you to my sitting room today?" she asked, oblivious to the little dog's squirming.

"Only my desire to call on you, my lady. My mother speaks so very highly of you, and I had always thought that when I've come out, I shall go and pay my respects to Lady Southbridge."

Lady Southbridge smiled broadly at that, her cheeks balling up like two lumps of dough. "What a thoughtful dear you are!" she cried. "When *who* comes out?"

"When *I've* come out," Emily said again, but louder.

"Really, you *must* practice your enunciation, Miss Forsythe. You've an awful habit of mumbling! Oh, I *adore* callers, and you are the perfect antidote to an otherwise dreary afternoon! I'll just ring for tea," she said and picked up the little bell next to her day couch.

The sun was shining for the first time this week, but Emily smiled nonetheless and put her hands in her lap as Lady Southbridge rang for her butler.

They chatted over tea, gossiping about all the debutantes, with Emily professing a dislike for most of them. Lady Southbridge was accommodating in that—if Emily professed a dislike for another debutante, her ladyship was quick to offer up a juicy little tidbit about the offending young woman.

But when Emily had been in her company for three-quarters of an hour, she was growing desperate to plant the next seed to detach Montgomery from the widow. Fortunately, Lady Southbridge gave her the opening she needed.

The old woman was really something of a remarkable windbag, and she was droning on and on about someone, a friend's sister by marriage, some such relation, and that she'd done the most awful thing by consorting with a high-ranking official in the House of Commons. "Her reputation is *ruined*," Lady Southbridge said with disgust as she examined the biscuits. "She shan't show her face in London again, mark me. It was all really quite scandalous," she said with a shake of her head as she selected another biscuit.

"I should think not as scandalous as consorting with a vicar's wife," Emily quickly interjected.

"Eh? What's that?" Lady Southbridge asked, her head snapping up so quickly that Emily briefly feared she might choke on the biscuit she'd just shoved in her mouth.

"I said, I should think not as scandalous as a *vicar's wife*!" Emily shouted.

"For goodness sake, I *heard* you, dear! What I mean to understand is *which* vicar's wife?"

"Oh," Emily said and coyly sipped her tea. "I shouldn't have uttered a word, Lady Southbridge. I'm certain I'm quite wrong, and I should just as soon cut out my tongue as speak ill of anyone—"

"Yes, yes, but *who?*" Lady Southbridge insisted.

Emily put her teacup down. "All right then. But please, you must give me your word you won't repeat what I'm to say to another living soul."

That earned a groan and a roll of Lady Southbridge's eyes as she fell back against her day couch. "I should be insulted, were I not as old and wise as I am, for I am hardly the sort to wag my tongue!" she exclaimed heatedly.

"I beg your pardon; I never meant to imply that you were, mu'um. It's just that . . . it's so scandalous, that I *scarcely* believe it, and I should perish away if anyone were to credit *me* with having suggested anything so morally despicable!"

Lady Southbridge's tiny eyes widened, and she sat up, pushed her two dogs off the day couch in one sweeping movement that left them whimpering, shoved her legs off the side, and leaned forward, so that she was almost nose to nose with Emily. "What on earth are you saying? That *our* vicar's wife has done something *morally despicable*?"

"No, not *our* vicar's wife," Emily quickly assured her, wondering how Lady Southbridge could believe that a woman nearly seventy years of age was doing something despicable. "The *former* vicar's wife," she said, and leaned in to whisper, "The *Widow Becket*."

Lady Southbridge gasped; her mouth formed a tight little bud as her eyes narrowed. "Mrs. Becket!" she cried in disbelief. "That sweet angel! What possibly might she have done?"

Emily was starting to feel a bit warm beneath her collar. "I, ah . . . I can't say for certain that she's done anything, my lady. But one would think a woman of her precarious position would be far more careful in comporting herself than to spend time, *unescorted,* with a high-ranking lord. But perhaps . . . perhaps that is just the way of the Methodists."

Lady Southbridge's gasp was so audible and forceful that Emily felt pushed back by it. But she held her ground, nodded solemnly as Lady Southbridge's little eyes got bigger and bigger. "A *Methodist?*" she squealed.

"She is indeed," Emily said apologetically.

The old woman put her hands to her knees, leaned even closer to Emily. "*Which* lord is it?"

Emily glanced over her shoulder, saw nothing but the two dogs wanting out, and leaned close to Lady Southbridge's ear. "*Lord Montgomery,*" she whispered.

Lady Southbridge instantly reared back, and her eyes were crinkling. "Oh *dear,*" she said, but she looked quite delighted by the news. She daintily picked up her teacup. "Finished with your tea, dear? Oh, I do thank you for calling, Miss Forsythe. I hope you shall call again, and very soon. It's been so lovely chatting with you."

Emily recognized her cue to leave, and carefully stood up, thanked Lady Southbridge profusely for receiving her, and with her back to the grand dame of rumor and innuendo, she smiled. Her mission was complete. Lord Montgomery would soon be forced by untoward talk to rid himself of the pesky widow. And then he'd be one step closer to seeing his way to making an offer for her.

An hour later, after Lady Southbridge had finished off what was left of the biscuits, she asked her butler to round up her coach, and gave the driver the direction of Lady Marlton, her dear old friend. She knew that Martha would be as interested as she was to learn that the old scoundrel Lord Connery, who happened to be married to Martha's cousin, had failed once again to keep his trousers securely fastened, and was up to his old tricks in seducing the vicar's widow.

Chapter Five

At his gentlemen's club a few days later, Darien heard the rumor about Lord Connery—a scoundrel by anyone's measure—and the Widow Becket from his friend Freddie, who relayed the news to him, having just come from a card table where, he lamented, he had lost forty pounds.

"Connery's the cause of it," he said, his chin on his fist.

"Connery!" Darien said with a laugh, and chomping down on his cigar, he grinned at Freddie. "Is there nothing to which you will not stoop in blaming your losses?"

"I swear, it was Connery! I knew him to be a scoundrel . . . but the vicar's widow?"

Darien almost choked on the cigar. "Beg your pardon?" he asked, lowering the paper he had been reading.

"Ah, well then—that has your attention, does it not?" Freddie said. "Even a scoundrel such as you must be nonplussed by it, eh? Quite shocking, really."

"What exactly did you hear?" Darien pressed him. "I am acquainted with the vicar's widow, and I can assure you, she'd not consort with anyone, and particularly not the likes of Connery."

"Tell it to Westfall, then, will you? He claims to have it on very good authority that Widow Becket has been seen about town with Connery, and in some locations that are of less than good repute," Freddie said as he casually looked about the roomful of gentlemen.

"Westfall is quite certain of it, is he?" Darien pressed.

Freddie chuckled. "What then, Montgomery? Jealous, are you?"

Darien frowned lightly at the news.

"What now?" Freddie exclaimed. "You're positively sullen!"

"I wouldn't want to see a good woman debauched, that's all." He instantly wished he hadn't said it—now Freddie was watching him intently. So he added, "Unless I'm the one to do the debauching."

Freddie laughed roundly at that, slapping his hand on the table and drawing the looks of a few.

He waited on the corner of Park Lane, near the Hyde Park entrance, because he knew she'd come across the park on her way to the church, just as she did every Wednesday when returning from her rounds. He had in his hand a bouquet of spring flowers, purchased for a tidy little sum on Bond Street.

He stood back, out of the heavy foot traffic, smiling and nodding politely at the many ladies who promenaded past, winking at those who dared to stare back. He might, had he been more engaged in the art of flirtation, involved one or more of them in light conversation, but he could think of little else but Mrs. Becket.

When at last she appeared, striding across the park, her feet encased in sturdy boots, her bonnet a bit askew, and the empty basket on her arm swinging in a rhythm only she knew, he thought she was a most desirable woman, far more desirable than any other woman on the street just then.

She did not see him as she darted across the street, dodging carriages and horsemen and hacks; and she seemed quite caught up in her thoughts as she strode purposefully along, one hand on the top of her bonnet to keep it from sliding any further. It wasn't until he stepped into her path that she came out of her fog, and her face, rosy from her walk, broke into the wreath of her smile. She was, he noted, quite happy to see him.

"My Lord Montgomery!" she exclaimed as she came to a halt and peered up at him with her soft green eyes. "You must truly enjoy walking in the park, sir, for rare is the sunlit day that I do not encounter you here."

"Do you honestly believe it is merely the park that brings me here, Mrs. Becket?" he asked, smiling lopsidedly at her coy remark. "Indeed it is not, for I have professed my esteem of you on more than one occasion," he said and pulled the flowers from behind his back, holding them out to her.

She gasped with surprise and delight, her face lighting up, and she instantly clapped her hands together at her chest. "What beautiful flowers! They look as if they belong in the king's garden!"

"A king's garden?" He scoffed. "Their exquisite beauty and vivid colors bring to mind a certain widow. They belong with you, Mrs. Becket."

She laughed as she stepped forward to inhale their scent. "You are too kind, Lord Montgomery, indeed," she said, stepping back again. "But you know very well that I cannot accept such a token from you."

"And why on earth not?" he demanded.

"Because, my lord, it is improper."

"Ach!" he said with a dismissive flick of his wrist. "What is proper, I ask you! Shall I bring you flowers when they've laid you in your grave? No, madam, I refuse to honor your maidenly notions. If I admire a beautiful woman, I will not be ashamed to let her know that I do," he said and stepped closer, pressing the flowers toward her.

With another pleasing laugh, Mrs. Becket took the flowers. Her long fingers brushed lightly against his; she put her face to the flowers and inhaled, then carefully put them in her basket. As a breeze wafted through, she caught her bonnet atop her head and smiled up at him. "I wonder," she said, her eyes narrowing playfully, "how many bouquets have you delivered this fine day? Surely I am not the first woman to cross such a public path as yours today, sir."

"There have been scads of women before you, all worthy of my admiration. But you are the only one to receive my bouquet."

"Mmm," she said skeptically.

"Shall we walk?" he asked.

"Oh no, my lord!" she exclaimed, smiling. "You have undoubtedly noted that my father is not in my company this afternoon! It would be imprudent of me."

"Now you're being coy, and well you know it," he said cheerfully. "You are a widow, madam, not a debutante, and I am a respected lord. We are two adults, free to walk on to the church and chat about the good works of the Lord." With that, he put his hand to her arm, urging her forward.

She went along with him, her body brushing against his in the crush. "That's rather tidy and convenient, isn't it, using the church to walk about? And here I had been given to understand that you prefer finding places far from the curious eyes of the *ton* for your seductions."

Startled, he glanced at her and instantly noticed the smile playing at the corner of her lips. "Meaning?" he asked.

"Meaning, sir, that there are those who say you are often seen with less than reputable women in the less than reputable corners of London."

Darien was accustomed to the rumors that floated around about him, but nevertheless lifted a brow of shock for Mrs. Becket's sake. "My good Mrs. Becket! Do you believe me to be less than honorable in my intentions?"

She laughed gaily. "How could I possibly believe you to be anything but?"

"Touché, madam," he said with a grin. "And I suppose your conscience is quite clear, is it? What with all the calls being paid to you by a certain rakish gentleman."

"A rakish gentleman?" she asked thoughtfully. "You mean one in addition to you?" she asked, and laughed, pleased with her jest.

Darien laughed, too. "I was in fact referring to Lord Connery."

"Lord Connery!" she cried in surprise, and came to a halt, turning to fully face him. With laughter in her eyes, she peered up at him. "Are you implying that I would allow *another* man to scandalize me?"

"I beg your pardon, Mrs. Becket, but *I* do not scandalize you. I merely adore you," he said, and took her gloved hand in his, bowed over it, and brought it to his lips.

"Well then, you have my leave," she said softly as he kissed the back of her hand. "Adore at will."

He chuckled low, turned her hand over, and pressed his lips to the smooth skin of her wrist, just above the frilly trim of her glove. He heard her slight intake of breath and smiled as she carefully withdrew her hand.

"Then what of Connery?" he asked. "Do you intend to break his heart as you will surely break mine?"

"How odd that you should mention Lord Connery. He did call on me, just this morning, and quite unexpectedly. Frankly, it has been so long since I've seen his lordship in church that I wasn't entirely certain of his identity."

Darien laughed.

"I'm quite serious, truly I am! I asked if I might have known him from Shropshire. He explained that he had met me at church and I recalled, after his lengthy explanation, that I did indeed make his acquaintance before my husband died. I suppose his lordship left in a bit of ill humor, as he had hoped my recall would be perfectly clear."

Darien laughed at the image of Connery, his dishonorable hopes quite dashed. "Then you won't deny it," he said jovially.

With a roll of her eyes, she tossed her head pertly. "I will not deny the man has called, but I cannot decipher why he should. And *you,* sir," she said, glancing at him from the corner of her eye. "Do you deny that you have escorted disreputable women about?"

"Ah, that old rumor."

"Persistent one, is it?" she asked laughingly as they turned down a side street that led to the back of St. Johns Church. "May I assume it is true? That you would declare your undying esteem of one woman, while escorting another one about town at night?"

"Escort her? No," he said shaking his head. "Visit her bed? Well now, that is another matter entirely."

The suggestion colored Mrs. Becket's cheeks, but she looked at him with a bold little smirk.

"What is it then, Mrs. Becket? Have I offended you? Have you not, in truth, wondered, if only a little, if I had indeed done so?" he asked pleasantly. "If I am not a man, and therefore, in search of certain pleasures?"

She opened the wrought-iron gate that surrounded the

cemetery, banging him in the hip in her haste to do so. "You presume too much, sir. I am not in the habit of wondering about parishioners in the least," she said and strode through the gate.

Darien easily kept stride with her. "But I am not just any parishioner," he pressed nonchalantly. "I am a man who has made it clear that he esteems you. And I should think a woman of your youthful years, having enjoyed the fruits of a marriage bed, then having lost them, might wonder about it from time to time."

"Mmm," she said pertly. "It would seem as if you have an inordinate amount of time to sit about speculating on any number of things." She paused at the first tombstone and took one of the flowers from his expensive bouquet and laid it at the head of the grave, and did the same at the next.

"I suppose I do," he agreed, calmly watching her dismantle the flowers he had given her. "For I have also imagined, if only a little, what it might be like were I to visit *your* bed."

Mrs. Becket almost tripped over a crooked grave marker. Darien laughed, grabbed her wrist, and pulled her around a neighboring obelisk that rose over some ancient ancestral grave, and lightly pushed her against it, holding her there with his body, his hands on her waist, his legs braced around her skirts. She tilted her head back with a challenge in her eye.

"I have wondered what heaven it would be to kiss your breast," he said low, smiling lopsidedly as his hand glided up to cup the mound of her breast. Mrs. Becket drew a quick breath, and her eyes fluttered closed.

Darien's smile deepened. "And I've wondered at the heat of our bare skin as we lay together," he murmured, dipping to kiss her neck. "Or even how my hands might feel on your bare bottom in the throes of lovemaking," he said against her skin as he squeezed her hips.

She gave a throaty laugh before she pushed him away. Darien instantly stood back. He grinned at her. Her eyes were sparkling with amusement, and she did not seem the least bit intimidated by his bold gesture.

"I have certainly *not* wondered about it," she said pertly but with a coy smile. "Are you determined to make your point by ravishing me in a church cemetery?"

"Don't tempt me, madam." And he meant it, as he took in her face, her full lips, the way her nose upturned just so, and her eyes, always glittering with something deep within. There were times, like now, that he looked upon her and thought he'd perish if he didn't have her.

But he laughed, stroked her arm. "Don't deny it, Mrs. Becket. You've wondered what it must be like to feel my body against yours. . . ." He leaned forward, so that his lips were against her ear. "Or *in* yours."

"I haven't," she said unconvincingly.

"You have," he insisted, his gaze dropping to her lips again. "And I further believe you have thought often about the kiss we shared, and perhaps wondered if it was real, or if your memory had played a trick on you and made it into something so spectacular that your heart took wings."

She gave him a saucy toss of her head. "You must be speaking of your own heart."

"Perhaps I am," he said, slipping his hand beneath her chin and turning her face so that he could graze her lips with a kiss. "My heart did indeed take flight that night. But I am quite certain mine was not the only one, Mrs. Becket. I felt your heart beating just as rapidly against mine."

"You are trying to seduce me!"

"No, madam, I am trying to love you."

Her lips curved with a soft sigh. "Are you not fearful of being seen?" she whispered, her gaze dipping to his lips.

"I am only fearful of never kissing you again." He touched his lips to hers.

He felt her body stiffen with the first glance of his lips, and he moved closer, angling his mouth across hers, kissing her softly, just feeling the flesh of her mouth against his. But then he felt her rise up like a mist, so slowly and gently that it was almost imperceptible, until her body was touching his.

Darien slipped his arm around her waist, pulled her into him, away from the obelisk, and kissed her like a woman then, not some maiden to be gentled, but a woman who had known the touch of a man and had gone without it for two years now.

Mrs. Becket opened her mouth beneath his and drew his breath into her; he heard the clatter of the basket as it fell to the ground and hit a grave marker as her hands went around his neck. Her body felt firm and supple and alive against him; she was perfect in his arms.

And then suddenly she forced her hand up between them and pushed hard against his chest, forcing him to let go. She stepped back, bumping up against the obelisk, blinking up at him.

Darien refused to let go and merely smiled.

So did Mrs. Becket. "That was a terribly wicked thing to do," she whispered.

"Yes, it certainly was. I'm a heel, a *roué*. A rotten bounder. But I adore you."

Her smile deepened with pleasure, and she playfully shoved him away. Darien let go, stepped backward. She slid down the obelisk and reached for her basket, carelessly tossing the flowers into it before rising again. "I must insist you not behave in such an objectionable manner again."

"Of course not," he said, bowing his acquiescence.

She smiled, righted the bonnet which had slid off the back of her head, and put the basket on her arm. "And now, I will take my leave of you, sir, for you cannot be trusted with my good virtue."

"You are quite right. I most certainly cannot."

With an impertinent smile, she began walking.

Darien watched her for a moment, the smooth swing of her hips, and suddenly called out, "Kate!" He stopped her with the use of her Christian name, the first time he had ever uttered the name aloud, except to whisper it on those occasions when he longed for her the most.

She did not turn round but slowly glanced over her shoulder. "My lord?"

"Do you care for picnics?"

She said nothing at first, turned halfway toward him, assessing him. After a long moment, she smiled again. "I do," she said, and with a laugh, she turned and glided away from him, her basket swinging carefree in her hand.

Chapter Six

Lords Montgomery and Frederick arrived at the Wither-spoons' May Day Ball, the two of them striding into the ballroom looking quite dashing in their black tails and black waistcoats over pristine white shirts.

They paused just inside the entrance of the ballroom and casually glanced about, seemingly oblivious to the young debutantes who coyly eyed them from behind their ornate fans. Spying a group of men, the two proceeded forward to join them.

On the other side of the dance floor, Emily watched Montgomery as he chatted with the other men, absently looking about, openly eyeing the ladies who twirled about the dance floor as well as those who lined the wall, not so fortunate to be standing up with their favorite beau.

This was the second time in as many days Emily had seen the viscount. Yesterday, it had been in Hyde Park, where she had been riding with her mother. They had happened upon Montgomery, who was likewise on horseback, and Emily's mother, sensing her interest, had invited him to join them for a leisurely ride about the park.

That was how Emily learned he had not intended to be in London this season at all but had meant to be abroad, but that something had cropped up at the last moment, and he had remained in London. He claimed to be happy for it, as things seemed, he said, infinitely brighter this season. He'd been looking at her when he said so.

Emily believed he intended to convey something personal to her with that remark, and after a full day of stewing about it, she was feeling rather confident about her prospects with Lord Montgomery and his forty thousand pounds a year.

So confident that she took Tabitha by the hand and made her promenade about the dance floor with her, finally easing to a halt near the group of men who were laughing together at something one of them had said.

Tabitha instantly realized what Emily was doing and hissed, "What do you mean to *do*?" as she self-consciously fidgeted with the pale blue ball gown Emily knew she'd wear.

"Would you care to dance, or stand aside all night, looking quite indistinguishable from the pattern of the wall covering?" Emily hissed back.

Tabitha was clearly taken aback by her remark and reluctantly nodded and bowed her head.

Emily straightened, her back stiff as a board and pretended to watch the dancers while she tried to listen to the gentlemen's conversation. Unfortunately, what with the music and din of conversation in the room, she could make nothing out but the occasional round of laughter. She moved slightly, turning her head just a bit, and therefore missed the approach of Lord Dillingham.

The instant she realized that someone had joined her and Tabitha, she quickly extended her hand—but Tabitha's hand was already in Lord Dillingham's.

"Miss Townsend," he said, bowing over her hand and lingering there for a moment before slowly lifting his head and smiling warmly at her. "You look quite lovely this evening."

Tabitha nearly swooned.

Emily cleared her throat; Lord Dillingham shifted his gaze to her. "Miss Forsythe," he said, not quite as warmly. "How do you do?" He bobbed a little over her hand and quickly let go.

"Very well, thank you, my lord," Emily said stiffly.

Lord Dillingham turned to Tabitha again with that warm smile. "Miss Townsend, would you please do me the great honor of standing up with me at the next dance?"

Tabitha was at least as shocked as Emily by the invitation. Her mouth fell open; she looked at Emily and blinked like an old cow, then looked at Lord Dillingham again. "My lord! I'd be *delighted*!" she cried happily.

He grinned. "Oh . . . hear it? They've just finished the quadrille. I believe a waltz will be next, if you'd like."

"Yes, my lord . . . I'd like," Tabitha stammered, and with a beaming smile for Emily, she put her hand in Lord Dillingham's. "Please excuse me, Miss Forsythe." And she practically bounced off to the dance floor, her beaming smile now directed at her partner.

Of all the . . . Emily mentally crossed Dillingham off her list of potential husbands. No loss, really—he'd been rather far down the list to begin with.

But now that she was left standing alone, much like an old spinster, Emily tried to keep from fidgeting with her gloves and the ribbons of her gown, tried to keep her sights trained on something more appealing than all the other girls who were fortunate enough to dance. And just when she thought she'd go mad with all the trying, the gentlemen behind her moved forward, so that they were standing very near to her.

Emily glanced at them from the corner of her eye. As fortune would have it, Lord Montgomery was standing directly beside her, and Emily seized her opportunity.

"How do you do, Lord Montgomery?" she asked loudly.

It worked—the gentlemen stopped their chatter and all five of them turned to look at Emily. Lord Frederick eyed her from the top of her head to the tip of her slippers, while a smiling Lord Barstow elbowed him and snickered. The fourth gentleman, whom she did not know, looked absolutely horrified by her boldness.

Montgomery was the only one to smile at her; he bowed. "I am quite well indeed, Miss Forsythe. And how do you do?"

"Very well," she said, clutching her fan so hard that her fingers ached. "I was just admiring the dancers," she said, and looked meaningfully at the dance floor.

Montgomery looked at the dance floor, then at Emily, gallantly ignoring the sniggering at his back from Barstow and Frederick. "Would you care to dance, Miss Forsythe?"

Emily's heart winged almost free of her chest. "How kind of you to ask, my lord," she said, and in her haste to put out her hand, lest he retract his offer, she dropped her fan. Montgomery stooped down and picked it up, put it solidly in her hand, then even went so far as to curl her fingers around it so that she did not drop it again, before holding out his arm to receive her hand.

Emily laid her hand on his sleeve. He put his hand over hers, his fingers warmly surrounding hers, and she smiled brightly.

He led her to the edge of the dance floor where the waltz was starting. Emily curtsied deeply; he gave her an

amused smiled and bowed with a flourish before helping
her up. With her hand securely in his, he stepped forward,
put his hand lightly on her waist, and Emily sucked in her
breath as she put her hand on his shoulder.

As he pulled her into the dancing, she felt a thousand
butterflies in the pit of her belly, waltzing about on their
own as he smoothly led her in time to the music. He moved
so elegantly, so expertly, all the while smiling down at her,
his eyes warm and liquid, and the very color of fine tea. *Oh
yes, oh yes, this was the man she would marry!*

"And have you found the May Day Ball to your liking,
Miss Forsythe?" he asked, his eyes never leaving her, one
hand gripping hers firmly, the other riding high on her
waist and covering her ribs.

"Quite," she managed to get out, unthinkingly staring at
his remarkably full lips. Full and glistening and—

"I've always found the spring season to be the best time
of year for balls, as it is neither too cold nor too warm."

Actually, Emily felt a little warm. "It's quite lovely," she
rasped. "Perhaps the loveliest of all that I've attended thus
far. Yet I understand that the annual Charity Auction Ball is
much grander than this. Have you attended in the past?"

"I have, from time to time."

"Do you think it is more or less grand than the May Day
Ball?"

He chuckled at her eagerness. "In truth, I have not given
it as much thought as that. I suppose I find all balls rather
grand."

"Then do you plan to attend this year's Charity Auction
Ball?" Emily asked, immediately regretting her words, realizing how forward she must seem.

As if to confirm it, he cocked one brow high above the
other. "I have not as yet made plans," he said politely.

Anxious to cover her gaffe, Emily quickly stammered, "You . . . you are a wonderful dancer, my lord."

"How kind of you to remark. But I must give all credit to my partner, for she makes it quite easy to move about the dance floor," he said, and twirled her around, pulling her closer as he did. Emily could only hope that her knees wouldn't buckle with the force of her exhilaration.

She stared at his perfectly tied neckcloth for a moment, trying to push the feel of his hands on her body out of the forefront of her mind. When she looked up again, she noted that his gaze had shifted away from her; he was looking at someone else. "My mother and I enjoyed our ride in the park," she said quickly to draw his attention back to her.

"Did you? I found it quite pleasant, particularly after the rain we've endured."

"Yes indeed . . . I am glad the rain has gone for the time being, but I'm rather impressed with the spring flowers that have begun to pop up. They are flourishing in the park."

"Quite right, Miss Forysthe. I am certain that in a fort-night's time, the blooms will be a magnificent sight to be-hold." He twirled her one way, then the other.

"Yellow tulips are my favorite," she added breathlessly, and had a sudden image of him on her doorstep, an enor-mous bouquet of yellow tulips wrapped in bright paper in his arms.

"Mmm," he said, twirling her around again.

"Do you have a favorite flower, my lord?"

The question seemed to take him aback; he blinked. "I don't believe I have a favorite, Miss Forsythe. I like them all, I suppose. Including your yellow tulips."

Emily beamed up at him. He smiled again, then shifted his gaze above her head, and spun her into the thick of the dancers. He did not speak again, and Emily, having quite exhausted her repertoire of suitable things to discuss with a gentleman when one is dancing, could not seem to find anything to say. It was as if her mind was completely blank, save the incredible sensation of his hands on her body.

As the dance came to its conclusion, Montgomery stepped back and bowed, and Emily curtsied, frantically thinking of how to keep his attention. As he escorted her from the dance floor, she could think of absolutely nothing civilized with which to keep him engaged, and in a moment of sheer insanity, she put the back of her hand to her forehead and said in a whimper, "I feel a bit weak."

Montgomery instantly put his hand on her back to steady her and grabbed her arm. "Are you quite all right, Miss Forsythe?"

Not entirely, for she hadn't thought past this bit of drama, and now she felt as if she'd gone too far with it. She didn't know what to do—other than faint.

Right into his arms.

She heard the shriek of a woman, heard Montgomery bark for someone to clear the way, felt him pick her up, one arm beneath her knees, the other beneath her back, and carry her—*carry her!*—to the chairs along the wall. As he put her down in a chair, he pressed his palm to her face. "Miss Forsythe!"

Emily slowly opened her eyes—he was kneeling before her, looking terribly concerned. She had not imagined a moment such as this could be so unbearably romantic and chastised herself for not thinking of it weeks earlier than this. What if she'd fainted at the church social? That would have sped things along quite well.

"Dear God, Miss Forsythe, are you quite all right? Do you feel ill?"

"I . . . I don't know," she said weakly.

"Stand aside, son—I'm a physician," an old man said and leaned down before Emily. Dr. Hamblen's face loomed so large as he peered into her eyes that she could no longer see Lord Montgomery. Blast it all, Dr. Hamblen was ruining everything! Even worse, several people had gathered round her and were staring at her with fright and concern. All but Tabitha, that was, who appeared on Emily's left and gazed down at her with complete disdain.

Emily ignored Tabitha and strained to see around Dr. Hamblen—who was now holding two fingers against the pulse in her neck—to see Montgomery.

He was standing back, his hands on his hips, his legs braced apart, watching intently as Dr. Hamblen examined her.

"Her heart is racing a bit, but I think it nothing to fret about," the doctor proclaimed, straightening, and turning to Montgomery. "She's a healthy young lady. I've seen this sort of thing more than once—young ladies just out become caught up in the sights and sounds of a ball, you see, but their tender constitutions are not mature enough to endure all the excitement."

"Thank God it's nothing serious," Montgomery said and looked at Emily. "My dear Miss Forsythe, you gave me quite a fright," he said kindly. "I should not have stayed with you so long on the dance floor."

"Oh, no!" she insisted weakly. "It is not your fault, my lord! I am certain it's the heat—I find it rather warm in here."

"A spot of punch will cool her down," Dr. Hamblen said.

"I'll fetch it," Tabitha sighed wearily.

Dr. Hamblen looked at Montgomery and smiled. "You need not fret, my lord. I suggest you go about your evening.

I shall keep a close eye on her for a few moments and en-
sure she is suitably recovered."

"You're quite certain?"

"Absolutely," he said, and Emily imagined kicking the
good doctor in the arse.

Montgomery nodded, stepped forward, and lifted Emily's
limp hand to his lips. "Thank you for the honor of your
dance," he said. "And promise me that you will be more
careful of vigorous dancing in the future."

"It wasn't the dance," she said again. "I felt perfectly
fine. More than fine, really."

He chuckled as he stepped aside so that Dr. Hamblen
might put his hand to her forehead.

A few moments later, when Tabitha returned with the
punch, most of the onlookers had wandered off, including
Dr. Hamblen, who had peered at her closely and proclaimed her quite recovered. Only two debutantes remained
behind, their backs to her, but whispering to one another as
they stole glimpses of Emily over their shoulder.

Tabitha sat on the edge of a chair beside Emily and
handed her the punch. "How do you feel?" she asked with
a bit of sarcasm in her voice that Emily did not care for.

"I am improved, but not fully recovered." She sipped
the punch.

"I'll stay until you are," Tabitha said with a sigh, and
leaned back in her seat, to have had a look around the
room. "Oh!" she exclaimed. "Look who's come, will you?
It's that scoundrel, Lord Connery!"

Emily looked to where Tabitha indicated. "The scoundrel?"

"Have you not heard the rumors about him?" Tabitha
asked, lighting up. "Do you recall that we were speaking of
the vicar's widow?" she asked excitedly.

"Yes."

"Well." Tabitha paused, glanced around them to make sure no one was too close. "I attended a tea at Lady Southbridge's just two days past and overheard her remark to Mrs. Bledsoe that Widow Becket would do well to have a care for her reputation, for more than one trustworthy person had seen her traipsing carelessly about Mayfair, unescorted, in the company of Lord Connery!"

"The devil you say!" Emily whispered harshly.

"It's quite true!" Tabitha insisted. "Lady Southbridge said that they had been seen together in some scandalously disreputable locations and that honestly, it was not the first time since her husband's tragic death Widow Becket had demonstrated a lack of care in either her whereabouts or the company which she keeps!"

Ah, for the love of God! Emily closed her eyes and leaned her head against the wall. Lady Southbridge's atrocious lack of hearing was to blame for this mess. *Not* Lord Connery! *Lord Montgomery!* And now what was she to do?

"I really had never thought of her at all until you mentioned it," Tabitha said.

"Widow Becket is quite free with her affections, you may be sure," Emily muttered irritably. "Lord Connery, Lord Anyname, it matters not to her!"

"No!" Tabitha gasped loudly.

"Yes!" Emily said. "I've even heard it rumored that she's been in the company of Lord Dillingham."

That was met with cold silence from Tabitha.

"I've a horrid ache in my head," Emily moaned, as she tried to make sense of her thoughts.

"Oh come now, you needn't pretend with me," Tabitha chastised her and took the cup from her hand. "I know what you're about."

At that moment, another, better idea occurred to Emily, and she opened her eyes. "What *I'm* about?"

Tabitha rolled her eyes and slumped back in her chair. "That bit of fainting—it was for his lordship's benefit. Admit it."

Emily gave her a wry smile. "You are ignorant at times, Tabitha," she said with much superiority. "I don't suppose you've heard the rumors about Montgomery, then, have you?"

"No. I suppose even *he's* been seen with Widow Becket?"

"Not about Widow Becket!" Emily said crossly. "About for whom he intends to offer!"

Tabitha sat up now and scooted to the edge of her seat. "No! Who is it, then? Please don't say that wretched Miss Smythe. She thinks herself so superior to us all!"

Emily chuckled low, took the cup of punch from Tabitha's hand, drank her fill, set it aside, and clasped her hands in her lap.

"Emily! Don't be coy!" Tabitha cried. *"Who?"*

"Really, can't you see it with your very own eyes?" she asked, laughing at Tabitha's eagerness. "Who did Lord Montgomery seek out and accompany on a long ride about Hyde Park just yesterday? And who is the first person he danced with upon arriving at this ball? And might you guess *who* he inquired as to her favorite flower, then declared it *his* favorite flower, too, and furthermore, how early spring, what with all the *dancing,* and the *flowers,* and the *rides about the park,* is his favorite time of year?"

Tabitha's eyes widened.

"That's right," Emily said, nodding. "He's a particular interest in *me,*" she said, and watched Tabitha's eyes widen with surprise. And all right, then, a bit of shock, too.

Chapter Seven

A few days after the May Day Ball, Kate and her father returned from their weekly calls to the elderly in a bit of a deluge; it was as if the heavens had opened up and poured out a sea of water on London. They were met in the foyer by William, a servant in the vicar's employ.

"Beggin' yer pardon, Mrs. Becket, but ye've callers," he said, taking her reticule from her.

"Callers? In this storm?" Papa asked, and exchanged a curious look with Kate. Together, they walked to the door of the small parlor of the vicar's guest house and peeked inside.

There were four men inside, all right, and they surged to their feet almost as one the moment they saw Kate. Papa strode into the room; behind him, Kate hastily removed her bonnet and tried to smoothe her hair before following him.

"Mrs. Becket," they muttered in unison. "Mr. Crowley."

"Rather a nasty day to be about making calls, sirs," Papa remarked dryly.

"Ah, but what better opportunity to call on the fair Mrs. Becket," Lord Connery said and quickly stepped forward from the pack of men and extended his hand to Papa. "She knows me well."

"Does she indeed?" Papa drawled, squinting up at Connery. "And here I believed her to have only a passing acquaintance with you, my lord."

Lord Connery was not the least bit intimidated by Papa's challenge; he grinned and bobbed his head at Kate as a rotund gentleman elbowed his way in front of him.

"I daresay I've not had the pleasure of making Mrs. Becket's formal acquaintance," the rotund man said, bobbing at Papa before turning to Kate. "Madam, if you will allow me. Lord Moreland at your service," he said, and bowed low.

"Mr. Anglesey at your service, too!" another gentleman all but shouted from the back.

"And lest I be overlooked, madam, Baron Hardwick." You may recall that we met at church services approximately two months past."

"I, ah . . . I am certain I will recall it in a moment," Kate said, feeling a bit flustered by all the attention. And confusion as to *why* the sudden attention.

Papa was confused, too, judging by his suspicious expression as he eyed them carefully. "Seems rather odd, the four of you calling on my daughter all at once and in a bad rain."

"I am certain I mentioned I'd be calling the last time I had the pleasure of Mrs. Becket's company, sir," Connery said with that despicable smile of his.

"You did not have my company, my lord," Kate reminded him.

That earned her an oily smile and a shrug from him.

"Nevertheless, no one has asked my daughter if she is disposed to receiving so many gentleman callers today," Papa said sternly and looked pointedly at Kate.

Hardly—she was wearing a drab gown, her hair was mussed from her hard walk across Mayfair in a downpour, and her feet, while shod in her best walking boots, were killing her. Not to mention her general confusion as to why this spate of callers were at her door to begin with. She'd rather thought that a gentleman called as the result of some mutual understanding betwixt himself and the lady. She had no such understanding with any of these gentlemen. Or the three who'd called earlier this week.

Nevertheless, the four gentlemen looked at her expectantly as they jostled about a bit to stand before her. Kate self-consciously put a hand to her hair and said, "I beg your pardon, good sirs, but I am not, at present, quite prepared to receive callers. I've had a rather arduous morning and really must tend to my father's, ah . . . business this afternoon."

The four men looked at one another. Lord Moreland was the first to waddle forth; he paused before Kate and snatched up her bare hand, pressed his thick lips to it before looking up and pinning her with a very strange look. "I shall call again if I have your leave, madam," he said low. "I think you will find me a most *pleasant* companion."

"Oh! Ah . . . I'm, ah, certain that you are, my lord," she said, having no earthly idea what to make of it.

Mr. Anglesey and Baron Hardwick both sought to take their leave next, and Kate had to suggest that perhaps Mr. Anglesey go first, as he was closest to her. Both men exited quickly, eyeing Papa nervously as they vowed to call again at a more convenient time.

Lord Connery, naturally, was the last to leave, and he

sauntered toward her, his head lowered, his gaze prurient. "Lovely Mrs. Becket," he purred over her hand. "How long shall you keep me waiting for the pleasure of your company?" He bent over her hand and pressed his lips to it. She felt the tip of his tongue flick against her skin and quickly jerked her hand back.

"I thought I had been perfectly clear on that, my lord," she said, smiling sweetly. "You shouldn't wait at all, as I do not intend to grace you with my company."

He was completely unrattled by her, and simply smiled in a way that made the hair stand up on the back of her neck. "Very well then. I shall wait," he said, and with a wink, nodded his good day to her father and continued his affected saunter out of the parlor.

Kate and her father walked to the front of the parlor room and looked out the window at the departing gentlemen as they walked quickly across the lawn, their umbrellas bobbing above them.

"Like rabbits, the lot of them," Papa said, scowling. "Hopping eagerly about when the widow comes out of her weeds. There's not an honorable one among them, I'd wager," he opined and turned from the window.

"I can't understand it, Papa. I've scarcely spoken to any of them, other than to greet them at church."

Her father laughed. "You are not aware of your charm, Kate. But I think that just as well, for there is nothing more appalling than a woman convinced of her own appeal. In the future, mind you have a care about the bachelor gentlemen of our church."

Kate laughingly agreed and glanced over her shoulder at her father. "You should rest, Papa."

"I am rather tired," he said, nodding. "Have William wake me before supper, will you?" he asked, and with a yawn, walked out of the parlor.

Kate thought to rest, too—the trek through the rain had been grueling. Perhaps she would lie down for a few moments in here, in the dark of the parlor. She turned round, went to the window again to draw the drapes closed, but she noticed someone standing at the gate. She stepped closer to the window and peered out.

It was Montgomery, leaning up against the wrought-iron fence, one leg casually crossed over the other, holding an umbrella over her his head as he absently twirled a timepiece around his finger, then out again, then in. He nodded in something of a silent greeting.

A smile, golden and warm, slipped across Kate's lips. With a furtive glance over her shoulder to assure herself her father had gone, she looked out the window again and could not help the small laugh that escaped her; Montgomery had moved forward and was standing now, his legs braced apart, one hand shoved deep in his pocket, staring up at the parlor window.

There was something about that man that drew her like a magnet, and Kate pressed her hand against the glass pane. From where she stood, she could see that he grinned. She abruptly whirled about, walked to the door of the parlor, gathering her bonnet from the chair where she'd dropped it as she went into the entry hall. Picking up the umbrella William had put next to the door, she slipped out.

He was standing beneath the overhang of the small front porch. "Good afternoon, Kate," he said, quietly smiling.

The tenor of his voice reverberated in her chest, almost stealing her breath. "My lord," she said, returning his smile. "What an unusual way you have of calling."

"I would have presented myself, but it seemed rather crowded within." He closed his umbrella. "I thought it best to wait under the old oak," he said, nodding to a tree at the corner of the guest house, which could not be seen by the departing gentlemen, lest they turned fully around.

Kate laughed. "And did you not think, sir, when you saw the other gentlemen depart promptly, that perhaps it best if you joined them?"

"What? And leave you quite alone?" he asked playfully, tapping the tip of his umbrella against hers. "It was quite clear to me that you were sending them forth so that you might honor *me* with the particular pleasure of your company."

Another warm smile soaked through her. "My, my, your flattery grows more eloquent with each passing day!"

"That is because I cannot possibly adore you enough," he said with a smiling bow. "Casual words are increasingly in-sufficient to describe my esteem for you, so I must improve my thoughts and speech to capture your lovely essence."

"That's really very lovely," Kate said with a coltish tap of her umbrella against his boot. "But I confess to being quite in the dark as to the true motives behind such elo-quence, my lord."

"My lord, my lord . . ." He sighed wearily. "When will you take leave to call me by my given name, Kate? I shall remind you once again that it is Darien, the name of my grandfather, and his father before him. As to my motive, I think you have deduced it quite accurately—it is simply to hear my name on your breath as I make you succumb to pleasure." He gave her an easy, roguishly charming smile.

A blush spread rapidly across her cheeks. It was strange, she thought, how this sensual banter between them never failed to both appall and appeal to her. Certainly Richard had never spoken to her in this way. She was glad of it. Richard had not been as . . . *exciting* . . . or dangerous . . . as Lord Montgomery.

Kate leaned forward onto her umbrella so that she was

only inches from him, and tilted her face up to his. "You shall hear that name on my breath, *Darien,* when I accuse you once again of being a *roué.*"

"Ah," he breathed, and clapped a hand over his heart, closed his eyes, and laid back his head. "'Tis as sweet as I've imagined." With a chuckle, he lifted his head and held out his hand to her, smiling broadly. "Yet there is so much more I've dared to imagine. Come with me now, Kate."

"Come with you?" She laughed. "Are you mad, sir?"

"Yes, quite. Mad with thoughts of you, constant and un-abashed thoughts of you and your shimmering green eyes and creamy skin and golden-red hair. Come with me, Kate—I'm so bloody mad that I've arranged a picnic, in your honor, just for you."

"A picnic? Today?" she cried, and laughed again. "Have you not noticed, my lord, that the skies are pouring rain?"

"I hardly notice the earth or the sun or the moon in your presence, Kate. You overshadow them all."

That prompted a hearty laugh from her that had him smiling. "I could never fault you for being less than poetic in your persistence, but you know very well that I cannot possibly attend a picnic with you!"

"Why not?" he demanded, leaning forward on his um-brella, so that she could not miss the shimmer in his eyes, nose to nose as they were.

"I've *explained,* have I not?" Kate demanded, poking him in the chest with her finger. "Very well, then, I shall en-deavor to explain it all again. It would be unseemly of me to go off with you, a confirmed bachelor, without escort. Can you not imagine what the parishioners might think?"

"I have not a care for what they might think," he insisted sternly. "I have often been the subject of wretched specula-tion. Just this week, I have heard tell that I intend to offer very soon for a debutante, can you imagine? Yet I give it not a thought, for I know what is in my heart, Kate. There is no debutante, there is you, only you, and has been you since almost the moment I laid eyes on you, there in the church, beneath the organ pipes, looking quite angelic."

Kate knew better than to allow flattery to seduce her, but how could she help the butterflies that winged in her belly when he spoke to her so earnestly, his dark brown eyes glowing deeply? "You may not have a care, sir, but I do. And what of my father? Have you a care for what he believes?"

"Where is he, then?" Montgomery demanded. "I shall at once beg his leave that you may accompany me to a picnic!"

With a laugh for his bravado, Kate playfully pushed him back. "He's resting! And I shan't wake him for your amusement."

"Ah, there, you see?" he asked, grabbing her hand and holding it tightly in his, bringing her knuckles to his warm lips. "It is our good fortune to be blessed with such a dreary spring day, while your father rests and the parishioners sit about their drawing rooms, moping," he said with a wink. "Fate is smiling on you, Kate. Don't be so foolish as to turn your back on it."

"And now you would have me believe it is fate?"

He pressed her hand against his chest, covering it with his big hand, and the smile faded from his face. "I certainly do. I say this not to amuse you but to convey nothing but the utmost respect and adoration that I have come to hold for you. I only want to be with you, Kate. Rather, I *must* be with you, or I will truly go mad. Say yes, say you will spare this poor man's heart. *Come with me.*"

There was something in his voice that rang true; she forced herself to drag her gaze from him and look about. Fortunately, as the guest house was stuck in the corner of the vicar's Mayfair estate, no one could see them, save her father and their man William, were he of a mind to look out the window.

"You mustn't fret about prying eyes. I've taken care of everything."

"What do you mean? And how can you possibly intend to picnic in this rain?"

A grin, boyish and pleasing, turned the corners of his mouth. "You must come with me to have your answer. I promise a picnic for you, a perfect setting and fit for a princess, if I do say so myself," he said, bowing slightly. "Come with me, Kate," he urged, stepping backward now and tugging her along.

Come with me, Kate. Her heart was beating rapidly, the blood flowing hot through her body. She could not deny the desire she had to be with him, either. The kisses they'd shared had awakened the dead and shriveled-up woman inside her. She felt as if she'd literally come alive these last few weeks, and at the moment, she was feeling her body and her heart push her toward him.

"No one shall ever know; I give you my word," he vowed.

As much as she wanted to go, as much as she longed to go, she knew what sort of man he was, and she knew very well what a man like him would want with a widow. Hadn't her father just said as much? And as much as she might want the same, she could not risk her honor. "I scarcely trust a man with your considerable reputation, sir."

"Aha. Then you have heard me labeled a scoundrel, have you? I will freely confess to being a scoundrel and more, if it pleases you," he said, with a fetching grin. "It's all quite true; I will not lie. But that was all before *you*, Kate. You have my word that I will honor you, as you have my word your honor will be protected always with me."

When she did not immediately respond, he tugged her closer. "You know I adore you. You know I want you. And if that desire is unrequited, I scarcely care—I will honor your wishes if you will just be with me for the afternoon." And then he smiled in that devilishly charming way he had, tugging lightly at her hand, and Kate felt herself light up inside like one thousand beeswax candles.

"You must fear for your eternity, my lord," she said, taking a tentative step toward him. "For you will surely suffer the consequences of spiriting a widow away from her father's home."

"Madam, I am more than prepared to suffer the fiery pits of hell for it," he said cheerfully and popped open his umbrella as he carelessly pulled her into the rain.

Chapter Eight

They ran across the manicured lawn beneath their umbrellas, Kate's bonnet dangling from her hand, through the mews that ran along the side of the vicar's house and out to the main street.

At the gate, Montgomery stopped and stood on tiptoe to peer out through the ornate wood carvings that adorned the top of the fence. "Perfect," he said low. "There's no one about in this wretched weather." He grabbed the gate handle, pulled it open, then took Kate's free hand securely in his and pulled her along behind him, through the gate, and to the left, striding purposefully down the walkway, Kate running to keep up.

She felt as if she were eloping, running off to something spectacularly secret.

At the corner of the street, there was a large black landau coach, fully closed, with a gold crest painted on the side, attached to a team of four grays. Two men were perched atop the driver's seat, their hats pulled low over their heads and the collars of their greatcoats turned up around their ears.

Upon seeing the viscount, one of them hopped down and quickly put down a small footstool before the coach door.

He pulled open the door as they reached the coach. "Milord," he said, bobbing his head.

"Thank you, Percy." Montgomery held his umbrella high over Kate, took hers, and handed it to the man before helping her into the interior of the coach.

Kate gasped as she settled onto the velvet bench; the interior walls were covered with red silk; the two opposing benches were covered in bloodred rose petals that filled the coach with a heavenly scent.

Montgomery came in behind her, landing directly across from her on the dark velvet squabs, his knees almost touching Kate's, beaming proudly as the door swung shut behind him. "What do you think? Is it to your liking?"

"It's *lovely,*" she said. "Breathtaking. I shudder to think how many innocent roses met their demise here."

He laughed, tapped the ceiling, and the coach lurched forward.

"Was it some sort of accident?" Kate asked, looking at them scattered on the floor, on the bench, and sticking to his wet boots and her wet hem.

"*Ach,* have I failed so miserably? I rather hoped you'd find the look and scent of them appealing."

"Oh, of course I *do,*" she said laughingly. "But it's a pity that they'll lie inside your coach while we . . . while we are elsewhere? Or do you intend to picnic in the coach?"

"There are plenty of roses in England. A veritable army of them, actually," he said with a wink, and leaned over, withdrew a small flagon of wine from beneath the bench and then a small glass. And another. "It seems as if my genius is not yet apparent to you."

"On the contrary—a picnic in a coach is quite imaginative. Some might even be moved to call it genius."

He grinned, obviously pleased by that. "Imaginative, perhaps, but a bit close, wouldn't you agree? No, the picnic is somewhere else entirely," he said as he poured a small amount of wine into a glass and handed it to her. "We shall be leisure in the course to our destination, where you will dine on roasted hen, tender leeks, and sweet pudding."

"How lovely," Kate murmured and sipped her wine, felt a warm glow from it and the knowledge that the handsome man sitting across from her had gone to so much trouble on the slim chance that she might agree to his insanity.

It was beyond her ability to comprehend, really. A wealthy viscount, a vicar's widow . . . it was scarcely the sort of affair that the *Morning Times* alluded to among the *ton*. Men of Montgomery's stature attracted any number of women—in fact, she'd read such speculation about him on more than one occasion. But he had been steadfast in his pursuit of her, and at the moment, she hardly cared of his motives. The butterflies he always seemed to put in her belly had somehow expanded into an entire aviary of wings beating away inside her, making her feel giddy with wild excitement.

It felt as if she had scarcely sipped her wine when the coach came to a halt. She detected the pungent scent of fish and heard the voices of several men.

"Where are we?" she asked.

Montgomery smiled enigmatically. "At the river's edge," he said as the door swung open. "We're to take a short journey upstream," he added and disappeared through the open door, then extended his hand to help her down.

Kate didn't know precisely where on the Thames they

had come to. They hurried across a rain-slicked dock to a waiting barge. In the middle of the barge was a large, box-shaped enclosure. Three boatmen were on board, two with oars in hand, and another at the rudder. A fourth waited patiently on the dock, next to a thick rope that anchored the barge to the dock.

"Mind your step," Montgomery warned her and hopped onto the barge, then caught her by the waist, lifted her off the dock, and swung her down onto the barge. With a boyish smile, he grabbed her hand, pulled her into the boxed enclosure.

She made a sound of surprise as she ducked and entered the enclosure. The small area was furnished with thick brocade pillows. The walls were velvet, and two tiny port-holes graced each side. There were candles in the sconces, a basket at the opening, and rose petals everywhere. *Everywhere.* They covered the cushions, the blankets, the baskets.

Kate was so awed by the sight of it that she scarcely noticed Montgomery was helping her in, seating her on a pile of cushions next to the porthole. He covered her with a blanket, then took his place next to her. From their vantage point, they had a view of the river as they headed upstream.

Water lapped gently at the sides of the barge as the boatmen made the final preparations to launch in the thick rain and mist. Kate watched them move back and forth before the enclosure until the barge glided away from the dock and started upriver. Then she shifted her smiling gaze to Montgomery.

"What's this?" he asked, looking at her soft smile. "Ah, I expected as much," he said and reached for the basket, his arm brushing carelessly against her as if they were quite accustomed to one another.

He placed the basket on his lap. "I should not expect

you to ride very far without some sustenance," he said as he unfolded the linen cloth in the basket. It was filled with tiny sweet biscuits of various shapes and varieties. "What would you like?"

Kate leaned forward, glanced at the biscuits in his lap, then lifted her gaze. "What would you suggest?"

With a low laugh in his throat, Montgomery put aside the biscuits and put his hand on her neck. "I would suggest," he said, leaning closer, "this." He pulled her to him, kissed her soft and wet as they floated into a thickening mist.

Neither of them noticed.

They kissed, ate biscuits, and kissed again until the barge bumped up against a pier sometime later. Darien lazily lifted his head and leaned to one side, peering at the port-hole to have a look, and turned a beaming smile to Kate.

She was turned to one side, lying against the cushions. A part of a rose petal had adhered itself to her cheek, and another was tangled in her hair, which had come quite undone. Her lips were slightly swollen and glisteningly moist. Through half-closed eyes, she smiled dreamily at him. "Where are we?"

"You must come have a look for yourself." He helped her up; Kate leaned across his lap and looked out. Her brow puckered slightly as she tried to make out where they were. "It's a boathouse."

"That it is." But it wasn't just any boathouse. It was the grand old boathouse on his uncle's estate. His uncle, who was well past his eightieth year, neither cared nor noticed that his nephew was borrowing the boathouse for the after-noon.

Darien had sent his butler Kiefer this morning to arrange it all. The boathouse had a pair of doors that opened up to the river, so that boats could be launched from an enclosed dock.

"Oh my," Kate whispered, taking in the grassy slope of lawn that stretched from the water's edge up to his uncle's magnificent estate. "It looks like something from a picture book."

Darien laughed, urged her up and helped her from the barge. He let the boatmen go, giving the captain a handful of coins to disappear for a couple of hours, then led Kate across the exterior dock to the boathouse.

Her blue eyes widened when they entered the interior. Near the open doors, two piles of rich brocade cushions lined either side of a damask tablecloth. On the tablecloth, a pair of silver candelabras rose above several covered platters. Two bottles of wine were nearby, as were china plates and silver cutlery. In the boat slip, candles floated, bobbing languidly in time to the rain on the roof.

And everything was covered in rose petals.

Darien glanced at Kate. Her lips had parted slightly; her eyes were wide as she tried to absorb what he'd done for her. Actually, he was rather impressed himself. He had described what he envisioned to Kiefer, but he'd never dreamed it would look as good as this. The man had outdone himself, and Darien made a mental note to commend him for his mastery.

"I'm . . . astounded," Kate said at last.

"I'm rather astounded myself," Darien said.

They sat on the cushions; Kate gazed out the doors open onto the river as he lit the candelabras and poured the wine. "I can scarcely believe you've done all this . . . for *me*," she said softly, gesturing to the picnic.

"Why can't you?" he asked, tipping his wineglass against hers and lifting it in a salute before drinking.

"No one has ever been so considerate of me," she said

thoughtfully and smiled warmly. "I've never been given a picnic. It rather warms the cockles of my heart, my lord."

Darien grinned. "That's all the thanks I need," he said and put aside the wine and lifted the dome from the first platter. Roasted asparagus. "I should think your husband, may he rest in peace, might have treated you to a picnic now and again," he said, broaching the subject that had weighed heavy on his mind these last few weeks.

"No," Kate said, shaking her head and drawing her legs up against her chest. "Richard was a good husband. But he was not as creative as this."

"Asparagus?"

"Please."

"Your husband was a clever man. I rather enjoyed his sermons. But I must confess, Mrs. Becket, that I have often wondered if he knew about the Christmas soiree." He glanced at her from the corner of his eye.

Her eyes filled with a regret that speared him, and she dropped her gaze to her lap as she shook her head.

Darien said nothing. He regretted it, too, and feeling awkward now, he busied himself with putting chicken and roasted potatoes on her plate.

"He was fond of you, you know," she said after a moment.

That surprised him greatly; he looked up to see if she was jesting as he handed her the plate. "Of *me?*"

"Mmm. He once said that your reputation was born of what little society really knew about you, but that you were far greater than they knew."

Darien arched a brow in surprise. "He said that of me, did he?"

She nodded, bit into the chicken. "It's delicious!" She gave him a pleased smile that he rather suspected would entice men to move mountains. "Richard knew of your charitable works, of course. And your endowment for the boys' school."

It was Darien's turn to color slightly—his endowment was not something about which he cared to speak. That sort of information invariably brought beggars and charlatans crawling out of the woodwork looking for money.

"Does that disconcert you?" she asked, smiling softly.

"A bit," he admitted with a wry smile. "But not for the reasons I think you'd believe. It's just that I'd rather keep that sort of effort to myself."

"Your secret is quite safe with me," she said lightly. "And besides, I rather enjoy hearing the other things people know about you. I'd hate to cast you in a favorable light and dash all their presumptions to pieces."

"What other things, if I may?" he playfully demanded.

Kate shrugged and bit the top off the asparagus spear. "I can hardly be specific, you know. There are so *many* things said. And written. And debated."

"Are there, indeed?"

"Mmm. The *on-dits* in the society pages, you know. Whether or not you were actually seen at Vauxhall Gardens with Lady Spencer on your arm, or was it, perhaps, Lady Penshurst?"

"Lady *Penshurst?*" Darien cried, almost choking on the roasted chicken. "Madam, I'd rather be drawn and quartered than accompany Lady Penshurst so far as the garderobe!"

"My lord!" Kate cried with a burst of laughter.

"I'm quite serious," Darien insisted. "There was never a more disagreeable woman in all of England, you may rest assured!"

"But you do not object to Lady Spencer?" she asked coyly.

Darien lifted a brow. "No more than you object to Connery, or Anglesey, or—"

"Yes, yes, I take your meaning," she said with a dismissive flick of her wrist. "It seems as if my reputation has taken a rather strange turn, for reasons I am happily ignorant."

Frankly, Darien had wondered about that—oh honestly, when it came to Kate, he wondered about everything. What did she eat? When did she sleep? How did she look with her hair completely unbound and mussed? Did her sleepy morning eyes still shimmer with her spirit? What books did she read? What thoughts did she have? Who did she love?

"Do you miss him?" he suddenly blurted, and mentally kicked himself for voicing the question aloud.

To her credit, Kate did not seem either appalled or surprised. She put aside her plate and girlishly lay back on the pillows, rolling onto her belly. "I missed him terribly at first," she said, looking out at the rain. "But I don't think of him as often now." She glanced at Darien from the corner of her eye. "Do you think me horrible?"

"Not in the least," he assured her. "Time has a rather cruel way of marching on."

"Yes, rather determinedly, I've noticed. I still think of Richard, I do. And I treasure the time that we had. But it seems that as of late, there is someone else occupying my thoughts."

Darien stilled. "Is there?"

"There is," she said, smiling again, lifting her funny walking boots above her knees.

"Not Connery, I should hope."

She laughed lightly and rolled onto her side, propping her hand beneath her head, "It's hardly Connery. The man is intolerable."

Darien put his plate aside and calmly wiped his mouth with a linen napkin as he considered that. "Then might I be so bold as to inquire?"

She laughed, put her hand reassuringly on his forearm. "Can you not guess, my lord? After all, I turned the other gentlemen away."

The gentle, lusty timbre of her voice wrapped around him, and Darien impulsively reached for her hand. But Kate startled him by catching his hand in hers, her long, delicate fingers closing tightly around his.

"Can't you guess?"

The question sent a white-hot bolt of lightning through his body. Darien's blood was churning; he felt as if he was being swept away, carried off by the stream of her voice. She suddenly sat up, took his hand firmly in hers and laid it in her lap. With her other hand, she traced the lines of his palm, slowly to his wrist, and then back again, to the forefinger, her touch scorching him as she moved. It seemed minutes, if not hours, before she shifted her gaze from his face to his eyes. "Shall I tell you your future?"

"Not," he said hoarsely, "unless you are in it."

Her gaze calmly roamed his face. "Do you truly want me in it?"

"I want you, Kate," he confessed in a gruff whisper. "Is it not obvious to you by now? I've wanted you for my own the moment I laid eyes on you. I've wanted you so long and hard that my body aches with it."

She gazed at his lips for a moment. "Those words," she said, "which you speak so carelessly, are a salve to my wounded heart." She lifted her gaze to his, her green eyes almost the color of the ivy that grew along the riverbank. "But I fear for my heart, sir. I fear it will not withstand another blow. You will please forgive me, then, if I ask if I am the only one to whom such poetic and . . . stirring words have been spoken?"

Darien impulsively grasped her hand, leaned down to kiss her palm, his lips lingering there, wondering how in

God's name he might convince her of what was in his heart. But then Kate withdrew her hand and laid it tenderly against his cheek, and Darien lost all reason.

He reached for her, seized her, really, and pulled her hard to him, then bore her down into the cushions. He pressed his mouth against her cheek, then her eyes, and slid to her lips, drinking in the wine she had drunk, the saltiness of the roasted chicken. He felt the succulent surface of her lips and held fast there, relishing the feel of her in his arms.

"Only you, Kate. It has been only you these last few years," he said hoarsely. "I bare my soul to you now. I'll not tease you about something so important as this."

It was Kate who moved first, Kate whose fair lips parted slightly, Kate's tongue that dipped between his lips to touch him. And then Darien was falling, drifting down like a feather onto the field of gold where she pushed him.

He rolled onto his back, bringing Kate with him, on top of him, his hands on either side of her head, his lips covering hers, and her face, her ears, and neck. He devoured her soft lips, inch by extraordinary inch. Then he tasted the inside of her mouth, reveled in the feel of her teeth, her tongue, and the sweet, smooth flesh of her mouth. One hand fell to the slender column of her neck, drifted down to the wool cloth that covered her bosom, cupping the pliant weight of her breast before fumbling with the dozens of small buttons that kept her from him.

Heedless of anything but her body, her scent, and the feel of her skin, he slipped his hand inside the gown, felt the warm, smooth skin of her breast, swollen with desire, and her taut nipple.

Kate gasped softly in his ear as he squeezed her nipple between his fingers, and pressed herself against him, her body stretched the length of his, firm and supple and young.

Darien twisted again, rolling her onto her back and coming over her, one hand in her hair, long, golden-red hair that had come completely out of its carefully constructed coif. She was amazingly soft, astoundingly plush, and her breasts supple and ripe. Darien inhaled deeply, touched his lips to her neck, and shuddered when Kate whispered in his ear, *"It's been only you, too, Darien . . ."*

Purely male instincts took hold of him—he was without conscious thought, filled with a longing so strong and powerful that he felt completely out of control. Her hand, her slender, perfect hand, slid to the nape of his neck, her fingers entwining in his hair, then down his arm, squeezing it, her fingers kneading the muscle, then inside his coat, feeling his rib cage, his back. Darien kissed her wildly, deeply, his heart and mind raging to be inside her . . . and he was, he realized, through the fog that had shrouded his mind and all common sense, just moments away from *being* inside of her.

He suddenly sat up, clawed his way out of his coat and waistcoat, ripped at the neckcloth that confined him, yanking his shirt from his trousers. Kate laughed at his determination and calmly unbuttoned her gown.

When she had freed all the buttons, Darien caught her hand, stilling her. He rose to his feet, then held out his hand to her. Without question, Kate put her hand in his and let him pull her to her feet. No words were necessary; she lifted her arms in the air, allowed Darien to pull the gown over her head and lay it aside. "Are you frightened?" he asked.

"No . . . I am breathless."

With a growl, Darien shed his shirt, kicked his boots from his feet, and loosened his trousers. He could scarcely bear to see her standing there in a plain cotton chemise and not touch her. So he put his hands on her shoulders and carefully pushed the chemise down her arms. It fell to the floor in a cloud of white, leaving her to stand before him, naked in her splendor.

She was beautiful. "Good God," he muttered in genuine appreciation. She was so unlike any other woman he had ever known. There was no pretense about her, no cosmetic— she was curved in all the right places, round where a man desired it most.

"I knew you would be beautiful," he said and palmed a dark areola that stiffened quickly with his touch; his fingers splayed across her breast and nipple and squeezed gently.

Kate gave him a terribly seductive smile, and Darien covered her mouth in a stupefying kiss as his hands found her waist. Kate lifted her arms, put them around his neck, and pressed her bare torso against his. A groan of ecstasy escaped him, and he suddenly and effortlessly lifted her in his arms, fell to one knee, and placed her on the cushions.

He quickly shrugged out of his shirt. She lay before him, watching him, as he had, on so many sleepless nights, imagined her. Golden, silky hair framing her. Firm breasts, a slender waist that curved into narrow hips, and long, shapely legs brought together in the gold triangle of curls. In the candlelight, her skin glowed radiantly.

Kate lifted her hand, touched his face. Darien shed his trousers, carefully lowered himself to her and kissed her, probing deeply within her until he could bear it no more. He lifted his head; her gaze slipped to his mouth, and she put a finger on his bottom lip, ran it lightly across.

He smiled gratefully; his pulse was now coursing hard in his neck. He moved lower, to her breasts. One hand floated down her side and across her flat abdomen as he moved against her, his cock thickening impossibly with only the contact of her skin. When his fingers brushed deliberately against the inside of her thigh, she inhaled softly.

Lying beneath him, Kate was not conscious of anything

but his touch, both alarmed and titillated by the response it evoked deep within her. She gasped when he brought his mouth to her breast, but came out of her skin when his hand slipped between her legs and stroked the silken folds there. She was fast losing control, felt her thighs parting for him, urging him deeper.

It had been so long, an eternity perhaps, since she'd felt a man's touch. Yet it seemed as if she had never known a man, not like this, not with her blood pounding in her ears and her heart beating hard in her chest. Then Darien muttered something incomprehensible against her breast and slipped his fingers deep inside her sheath, and Kate instantly lifted against his palm.

She was lost.

It was not supposed to be like this, she was not supposed to revel in her complete seduction, but she pressed against his hand nonetheless, a curious but familiar mix of pleasure and anxiety spurring her.

His fingers gently but expertly moved in her, then slowly withdrew to stroke her. Kate felt herself falling away, and she pushed her hands against the side of the boathouse, moaning softly.

"Not yet," he murmured against her stomach. "No, no, I will not let you go so easily, Kate. Have you any notion of how I have longed for this moment? How I have dreamed of giving you pleasure you have never known?"

The question compelled Kate onto her elbows; with her hand, she cupped his face, made him rise up so that she might kiss him hard and deep. "Then give it to me," she rasped. "Give me pleasure I've never known. Give it to me *now*," she whispered.

Darien grinned. "God blind me, Kate Becket, but I've never adored a woman as I adore you this very moment."

And with that, he moved his thigh in between her legs, pushed them apart, and lifted himself over her.

He languidly kissed her breast while he laced her fingers with his above her head. With his other hand, he guided her to feel his passion, held her hand firmly there while he brushed the tip against her, and again, only deeper. She was shuddering, astonished by the waves of passion crashing through her. Darien smiled at her gasping and slid inside her, slowly at first, his eyes on hers, watching her closely as he adjusted himself to her body surrounding him, then sliding deeper with small, rhythmic movements.

Her control was at an end; she did not think she could contain the ecstasy that was building in her a second longer. He felt hot and thick inside her; she arched her pelvis against him and instinctively demanded more as she gasped for her breath. Darien moaned, and covering her mouth with his, he thrust powerfully within her. Kate cried out with pleasure against his mouth, then let her head fall back as her body rose to meet him with the next thrust, and the next.

His strokes lengthened within her; her knees came up on either side of him, and she lifted her pelvis to match his rhythm. She felt herself falling swiftly away, falling from this world and everything but Darien's body. His breath was hot on her shoulder, his grip of her hand almost painful, his body long and deep within her.

"Dear God!" she whispered, wildly anxious as the pleasure began to mount toward its inevitable, explosive end. She gripped his shoulder, lifted herself higher, meeting his hard strokes. *"Darien!"* she whispered frantically in his ear.

It happened—wave after wave of pleasure erupted within her, carrying her swiftly away from even Darien.

She threw her head back and arched her neck as the release flooded from every pore.

"Kate. Dear Kate," he gasped, and cupped her bottom, drove into her once more, erupting powerfully inside her, filling her completely as the rapture continued to wash over her. She collapsed backward, tightening around him, never wanting the incredible experience to end. Somewhere, above her, Darien called her name on a soft groan.

Kate opened her eyes. He was holding himself above her, his arms muscular and strong, an unfathomable look in his brown eyes. Carefully and tenderly he lowered himself onto his elbows and cupped her face in his hands while his gaze roamed her features. *"God, Kate,"* he whispered.

Yes. Oh, God.

Chapter Nine

Eventually, and very reluctantly, they left the boathouse behind and returned to Mayfair, wrapped in one another's embrace as they floated down the Thames.

Darien hadn't felt so bloody alive or so much a man as he did that afternoon. He had an urgent desire to hold her always, to keep her very near.

Of course he intended to offer for her—he'd reached that conclusion the moment he'd really touched her, in the very same moment he realized she could never belong to any other but him, and he said as much to her. "I shall keep you near me always," he'd said, but Kate laughed and kissed him, and he was not entirely certain if she truly believed his intentions.

Nevertheless, he was determined to offer, and to do so properly, perhaps after the Southbridge Charity Auction Ball, in which he knew she was rather involved, and after which the season would begin to wind down. There'd be less distractions then . . . less talk, too, for it was not often a man of his social rank took a vicar's widow to wife.

That gave him a little over a fortnight to prepare his offer and his home for her.

When they reached Kate's street, Darien signaled for the driver to stop, and gathered up her umbrella and bonnet and handed them to her, then set about straightening her clothing, unbuttoning and buttoning the gown again, as Kate had managed to do it crookedly.

She laughed as he deftly repaired her. "Oh my," she said, her cheeks flushed and her eyes sparkling. "I'm so terribly clumsy. One would think I was a girl who'd received her first kiss."

"One look at you, madam, and one would rather believe that there walks a woman who is true to herself and her passion," he said with a wink.

Her flushed cheeks turned cherry red, and she playfully slapped his hand away, finished the buttoning herself, as he sought to tame errant wisps of her hair and tuck them behind her ears. "You're a wicked man, Darien," she said, but she was smiling. "You've led me quite astray with your picnic."

"I should like to lead you much further than that."

With a laugh, she smoothed the front of her gown, then looked up, cupped his jaw with her hand. "You're a scoundrel, my lord. What would my poor father think?" she asked, and impulsively lifted up, kissed him fully before abruptly breaking away and grabbing her things. "I must hurry," she said, and reached for the coach door. "It's quite late."

"Kate!" Darien said sternly after her as she poked her umbrella outside and opened it. "I shall call again."

She smiled at him over her shoulder. "I must go now." And with that, she was gone.

Darien pulled the door to, then pushed aside the curtains and watched her striding purposefully through the rain, her head held high, her bonnet hanging down her back. And her chemise, unfortunately, hanging below the hem of her day gown. He couldn't help but smile, and reluctantly, he let go the small drape, tapped on the ceiling to send the driver on, and leaned back against the squabs, wondering if he could possibly bear it until he saw her again.

William's wife, Mary Beth, served leek soup for supper that night. Kate sat across from her father, a bit fearful that he might note the flush in her cheek or inquire as to her whereabouts in the afternoon while he lay napping. But if he noticed any change in her, he said not a word and talked on about a game of cards he had enjoyed in the past week with the vicar.

That evening, after reading to her father as she did every night, Kate at last lay on the small four-poster bed in her room, reliving every moment of this astonishing afternoon. She stared blindly at the peeling wallpaper and faint cracks in the ceiling, giggling at the prospect of being completely and inexorably in love again.

There had been a time, shortly after Richard's death, that she was quite certain she'd never loved anyone before him and would certainly love no one after him. The young men with whom she had flirted and shared an occasional kiss before Richard were sweet memories, but she never felt the same sort of deep esteem for them that she had for her husband.

She regretted never telling him about the kiss she shared with Darien. It had been a colossal mistake, and she'd been so fearful of what he might do or think, of losing his respect. In hindsight, however, with time and grief having dulled her girlish feelings, she believed he might have understood and forgiven her.

Would he forgive her now? For being so wanton as to sleep with a man out of wedlock? For wanting to feel love again? And she did *so* want to feel love again, to know, with all certainty, the strength of a man's love for her, to feel his arms around her, protecting her, holding her. She had convinced herself she'd not know such love again, that she'd spend the rest of her days doing charitable works and looking after her father.

And she'd be quite content with it, really, for hers was a good existence. As a widow, she was not as restricted as the unmarried girls about town. In truth, she was free to come and go as she pleased, to speak freely with gentlemen at church, to live her life as *she* wanted, and not the way a man might dictate.

There were, of course, drawbacks to her carefree life. Her current spate of callers for example—Kate had not heard anything in particular about herself, but she was beginning to have the uneasy feeling that something untoward had been said about her, something that was being passed around as truth. She knew that certain widow's were rather free with their affections. Had that been said of her?

As to the matter of her physical being, she had not realized how, having known a man's love, she might yearn for it again. Oh, she yearned for it, all right. Yearned for it so hard that sometimes she lay awake at night, felt the ache of it deep in her marrow, making it impossible to sleep. And now, to have experienced that most elemental, primitive pleasure again, the ache had spread to her heart and head.

Kate rolled over, balled the pillow up beneath her head. *Did she love him?* Or did she merely enjoy the attention? And did he love her? Or was he really the sum of his reputation? A man who, by most accounts, was a *roué,* a rake, pursuing physical pleasure and careless with the hearts of the ladies—and widows—he knew?

It was hard to believe it of him. Since the first day he had appeared quite unexpectedly to walk with her as she made her calls to the elderly, and every day he appeared after that, she had never sensed anything but the most genuine of affection and esteem from him. Certainly today he had shown her his esteem—he was a powerful yet gentle lover, more concerned with her pleasure than his own. And he spoke so poetically, spilling words of passion and adoration for her that made her swoon.

Yet she could never shake the feeling that perhaps, just perhaps, his was the language of practiced courtiers, that he spoke those poetic words to other ladies as well. But he'd seemed so terribly sincere when he had spoken them to her! *Only you, Kate, it has been only you these last few years. . . .*

Kate sighed dreamily. Whatever the truth, it had been a most exquisite afternoon.

Downstairs, the clock struck a quarter past one, and Kate sighed and closed her eyes, drifting off to sleep and a dream of what their children might look like. Strong and handsome children, with laughing eyes, just like their father.

Darien did not appear Wednesday when Kate and her father took their rounds. At the outset, Kate thought nothing of it, in spite of her father's wondering aloud what had happened to her constant escort. She had every faith he would call when he could and rather imagined he might appear a bit later on their route. If not, she would assume some order of business had cropped up and kept him away.

It was Mrs. Biddlesly who wedged the first sliver of doubt into her opinion.

Kate had arrived with a basket of fresh fruit, just as she did every Wednesday. *"Fruit!"* Mrs. Biddlesly had cried with great disgust. "Would that you'd bring an old woman something other than *fruit!"*

"What would you like, Mrs. Biddlesly? I shall endeavor to bring it to you," Kate asked patiently.

"A spot of good brandy, that's what! And a girl like you ought to know where to put her hands on it!" she said, flicking her wrist at Kate.

"A girl like me?" Kate asked airily, as she handed the basket to the footman, quite accustomed to the old woman's ranting, and just as accustomed to ignoring it altogether.

"Yes, of course a girl like *you,*" Mrs. Biddlesly said, but with a venom that startled Kate. She turned to look at the old widow.

"I've a mind to tell the vicar not to send your sort round anymore! I don't care for your reputation! You mock your good husband's memory!"

"I beg your pardon, Mrs. Biddlesly! What of my reputation?" Kate demanded hotly. "What could you possibly mean?"

Mrs. Biddlesly folded her bony arms over her sagging bosom and glared at Kate. "As if you don't know! Cavorting about with men, appearing in places of ill repute! Having a time of it, aren't you, Mrs. Becket, now that you're out of your widow's weeds? And after all the dear late vicar did for you! Bringing you out of the country to a grand house and a grand existence!"

Fury and confusion erupted in Kate; she glared at the old bag. "I beg your pardon, Mrs. Biddlesly, have you quite lost your mind, or have you any idea what vile things you are implying?"

"I may be old, but I'm not a fool!"

"You've no cause to make such appalling accusations!"

"Don't I, indeed? It's quite common knowledge, you strumpet! It's said all about town!"

Kate's stomach dropped. *Said all about town* . . . Her fear was borne out—something horribly unkind had been said about her, something to make men believe they might have their way with her, and, if one were silver-tongued, then he might possibly—

No! She whirled away from the old woman, reached for the door. "You'll do well to ask the vicar for another caller, Mrs. Biddlesly," Kate said hoarsely, "for I shall never bother with you again!" She yanked open the door, stepped outside, and slammed it soundly behind her.

On the street, her father looked up in shock as she came running down the steps. "Kate! What's happened?"

"Nothing, Papa. Nothing but the ranting of an impossible old woman!" she cried, and grabbed up the next basket, then marched forward, ahead of her father, so that he would not see the tears of fury glistening in her eyes.

Whatever the old woman thought she knew, Kate could not believe Montgomery would have talked about them. He'd said such beautiful things, had given her his word he'd protect her virtue. He'd *promised!* Her heart refused to believe it, but with every step, her doubt weighed heavier. She didn't want to believe that he'd used her so shamelessly. She didn't *want* to believe it. . . .

She made the rest of her rounds in something of a fog. Papa worried about her; she told him she was feeling a bit ill, so he insisted on carrying in the last three baskets. That afternoon, she went straight to her room and lay down, and stared through tears at the ceiling above her, her mind twisting impossibly with doubts and her desperate attempts to reassure herself.

That evening, at supper, Papa told her that Lord Montgomery had called, as had Lord Connery, and that he'd informed them both she was indisposed.

Kate said nothing, merely nodded.

The next day, she awoke feeling old and used up. But she forced herself out of bed and to wash and comb her hair, as today was the final meeting of the Ladies Auxiliary before the Southbridge Charity Auction Ball, their main event each year. Kate had little heart for it but forced herself to dress in a bright yellow day gown, hoping it might cheer her.

She left for the church early, to be away from Papa's prying eyes.

The ladies began to trickle in shortly before noon. Was it her imagination, or did some of them greet her a little coolly? None of them offered to help her set the table where they would gather, but then again, Kate reminded herself, they rarely did. She was imagining things. Mrs. Biddlesly was an old woman who had several bats in her belfry. No one else believed she was a strumpet.

So Kate went about her business alone, scarcely hearing the ladies' chatter and trying to ignore any whispering, even when it seemed so loud as to be deafening to her.

Mrs. Forsythe and Miss Forsythe were the last to arrive, and Kate smiled as they walked in the door, called her greeting. Mrs. Forsythe did not seem to hear her, even though Kate was only a few feet away.

It was Miss Forsythe who garnered everyone's attention, however, with the news apparently making the rounds of the *ton*. News Kate had not heard.

"Ah, there she is, the belle of the ball!" Lady Bristol cried happily. "Now don't be coy, Miss Forsythe, but tell us, will you, if you are considering his offer?"

Miss Forsythe blushed prettily and looked demurely at her mother.

"Lady Bristol, we mustn't speak of any offer, as one has not yet been made," Mrs. Forsythe said, but a smile was playing at the corners of her thin lips.

"Honestly, Mrs. Forsythe!" Lady Cheevers scolded her. "You are among friends here! We *know* no offer has been made, for certainly you would have crowed it like a rooster the moment you walked through the door!"

That remark prompted a laugh from the other ladies, and even Mrs. Forsythe laughed a little.

"It's all about the town," Lady Cheevers cheerfully continued. "It is a matter of when, not *if*," she said authoritatively. "A man in his position would not allow it to go so far as this if it weren't true."

"Oh dear, I can't be so sure as *that*," Miss Forsythe said nervously, and the ladies rushed to assure her that a rumor of this magnitude would not have been repeated were it not true.

Kate's heart began to pound. She recalled Darien saying that there was some speculation that he would offer for a debutante, and had dismissed it as if it were ridiculous. Why should she doubt him? But after a few more minutes of the ladies gushing over Miss Forsythe, Kate cleared her throat and interjected shakily, "I beg your pardon, but I've not heard. . . . Who is it that seeks your hand, Miss Forsythe?"

Lady Cheevers and Mrs. Forsythe glared at her. The other ladies looked around the room. One might have thought she'd just announced she was having an illicit affair with the archbishop.

"I can't say as anyone seeks my hand, really," Miss Forsythe said kindly. "It's all a bit of speculation. But I suppose there are a *few* signs that would indicate—"

"A *few* signs?" Lady Bristol cackled. "My dear Miss Forsythe, a gentleman does not seek your particular company in a public park, or at a public church meeting, or certainly not at a public ball, and then tend to you as carefully as he did when you fainted, if it's merely speculation. The viscount intends very well to offer for you!"

"Not to mention the things he has said to her," Mrs. Forsythe said proudly. "Privately, that is."

A viscount. Now Kate's heart was in her throat. She managed a smile for Miss Forsythe, who was looking at her curiously. Kate nervously tucked a strand of hair behind her ear. "How wonderful for you, Miss Forsythe," she managed to say. "Pray tell, which fortunate gentleman holds you in such high esteem?"

Miss Forsythe gave her a strange, ugly little smile, and said, "Have you truly not heard, Mrs. Becket? It's been remarked for a fortnight now. It's Lord Montgomery."

It felt as if the ground buckled beneath her feet. Kate reached for a chair and slid into it while she tried to keep smiling and tried to keep from sobbing or gasping or crying out to the heavens. "How marvelous for him," she said unevenly. "He'd have quite a catch, were he to offer."

"Yes," Miss Forsythe said, taking a step toward her. "Wouldn't he?" But then she whirled around to the other ladies. "I mean to say, it would be marvelous if he truly esteemed me in that way."

Once again, they all hastened to assure her that he did, and that his imminent offer would certainly come at the Southbridge Charity Auction Ball. One of them vowed that Lady Southbridge had said, in fact, that she had it on very good authority that was precisely where he intended to make his offer, in grand fashion, just as they used to do in the olden days.

How Kate managed to endure that luncheon was quite beyond her comprehension. She could not look at the fair Miss Forsythe and not see that it was true. Of *course* he would offer for her—it made perfect sense. The girl came with a respectable dowry, was properly credentialed in the eyes of the *ton,* was the perfect wife in every way for a man of his stature. She was a vicar's poor widow. And when he'd said he should always keep her near, he meant something entirely different than a legitimate offer of marriage.

How pathetically foolish she had been to believe otherwise! He'd wanted beneath her skirts, that was all! He'd seen a widow and had acted upon his male instincts, just as Lord Connery hoped to do. And even though she could believe that Montgomery did indeed esteem her in some way, it was clear to her that he'd never intended to have more than what she had so freely given him, and more the bloody fool that made her, for she was not a young miss. She understood the way of men and women, yet had chosen to believe her silly, childish fantasies!

Her bloody heart felt as if it had been crushed to tiny pieces.

At the end of the Ladies Auxiliary meeting, Emily watched Mrs. Becket clear the cake plates. She moved lethargically, as if she had been dealt a tremendous blow. It was strange, Emily thought, as she gathered her gloves and reticule, that it did not bring her the pleasure she had imagined. It seemed as if the woman had been mortally wounded, and she imagined how the vicar might find her Sunday morning, sprawled in the church's kitchen, an arrow through her heart, the very life bled out of her.

The image was so strong that as she walked down the

street, lost in thought, her mother mistook her silence for fretting, and put her arm around Emily, drawing her in close to her side. "You mustn't fret, Daughter," she whispered reassuringly. "Lady Cheevers is quite right. The rumor never would have carried so far if there were not some truth to it. It was obvious to all in attendance at the May Day Ball that he held you in highest esteem. Lady Southbridge said he looked after you quite lovingly."

Only because she had told Lady Southbridge that he had.

"Now when your father returns from the country, he'll pay a call to Montgomery and determine what he's about."

A knot formed in her belly; Emily looked down at her feet.

"There, now," her mother said again. "Your father is quite adept at this sort of thing. I'd wager by the time he leaves Lord Montgomery's study, his lordship will wonder why he waited so long to make an offer for the fair Emily Forsythe, mark me."

Unless, of course, his esteem of her had been manufactured and planted in her mother's head, just as it had been deviously planted in every feminine head among the *ton.*

But then again, Emily thought brightly, perhaps the gems of gossip she had left behind in all those drawing rooms might somehow work together to convince Lord Montgomery that he did, in fact, esteem her as he ought. Perhaps, when her father called, he'd be begin to see it, and if not, her father would help him to see it. She imagined Montgomery imagining her walking through a field of flowers, a garland in her hair, and resisting the urge to run to wherever she might be at that moment.

She lifted her head, smiled at her mother.

"Ah, there's my darling! The world is a much brighter place when you smile, Emily. I am quite certain that Lord Montgomery noticed it instantly the night you came out. I recall that he watched you very closely the entire evening of your debut," she said, and seemed firmly convinced of it.

Perhaps, then, Emily thought as she marched alongside her mother, her plan wasn't so very far-flung after all. Perhaps she had only aided the inevitable.

Chapter Ten

By the time Sunday morning rolled around, Darien was feeling a bit frantic. He'd not been successful at seeing Kate since the day of the picnic. His calls to her house were rebuffed by her father, who said she was, alternately, ill, indisposed, then ill, then indisposed.

He could not begin to understand why she might be avoiding him. The afternoon they had spent in the old boathouse had been the most blissful of all his days on this earth, and he was at a loss to understand how she couldn't feel at least a bit of that, too.

Naturally, he imagined all manner of things—she regretted their lovemaking (but what living, breathing adult could regret that fantastic experience?); she had been found out by her father (but the chap seemed rather cheerful, all in all); or that she was truly ill (but she had been the picture of health).

Nothing made sense.

One thing Darien knew in all certainty—she'd not miss church services, and that morning, he donned his finest clothes and strode to church quite early. So early, in fact, he arrived before the vicar.

As the other parishioners began to arrive, he stood on the church steps, watching closely for Kate, greeting friends and acquaintances rather gruffly so that he'd not be engaged in some lengthy conversation and miss her slipping by.

His best friend, Freddie, found his behavior insupportable. "I'm not in the habit of remarking on your bad manners, my lord," he said with a sniff, "but that was the prime minister you just cut."

"I have no doubt that the prime minister will recover from any perceived slights," Darien said, scanning the crowd.

"What in the devil has you so wrought?" Freddie demanded. "I've not seen you this way in all the years we've known each other!"

Darien said nothing but managed more of a smile for the Forsythes as they climbed the church steps toward him.

Freddie followed the direction of his smile and laughed. "Aha! I should have known that the rumors are true, eh, Montgomery? You've set your heart on a female, have you?"

"W-what?" Darien stammered and jerked his gaze to Freddie; his first awful thought that Freddie somehow knew about Kate. "What did you say?"

Freddie laughed again and clapped him soundly on the shoulder. "You needn't be coy with me, my friend. You are, after all, quite human, and therefore, it stands to reason that even *you,* a confirmed and steadfast bachelor, might find happiness with a budding debutante. I daresay you've chosen one of the comelier ones. Dear God, there were some frightfully ugly ones in this year's crop, but I've quite admired this one myself."

It took a moment for Darien to understand what Freddie was saying, then found it incredulous that his oldest and dearest friend could possibly believe that a man of his years and experience would be smitten by a mere child such as Miss Forsythe.

"My lord!" Mr. Forsythe called.

Darien forced himself to turn and greet the Forsythes cordially, and as he did so, he couldn't help but look long and hard at Miss Forsythe. He supposed she was pleasant enough, but she could not have been more than seventeen, perhaps eighteen years of age. She blushed furiously when he looked at her, and clasped her hands tightly together while her beaming mother proudly looked on, and her father herded the family inside.

Freddie chuckled again. "Rather shy, ain't she?"

Darien frowned at Freddie. "I've not the slightest interest in her," he said sternly. "Anyone who says I do is quite mistaken."

"Not me," Freddie said, throwing up his hands. "I've only heard it. Lady Southbridge told me at tea just yesterday."

"Good morning!" Mr. Anglesey called out as he passed them with his aging mother.

"Morning," Darien and Freddie echoed, and as he passed, Freddie nudged Darien. "There's another one," he said low.

"Another what?"

"Another bachelor who has called on the vicar's widow of late. Had that at tea, too, you know. Seems rather a string of them have been calling, hoping to find the same success as Connery."

Darien glared at Freddie. "The same success?"

Freddie chuckled. "You're intent on slaying the messenger, are you, my lord? Just another bit of gossip from Lady

Southbridge. It would seem the widow has removed her widow's weeds and embraced life," he said with a wink.

"I shan't allow you to speak of Mrs. Becket thus, Frederick," Darien said icily. "Hasn't the lady suffered enough without the entire *ton* speaking ill of her?"

Freddie's eyes rounded wide. "My, my, Lord Montgomery. I had no idea you were the defender of widows and the suitor of young girls. And here I believed I knew you well."

"You know me well enough," Darien snapped as the church bells began to toll for the final call to services. "And now, if you'll excuse me, I should join my sister and her family."

Freddie very sarcastically extended one leg and bowed long over it as Darien passed by on his way inside. He didn't care in the least; his mind was churning with what Freddie had said.

He took his customary seat next to his sister and glanced to the left, to the place Kate always sat, her eyes keen on the vicar, her sweet voice rising above the others in song. She was not there. For the first time since he could remember, save the Sunday following her husband's death, Kate had not come to church services.

That was when the panic sank its tentacles firmly in him, twining around his heart and all but squeezing the very life from him. Something was horribly, terribly wrong.

The Southbridge Charity Auction Ball was to be held Friday evening, and it was the last place Darien hoped to speak with Kate before resorting to more drastic measures, of which he had not yet divined—so unaccustomed was he to this particular game of the heart—but that he *would* divine before he let her slip through his fingers.

In fact, it was the more drastic measures he was mulling over a very cold and wet afternoon, not unlike the afternoon that reminded him of the one he'd spent with Kate. That day was indelibly scored in his mind, a day he could not stop thinking about, could not stop reliving, every moment, every snippet of conversation, looking for a clue.

He was sitting before the fire in his study, a glass of whiskey dangling between two fingers, his legs stretched negligently before him when Kiefer entered to announce a caller. "Mr. John Forsythe," he said as he presented the man's card.

Bloody hell. Darien didn't bother to pick it up—he imagined the man's wife had put him up to it, if not the girl. "Show him in, will you, Kiefer?"

Kiefer returned a moment later with Mr. Forsythe in tow.

Darien managed, in his lethargy, to come to his feet and extend his hand in greeting. "Mr. Forsythe," he intoned. "Frightful weather to be out and about."

"Indeed it is, my lord. But I felt it imperative that I speak with you."

"Imperative?" Darien asked, cocking a brow as he gestured for Forsythe to sit. "We've no business that I am aware."

Forsythe laughed nervously, and flipping the tails of his coat, sat where Darien had indicated. Darien sat, too, picked up his whiskey. "A bit of whiskey to warm you, Forsythe?"

"Please, my lord."

Darien nodded at Kiefer, who poured the man a generous amount before leaving the study and pulling the door shut quietly behind him. Darien waited for Forsythe to taste the whiskey, then lazily lifted his glass to him before downing the rest of his. "Very well, then, Forsythe. What business have we?"

Forsythe laughed again and cleared his throat. "I recognize that this might be a bit premature, my lord, but what with all the rumors going about, I thought it was prudent of me to have a chat, man to man, about . . . about what the future may hold."

"And are you privy to what the future holds, sir? If you are, I'd very much like to know."

That seemed to rattle Forsythe a bit; he cleared his throat again, put the whiskey glass down, and fidgeted nervously with his neckcloth. "Surely, my lord, you are aware that rumors continue to circulate about the *ton* as to your intentions."

Darien chuckled. "Rumors of my intentions have been the rule rather than the exception for years now, Mr. Forsythe. I rarely pay them any heed at all."

"Ah, well," the man said, looking a bit ill at ease, "as these particular rumors involve my daughter Emily . . . I hope you can see the need for a bit of a chat."

He'd just said he paid the rumors no heed, implying that perhaps Forsythe shouldn't, either. With a shake of his head, Darien flicked his wrist and said, rather insouciantly, "Chat as you like."

Mr. Forsythe frowned at his lack of regard and looked down at his hands for a moment before speaking. "We've heard, on more than one occasion, that your interest in our daughter has . . . *blossomed* . . . and that you might be considering something perhaps a little more . . . long-term."

"And where have you heard this blossoming rumor?" Darien asked, refraining from chuckling at his own jest as Mr. Forsythe was beginning to look a bit like a pomegranate in the face, which, already quite round, was getting redder.

"Where? I, ah . . . well, then, I can say in all certainty that our Emily has been apprised by Lady Southbridge.

And, ah . . . Ladies Cheevers and Bristol, and, I believe, Ramblecourt."

Now there were four women with nothing better to do than wag their bloody tongues all day, Darien thought. But he did think it rather interesting that Forsythe credited Emily with the repeating of the rumors. "And your wife, Mr. Forsythe? Has she attributed these rumors to the same sources?"

"I . . . I believe she has, my lord," he said, looking a bit confused. "But as Emily is the one who is out in society, more so than her mother, you see—that is to say, she is fond of calling on Lady Southbridge, for example, to talk about upcoming events, that sort of thing."

"I know very well about that sort of thing," he said with sly smile, and thought it curious that Freddie had attributed the rumors about Kate to Lady Southbridge as well. The old woman was certainly busy this season. But while Lady Southbridge was notorious for spreading gossip, she was not, as far as he knew, given to fabrication. No, fabrication and deceit were the handiwork of young girls. Girls like Emily, for example, who feigned fainting at large balls.

"No matter how the rumors are started, my lord," Mr. Forsythe said, as Darien looked at the fire, his mind starting to turn, "it is my duty to inquire as to your true intentions for my daughter."

Darien suddenly remembered the day at the church spring social, when Emily had so boldly approached him while he was conversing with Kate, and something clicked in his brain.

"Of course," Darien said absently. "No matter how these rumors are started, no matter who they harm."

"I beg your pardon?" Forsythe asked, confused, his face getting redder. "Might you speak of your intentions, my lord?"

A light was suddenly dawning, and while Darien wasn't certain what to make of the things he was thinking, or how they might all fit, his suspicions of Emily Forsythe were suddenly raging. But before he could sort it all through, he had to rid himself of her hopeful father.

He smiled at Forsythe, lifted his glass, and said, "Mr. Forsythe, I am touched by your concern for you daughter. I hope to make my wishes known at the Southbridge Charity Auction Ball."

Forsythe blinked. He opened his mouth, then closed it again. And then he smiled and sat a little straighter, having obviously reached the conclusion Darien wanted him to reach. A conclusion he hoped the man would repeat to his chit of a daughter and anyone else who would listen.

"I think I take your meaning very well, sir," Forsythe said, sounding decidedly happier than a moment ago. "Yes, my lord, I do indeed take your meaning! Well then," he said, coming to his feet, "I believe I have taken enough of your time."

Darien smiled, too, and gained his feet. "I believe you have," he said and, clapping the man congenially on the back, he showed him the door.

Chapter Eleven

No one, unless they were dead or in the process of dying, missed the Southbridge Charity Auction Ball.

It signaled the home stretch of the season and was the event where debutantes who had not received an offer, and dandies who were toying with making an offer, wanted to see and be seen. It was the event where the next year's crop of debutantes was talked about, and speculation made as to how they might be paired up with the idle young men of the *ton*.

Married couples looked to the event as the last time they might see their lover, either real or potential. The older couples relished the hijinks of the young and speculated openly as to their various chances for success.

The event was held annually at the Southbridge mansion, in the grand ballroom that some said rivaled that of Carlton House, and was, according to most, just as elaborate as that of Carlton House. The walls were covered in blue silk that matched the paint on the ceiling, where a scene depicting heaven, complete with clouds and angels and naked cherubs playing their trumpets of love, had been artfully portrayed. The room was so cavernous that it required a twelve-piece orchestra, positioned in an alcove above the dance floor, which had been polished to perfection with hundreds of beeswax candles and dotted at its borders with potted orange trees.

At the other end of the ballroom, a platform had been erected, and it was from that platform the auction would commence at precisely midnight. In addition to being *the* event of the season, the Charity Auction Ball could also be credited with raising hundreds of pounds for the Ladies Auxiliary Charitable Works Benefiting Orphans and Pensioners.

Up until the auction commenced, and for hours long after it was over, there would be dancing in the main ballroom, gaming for the gentlemen across the way in the library, and supper served in the formal dining room for those in need of sustenance.

It was *the* place to be, and the last place Kate wanted to be.

If it hadn't been for Papa, she wouldn't be in attendance at all. But he'd been quite firm in this—he'd insisted she attend ("You're not getting a day younger, Kate,") and had even commissioned a lovely pale gold gown for her, made of gossamer silk with a train studded in tiny crystals that swept down from the middle of her back. Certainly it was the loveliest gown she'd ever worn, and even she could agree that the pale gold complemented her coloring.

But she'd been appalled when he'd first presented it to her, arguing that a vicar's widow did not wear something so lovely, and in addition, he could not afford something so fine on his pension.

"I suppose I can, and I did," he'd said gruffly.

"But *why,* Papa?" she'd asked as she had taken the gown from the modiste box to admire it.

"Is it not obvious, Kate? You are a young woman in the prime of her life. I can't bear to see you sitting about this tiny house wearing that drab vicar's wife gown, reading to an old man night after night! You deserve happiness! You deserve the very best this life has to offer! But you'll not find it rapping at your door—you must seek it, and I'll be damned if I'll allow you to seek it looking like a martyr."

Kate loved her father dearly. And on any other occasion, she would have been proud to wear the gown, thrilled with the luxury of it. But on this occasion, she felt nothing but dread. How could she see him, see his eyes and his mouth and his broad hands, and watch him publicly offer for Miss Forsythe? She'd die of heartache; she was certain of it.

It was not to be borne.

But she'd not had the heart or the courage to tell her father what had happened between her and Montgomery, and therefore could do nothing but don the gown and attend.

Her resolve crumbled quickly once she reached the ball and saw her father into the gaming room, however, for everyone was whispering about the impending offer Lord Montgomery would make for Miss Forsythe. "He's forty thousand pounds a year," Mrs. Peters whispered to Kate as she helped herself to punch. "That will make Mr. Forsythe quite happy, I assure you, as his fortune has dwindled somewhat with his son's gambling debts."

"Forty thousand pounds a year," Kate said evenly. "That's almost impossible to comprehend, is it not?"

"Not if you're Miss Forsythe, I assure you," Mrs. Peters said with a decided smirk.

"It happened at the May Day Ball," Kate overheard one young woman say to another. "He was very attentive to her."

"Because she *fainted*," the other woman said, clearly not as impressed with the events of the May Day Ball.

"And you wouldn't do the same," the first woman chastised her friend, "if Lord Montgomery had whispered decadent thoughts into *your* ear?"

Kate tried to stay away from the whispering and conjecture, and busied herself with the preparation of the night's auctions. It was an exercise in futility, for it seemed that everywhere she looked, Darien was standing there, looking magnificent in his formal tails and snowy white waistcoat, his eyes gleaming as he chatted with other guests. And if she felt her heart start to tear in two again, she would turn away from him, only to see Miss Forsythe, looking quite serene in her gown of pink and green.

Worse yet, more than one woman looked at her with some disgust. Or in the case of men, with lust.

Emily's court gown, as she explained to Tabitha, was made by a *French* modiste. Tabitha declared she couldn't possibly tell if it was French or English, but that it was perfectly lovely for such an important occasion. Emily thought it was more than perfectly lovely—it was the grandest gown in the entire room. When Montgomery offered for her, she'd be the envy of every woman in attendance.

In truth—not that she'd admit this to another living soul—she'd been rather anxious when she and her family had arrived tonight. Even though her father returned home from calling on Montgomery with the news that he would offer for her this very night, Emily had been bothered by the small detail that he'd not called on her personally to say as much. Shouldn't he have done so? Her mother said no, that it was not absolutely necessary to do so, seeing as how he'd already spoken to her father.

Perhaps not. But still . . .

When the Forsythes had arrived earlier, it seemed as if everyone in the entire ballroom knew about the supposed offer that was to take place. Emily was aware of heads turning toward her, whispers at her back. And when Montgomery made his entrance with Frederick, calm and perfectly poised, she'd known a bit of panic. How could he possibly be so calm if he contemplated making a public offer that would impact the rest of his life?

But then Montgomery had walked very near her, and had paused, turned round, and walked to her. "Miss Forsythe," he'd said, bowing low.

"My lord," she said and curtsied as she offered him her hand, as she had practiced dozens of times in the privacy of her chambers.

"It gives me great pleasure to see you this evening."

Emily's heart dropped to her toes. She beamed up at him. "Thank you!" she gushed.

With a subtle wink, he walked on in the company of his friends, one of whom said, in Emily's hearing, "You'll have her eating from your hand before the vows are even said." For some reason, that remark caused the other gentlemen to laugh heartily. Emily didn't care—let them laugh, for she'd have the last laugh as Lady Montgomery.

Darien's show of the carefree bachelor was merely a facade; inside, he couldn't have been more anxious. All around him, gentlemen were making remarks about how the mighty had fallen. They referred to him, of course, and what they believed to be an imminent offer for Miss Forsythe's hand.

Their remarks didn't bother him. Nor did his plans for Miss Forsythe. It was Kate that had him all in knots. He had no idea how she'd react to what he planned. For all he knew, given her sudden abhorrence of him, she might slap him across the face.

Darien surreptitiously scanned the crowd, looking for her, putting down the fear that perhaps she hadn't come at all. But then he caught a glimpse of her near the auction table, and his heart skipped a beat or two. He'd never seen her look as lovely as she did this evening in a dress that sparkled with the light of thousands of candles, her hair elegantly arranged and bound with ribbons. It was truly, he thought, like looking at an angel sent from heaven.

As he stood gazing at her, she glanced up and caught his eye. For a moment, a single moment, it seemed as if time stood still, as if there was no one in the room but the two of them. Darien felt it so strongly that he took one step toward her—but Kate quickly looked away and walked to the far side of the room.

He debated going after her. When the orchestra struck up from having taken a brief respite, he made up his mind. Making his apologies to the men around him, he stepped away, then strode to the far side of the ballroom. Heaven was with him—Kate didn't see him coming; she had stopped to admire a stand of roses and was caught completely off guard when he touched her shoulder.

She gasped and twisted about. Her jaw fell open, and he could see in her eyes that she looked for an escape. "No, Kate," he said firmly. "You've evaded me for more than a week. I will not allow you to do so now."

Her eyes narrowed. "And how do you propose to stop me, my lord?" she asked in a hot whisper.

"Do you doubt I will? And I'll have no qualms about doing it publicly, madam. Do you dare test me? Or would you rather stand up this waltz with me and be done with it?"

Kate seemed to be considering her options, her eyes

darting to the door leading to the corridor, then to the crowd at Darien's back.

"Not an easy escape this time, is it, love? Come on then, Kate," he said, holding out his hand, palm up. "Come with me."

She made a sound in her throat—a cry, a sob, he wasn't certain—her eyes filled with tears, and she looked dangerously close to breaking apart.

"One dance," he said quickly, feeling sorry for her. "Just one dance." There was, he knew, no escape for her unless she wanted to create a scene by cutting him. Kate knew it, too, and she slowly, reluctantly, slipped her hand into his palm. Darien instantly closed his fingers tightly around hers and released a small sigh of relief.

"A waltz," he said low. "Do you know the waltz?"

She nodded and allowed herself to be led onto the dance floor. Darien was aware of the many pairs of eyes on them, the sound of whispering as he led her out. He could almost feel the shock of surprise ripple through the crowd and supposed his asking the vicar's widow to dance was akin to the parting of the Red Sea. It certainly wasn't any less dramatic.

On the dance floor, he bowed, and Kate, her eyes downcast, curtsied. He put his hand on her waist and remembered, with achingly vivid clarity, the curve of that waist into her naked hip.

The waltz began, and he pulled her close to him and swept her into the stream of dancers. "Look up at me," he commanded her. "You can't avoid me now."

She looked up. To his neckcloth.

"And now that I have your undivided attention, perhaps you might tell me why, after the most glorious afternoon of my life, that you would work so hard to avoid me?"

"How can you ask that?" she demanded on a strangled

laugh. "I should think the answer to that is obvious, my lord!"

"My lord! What happened to Darien? What happened to *us*, Kate?"

She shook her head, pressed her lips together, and glanced over his shoulder.

"Obviously, you think I have wronged you somehow," he said, feeling his heart slipping with the utterance, "but for the life of me, I don't know what I've done."

"You haven't *done* anything," she said morosely. "The blame lands squarely on my shoulders. I am nine and twenty—not a naive girl. I freely accompanied you, and I knew exactly to what end." This she said with a sidelong glance at those around them.

"Then *why?*" he asked, gripping her hand in his.

She looked up at him then, her green eyes studying him, as if she tried to make sense of something only she could see. "*Why?* As if you don't know why!" she said sharply, and her eyes were suddenly blazing. "Does it give you some sort of perverse pleasure to ask me this?"

Darien blinked. "You think I *lied* to you?"

Kate said nothing but continued to look at him with fire and hurt in her eyes. Anger swelled in his chest, and he twirled her roughly round the corner of the dance floor, catching sight of several guests standing off to the side as he did, watching them intently, and whispering to one another.

Darien suddenly realized that not only had Kate heard the rumors, she had believed the gossip that he would offer for Miss Forysthe. And therefore believed that he had used her. Silly, silly woman! Could she not see the way he looked at her? Could she not feel his longing?

He sighed wearily and shook his head. "How could you not believe me, Kate? Of course I never lied to you!"

For some reason, that made her smile sadly. "I know

you didn't lie, my lord . . . but perhaps you were very artful in the manner in which you spoke to me. Perhaps you chose your words carefully."

Now the anger swelled like a rough sea in him. "You impugn my integrity, madam. I never lied to you, and furthermore, the truth will be revealed, here tonight, you silly little chit."

She gasped with indignation. "Marvelous!" she said, tossing her head back and glaring up at him. "I thought as much, my lord! Miss Forsythe is a delightful girl. I am certain you will both be exceedingly happy. But you will not have *me* to warm your adulterous bed," she whispered hotly.

Darien chuckled low and pulled her close. "Would you like to place a wager on that, Mrs. Becket?" he asked icily.

Her eyes narrowed. "You must be as free with your money as you are with your words."

"I'm not free with either. I use them only when necessary and never frivolously. And before you say another unkind word, let me say that I shall look forward to the truth being revealed, and I will demand that you promise one thing."

"Which is?"

"When you hear the truth revealed," he said with a wicked smile, "you will acknowledge it as the truth, and do so graciously, like a lady ought."

Her brows formed something of a furious vee above her glittering green eyes. "I vow to be as gracious as you are ever faithful, my lord."

"Then you might do it with a smile. Grace is all the lovelier with a smile."

"I would not smile if you were the last man on earth," she said evenly, her eyes narrowing even more as the waltz drew to a close.

Darien chuckled and squeezed her hand before he let her go. "Before you stick your foot completely in your mouth, Kate, remember what I said. There is no one but you." And with that, he dropped her hand, stepped back, and bowed deep.

Kate gave him a skeptical look, then turned and walked away from him on the dance floor.

Darien smiled at her departing back and strolled away in the opposite direction, in search of Emily.

He found her sitting with Miss Townsend on chairs that lined one wall. She tried to be coy as he approached, tried to pretend she didn't see him, and very poorly pretended to be surprised when he clicked his heels before her and bowed low. "Miss Forsythe, how do you do."

"Oh! You startled me sir!" she cried with a false laugh. "I do very well, indeed."

"Will you do me the honor of giving me this dance?" he asked, extending his hand. "Unless, of course, you are already spoken for?"

Miss Forsythe looked at her friend, who was still staring at Darien as if she couldn't quite believe he'd asked. "I'd be delighted," Miss Forsythe said, and nudged her friend before rising to her feet and accompanying him to the dance floor, smiling broadly for everyone to see.

The dance was a quadrille, and Darien took his place across from her, bowing low. As the music started, he took his steps toward her and around her. "You look resplendent."

She blushed.

"You must be expecting an extraordinary evening."

The girl blushed again, looked a little nonplussed, as if she didn't quite know how to respond.

"I know that I am," he said, smiling. "An *extraordinary* evening."

Now she beamed at him. "Oh dear, my lord, you are making me quite nervous! When will you do it? At the auction?

Lady Southbridge said these sorts of things were always done at the auction in the past."

"What sort of things?" he asked nonchalantly, and had to keep from laughing when the girl stumbled in her effort to retract what she'd said.

"I, ah . . . I'm not really certain what she meant."

"I was rather surprised to know that Lady Southbridge knew of my intentions, frankly," he said evenly, watching her closely.

The girl averted her gaze. "Were you?"

"Or your father, for that matter. How do you suppose your father knew?"

"Oh! I, ah . . . I suppose he, ah heard my mother speak of it."

"Hmm . . . and do you suppose Lady Southbridge heard your mother speak of it?"

He could almost hear the conniving little wheels turning in her head as she tried to sort her way through this mess. Her color was high—a casual observer might think he was whispering decadent things in her ear as they danced. At any other dance, under any other circumstance, he might have done so.

"I suppose she did, my lord," Miss Forsythe said, and nervously cleared her throat as she twirled around, then back again.

"How odd. I had not mentioned it to your mother."

Miss Forsythe shrugged and in doing so, missed another step.

"Lady Southbridge surely heard it from someone else. I shall have to inquire, I suppose, for I cannot let our personal affairs be fodder for the *ton*'s appetite, can I?"

"Of course not," she said weakly.

A thin sheen of perspiration had appeared on her forehead. Pity, that, what with the worst yet to come. Poor girl.

He stepped toward her and asked, "Do you suppose Lady Southbridge heard something untoward about Mrs. Becket from the same source?"

The color rapidly bled from her cheeks. She struggled to look serene, but any confidence she had was melting away. "I ah . . . I suppose it's possible, my lord," she said in all but a whisper.

"Interesting," Darien said, and left it at that for the remainder of the dance. As the quadrille closed, he bowed once more, offered his arm to Miss Forsythe, who seemed almost reluctant to put her hand there. He led her to the edge of the dance floor. "Now don't go anywhere, will you?"

"No?"

"I shouldn't want you to miss any of the auction."

"The auction," Miss Forsythe echoed dumbly.

"That's right, the auction. I shall want to see you clearly when the time comes."

Miss Forsythe nodded, and Darien wondered if this time, her faint might be real.

Chapter Twelve

She had no idea what he planned; neverthless, Kate wished she could crawl beneath the floorboards and disappear. There were only four items left on the auction table, and the crowd was literally buzzing with the anticipation of what was quickly becoming the greatest offer ever made in the history of the *ton*.

The buzz was quite irrespective of the two main parties, as they had not spoken since dancing the quadrille. Of course Kate had seen them—she couldn't help but watch. And she'd been appalled by the frenzy of whispering and conjecture as they'd danced. Lady Ramblecourt insisted there would be an August wedding, that she had overheard Lord Montgomery's sister discuss it with Miss Forsythe. On the other side of the room, however, where Kate had gone to escape Lady Ramblecourt's talk, she had been the recipient of Lady Cheevers's speculation.

"He'll ask for a dower too large for Forsythe, mark me," she said with a superior sniff. "The Forsythes would do well to keep their enthusiasm under their own roof, if you take my meaning."

"Yes, my lady," Kate said miserably, at which point Lady Cheevers had turned a judgmental eye to her.

"You might have done as well for yourself, dear, had you been more circumspect."

Kate certainly didn't argue that.

At the moment, however, Lady Southbridge was announcing the last of the items to be auctioned—a pair of silver candelabras that had been the gift of Prinny to Lord Daniels. As the bidding started—it was a coveted item—Kate used the opportunity to drift farther back, away from the crowd.

But as Montgomery made his way to stand next to the platform, he let his gaze idly roam the crowd, and it eventually landed on her, standing in the shadows. A small smile tipped one corner of his mouth; a brow cocked high above the other, and she wondered why he must taunt her at this wretched moment.

She wished she'd never met him. Honestly, she did.

"Oooh," Lady Southbridge trilled when the candelabras had been auctioned off for two hundred pounds. "I do believe that brings us to the last item to be auctioned for charity. Stevens, what is the final tally, if you please?"

"One thousand forty-two pounds, my lady," her secretary called out. "A new record!" A round of applause went up from the crowd.

"I'll add a thousand pounds to the total," Montgomery called out to the delight of the crowd, and Kate rolled her eyes at the very same moment she felt her stomach roil with her bloody nerves.

"Oooh, do come up, my lord Montgomery!" Lady Southbridge cried happily, and endeavored to move her

girth aside to allow him room. "Two thousand pounds indeed! That's quite generous, my lord!"

"Ah, that would be a thousand," he kindly corrected her as he gracefully hopped onto the platform beside her.

"Go on, then, Montgomery, make your offer!" a man shouted, and a cry of howling laughter rose from the crowded ballroom.

No matter how she despised him, Kate couldn't help but admire his calm in the face of this half-drunken, half-deranged crowd. He smiled, nodded as the laughter died down. "My offer to you sir, is a carriage and a driver," he called out cheerfully, and earned another round of laughter from the crowd.

Lady Southbridge, obviously not pleased that attention had been turned from her, managed to wedge herself in front of Montgomery and the crowd, her arms high in the air as she tried to quiet them all. "Hear, hear!" she shouted. "Lord Montgomery has made a very generous offer of two—"

"One," he quickly interjected.

"One, is it?" she asked, clearly disappointed.

Smiling, he nodded. *"One."*

"One then," she said in a bit of a huff. "He's made a very generous offer of one thousand pounds to the Ladies Auxiliary charitable fund, and the least we might do is hear his terms!"

"His terms, his terms!" the crowd began to shout, and a few sympathetic debutantes began to form a protective circle around Miss Forsythe.

Kate stepped deeper into the shadows as Montgomery moved forward and raised his hands, gesturing for the crowd to quiet.

"My terms," he said thoughtfully as the laughing crowd began to quiet. "Are quite simple, really. I will give one thousand pounds to the Ladies Auxiliary in exchange for the repair of my heart, for it has been quite irreparably damaged, I'm afraid. Unable to function, as it were . . . incapable of beating properly."

The crowd grew very quiet. Kate closed her eyes and drew a tortured breath; she knew of damaged hearts. He couldn't *possibly* know about them, how they weighed a person down, snatched a person's breath away, what with all their thrashing about like a wounded bird, beating harshly and erratically.

"I had not known before now how useless a broken heart can be," he continued to a rapt crowd. "It does not regulate the body properly and puts everything at sixes and sevens. Day becomes night, night becomes day, and a man is given to wandering about aimlessly."

What had this to do with Miss Forsythe? Confused, Kate opened her eyes and looked to where Miss Forsythe was standing. She was not alone in her confusion; several heads swiveled between Miss Forsythe and Montgomery.

"Having suffered this horrible predicament, I've come to the conclusion that there is only one thing to be done for it. A lady—"

A collective gasp went up from the crowd.

"For whom this old heart is destined, must take it and repair it—nothing else will do. And not just any lady, but one who is kind and charitable. One with eyes as deep as the sea and the warmest smile in all of England, who has a good keen wit about her so that she may keep me quite on my toes, and never let me believe I am more than I am.

"What I am, ladies and gentlemen, is a man who is quite impossibly in love. There is only one woman who will do for me, and if she refuses me, then I might as well give this heart of mine to the Ladies Auxiliary, too."

Now the crowd was wild with anticipation, and Kate felt her own heart sinking deep into confusion from which she was sure she'd never be able to retrieve it. What was he doing? She wanted to cry out, to vomit, to do something, *anything* but stand here and listen to him profess his love if it was for another woman, for now her hope had been raised up from the dead. From where she was standing, she could see Miss Forsythe staring up at him with an expression of pure fear. She, too, thought this declaration of love was for another woman. Kate's hope surged.

"Therefore," Montgomery said, riveting everyone's attention on him again, "I am prepared to offer my name and protection and my lifelong love and adoration to the woman who can repair this heart of mine, if she'll have me."

One could hear the crowd draw their breath and hold it.

And then Montgomery did something extraordinary. He looked to the back of the ballroom, to where Kate was standing—no, to where she was bleeding—and said, so gently that she wasn't very certain she heard him, "Will you have me, then, Mrs. Becket?"

Something snapped inside her—a flood of relief overtook her grief, light covered the dark thoughts she'd had in the last several days. Someone, perhaps Miss Forsythe, cried out, and Kate could hear voices all around her, could feel eyes on her, as she tried to catch her breath.

Someone shouted that Miss Forsythe had fainted, and Kate was certain she would, too, at any moment, for it seemed as if her knees had ceased to exist; there was nothing to hold her up.

Pandemonium erupted; people crowded around her, some smiling, some frowning, but the only one she wanted to see was Darien. And then he was there, standing before her—she hadn't even realized she'd made it halfway to the platform to reach him until she felt his hand on her arm, the other on her waist, steadying her.

She tried to smile, but she was so shocked, she couldn't

even breathe. "Kate," he said, his voice penetrating the din around them. "Come with me, Kate, say you'll come with me now," he said earnestly.

"Anywhere," she whispered hoarsely, and impulsively threw her arms around his neck, oblivious to the cheers surrounding them, oblivious to everything but Darien's arms around her, holding her tightly, his face in her neck, breathing her in.

Several days passed after the Southbridge Charity Auction Ball, the newspapers ceased to carry the *"Montgomery Offer,"* as it had been dubbed, in the gossip columns, and turned instead to the speculation of whether or not Lord Frederick, a close and personal friend of Montgomery, would offer for Miss Forsythe in the wake of this trauma.

She was reported to have said that she would have refused Montgomery's offer, had it been made to her, and that she never expected such a thing.

Darien and Kate never heard the latest gossip flowing in and out of salons in Mayfair, for they had departed London a scant two days after the Southbridge ball for Gretna Green, along with Darien's sister and her family, and Kate's father. It was the third Sunday church service Kate had missed since arriving in London.

After a fortnight had passed, the weather was so fine that Lady Southbridge decided to take her two dogs on a doggie walkabout, and had her butler leash them up properly while her lady's maid saw to it that Lady Southbridge was properly leashed up. In Hyde Park, where she had paused and instructed her footman to see to the dogs' needs, preferably behind the bushes, she had occasion to meet Lady Ramblecourt.

The two friends exchanged pleasantries, and as they

waited for the footman to return with the two yapping dogs, Lady Ramblecourt said, in a soft voice so that no passersby would hear, "Have you heard, Elizabeth? The child?"

"W-what?" Lady Southbridge demanded, focusing all her attention on Lady Ramblecourt.

"The *widow,* of course!" the woman hissed, looking around them covertly. "They say she's with *child!*"

"No!" Lady Southbridge said, aghast.

"Mmm," Lady Ramblecourt said, nodding adamantly. "That explains quite a lot, wouldn't you say?"

"Indeed it does!" Lady Southbridge loudly agreed.

And in truth, the information bothered her the rest of the afternoon. It was a mystery, she confessed to her good friend Lady Marlton, why Mrs. *Kimbro* would want another child, having birthed six of them already.

"Because," Lady Marlton said authoritatively. "She's taken a lover."

"Who?" Lady Southbridge demanded.

"Lord Tarelton."

Lady Southbridge fell back in surprise. Lord Darlington was at least ten years Mrs. Kimbro's junior. Would the wonders never cease?

Clearly a Couple

Rebecca Hagan Lee

Chapter One

"I don't know what to do with her," Lord Admiral Sir Harold Gregory admitted to his friend, Lord Davies. "Or what to say. She's spent five years in the Topkapi." Sir Harold threw up his hands. "Her whole world has changed, and everyone she loved is dead."

"Except you," Lord Davies pointed out.

Sir Harold snorted. "I was away so much she barely knew me." He took off his hat, tossed it on a chair, then raked his fingers through his hair. "This was all my fault."

"How so?" Lord Davies frowned. "Unless you've begun underwriting Barbary pirates . . ."

"I insisted that Louisa—" He squeezed his eyes shut at the sound of his daughter's name. "And Travis send India to us so her grandmother and I would have an opportunity

to get to know her. But Louisa didn't want to let her go."
He opened his eyes and looked at his friend. "She had suffered so many disappointments. . . . Lost so many babies.
India was her little girl. Her only little girl. And Louisa refused to send her until India was old enough to begin
preparing for her presentation at court." He snorted once
again. "That's how we . . . how *I* persuaded my daughter to
part with her only child. . . . I reminded her that India
needed a proper English education in order to make her
curtsy to the king and her debut into London society." He
paused to gather his thoughts. "In truth, it was simply a
way for her grandmother and me to get to know our granddaughter." He scratched his head. "I saw her several times
over the years. I made it a point to see her whenever I
sailed to India, but Jane . . ." Sir Harold closed his eyes
again at the memory of the wife he'd loved for so many
years, the wife who had died alone while he was at sea
fighting Bonaparte's navy. "God rest her soul. Jane was a
terrible sailor. She'd only seen India four times in fourteen
years. I wanted Jane to have the chance to spend time with
Louisa's child. And I wanted India to get to know England
in the hopes that she would consider it as much home as
she did the country for which she was named."

"Nothing wrong in that," Lord Davies pronounced. "I
would have done the same. She was born in Calcutta, but
she's English."

"If I hadn't insisted she come to London, India wouldn't
have become so homesick for her mother and father that
we feared for her health. It broke Jane's heart to see her
suffering. Still, I shouldn't have *sent* India back to Calcutta. I should have taken her myself." Sir Harold sighed.
"Lud! She hated it here. I suppose she loved us, but Jane
and I were strangers to her. And she hated the cold and the
damp. India found London colorless, and no doubt it did

seem colorless to a girl who had spent her formative years in the tropics." He looked over at his friend, allowing Lord Davies to see the stark pain in his eyes. "So I bought her passage back to Calcutta. *I* put her on that ship. . . ."

"You could not have known it would fall prey to pirates," Lord Davies said. "I've lost three of my ships to the scurvy bastards in the past two years, and I never dreamed pirates were operating in those waters." Lord Davies shuddered. "We knew the French were a threat, but not pirates."

The loss of a vessel was always tragic for navy admirals like Sir Harold and for owners of merchant ships like Lord Davies. Lord Davies had experienced the devastation of losing lifelong friends—captains and crewmembers—who had been with him from the beginning. He understood the value of a lost cargo, but he couldn't begin to fathom the pain of losing a wife, a daughter, a son-in-law, or a granddaughter. Over the course of five years, Sir Harold had lost his wife to consumption, his daughter and son-in-law to a cholera epidemic that swept through Calcutta, and his granddaughter to Barbary pirates. Lord Davies couldn't imagine the pain his friend had endured.

"India left England a schoolgirl," Sir Harold continued. "And she's returning from a life as a concubine."

"Through no fault of her own," Lord Davies reminded the admiral. "The important thing is that you managed to capture the ship responsible for taking the *Portsmouth*. The important thing is that you persuaded that knave of a captain to save his own neck by providing you with enough information about India and her governess's whereabouts to pressure the sultan into accepting payment for them. The important thing is that she's returning. It's a miracle she survived the ordeal at all. Her governess did not."

Sir Harold squeezed his eyes shut and fought to maintain control of his emotions. "And she's ruined." He opened his eyes. "What are her chances of making a life for herself here now? When everyone knows what happened to her? Where everyone knows she spent five years in a harem? What gentleman is going to offer for her under those circumstances? Especially when she cannot be presented into society?"

"You might be surprised," Lord Davies told him.

"I'm not a nabob like you," Sir Harold replied. "I'm comfortably well off, but I can't afford to provide a dowry generous enough to persuade a gentleman to overlook her loss of virtue."

"The right gentleman won't require it." Lord Davies gave a slight smile. A year ago, his daughter, Gillian, had foolishly eloped to Scotland with a scoundrel who abandoned her there after their wedding night. And while it was true that he had offered his current son-in-law a considerable fortune to marry Gillian in order to save her reputation, Colin had wanted Gillian more than the fortune. No one looking at Colin and Gillian today would ever guess that Lord Davies had blackmailed Colin McElreath, Viscount Grantham, into marrying his only daughter. Their marriage of convenience had turned out to be a love match. "There are men who will see India for the courageous young woman she is. Men who will admire her for surviving her ordeal, rather than condemn her for the manner in which she survived it." He looked at Sir Harold. "But I think we may be getting a bit ahead of ourselves. First, we bring India home safely and allow her to settle in before we begin worrying about providing for her future."

"That's just it," Sir Harold answered. "The horns of my dilemma." He took a deep breath. "That's why I've come to you. I've arranged the transfer of cash and securities into gold as the sultan requested. But I'll need someone completely trustworthy to deliver it. As an admiral in His

Majesty's Navy, I cannot put into port in Turkish waters. *I* cannot bring India home to London," he admitted. "At least, not yet."

Lord Davies frowned. "Why not?"

"The Admiralty wants to send a diplomatist to deliver the ransom so they gain access to the Topkapi, claim success for recovering India from a fate worse than death, and then use her to gain information about him and his alliance with the French. But the sultan insists that if our government becomes involved or interferes in the negotiations in any way, the deal will be nullified, and my ransom and India's life will be forfeited. I refused to jeopardize India's life by allowing the Admiralty to send a diplomat, but the Foreign Office is convinced that sending one is the best course of action." He sighed. "They don't believe the sultan will harm India. But she's suffered enough and I cannot gamble with her life." Sir Harold looked his old friend in the eyes. "I need to recover my granddaughter before the Foreign Office sends a diplomatist to Istanbul. And it must be done in complete secrecy. The first lord of the Admiralty has placed my ship at the diplomatist's disposal, but the Turkish government refuses to allow a British naval vessel into their waters. Negotiations to gain entrance to the port are set to begin at the end of next month."

"That means you've less than a month to arrange the transfer of funds and to recover India before our government calls the sultan's bluff."

Sir Harold nodded, then raked his fingers through his hair. "And although she cannot be presented to the regent, the first lord is planning a huge celebration once India is back on English soil and the season gets under way. I'd prefer India arrive home alive without any fanfare. We don't know her condition or her mental state. I haven't the foggiest notion of how to proceed with her, but I know exactly how I shouldn't proceed. And that's to bring her to London during the height of the season, where she'll be picked apart by curiosity hounds and gossips."

Lord Davies nodded thoughtfully. "I concur."

"Unfortunately, Lord Middlebrook is my commanding officer, and Lady Middlebrook appears to be his." Sir Harold furrowed his brow. "The best I can hope to accomplish at the moment is to bring India home on a privately held vessel and hold the admiralty at bay for as long as possible. If I bring her home, there will be no keeping it quiet from my superiors and I'll be obligated follow orders. But if I were to charter a private ship to fetch her home and keep her someplace outside London, I might buy India some time before she's forced to confront London society."

"I still have Plum Cottage," Lord Davies offered. "It's small, but it's clean and comfortable." He smiled. "I don't travel to Dover much anymore, and Julia and I seldom use the cottage. We held on to it for sentimental rather than practical reasons. I gave my son-in-law a key to it last season so he and Gillian could spend part of their honeymoon there, but they shan't be using it this season." Lord Davies walked over to his desk drawer, unlocked it, then pulled out a key on an iron ring and handed it to Sir Harold. "You're welcome to Plum Cottage and the services of the couple in the village who maintain the house and grounds. It's private and available, if you want it."

Plum Cottage and its adjoining neighbor, Primrose Cottage, shared a small acreage along the route from London to Dover. The cottages weren't a vast distance from town, but they were far enough outside the city gates and far enough away from Brighton to be considered beneath notice of the fashionable set. "And I'll set sail right away."

Sir Harold shook his head. "I hoped you would offer, but

you haven't sailed on one of your vessels in years. How will it look if you do so immediately after I've paid you a visit?"

"It will look like I'm doing a very important favor for an old friend," Lord Davies conceded.

"Send someone else," Sir Harold advised. "Send a vessel no one will question. One that sails those waters and with a captain you trust implicitly."

Lord Davies thought for a moment. "That would be *The Bengal Princess*. Hers is the closest route to Istanbul. Her captain is a man I'd trust with my life, and she sails in a week." He smiled at his old friend. "I'll meet India when she arrives at Plum Cottage. . . ."

Sir Harold let out a sigh of relief. "Thank God."

Chapter Two

Four months later

"We won't make London tonight, Fellow." Jonathan Manners, eleventh Earl of Barclay, shivered in his heavy overcoat and readjusted his hat so the rain pooling on the brim dripped down his collar instead of into his eyes. Pausing, he gauged his surroundings and calculated the miles left to London. He had hoped to make it back to his own bed before daylight, but the going was slow, and he had one more item on his list of assignments.

Jonathan didn't mind the rain, but the wind and the rumbling thunder and chain lightning accompanying the early summer storm made his travel treacherous. And trudging through the mud on foot had cost him a great deal of time and strength. He couldn't recall the last mile marker posted alongside the road or remember turning left at the crossroads, but he must have, because he was on the road to London despite the fact that the last six or seven miles were a blur of cold rain, gusting wind, mud, and sheer determination.

Determination not to disappoint his Free Fellows brethren. Determination to press on rather than turn back. Determination to walk rather than ride, to trudge through the mud with his horse at his side. Determination to complete the mission to which he'd been assigned with as few complications as possible. And he'd nearly succeeded.

In the week since he'd left town, Jonathan had crossed the Channel three times, leading a series of clandestine missions to deliver desperately needed supplies to the network of English agents spread out along the coast on both sides of the Channel. He was wet, cold, hungry, and teetering on the brink of complete exhaustion, but he'd accomplished his mission in record time, successfully eluding both the French and English frigates patrolling the Channel as well as the French agents sent to stop him.

All he had left to do was stop at Plum Cottage and pick up a parcel Lord Davies needed in London. Colin had planned to retrieve the parcel his father-in-law had requested himself, but Jonathan had been scheduled for the next Channel crossing, and since his clandestine mission would take him within a few hundred feet of Plum Cottage's front door, Jonathan had offered to do it for him.

And now he was glad he had. Neither he nor his horse could go much farther without rest, and spending a night in a warm bed and dry stable at Plum Cottage would go a long way towards restoring both of them.

Reaching up, Jonathan ran his right hand beneath his horse's mane, feeling the heat of exertion through the soft leather of his riding glove. He'd have collected the parcel and been home hours ago if his horse hadn't thrown a shoe several miles past the last coaching inn.

Jonathan rubbed the horse's neck once again. He didn't know the horse's name, but he knew that allowing this particular horse to continue to carry him was out of the question.

The horse snorted, jigging sideways, as a gust of wind sent rain spiraling in front of him. "Easy, boy." Jonathan caressed the gelding's nose, soothing him with his voice. "It's only rain and wind, and we'll have you out of it soon." He hoped.

Jonathan squinted into the darkness, through the wall of rain, and recognized a familiar landmark, a white stone corner post that marked the boundary of the property he had hoped was close by. Smiling, Jonathan urged the gelding forward and quickened his pace. "We'll have you settled into a nice warm stall and me into a nice warm bed before you know it."

Plum Cottage was straight ahead. Jonathan said a prayer of thanks as he led his horse past the stone marker and the front of cottage, around to the path on the side.

Lord and Lady Davies owned Plum Cottage, but they had granted their daughter, Gillian, and her husband, Lord Grantham, full use of it, which was fortunate, because Colin McElreath, Lord Grantham, happened to be Jonathan's friend and one of the three—along with Griffin Abernathy, Duke of Avon, and Jarrod Shepherdston, Marquess of Shepherdston—founding members of the secret Free Fellows League. Jonathan was also a member of the League— one of the newest—and Colin had entrusted him with this mission and a key to Plum Cottage.

Colin had spent part of his honeymoon with Gillian at the cottage and had fallen instantly in love with the place. But Colin had also recognized Plum Cottage's potential as a resting place for the Free Fellows engaging in the clandestine fight against Bonaparte.

Its location outside of London on the main road to Dover and the other Cinque Ports towns along the Kentish coast made Plum Cottage ideally suited for the work of the Free Fellows League. The closest neighbor had been an elderly widow who owned Primrose Cottage. Plum Cottage and Primrose Cottage adjoined at the garden and shared a stable and small paddock, but the widow had been too old and feeble to make use of any of it. When she'd passed away and Primrose Cottage became available, Colin and Gillian had quietly purchased it. Unfortunately, Primrose Cottage had been neglected for far too many years and was in danger of falling down around their heads. It required extensive renovations, and the going was slow, since Colin refused to hire laborers to do the job until he was certain they were laborers, not agents in service to the French or English governments. And Colin's evaluation process was very deliberate, quite thorough, and time consuming.

The fact that Primrose Cottage was unoccupied made Plum Cottage all the more appealing as a hideaway and provided the four Free Fellows whose regular missions carried them to the Cinque Ports of Hastings, Romney, Hythe, Dover, and Sandwich with a purpose for their frequent visits to the cottage just south of the small village of Pymley and a reason for making local inquiries. They could pose as gentlemen looking to purchase the property, as the factors sent to attend to the hiring of workers to renovate it, or as butlers, valets, or other various members of the owner's staff.

Jonathan had never made use of the cottage, preferring to sleep in his own bed in his apartments in fashionable Albany, but he had memorized the layout from a sketch Colin had given him along with the key to the back door. He knew the location of the stables and the paddock, knew that the small stable contained the fresh hay and grain necessary to see to his horse's comfort, and knew that the cottage was stocked with the items necessary to see to *his* comfort. Tonight, Jonathan intended to retrieve Lord Davies's parcel and to enjoy the man's hospitality in order to grab a few hours of much-needed rest.

The gelding whinnied softly as Jonathan unlatched the paddock gate and led him inside the stable. Jonathan's teeth chattered with cold, and his hands shook as he removed his leather gloves and fumbled in his pockets for his tinder and flint to light the lantern hanging just inside the stable door.

After untacking the horse and removing his saddle pouch, Jonathan lifted his horse's left foreleg, feeling for heat and swelling. It was warm to the touch, but only slightly swollen. Gently lowering that foot to the ground, he then lifted the right foot and repeated the procedure. Discovering that the shoe on the right foot was also loose, Jonathan set the horse's foot down, then rummaged around the small stable until he located the toolbox. In minutes, Jonathan had pulled the other front shoe off. He hadn't the tools to fashion new shoes—that would require the services of the blacksmith, but pulling the loose shoe would allow the horse to stand more comfortably.

"There," Jonathan soothed, caressing the horse's neck before running his hand down the horse's left leg, "you'll rest better on equal footing."

The horse nickered softly as Jonathan rubbed him down with a handful of straw from the stall floor and a length of toweling from his saddle pouch, then fed and watered him.

When he'd done all that he could do to provide for his horse's comfort, Jonathan gave thought to his own.

He was so tired he briefly considered bedding down in the stable with the horse, but he craved a warm fire, a hot meal, a glass of brandy, and a bed big enough to allow him to stretch out for the first time in days for a few blissful hours of uninterrupted sleep.

The stable was warm and dry, but it offered none of the other amenities and while Jonathan had grown rather fond of the big bay gelding, he didn't relish sharing sleeping quarters with him. Not when there was a cottage and clean sheets nearby.

"Good night, fellow," Jonathan whispered as he slung his leather saddle pouch over his shoulder and extinguished the lantern. "I'll see you in the morning."

Closing the stable door behind him, Jonathan made his way down the path to the back door of Plum Cottage. He looked back over his shoulder, then glanced around the back door before removing the key from inside his coat pocket and inserting it into the lock. Jonathan didn't expect to find the parcel outside. Lord Davies had told Colin the parcel was inside the cottage, but Jonathan checked his surroundings just the same. He unlocked the door, nudging it with the toe of his boot before pushing it open. Recalling Colin's warning to mind his head when he entered the back door of the cottage, Jonathan ducked under the lintel and stepped over the threshold into the kitchen.

He took off his hat, then shook the rain from his coat and hung it on a peg beside the back door.

He felt the movement, the whisper of air, as the fine hairs at the back of his neck prickled in warning. But his senses were dulled with fatigue, and the warning came a fraction of a second too late. Jonathan struggled to keep from tensing his body at the feel of the cold steel of the curved blade at his throat.

"Move and you die, infidel."

The high-pitched whisper was spoken in heavily accented French.

Jonathan wondered fleetingly if this was what Colin meant when he'd warned him to mind his head. Had Colin installed a French-speaking Saracen with a curved blade on the premises to protect the property? And there was no doubt that the man gripping his shoulder and holding a blade to Jonathan's throat was a threat. Or a Saracen. A giant of a Saracen who wore flowered brocade robes that smelled of heavily scented oil and Turkish tobacco. For who else but a follower of Muhammad would call him an infidel? And who else but a giant could hold a knife at his throat so effortlessly? Jonathan stood an inch over six feet without shoes or boots and weighed thirteen stone, and the Saracen stood half a head taller and outweighed him by fifteen stone or more.

He hadn't moved an inch, but the blade bit into the tender flesh of his throat just the same, and Jonathan gritted his teeth and cursed the fact that he was unable to reach the firearm concealed in the inner pocket of his coat.

Chapter Three

"Mustafa?"

The Saracen giant turned at the sound of the softly spoken query. And Jonathan was forced to turn with him.

A woman carrying a small oil lamp entered the kitchen and hesitated in the doorway when she realized the man she called Mustafa wasn't alone.

She stared at him, and Jonathan returned her gaze, barely registering the pain as the curved blade drew a thin line of blood just below his ear as he got his first look at his savior.

Half of her face was shadowed, but the visible half was extraordinary, and her figure . . . Jonathan sucked in a breath. Her long, dark hair was loose, flowing down her back, caressing the curve of her waist. Her *bare* waist. Jonathan sighed. He'd never seen so much exposed flesh on any woman with whom he hadn't been intimate. And while this young woman wasn't entirely naked, she wasn't wearing a nightdress, either. She was wearing an abbreviated blouse that left her midriff bare and a pair of trousers with a waistband that dipped low, hugging her slim hips and covering the essentials, while surrounding her long, shapely legs with sheer blue fabric. Half a dozen tassels hung from the hem of her short blouse, and Jonathan noticed that the tassels swayed provocatively each time she moved, caressing her skin and releasing tantalizing whiffs of the light, appealing fragrance of delicate spices and lilies. Her feet were as bare as her middle, and she shifted her weight from foot to foot, clenching her toes against the cold stone floor, filling the small room with the scent of her perfume and the musical sound of bells. Jonathan searched for the source of the music and discovered it originated from a chain of tiny gold bells encircling her right ankle. She literally brought beauty, music, and perfume into the room, and the potent combination teased the senses, capturing his imagination as firmly as her alluring clothing. It was, quite honestly, the most captivating costume he'd ever seen.

And likely to be the last. Jonathan closed his eyes and expelled the breath he'd been holding. He didn't understand all of Mustafa's words, but he understood "infidel" and the Saracen's intent. Jonathan winced as the blade at his throat bit deeper into his flesh.

"Non!"

Jonathan opened his eyes once again, watching and listening in rapt fascination as the young woman began a heated discussion with Mustafa in a mix of French and a language Jonathan could only assume was Mustafa's native tongue.

"Non!" she repeated, shaking her head for emphasis.

"For God's sake, stop antagonizing the man," Jonathan muttered beneath his breath, catching enough of the French to understand that Mustafa considered it his duty to dispatch the infidel and be done with it. "Or he'll slit my throat just to have an end to the argument." She hadn't seemed to notice Mustafa's irritation, but Jonathan was well aware of the fact that Mustafa increased pressure on the blade at Jonathan's throat in direct proportion to the young woman's argument.

Suddenly, she broke off her argument and directed her next words at Jonathan. "You're English?"

"Yes."

Her face lit up in delight. "So am I."

Jonathan stared at her unusual garments and in a rare, unguarded moment said the first thing that came to mind. "I would never have guessed."

She caught the teasing note in his voice and smiled. "What would you have guessed?"

"An Arabian princess. Or a Greek goddess . . ."

"Then you would have been wrong," she pronounced. "For I'm English through and through."

"You don't look English through and through, and you don't sound it either," Jonathan told her.

She frowned. "How do I sound?"

"Like a French spy," he answered.

She bristled at that, and Mustafa reacted immediately, tightening his grip around Jonathan's shoulder. "I'm not French," she told him. "Or a spy. I despise Bonaparte and the whole French navy."

"I believe the lady doth protest too much," Jonathan quoted. "For you speak the language like a native."

"As do a great many other Englishwomen," she retorted. "And *men*. And if I speak French like a native, it's because I've had a great deal of practice. My English may sound faulty to you, but that doesn't change the fact that I'm English just the same."

Strangely enough, Jonathan believed her. There was something very real and very convincing about her declaration that she was English. If she was lying, she was an expert at it. She didn't seem to be trying so hard to convince him that she was English as she was herself. And Jonathan thought that if he accused her of being French one more time, she just might break into "God Save the King." So the question he had to ask was what an English girl was doing with a Saracen bodyguard at a cottage in Kent? Especially a cottage that should have been empty. Jonathan opened his mouth to ask her, but Mustafa stopped him with a torrent of unintelligible words directed at the young woman.

"What did he say?" Jonathan demanded a translation as soon as the giant Saracen finished speaking.

"He wants to know what you're doing here and why you broke in."

"I didn't break in," Jonathan told her. "I used my key." He slowly opened his hand, and the iron key he hadn't had time to pocket fell to the stone floor with a clatter.

The young woman set the lamp on the floor as she knelt to retrieve the key. And when she lifted the lamp once again, Jonathan could have sworn he saw the sparkle of a precious gem in the indention of her navel.

His mouth went dry as she moved closer, opening her palm so Mustafa could see the key and the tiny brass plum attached to it.

She listened intently while Mustafa spoke, then turned to Jonathan.

"Does he still intend to kill me?" he asked.

"That depends," she replied coyly. "Have you committed a crime for which you deserve killing?"

Jonathan smiled at her directness. "Not tonight."

"How do you feel about losing a hand?" she asked.

"I'm against it," Jonathan answered honestly. "As I'm opposed to violence against my person in any form."

"Then answer truthfully," she directed. "He may not speak English, but Mustafa is an expert at discerning lies. He can detect them in any language, and he believes you're a thief or an assassin who came by this key dishonestly. And in Mustafa's world, the punishment for thievery is the forfeiture of a hand."

"Dare I ask the punishment for would-be assassins?"

"Beheading," she answered.

"I'm neither a thief nor an assassin," Jonathan answered. *At the moment.* Although Jonathan silently acknowledged that his work with the Free Fellows League might require him to become both at any time. He looked the young woman in the eyes and discovered that her eyes were an extraordinary shade of blue. "I'm a traveler on my way home from the Cinque Ports."

"And you live here? In Plum Cottage?"

Jonathan started to shake his head, then thought better of it. "No. I live in London."

She swung the key from her fingertip. "Then why do you have a key to this house?"

"So I would have a warm, dry place to sleep should I desire to spend the night rather than continue my journey." He frowned at her.

"How did you come by it?" she demanded.

"The man who owns the cottage gave it to my friend, who gave it to me."

"And the name of the man who owns this cottage is?"

"Lord Davies," Jonathan answered. "Carter, first Baron Davies. And my friend is Lord Grantham. He's married to Lord Davies's daughter, Gillian, and is obviously unaware that you and your—whatever he is—are staying here, or he wouldn't have given me the key." He faced the young woman. "Now, if you'll be kind enough to ask Mustafa to release me, I'll forgo the pleasure of sleeping in Plum Cottage and join my horse in the stable."

To Jonathan's amazement, she grinned. "Then you weren't sent to spy on me? Or do me harm?"

"Do I look or sound French to you?" he asked.

"The French aren't the only people who employ spies," she replied.

That was true. As well he knew, since he was an English one. But she—whoever she was—hadn't been part of his assignment. Or anyone else's, as far as he knew. She was simply an unexpected complication at the end of a long mission. As far as the Free Fellows were concerned, Plum Cottage should have been empty.

Jonathan took a deep breath. "If I'd been sent to spy on you, I would have known you were here. And you would never have known that I was here. And if I'd been sent to do you physical harm, you'd be harmed. But obviously that isn't the case. The fact is that my horse lost a shoe several miles down the road. I'm cold and wet and tired and vastly disappointed to find that the one time I decide to make use of my key to Plum Cottage, it's already occupied. Even by someone as lovely as you." Jonathan sighed. "I hate to disappoint you, miss, but I've absolutely no idea who you are or why you're here."

She pursed her lips in thought and tilted her head to one side in a manner Jonathan would have found enchanting under different circumstances. "Although I have an idea of what you are, I have absolutely no idea who *you* are or if what you say is true."

"My horse is munching grain in the stable out back," Jonathan told her. "He'll vouch for me."

"Is he a talking horse that he can vouch for you and answer my questions?"

"Of course not," Jonathan replied. "But the mere fact that he's there will vouch for the fact that I'm telling the truth."

"What's his name?"

Jonathan frowned. "He doesn't have a name."

"Of course he does," she countered. "And if he belongs to you, you should be able to tell me his name." She pinned him with her gaze. "You don't know his name, do you?"

"I call him Fellow."

"Most original! Especially since you don't know his name."

"The fact is that he isn't actually my horse," Jonathan began.

"You said he was," she accused.

"He's borrowed."

She widened her eyes, toying with him, pretending to be shocked in order to test him. "So, Mustafa is right. You are a thief. A horse thief and a housebreaker."

"No, I'm not," Jonathan insisted. "One friend loaned me a horse, and another friend gave me the key and offered me the use of this cottage."

"You appear to be very fortunate in your choice of friends."

"That's true," he admitted. "I am extremely fortunate in my choice of friends. I don't have a cozy little cottage on the route to the coast, nor do I keep horses in London, but I have friends that do. Whenever I need a horse, I borrow one. I may not own the gelding in the stable, but we've been together long enough to get acquainted. The tendon in his left front leg is slightly swollen and feverish, and he's missing both front shoes. One shoe is buried in the mud somewhere between here and Dover. The other is hanging on a bent nail outside his stall door. I hung it there shortly after I removed it. Send Mustafa to check," Jonathan suggested. "I'll wait here."

She wrinkled her nose at him. "I don't know why, but somehow, I believe you."

"Why shouldn't you believe me?" Jonathan demanded. "Since I happen to be telling the truth. And my delight at garnering your trust is matched only by my desire to have this blade removed from my throat. So, now that we're acquainted, miss, do you think you could persuade this behemoth to lay it aside?"

"*Lady.*"

Chapter Four

Jonathan blinked in surprise. "I beg your pardon . . ."

"It's lady," she replied. "Not miss. I haven't used it in quite a while, but my title is lady. Lady India Burton. My father was—"

"Travis, second Earl of Carlisle." Jonathan had a talent for remembering family names and the titles connected to them, a talent that came in handy in his line of work and one that was second nature to him, since he'd spent most of his formative years memorizing every family name and title in Debrett's in preparation for his succession to the title. He might have been born the son of a younger son, but his mother had never given up hope that he might one day succeed to the title of Earl of Barclay. Lady Manners's hopes had been realized when Jonathan's uncle, the tenth Earl of Barclay and his father's older brother, died without male issue. Lady Bradford Manners's husband hadn't inherited the title, but her son had. And his mother considered Jonathan's succession and her insistence that he prepare for it her greatest accomplishments.

Lady India's face lit up as Jonathan completed her sentence. "You knew him?"

"I knew *of* him," Jonathan told her. "His success with the East India Company was legendary. My deepest condolences, Lady India," he offered. "I heard a distant cousin inherited the title." He stared at her clothes as a glimmer of a memory surfaced. "India Burton." He breathed her name. There couldn't be two Lady India Burtons. She had to be the one who had been abducted from the ill-fated HMS *Portsmouth* by Barbary pirates and—

"Yes." She knew the moment he recognized her name and realized what had happened to her. "I am *that* India Burton." She drew herself up to her full height, straightened her shoulders, lifted her chin a notch higher, and met his gaze without flinching. "And you are?"

"Jonathan Manners, eleventh Earl of Barclay. At your service," he drawled. "I'd bow and kiss your fingers, but I prefer to keep my throat intact."

India laughed in spite of herself. "Delighted to make your acquaintance, Lord Barclay."

Jonathan glanced skyward. "I wish I could say the same, but under the circumstances . . ."

Mustafa snapped an order at her in the language Jonathan assumed was Turkish, and to Jonathan's surprise, India retaliated in kind.

"Is this where he slices my throat? Or shall I simply bleed to death from the collection of cuts I garner each time you anger him?"

He spoke in a conversational tone of voice, and India was more impressed by Lord Barclay's courage than she wanted to admit. Lord Barclay might not realize the danger, but India knew that Mustafa was perfectly capable of slitting his throat or of strangling him without so much as a hint of remorse. She had seen him do both to wayward concubines and the lovers they'd met in the gardens or paid to have smuggled into the harem. The fact that she no longer belonged to the sultan and was no longer bound by the laws of the seraglio meant nothing to Mustafa. And the fact that the man who had breached the threshold of Plum Cottage was English and ignorant of the laws that governed the sultan's concubines and his chief eunuchs or the fact that he had broken most of them meant even less.

Mustafa was notoriously short-tempered, and India had spent the sennight since her arrival at Plum Cottage living in fear. The captain of *The Bengal Princess* had told her her grandfather had been delayed, but Lord Davies or someone else would come in his stead. Thank goodness he had. And thank goodness the man had arrived before the sultan's most trusted eunuch tired of waiting for someone to relieve him of the responsibility of the sultan's most troublesome concubine. India was acutely aware that Mustafa could have very easily disposed of her long before her grandfather or Lord Davies's emissary arrived.

"Mustafa ordered me to cover my face," India said. "He reminded me that to look upon my unveiled face carries a sentence of death for any man other than my lord and master."

"Am I now under Mustafa's sentence of death for looking upon your face as well as for being a suspected assassin?"

"You would be," India told him. "Except that I reminded Mustafa that we are in England because Sultan Hamid accepted my grandfather's gold in exchange for my return. I explained that Englishwomen are not required to cover their faces, and an ignorant English infidel could not be expected to know the sultan's customs or laws or recognize him as my lord and master."

"I can tell how well that explanation sat with Mustafa by the length and depth of the fresh cut upon my neck," Jonathan replied. "Do you think that for the sake of my neck and our newfound friendship, you might refrain from arguing with the man at least until he releases his hold on me?"

"I can try," she agreed, "but I can't promise."

In that case, Jonathan decided, it was better for him to take care of the ill-tempered giant himself. "Prick me once more with that blade," Jonathan warned, "and you will live to regret it."

"He doesn't speak English," India reminded Jonathan, gesturing for Mustafa to release him.

"He understands," Jonathan said, knowing instinctively that the Saracen giant understood exactly what he meant; he had simply chosen not to heed the warning.

Lady India gestured once again for Mustafa to release him, but the Saracen balked. He released a tirade of Turkish and French in a high-pitched voice that grated on Jonathan's nerves, pressing the knife blade into Jonathan's neck once again, turning it so the tip nicked his earlobe.

Jonathan exploded in a flurry of action. Realizing the Saracen's brocade slippers were no match for his boots, Jonathan lifted his right foot and stomped down as hard as he could on the other man's right instep. The Saracen gave a high-pitched yelp and abruptly released his hold on Jonathan. Jonathan ducked beneath his massive arm and repeated the maneuver on the opposite instep, then shifted his weight and put the full force of his thirteen stone into the blow as he elbowed the Turkish giant in the chest hard enough to cut off his wind. The curved blade clattered to the floor as the huge man bent double in a futile effort to replace the air that Jonathan had forced out of his lungs.

India scrambled to retrieve the knife while Jonathan waited patiently for the giant to lift his head before rudely greeting him with a combination of left cross and right uppercut to the jaw.

Mustafa fell back, hitting the stone floor with the force of a boulder, rapping his head against the door frame as he fell.

"How?" India's eyes were as big as saucers as she stood looking up at Jonathan.

"Three mornings a week at Gentleman Jackson's Boxing Academy on Bond Street," Jonathan announced triumphantly. "Like most bullies, your Saracen friend relies on his bulk instead of his brain. And he's soft," he added. "All flab. No muscle."

Strangling concubines a quarter of his size with a silk cord didn't require muscles or brains, India thought. The only requirements for that were unlimited power of life and death over the women in the harem and a complete lack of compassion, and Mustafa qualified on both accounts. She moved closer. "Is he dead?" she asked with a tremor in her voice.

Jonathan shook his head. "No."

"A pity," India replied.

"My sentiment exactly," Jonathan agreed, reaching up to swipe at the rivulet of blood running down his neck. "But I didn't want to take the chance of having the sultan lodge a complaint with His Majesty's government if I killed him. That would require an explanation, and an explanation might do irreparable damage your reputation."

India almost smiled at the irony of Lord Barclay worrying about her reputation, when he had to know that nearly five years in a sultan's seraglio had already damaged it beyond repair. "I suppose it's just as well," she said with a touch of wry humor. "For he must weigh a ton. I doubt that we could drag his body out of the cottage, and leaving it here would be a terrible abuse of Lord Davies's hospitality."

"Then the least we can do is bind his arms and legs so we won't have to worry about him for the rest of the night."

India leaned over the fallen eunuch and carefully pulled a long red silk cord from the pocket of his caftan. "Will this do?"

"It's perfect." Jonathan took the cord from her, then rolled the giant onto his stomach and secured his hands behind him. He glanced around for something with which to tie his legs, and India came to the rescue once again. She untied the flowered brocade belt at Mustafa's massive waist, tugged it free, and handed it to Jonathan.

Jonathan grinned at her. "Thank you, my lady."

"You're very welcome, my lord."

Their eyes met.

"You're quick on your feet," Lord Barclay complimented her as he tied the belt around Mustafa's ankles. "And you've a talent for improvising. You'd do well at Gentleman Jackson's." He looped the excess length through the bindings he'd just tied before pulling it up and tying it to the silk cord securing Mustafa's arms. When he'd finished trussing Mustafa like a stuffed Christmas goose, Jonathan gave Lady India another grin, then rolled the huge man onto his back where Mustafa's massive bulk would prevent him from working the bindings on his hands and feet and would prevent him from moving at all, because by morning the giant Saracen's arms and legs would be completely, painfully numb. "If you were a man—"

"I *am* wearing trousers. . . ." she ventured, warming to his praise.

"That you are," Jonathan agreed. "But you still couldn't gain admittance—even wearing trousers—for no one would ever mistake you for a man."

"A pity." India glanced down at Mustafa and sighed. "For I think I might enjoy hitting something."

"I see no reason why you shouldn't . . . enjoy it . . ." he told her, "so long there's no harm done. . . ."

India waited until Lord Barclay finished tying Mustafa, then motioned for him to follow her into the kitchen. She set the lamp in the center of the table and gestured toward a kitchen chair. "Sit down," she instructed. "You're bleeding."

Jonathan gave her an odd look. "Yes," he managed finally. "When one spends several minutes with an angry giant holding a knife to one's throat, bleeding usually plays a part in the outcome."

India scanned the tidy kitchen. "There must be something here that you can use to attend to your wounds."

"Thank you," he said. Jonathan had expected her to offer to tend to his wounds. He had expected her to produce a basin of water, a salve or an ointment of some sort, and fresh linen to wash away the blood, but Lady India Burton surprised him once again by standing in the center of the kitchen, staring at him.

She held up her hands in a helpless gesture. "I'm not sure what you require. Or where to find it."

Jonathan winced, hissing through clenched teeth, as he reached up to untie his cravat. "A mirror would be nice," he told her. "A basin of water. Fresh linen and . . ." He looked up to find her still frozen in place. "I've everything except a basin of water in my saddle pouch. On the floor," he said. "In there." He unwrapped the length of his cravat from around his neck and frowned at the amount of blood staining it, then unfastened his collar and nodded toward the back door. "I dropped it when your knife-wielding giant accosted me."

The mention of Mustafa spurred her into action. India left the kitchen and returned moments later with Jonathan's leather saddle pouch. She set it on the table within his reach, then retreated a few steps.

"More light," he suggested, shrugging out of his coat before unbuttoning his waistcoat and opening the front of his shirt in order to reach the blood trickling down his collarbone.

"Oh." India leaned across the table, stretching to turn the wick of the lamp up higher.

Jonathan sucked in a breath, and the lower part of his anatomy tightened in response when he realized that she did, indeed, have a precious gem affixed in her navel. A blue sapphire. Jonathan stared in fascination at the perfectly faceted blue sapphire adorning Lady India Burton's smooth, flat stomach. Lowering his gaze, Jonathan surreptitiously studied the sapphire's unique setting and did his best to solve the riddle of what kept it in place.

"Water," Jonathan requested suddenly, swallowing the lump in his throat and shifting his position on the chair in an effort to relieve the unwanted and increasingly insistent ache in his groin.

"Of course." India turned away and began to bustle around the cottage.

After what seemed an extraordinarily long time, she produced a blue basin filled with water. Her hands shook as she set it on the table, and Jonathan reached up and caught hold of her arm, gently wrapping his fingers around the delicate bones of her wrist.

She froze, inhaling sharply, as his thumb brushed the place where the blue lines of her veins beneath the pale skin of her inner wrist exposed the beat of her heart.

The feel of his hand on her arm, the feel of his fingers on her wrist, the feel of his thumb pressed against her pulse sent shivers up and down India's spine.

Jonathan felt it, too, and quickly let go of her, more disturbed than he'd like to admit. "I'm not quite sure what you said to Mustafa," he remarked, attempting normal conversation as he opened his bag and removed his shaving mirror, a bar of bay-scented soap, a length of toweling, a carefully folded shirt, and fresh cravat. "But it did nothing to improve his mood." He set his shaving mirror on the table, angling it so he could see the assortment of cuts Mustafa had inflicted, then dipped a corner of the towel into the basin of water before rubbing it across the bar of soap and diligently applying it to the cut behind his ear, along the line of his jaw, and on his neck.

"I told him that he couldn't kill you."

Jonathan blew out a breath, whistling through his teeth as the soap stung badly enough to bring a sheen of tears to his eyes. "I'm delighted to hear it," he managed through clenched teeth. "May I ask what you said that changed his mind?"

"I told him that you weren't a thief or assassin, but the personal emissary of the English king." India hoped Lord Davies wouldn't mind being replaced by the king, but invoking her savior's name didn't sound nearly as powerful or as impressive as invoking the sovereign's name—despite the fact that Lord Davies, the extremely wealthy owner of a fleet of merchant ships, had recently been elevated to the ranks of the aristocracy. "Sent by the king and my grandfather to escort me to London and that if any harm came to you, the king, like the sultan, would consider it a grievous insult and hold Mustafa personally responsible."

"That might be hard for His Majesty to do, since His Majesty's madness has him currently confined to a house in Queen's Square under his doctors' care."

That bit of information gave India momentary pause.

When Lord Barclay released him, Mustafa would return to the sultan with the complete description of everything that had taken place since they'd left the Topkapi, and India wanted to be certain Mustafa understood her grandfather's influence and Lord Barclay's enormous power. She wanted the handsome lord to figure so prominently in Mustafa's tale that he became a legend in the seraglio. And she wanted Sultan Hamid, the dey of Algiers, and the Barbary pirates who had taken her from the HMS *Portsmouth* to know that her champion—Lord Barclay—was not a man with which to trifle—that he had the power of the English Crown behind him. "The king is mad?"

"Quite." Jonathan dipped another corner of the towel into the basin of water and rinsed the soap from the cuts, more than a bit dismayed to discover the water had taken on a distinctly rust-colored tinge.

India winced involuntarily and bit her bottom lip. "When did that happen?"

"He's always had bouts of madness," Jonathan said. "Everyone knows that." Gritting his teeth, Jonathan scraped the end of the towel over the soap once again, washing and rinsing his wounds a second time.

"I didn't."

She sounded personally affronted, and Jonathan couldn't help but smile. "Perhaps, you were too young to notice." *Or too busy surviving.*

"You missed one," India told him. "There's blood."

"Where?" He craned his neck, trying to locate the cut in the mirror.

She took a step forward and touched the small cut below his earlobe. "There."

Her fingertip was cool against his warm skin, and Jonathan discovered he liked the feel of it. And the scent of her perfume surrounding him.

A drop of his crimson blood marked her fingertip. India paled as she stared at it.

Jonathan noted her pallor and quickly swabbed his blood from the tip of her finger with the end of the towel. "There," he pronounced. "As good as new." He refolded the cloth and pressed the dry portion against his neck to stop the fresh flow of blood.

India took a deep breath. "Is the king's madness common knowledge?"

Removing the towel, Jonathan lifted his chin and turned his head so he could view the results of his ministrations in the mirror. Satisfied that the bleeding had stopped, Jonathan laid the towel aside. "The exact nature of his illness isn't common knowledge," he answered, "because no one knows the exact cause, but the fact that he's ill is known to almost everyone since the Prince of Wales was named regent two years ago."

"Oh." India thought for a moment. "The regent usurped his father's power?"

"In a manner of speaking," Jonathan agreed. "Parliament endowed him with a great many of the monarch's powers. But unlike your sultan, the prince regent does not have the absolute power of life and death over his subjects."

"The sultan considers the English form of government weak," India said. "He cares nothing about the workings of Parliament. But he understands a son's willingness and ability to usurp his father's powers. Sultans live in mortal fear of having their power usurped by sons, brothers, and nephews."

"No doubt the Prince of Wales does, too," Jonathan quipped.

"The fact that you're an emissary of the usurper will make you more powerful than the emissary of an older, weaker ruler," India continued. "We shall have to inform

Mustafa of that in the morning so he can relay the information to the sultan. He understands strength, and he relishes court intrigues."

"Unfortunately, this isn't one of them," Jonathan replied. "And I doubt your bodyguard is going to be impressed to learn that I'm an emissary from the prince regent or the king," Jonathan warned her, reaching up to trace the first painful souvenirs of Mustafa's distrust.

"He'll be impressed," she replied. "And he'll carry the tales back to Istanbul because he knows it's the truth."

Jonathan would have liked to have Mustafa impressed in a very different manner. Hard labor on a British naval vessel might do the man a world of good, but Jonathan also knew that impressing him would raise all sorts of questions better left alone, so he was willing to settle for having Mustafa placed on one of Lord Davies's merchant ships and sent back to his lord and master in Istanbul.

"The truth is that I'm *not* an emissary for anyone," Jonathan said. "Certainly not His Majesty or the prince regent. Lord Davies asked his son-in-law to retrieve a parcel from his cottage. Since I was coming this way on business, I offered to do it for him." Jonathan realized the truth the minute the words left his mouth. "Good lord! *You're* the . . ."

"Parcel," India replied.

Chapter Five

"I had no idea," Jonathan admitted. "I was expecting a crate of books or a bolt of cloth or a bottle of vintage wine. A parcel wrapped in oilcloth. Nothing like this . . ." He looked at India dressed in her incredibly tempting costume.

India returned his speculative gaze. "And I was expecting Lord Davies or at the very least, a serious man of business."

"Lord Davies's wife tripped over one of their dogs and broke her hip," Jonathan told her. "She's confined to bed and Lord Davies was reluctant to leave her, so he asked Colin to retrieve a parcel from Plum Cottage." He looked at India. "I knew I'd be coming within a few feet of the cottage on my way home, and I insisted that Colin stay home with his wife and in-laws while I retrieved Lord Davies's parcel for him. So you got me instead." He frowned. "What makes you think I'm not a serious man of business?"

"Because you have *adventurer* written all over you."

Jonathan laughed. He might have *adventurer* written all over him but only because he *was* a serious man of business. He'd wanted to be a member of the Free Fellows League since Griffin, Colin, and Jarrod had formed it while they were all schoolboys at the Knightsguild School for Gentlemen. He believed in the Free Fellows League. And he was proud to be a member. He took the work they did very seriously, perhaps more than any other member, for Jonathan had been too young and too small to be a founding member. He'd had to wait over twenty years to be invited to join.

"I hate to disappoint you, my lady, but my life has been anything but adventurous. Compared to yours, it's been quite mundane."

"I'm not at all disappointed," she said softly. "I knew you were the one the moment I saw the key." She glanced up at him from beneath her eyelashes. The look was coy, but her words were anything but. "I may have been unfortunate in other areas of my *adventurous* life, Lord Barclay, but I think I've been most fortunate to have you as my rescuer."

"Anyone could have produced a key."

India shook her head. "The captain of the ship that brought me here assured Mustafa and me that the house was private and safe. When he relinquished the key, he swore that there were only two, both marked with a tiny brass plum. Lord Davies had given one key to Captain Marks to give to me and kept the other. When you produced the key, I knew that you were Lord Davies or that Lord Davies had sent you."

"Except that Lord Davies *didn't* send me," Jonathan replied. "His son-in-law, *Colin,* gave me a key to the cottage."

"Then it's fate that you should rescue me."

"I thought I'd be collecting a shipment of merchandise, and I'll wager Colin thought the same, or he would never have allowed me to do him this favor." Still, Colin hadn't put up much of an argument. Jonathan thought it was because he'd wanted to stay with Gillian and her parents, but now he wasn't so sure. Because Colin had worn an oddly pained expression on his face when he'd given him the key—almost as if he'd wanted to reveal a secret, but couldn't.

"No matter." She shrugged her shoulders in an unconsciously elegant gesture. "Your being here isn't an accident or a coincidence."

No, it wasn't. His stop to retrieve the parcel from Plum Cottage had been planned. The only part of this mission that hadn't been planned was the lost horseshoe and the nature of the parcel he was supposed to collect. What concerned Jonathan most was that there were at least two people outside the Free Fellows League involved in the planning.

India continued. "The fact that you are the emissary, even if you were unaware of it, saved your life. If you had been anything else—a thief, an assassin, or an innocent traveler whose horse went lame on his way home—Mustafa would have been duty bound to kill you."

"Because I've seen your face?"

She shook her head. "Because you are a man, and your presence in my quarters is an insult to Mustafa and to the sultan. He only spared you because you possess a key to this house, because he realizes that even though your presence here is an insult to him and to the sultan, you're the instrument of his return to the Topkapi." She sighed. "Otherwise, he would have assumed that you were a robber or an assassin or that you had come to my quarters to . . ." She blushed and glanced down at her feet. "Share my bed."

India expected him to take offense at being accused of the intent to rape, murder, and pillage, but Lord Barclay surprised her.

"I can't fault the man's reasoning."

"I can," India said. "For Mustafa could kill us to defend the sultan's honor——"

"Hang the sultan's honor!" Jonathan exclaimed. "What about yours?"

"I am a woman," she said simply. "In Mustafa's world, women have no honor, and until I'm safely delivered into my grandfather's or his emissary's keeping, Mustafa is duty bound to remain by my side and to treat me as if I were still the sultan's property. Once my grandfather or his emissary takes possession of me, Mustafa will be free to return to Istanbul."

"Where is your grandfather?" Jonathan asked. "Why isn't he here to meet you?"

"My grandfather is a vice admiral in His Majesty's Navy. According to Captain Marks, Grandfather arranged for me to travel on Lord Davies's ship to avoid conflict with the Admiralty and the Foreign Office because the sultan, allied with Bonaparte, refused to allow a British naval vessel to dock in Istanbul. My grandfather planned to rendezvous with my ship en route and accompany me here, but his vessel was badly damaged in a storm around the Cape, and he was forced to put into port for repairs. Captain Marks brought me here and gave me the key to Plum Cottage. We assumed Mustafa would return to Istanbul on the next tide and that I'd be here alone until Grandfather arrived, but Mustafa received his instructions from the sultan, and he refuses to leave until my grandfather or his emissary relieves him of his duty."

"Captain Marks had a key to the cottage," Jonathan pointed out. "Why didn't *he* relieve Mustafa of his duty?"

"He tried," India told him. "But Mustafa refused to accept it. There was nothing Captain Marks could do except report to Lord Davies and sail back to collect Grandfather."

"He could have sailed up the Thames and taken you to London."

"Not like this." India glanced down at her Turkish garments and shook her head. "*I* refused to return to London dressed in clothing I've been forced to wear since I entered the seraglio or with Mustafa trailing in my wake." She fixed her gaze on Jonathan, pleading with him to understand. "I left London as an English lady," she said. "And I intend to return the same way, not shrouded in heavy black veils and watched by the sultan's minion."

Jonathan heard the note of steely determination in her voice and recognized it for what it was, but he was compelled to challenge it, to test the iron will that had enabled her to survive an ordeal that should have destroyed her. "What difference does it make how you return to London, so long as you return alive?"

India glared at him, and Jonathan felt the heat of her gaze all the way to his toes. "It makes a difference to me, Lord Barclay," she said fiercely. "I did not lose everything and everyone I've ever loved and endure years as a slave in a harem in order to return home in the same manner. I know my presence here has come as something of a surprise to you, Lord Barclay, but I hope it hasn't been an entirely unpleasant one. . . ."

"Not entirely," he admitted.

"Then won't you please relieve Mustafa of his duty so that he might return to his home and so that I might return to mine?"

"I've responsibilities of my own," Jonathan explained. "And people depending upon me."

"Like Lord Davies."

"Like Lord Davies's son-in-law," Jonathan corrected. "And he's depending upon my prompt return for reasons that have nothing to do with retrieving the parcel from Plum Cottage."

"I see," Lady India said softly. "You don't wish to assume responsibility for delivering me to London because *I'm* the parcel."

"I had already assumed responsibility for delivering a parcel to London," Jonathan replied. "But, Lady India, you are *not* a simple parcel, and if it becomes known that I accompanied you to London without benefit of a chaperone, you'll be ruined in London society."

"I'm already ruined in London society," she reminded him.

"I'm not," Jonathan said. "And if it's all the same to you, I'd like to preserve my good name."

India gave an unladylike snort. "If it's all the same to you, Lord Barclay, I'd like to preserve my neck. If it comes to losing my reputation or losing my life, I'll gladly forfeit my reputation and yours, too, if it's necessary. I don't have a choice. Gold has already changed hands. If you leave Plum Cottage without me, Mustafa will—"

"I'll take care of Mustafa," Jonathan vowed. "He won't hurt you."

"Mustafa will kill me," India said. "Unless you keep him from it and—"

"By this time tomorrow, Mustafa will be on his way to Istanbul."

"Can you be sure he won't bribe someone to let him go? That he won't come back here and strangle me once you're gone?"

No, he couldn't. He couldn't be sure of anything except that his life was about to change. But he didn't know if it would be for better or for worse. "I thought you said he's eager to return to Istanbul."

"He is," she confirmed. "But not until he fulfills his obligation to the sultan. And after what we just did to him . . ." She shuddered. "You don't know Mustafa. He's more afraid of failing the sultan than he is of you. If you don't relieve him of his duty now, he'll find a way to come back and kill me. Or pay someone to do it."

"How long have you been alone here with him?"

"A week."

"And he didn't harm you. . . ."

"He had no reason to harm me then," she explained. "Now, he does."

"What reason?"

"You," she said.

Jonathan groaned.

"And me," she added. "Mustafa hates women, hates traveling, hates being bested, and hates me."

Jonathan closed his eyes and thought back to the newspaper articles he'd read about the taking of the HMS *Portsmouth* and the murders and abductions of her passengers and crew by the gang of Barbary pirates who owed their allegiance to the dey of Algiers. "Why does he hate you?"

Lady India didn't answer.

Jonathan tried again. "How long have you known him?"

"Nearly five years," she answered. "He took charge of me the day I arrived at the Topkapi. We didn't get on well. And I've lived in fear of him ever since. . . ." India shuddered again as the memories of that horrible day came rushing back. She looked at Jonathan. "He was every bit as ill-humored then as he is now."

"Who chose him to accompany you? And why would he agree?"

"The sultan chose him," India said. "And neither Mustafa nor I had a choice. The sultan's insistence that a bodyguard accompany me was included in the terms of my release. And as the sultan's most trusted and highly regarded eunuch, Mustafa was the sultan's obvious choice."

Jonathan wasn't sure he'd heard her correctly. "Highly regarded *what?*"

"Eunuch," India answered matter-of-factly. "Mustafa is the chief eunuch of the harem. He resides in the women's quarters and presides over the harem. He has the power of life and death over all of us."

"Lud!" Jonathan swore, eyeing the giant with a kind of newfound and grudgingly wary admiration. No wonder the giant smoked tobacco and weighed over twenty-five stone. Food, drink, tobacco, and the hookah were the only pleasures of the flesh left to him. "I'd be ill-humored, too, if a sultan forcibly removed my . . ." Jonathan remembered he was in the presence of a lady and caught himself in time to choose his words more carefully. "If I had to live surrounded by women twenty-four hours a day and was unable to pleasure any of them."

India frowned at Lord Barclay's ignorance. "Mustafa still has his tongue and his fingers and toes."

Jonathan coughed, choking on her unadulterated frankness. Lady India was no ordinary young English miss. She'd been forced to live a life that few people, except perhaps prostitutes, could imagine. He lifted his eyebrow as she continued. "Like the other eunuchs, he is quite capable of pleasuring his favorites with those. But becoming a eunuch rendered him incapable of the primary means of physical pleasure. The only men, other than the sultan, allowed to look upon or touch any female in the harem, are eunuchs. That ensures that the children born in a sultan's harem are all his."

"But an *eunuch* . . . " Jonathan shuddered. "I can almost feel sorry for him."

India shook her head. "Don't waste your pity on Mustafa. He receives his pleasure in other ways."

Jonathan was almost afraid to ask. "What other ways?"

"He derives great pleasure from disposing of unwanted and troublesome concubines," she answered. "He is particularly fond of slowly strangling them with the silk cord you used to tie his hands. And that would have been my fate had the sultan decided not to release me."

Bloody hell. Jonathan really didn't want to know that. "Why did the sultan decide to release you?"

"I have blue eyes."

"Very blue," he agreed. "And quite becoming."

She blushed at the compliment. "Not to the sultan. He found them troublesome, especially since the women in the harem were convinced that I was the devil in female form. I caused Mustafa and the sultan no end of trouble because the women in the harem believed I was capable of black magic and of bewitching them."

"You mean you aren't?" Jonathan teased.

India blinked in surprise.

"Because I feel quite certain that you may have bewitched me."

Chapter Six

"Have I, my lord?"

An hour ago, Jonathan would have sworn that Lady India didn't engage in the fine art of flirtation, but now, he wasn't so sure.

"You must have." Jonathan looked into her dark blue eyes. "For it's the only explanation for what I'm about to do."

"What are you about to do?" she breathed.

Kiss you. Jonathan inhaled deeply, unable to stop himself as he reached out and caught her chin up with the tip of his finger. "I'm about to throw caution to the wind and relieve the sultan's eunuch of his responsibility and escort Lady India Burton on her triumphant return to London." He gave her every opportunity to refuse or to escape, but India stood looking up at him, and Jonathan gave in to the impulse. He tilted her face up to his, then leaned down and gently covered her lips with his own.

As she closed her eyes and accepted the kiss, it was quite obvious to Jonathan that it was her first.

But what she lacked in finesse, she made up for in sweetness and enthusiasm. Jonathan savored the taste of her, reminding himself that despite her ardor for kissing, she was untutored and deserved more tenderness than raw passion. And he devoted himself to giving India everything she deserved. He nibbled at her lips, then traced the texture of them, lightly brushing them with his. Jonathan touched the seam between her lips with the tip of his tongue, showering India with pleasure as he tasted the softness of her lips and absorbed the feel of her mouth; poring over every detail, every nuance of her lips and mouth and teeth and tongue, with a single-minded determination to give pleasure.

India moved closer, shivering in delicious response as Lord Barclay abandoned her lips and kissed a path over her eyelids, her cheeks, her nose; brushing his lips lightly over hers once again before he continued on his path to the pulse that beat at the base of her throat.

Jonathan broke the kiss the moment he felt Lady India trembling in his arms. He stepped away, silently cursing himself for his weakness, as he put some much needed distance between them. "I apologize, Lady India."

India opened her eyes and looked up at him. "For kissing me?"

"For taking liberties," Jonathan answered. "Because I'd no right to presume that you would welcome my attentions."

"You had every right to presume I welcomed your attention," India told him. "For it's true." She blushed. "I wanted you to kiss me. And if you hadn't kissed me first, I would have kissed you as soon as I determined the best way to go about it."

"Going about it is easy," he said, bending his head to her

upturned face once again. "Just close your eyes and offer an invitation. . . ."

He brushed her lips a second time. "It's the stopping that's hard."

"Then don't stop," she told him. "Do it again."

Jonathan knew he should refuse. But India was sweet, amazingly innocent, and incredibly tempting. As he used his tongue to tease and tantalize, he couldn't help but marvel at his good fortune. She had spent years in a seraglio, and yet Lady India had never been kissed the way he was kissing her. In some part of his brain he realized that if she was an innocent in the art of kissing, she might also be innocent in other ways. And he had no right to take that innocence away from her. He ended their second kiss and stepped back once again.

India opened her eyes, read the look on his face, and sighed. "Please don't tell me you've changed your mind."

Changed his mind? Lost it, perhaps, but not changed it. He had acted on impulse, given in to his desire, and kissed her. And he knew immediately that he'd made a huge mistake. It was all right to think about kissing her, as he had ever since she'd walked through the doorway, but actually tasting the sweetness of her lips, not once but twice . . . *that* was a mistake.

"About taking me to London?" she prompted when he took too long to respond.

"Well," he said with a shrug. "I can't leave you here."

"Oh, thank you, Lord Barclay!"

"Don't thank me yet," he warned. "Surviving a London season may prove every bit as challenging as surviving life in the sultan's harem."

India gifted him with a brilliant smile. "This is England, my lord. People in London may criticize me and gossip about me behind my back. Here members of the ton may crucify my reputation, but no one can ever force me to hide my face or bow my head again. And I'll never again have to worry about Mustafa strangling me in my sleep."

Her words tore at Jonathan's heart. He understood that sort of fear. He knew what it was like to lie awake at night, afraid to close your eyes for fear of the monsters that preyed upon you while you slept. Once upon a time, he'd been terrified of the monsters in the dark, convinced they would come for him in the deep of night and carry him off.

Once upon a time, he'd been the youngest and weakest boy in the Knightsguild School for Gentleman, and he'd lain awake at night frightened and alone and crying for his nanny. Knightsguild had been one long, unending nightmare for Jonathan. He knew what it was to fear the darkness, knew how it felt to pray for someone to watch over him, someone to reassure him and keep the monsters at bay. And he knew what it was like to wonder if his prayers would ever be answered.

Jonathan had been lucky. His guardian angel had occupied the cot beside him, and ten-year-old Jarrod Shepherdston, twenty-second Earl of Westmore, founding member of the Free Fellows League, hadn't failed him. Jarrod had sworn that he'd protect him and dispatch any monsters that dared to enter their dormitory or attempt to lay a hand on Jonathan. Jarrod had kept watch so Jonathan could finally close his eyes and sleep through the night. And Jarrod had protected him in other ways as well. He'd kept the bullies from using Jonathan as their whipping boy and deflected the instructors' and the headmaster's sarcasm and ridicule from Jonathan's narrow shoulders to his broader ones whenever Jonathan stammered in the classroom or struggled to keep up on the playing field. Jarrod Shepherdston had helped Jonathan build his confidence and to make friends with the other Free Fellows.

Jonathan stared at Lady India. She'd done nothing to deserve her fate. She had had every reason to believe she was safe the day she and her governess boarded the ship that would take her home to Calcutta. The HMS *Portsmouth* was, after all, one of His Majesty's naval vessels, and Lady India's grandfather one of His Majesty's naval commanders. She had no reason to think that she might fall into the hands of Barbary pirates who would sell her to a Turkish sultan for their own gain. And once she'd been imprisoned in the Topkapi palace, she had no reason to believe that she would ever be free again.

Jonathan let out a breath. He had waited most of his life to become a Free Fellow, and suddenly, remaining free from marital encumbrances in order to serve his country in the clandestine war against Bonaparte seemed far less important than offering this one young woman his protection. For if ever a lady deserved a champion to protect her from the monsters she feared and from the monsters she'd yet to meet, it was she. And Jonathan intended to be that champion. Fate had sent him to Plum Cottage, and fate wouldn't be denied.

"I promise you, come morning, you needn't worry about Mustafa ever again," Jonathan told her in an echo of Jarrod's long-ago promise.

"Must we wait until morning?"

"I'm afraid so," he told her. "Because, as you pointed out, we cannot move him without help, and my horse is in no condition to help. But he should be up to the task by morning. If not, I promise I'll find some other way."

"No promises," she whispered, "not unless you know you can keep them."

The village of Pymley lay two miles north of Plum Cottage, off the main road. There was a pub there and a blacksmith and livery. Colin paid the blacksmith in Pymley extremely well to keep Plum Cottage's stable in fresh hay and grain and to keep silent about it. And Jonathan had recruited laborers from Pymley for other tasks. They knew he paid extremely well for hard work and for prudence. He knew he could trust them to help him remove Mustafa from Plum Cottage to the coast and to keep silent about it.

"I can keep this one," Jonathan told her. "Tomorrow morning, I'll take care of everything. But now, I'm dead on my feet. All I want is a warm fire, a hot meal, a glass of brandy, a soft bed, and four or five hours of uninterrupted sleep." Jonathan heaved a sigh, then picked up his saddle pouch and turned toward the back door. "But under the circumstances, I'm willing to forgo the meal, the fire, the brandy, and the soft bed in exchange for the sleep."

"Where are you going?"

Jonathan recognized the fear in her voice. "To sleep in the stable."

"You're going to leave me here alone with Mustafa after what we did to him? What happens when he wakes up?"

"He'll be securely tied and unable to move," Jonathan replied. "Just as he is now."

India bit her bottom lip in trepidation. "You needn't forgo the soft bed, the glass of brandy, or the warm fire if you know how to build one," she told him. "The cottage has two bedchambers, both with soft beds and fireplaces. And there are decanters of spirits on the side table in the sitting room."

He was incredibly tempted. But he was a gentleman, and she was a young lady whose reputation had already been sullied through no fault of her own while she'd been the sultan's captive. He wasn't going to add fuel to the flame of gossip by compromising it once again now that she had finally returned home to England. "I thank you most kindly for the invitation," he said. "But as you are an unmarried young woman and I am an unmarried *gentle-man*," Jonathan stressed the word, reminding himself that was the case even as he informed her of it and inched toward the door. He was exhausted, but he wasn't dead. Or made of stone. Jonathan knew himself well enough to know that his state of near exhaustion made resisting temptation harder instead of easier. "Since we are unchaperoned, it's best that I seek shelter elsewhere."

"But we are chaperoned," she insisted. "Mustafa is here."

"A sultan's eunuch is hardly a suitable chaperone," he replied.

"On the contrary, Lord Barclay." India shook her head, focusing her gaze on his handsome face rather than the fascinating wedge of thick, dark hair that was visible through the opening of his shirt. "Chaperoning is what the sultan's eunuchs do best. After all, they chaperone and care for three hundred seventy of the sultan's concubines every minute of every day." She moistened her lips with the tip of her tongue. "What's left of my reputation is safe."

"Not with him unconscious."

India gave him a speculative glance, then turned and began to pace the confines of the small kitchen. "Did you know that the Admiralty and the Foreign Office wish to host a series of balls in my honor when I return?"

"No, I did not."

"Will you attend?"

Jonathan drew in a deep breath. "I don't generally move in Admiralty or Foreign Office circles."

"Would you attend if I invited you?"

"Lady India . . ." When she looked at him with those big, blue eyes, Jonathan found her almost impossible to resist.

"I don't know anyone in London except you."

"You'll meet plenty of other people at the Admiralty Ball," he said.

India nodded. "Yes, I'm sure I'll meet plenty of people at the Admiralty who wish to use me for their own purposes." She stared at Jonathan. "People who want to hail my return as a diplomatic triumph and trot me out and show me off at every opportunity."

"You don't know that—" he began.

"Yes, I do," she answered. "That's one of the reasons my grandfather asked to borrow Plum Cottage and sent *The Bengal Princess* to fetch me. Captain Marks gave me a letter from my grandfather. In it Grandfather explained that he couldn't fetch me in person without alerting the Admiralty and the Foreign Office, and he didn't want to alert the Admiralty or the Foreign Office because he didn't want my homecoming to become . . ."

"A political circus," Jonathan concluded.

Lady India nodded. "A *political frenzy* was the term Grandfather used."

"That was good of him," Jonathan replied, heartened by the news that her grandfather hadn't ransomed her from the sultan in order to throw her to the wolves. "Your grandfather seems like a fine man, one who has your best interests at heart. He must love you very much."

"I hope so," India said, "for I've caused him a great deal of bother and cost him an enormous amount of money."

"The fact that he was willing to pay it should tell you something."

"I don't know him very well," she admitted. "But I know that he always does his duty. Whether he ransomed me because he loves me or because he was duty bound to do so remains to be seen." She turned to Lord Barclay. "You were right, you know."

"Oh?" He raised an eyebrow in query.

"I'm not really English through and through. I was born in Calcutta."

"I know," he said.

She frowned. "You could tell that from my voice?"

He smiled at her and shook his head. "No, I read it in the newspapers after the *Portsmouth* . . ."

"Newspapers," Lady India mused sadly. "Imagine that. I forgot about newspapers or that there are places in the world where people are allowed to read them." She was quiet for a moment, then pinned him with her gaze. "Did you also know that I came to London from my home in Calcutta because my parents and grandparents wanted me to be presented at court like every proper English lady?"

"No," he answered. "I didn't know that."

"I left India in the summer, but it was cold when I arrived in London to live with my grandparents. Cold and dark and damp." She stopped to trace her finger along the back of one of the kitchen chairs and looked at Jonathan. "And I hated it. I longed for Mama and Papa and home. I longed for home so badly that I made myself physically ill. My grandmother took pity on me and asked my grandfather to arrange passage for me back home. My governess, Miss Lockwood, elected to accompany me." India paused. "She could have remained in London. Grandfather would have hired someone to accompany me back home, but Miss Lockwood had no family, and she said that all my wonderful tales of India had filled her with a burning desire to see it." She took a deep breath, swallowed hard, and toyed with a lock of her long, dark hair, winding and unwinding it around her finger. "Grandmother and Grandfather had engaged her services shortly before I arrived. I knew her less than half a year, but we became very close. So close that she wouldn't hear of sending me home alone. Besides, she said, she wanted to see the elephants parading through the streets on festival days all decked out in their bells and finery, and she wanted to see the huge temples, the fakirs, and all the tropical flowers. It was all arranged. Miss Lockwood would accompany me on my visit to see my parents in India, and then we'd return to London in a year to continue my English education and my preparation for presentation at court. My grandmother assured me that she loved me enough to grant me another year to become accustomed to the idea of life in England, and she was sure that Miss Lockwood would ease the pang of homesickness when we returned. Miss Lockwood promised my grandmother that she would prepare me so well that my London season would be a resounding success, and every gentleman with whom I danced would want to marry me. It was such a lovely dream." She bit her bottom lip and blinked back tears. "Miss Lockwood made a London season sound so wonderful. It was, she said, the most exciting time in her life, even if she had only had the one season. Even if she had failed to garner any proposals. She had still gotten to dance and had been partnered by the scions of some of England's greatest families. She loved to dance, and she had saved every dance card. She showed them to me and shared the family history of nearly every gentleman with whom she'd danced. And she taught me all the dances. We practiced for hours and hours every Friday, so that when I made my curtsy, everyone would name me the most elegant dancer in London. That was Miss Lockwood's dream for me. She wanted me to be the most elegant dancer in London so I might marry a handsome and wealthy young gentleman and have lots of children she could teach—" India took a deep breath and glanced down at her feet. "But now, I shan't make my curtsy or be presented at court or dance in the moonlight when I return to London. I won't be able to keep my promise to Miss Lockwood."

"Why not?" Jonathan asked the question without thinking and could have bitten out his tongue when she answered.

"You know as well as I do, Lord Barclay, that disgraced ladies cannot be presented at court. And I have definitely been disgraced. My reputation and my good name have been ruined."

"Through no fault of your own," Jonathan pointed out.

She shrugged her shoulders. "It makes no difference. The fact is that my chances of making a good match are gone—especially since my grandfather was forced to pay a fortune to ransom me. With my dowry in jeopardy, what gentleman would choose to take me to wife?" She looked Jonathan in the eye. "I lost my reputation when a Turkish sultan purchased me from a band of murderous pirates, took my virtue, and confined me to his harem. But there are no exceptions. It doesn't matter why I lost my virtue or how I lost it. The only thing that matters to the court and to proper English society is that I'm no longer a fresh, young maiden, and everyone in London knows it." She lifted her chin a notch higher. "No doubt they read all about it in the newspapers."

"Not everyone," Jonathan said, attempting to lighten her mood. "There must be quite a few eligible gentlemen ignorant of your past. Because there are lots of gentlemen in London who've never read a newspaper or anything else."

India giggled in spite of herself.

"Now there's a nice sound," he told her. "You must do it more often."

India blinked in surprise. "I'd almost forgotten how to laugh," she admitted. "It's been so long since I've had anything to laugh about or anyone to laugh with."

"That will change," he promised. "You'll see."

"How can you be so sure?"

"Believe it or not, there are gentlemen out there who value all the wonderful qualities you possess."

"What qualities?"

"Strength and pride and honesty and courage and beauty. And any gentleman who desires those qualities more than he desires cash would be proud to marry you," Jonathan said softly.

I would be proud to marry you. The thought came unbidden, and Jonathan could almost feel his bachelor status slipping through his fingers. He nervously cleared his throat and awaited the outcome of his impulsive declaration.

Lord Barclay's thoughtful answer touched India almost as much as it surprised her. He sounded almost as if he believed it. "Then I shall have to hope there is such a gentleman at the Admiralty Ball," she said. "And that he asks me to dance. In the meantime . . ." She hesitated, moistening her suddenly dry lips once again. "My invitation still stands."

"Invitation?" he croaked.

"The cottage has two bedchambers," she reminded him. "And you're welcome to one of them."

"No," Jonathan repeated firmly, keenly aware that his willpower was in danger of crumbling. "Thank you for the invitation, but no." He collected his coat and reached for the doorknob.

"Wait!"

Jonathan gave her a wary look.

"Please," she said. "Wait." She turned and walked out of the kitchen, disappearing through the doorway that led to the other rooms in the cottage.

She returned to the kitchen with a pillow and an armload of bedding in one arm and dragging a large, thick, red silk mattress behind her. "If you won't accept the offer of a bedchamber inside the cottage, then at least take this." She handed Jonathan the pillow and clean sheets, then maneuvered the mattress between them and offered him the thick loop she'd used to tug it out of the main bedchamber.

"What's this?"

"Mustafa's pallet." Lady India looked up at him. "There's no reason you shouldn't sleep in comfort, even if you are determined to sleep in the stable. After all," she said softly, "he won't be using it."

"No," Jonathan agreed, "I don't suppose he will." He touched her fingers as he took hold of the loop she offered. "Good night, Lady India."

"Good night, Lord Barclay."

"Pleasant dreams."

India shivered as if someone had walked over her grave. Five years in the seraglio had put an end to pleasant dreams. In the seraglio, troublesome concubines were strangled while they slept or were smothered, or poisoned, or had their throats cut . . . Sleep didn't bring pleasant dreams. It brought death. India had learned to fear sleep and she'd all but forgotten that there were people in the world who still had pleasant dreams. And someone to beckon them the way Lord Barclay had wished pleasant dreams upon her. "And to you," she called, as he closed the back door and headed for the barn.

"The infidel will die on the morrow."

India opened her eyes and sat up, pulling her knees to her chest, and wrapping her arms around them as she huddled against the headboard of the bed. From the other room she could hear Mustafa muttering a litany of malevolent threats and promises in the mixture of Turkish and French she had come to understand and fear.

"I know you do not sleep, English. I know you listen. I know you hear my voice."

India pressed her face against her knees, bit her bottom lip to keep from answering, and silently conjugated Latin verbs in a desperate attempt to block out the sound of Mustafa's voice.

"He will have to loose my bonds eventually," Mustafa continued. "And that will be his undoing."

The eunuch made a sound that might have been a groan, but could have just as easily been a chuckle. "His death will be slow and painful," he promised. "And you shall watch as he bleeds from a thousand cuts. You shall watch as the floor grows red and slick from his blood. You shall watch as I cut out his tongue and replace it with his rod and testicles."

"Be quiet!" India ordered.

Mustafa giggled. "And when I've taken his manhood from him, I shall cut his heart from his chest and let you watch as it beats in the palm of my hand . . ."

"Shut up!" India ordered again, louder this time, her voice vibrating with rage.

"You shall watch as I crush the infidel's heart in my fist and squeeze the life from it." He paused. "And after I kill the infidel, I shall take my red, silk cord, and wind it about your slim, white neck, and pull and pull until your face turns purple and your eyes and tongue protrude. I shall tighten my cord, until the bones in your neck snap and I force the life's breath from your body. And then I shall laugh . . ."

"Don't!" she warned. "Don't say another word!"

But Mustafa ignored her. "The way I laughed when I squeezed the life from your friend. And I shall take my blade and cut off your head, and keep it on a table beside my bed next to hers . . ."

India let go of her knees, reached beneath her pillow, and grabbed the knife Mustafa had held pressed to Lord Barclay's neck and had dropped when Lord Barclay had outsmarted and overpowered him. Launching herself from the bed, she hurried out of her bedchamber to the kitchen and beyond.

Mustafa's eyes grew as big and round as saucers when he looked up and saw India coming toward him, his curved blade in her hand.

"I warned you, you pile of dung! I warned you to hold your tongue! I warned you to be quiet! I warned you not to speak of what you did! But you wouldn't listen. So, I'm going to make certain you never speak of it again."

Mustafa opened his mouth and screamed loud enough to wake the dead.

Chapter Seven

The red silk pallet retained the scent of the oil Mustafa wore, but Jonathan ignored it. He'd slept with far worse smells assaulting his nostrils, and although the fragrance was heavier than he would have chosen for himself, it wasn't altogether unpleasant, and the silk pallet was a vast improvement on the mound of straw he'd fashioned in the stall adjoining Fellow's.

Jonathan maneuvered the silk mattress through the door of the stall and arranged it atop the pile of clean straw. He tossed the pillow onto the mattress, spread the sheet and blanket over it, then stripped off his waistcoat, shirt, and boots, unbuttoned the top three buttons on his buff trousers, and sank down onto the pallet and rolled beneath the sheet.

Jonathan exhaled a deep, satisfied breath. The mattress was big and thick and long enough to cradle his body in comfort, and Jonathan graciously succumbed to the luxury of a silk mattress and silk sheets. Closing his eyes, he fell into a deep, dreamless sleep.

He awoke several hours later to the sound of a shrill, high-pitched scream of terror.

"Bloody hell!" Jonathan bolted upright, tugged on his boots, and sprinted through the misting rain toward the cottage. He opened the back door and discovered Lady India Burton perched on the center of the eunuch's massive chest and holding the eunuch's curved blade against his throat with enough force to draw blood.

Mustafa's black eyes were wide with terror as he stared up at Lady India, and he whimpered as he tried to wiggle away from the knife and failed.

Tears streamed down Lady India's face, but she was unaware of them as she threatened the man beneath her in her mix of French and Turkish. Jonathan understood enough of her words to know that she wanted the eunuch dead and was frustrated by the fact that while she'd drawn his blood, Lady India could not bring herself to finish him off. Jonathan watched as she tried, once again, to slit Mustafa's throat and inflicted another in a series of thin, bleeding wounds.

Jonathan crossed the floor, hooked an arm around Lady India's waist, and lifted her off the eunuch's chest. "Torturing is allowed," he told her, "for I've no doubt that he deserves it, but I can't allow you to kill him." Jonathan set her on her feet and held her close to his chest as he pried the knife from her hand and tossed it aside.

"Please . . ." She clung to him and wept huge, hot, heavy tears into the mat of hair on Jonathan's chest. "Help me . . ."

"I *am* helping you, sweeting," Jonathan said.

She looked up at him. "Please, help me kill him."

He shook his head. "I can't."

"But I want him to die."

"I know you do," he soothed. "I know he can't die soon enough to make up for the five years of fear and suffering you've endured at his hands, but I cannot let you kill him. Not like this. Not when he's tied and as helpless as a stranded whale."

"Why not?" she demanded, years of anger and frustration evident in her voice.

"Because it would be murder," Jonathan said simply. "And you, Lady India, are not a murderer."

She fixed her gaze on Jonathan's face, silently pleading with him to understand.

But Jonathan stood firm. "And neither am I."

"But he . . ." India bowed her head as the tears continued to flow. She knew Lord Barclay was right. But she also knew that Mustafa deserved to suffer the way all those women in the harem had suffered.

Jonathan nodded in understanding. "I know he's a man who deserves to die for the crimes he's committed against the women under his control. I know you want to see him dead. I know you want to go to sleep at night without seeing his face or wondering if you'll be next, but my dear Lady India, none of your reasons for wanting him dead—as valid as they are—change the fact that killing him like this would be murder. And I'm not going to allow either one of us to use your need for revenge to compel us to become as cold-blooded as he is." He took hold of India's shoulders and forced her to face him. "You can hit him, kick him, bite him, spit on him, and carve your initials on his forehead for all I care. You can vent your spleen in any way you choose, short of murder. I can't let you become the thing you despise, eternally haunted by the blood upon your hands."

India buried her face against Jonathan's chest and sobbed.

Jonathan bent at the knees, scooped her up into his arms, and carried her out of the cottage to the stable. He entered the stall next to his horse's stall and carefully lowered himself and Lady India down onto the red silk pallet. He held her in his arms, cradled against his chest, and rocked her like a baby while she sobbed, and when she'd cried the five years of tears she'd been holding back, Jonathan encouraged her to talk. "What happened?"

"I incurred Mustafa's wrath the very first day in the women's quarters," she related. "And he's never forgotten it."

"What did you do?"

"I bit him on the hand when he ripped open my clothing and began his inspection of my . . ." She faltered. "My person. I had already been thoroughly inspected by the pirates who took us from the *Portsmouth*. We all were."

"How many of you were abducted?" According to the newspaper accounts Jonathan had read, eight passengers, including Lady India Burton and her governess, had been taken off the *Portsmouth* alive. The whereabouts of the other passengers were unknown.

"Eight of us," India replied. "Miss Annabelle Southwick, her brothers, Gordon and Craig, Miss Helen Winston and her companion, Miss Nancy Phillips, Patrick Joiner, Miss Dorinda Lockwood, and me."

"The newspaper accounts named seven passengers," Jonathan said.

"Patrick wasn't a passenger," India told him. "He was cabin boy on the *Portsmouth*." She closed her eyes and remembered the handsome cabin boy with white-blond hair and blue eyes and a youthful body bronzed by the sun. At four and ten, Patrick was two years India's junior and had been a cabin boy since the age of nine. "He was the only crew member taken alive. The other crew members were already dead or put to the sword." She shuddered at the memory.

"What happened to Patrick?"

"We were all sold to the dey of Algiers," India explained. "He decided our fate. He sent me and Miss Lockwood and the Southwick boys to Sultan Hamid as a gift. He kept Patrick for himself and sold Miss Southwick, Miss Winston, and Miss Phillips at auction." She exhaled sharply. "I never saw Patrick or the other ladies again."

"What about the Southwick brothers?"

"I don't know," she said. "Once we entered the women's quarters in the Topkapi, the only males we saw were eunuchs and the sultan. But I heard whispers that the older one didn't survive his punishment for trying to escape, and that the younger one was presented to one of the sultan's ministers as a gift."

Lady India had accounted for all the passengers taken from the *Portsmouth* except her governess. "What about Miss Lockwood?" Jonathan asked gently.

India's voice was wooden. "Mustafa strangled her with the red silk cord he keeps in his pocket."

The same red silk cord India had pulled from the eunuch's pocket and handed to Jonathan to use to tie Mustafa's hands behind his back. "What did she do to offend him?"

"Nothing," India replied.

"Then why?" Jonathan asked the question, even though he was afraid he already knew the answer.

"To punish me." India began to tremble uncontrollably. "For biting him."

Jonathan hugged her close. "Oh, my sweet . . ."

"She told me not to cry. Not to show any weakness." India closed her eyes. "And he murdered her. He murdered

my friend and my teacher. He murdered Miss Lockwood."
She looked up at Jonathan, and he saw the horror in her
face. "Oh, God . . ." She began to cry once again. "He
killed her because of me. . . . He killed my friend, and he
made me watch while he did it—even though I begged his
pardon. Even though I fell to my knees and begged him not
to hurt Miss Lockwood. Even though I promised to behave. He laughed as he strangled her. He enjoyed it. And
Miss Lockwood . . . Oh, God, Miss Lockwood . . ." India's
breathing grew ragged as she struggled to talk. "She was so
brave. So wonderful. When we were on the pirates' ship,
she made me promise to survive, made me promise to do
whatever I had to do in order to survive. When Mustafa
wrapped his red cord around her neck, she looked him in
the eye and spat in his face. Mustafa tightened the cord until she was dead, then dropped her body like a rag doll. I
crawled over to her and held her until he ordered the other
eunuchs to strip me and beat me with rods upon the soles
of my feet." She choked back a sob. "The sultan was very
angry with Mustafa when he heard about Miss Lockwood
and about my punishment because we were English and
because the dey had sent us as gifts and Mustafa had disposed of one of the gifts before the sultan had the chance
to see her and had damaged the other without the sultan's
permission."

"Who told the sultan about Miss Lockwood?"

"I did," India said. "When I was sent to the sultan's bed a
fortnight after Miss Lockwood's death, when I had recovered well enough from my beating to walk again. Mustafa
had told the sultan that Miss Lockwood died but not how
she died."

A muscle in Jonathan's jaw began to twitch when India
mentioned being sent to the sultan's bed. "You were able to
communicate with the sultan?"

India nodded. "He speaks perfect French and considers himself a very progressive ruler and a social reformer."

"For an absolute monarch with the power of life and death over his subjects . . ."

"Yes," she answered. "He thinks he's progressive, but his private world is no different from the previous sultans'. He wants to be enlightened, but he's as superstitious as the women of his harem. He is fascinated by blue eyes, light skin, and the red and blond hair color of European women. . . ."

"Yet your blue eyes troubled him . . ."

"Because he thought I saw too much. And because I told him that he was cursed because a blue-eyed, blond-haired innocent English woman had died at the hands of his chief eunuch and the all-powerful sultan was too weak to do any-thing about it."

Jonathan winced. "It's a miracle he didn't have Mustafa dispose of you."

"He would have," India said. "But he wanted what I had, so he punished Mustafa instead."

"Something other than your innocence?" Jonathan tried but failed to keep the sting out of his voice.

"He took my innocence as a matter of pride because he could," India told him. "But what he really wanted was knowledge. He couldn't take the knowledge locked in my brain or force me to share it. He had to persuade me to share it. And my cooperation came at a price."

"Why'd he bother?"

"Because he is allied with the French, but he fears Bonaparte's ambitions."

"He needed to learn English." Jonathan guessed.

"Yes," she said. "And about England. In secret so his ministers wouldn't know he was gaining knowledge or question his motives. The sultan is ignorant of nearly everything that goes on in the outside world. He relies upon his ministers, but he doesn't trust them. He spent the first thirty years of his life locked in the Cage, a vast warren of rooms beside the women's quarters, wondering if he'd live to become sultan or if he'd be dispatched to make way for one of the other princes locked in the Cage."

"Survival of the fittest," Jonathan said.

"Or at least the luckiest or the craftiest."

"Or the most ruthless." Jonathan smoothed a stray lock of long dark hair off India's cheek.

"Or the most ruthless," she agreed. "It is very important that the sultan be on the winning side of any conflict. And with England and France at war . . ."

"He's trying to hedge his bet."

"I don't know what that means," India told him. "But the sultan doesn't want his empire annexed by Bonaparte if France wins or carved up into little pieces if England is victorious."

Jonathan grinned. "You've just given a perfect example of a man hedging his bets, trying to be on the winning side regardless of who wins."

"Every time he complimented me on my knowledge, I reminded him that I had been taught by Miss Lockwood. That I knew only a fraction of what Miss Lockwood had known and that he could have learned so much more if Mustafa hadn't murdered Miss Lockwood. I tried to convince the sultan that the only way to gain favor with England was to release all his English prisoners." She looked at Jonathan. "I didn't know there were ransom efforts under way. I didn't know if there were survivors from the *Portsmouth* or that my father was paying for information regarding my whereabouts or that the trail had led to the dey of Algiers, and from there to the sultan. I didn't know that my father had worked to persuade the East India

Company to pursue ransom as a way to have me returned or that my grandfather was pursuing the same end in London until the sultan told me. All I knew was that I had promised Miss Lockwood I would do whatever it took to survive, and befriending the sultan seemed the best way. But in befriending the sultan, I made enemies in the harem."

Jonathan furrowed his brow. "Mustafa."

She nodded. "But we were at war with France, and I was afraid of becoming a traitor, so every time the sultan asked me to describe the vast numbers of wondrous ships of His Majesty's navy or to compare England's far superior modern weapons to his, I would smile and tell him that I was sure Miss Lockwood would have known the answer, but that she hadn't completed my military education, that I was sorry, but I couldn't tell a pistol from a rifle, and despite the fact that my grandfather was an admiral, all ships looked alike to me. Eventually the sultan tired of being reminded that his chief eunuch had murdered his greatest source of knowledge. But by that time, I was known in the seraglio as the witch who had enthralled the sultan. He used my eye color as an excuse to ransom me back to my grandfather, by saying that I was sorceress in human form."

"You did what you had to do to survive."

"Yes, I did," she said softly. "When the eunuchs dragged Miss Lockwood's body away, I swore I would survive. I swore I would keep my promise to her and that I would have my revenge on Mustafa. I hated every moment I spent in the sultan's company," India confided. "I would return from his chambers and scrub myself with the hottest water I could find, but I could still smell the stench of him. I'm afraid I always will." To her very great mortification, her tears came with the force of the monsoon rains. She who hadn't cried during her five years in a harem had turned into a veritable watering pot within a sennight of her return to England. She who had gone uncomforted and had not been allowed to mourn her dear friend suddenly had someone to hold her and comfort her and promise her everything was going to be all right. "I am so sorry, Lord Barclay. I don't usually cry, and I've suddenly become a watering pot."

"Sssh," Jonathan murmured, holding her against him. "There's no shame in shedding tears for people you loved or for yourself upon occasion. Some of the strongest men I know have shed buckets of tears at one time or another." He leaned closer and sniffed her ear. "And just so you know, you smell clean to me." He breathed in the scent of her fragrance. "Cleaner than a spring morning. Cleaner than a field of daisies. Cleaner than a brook babbling in Scotland. Cleaner than a ray of sunshine. Cleaner than the prince regent's wash on Monday morning. Why, I'll vow you're the cleanest girl in all of England."

India smiled through her tears.

"Nothing you did and nothing the sultan or his eunuch did to you can ever sully you in my eyes."

"Except murder," she reminded him, sobbing harder. "I wanted him dead. I tried, but I couldn't. I just couldn't . . ."

"That just proves how clean and good you are," Jonathan told her. "And believe me, by morning, Mustafa will wish you had. So, let him suffer. Let him live with the fact that you bested him, that you would have killed him had I not pulled you away. Let him live with his failure. That's a better revenge, because you'll be free to live your life however you choose, and Mustafa will be back in Istanbul."

"Back to his old life and his old ways," India replied bitterly. "Back to strangling troublesome concubines for pleasure."

"No," Jonathan told her. "Because by the time Mustafa returns to Istanbul, someone else will be sultan's most trusted chief eunuch. And if Mustafa ever sets foot on English soil again, it will be to stand trial for the murder of Miss Lockwood, I promise you that. Now," he whispered, "close your eyes and go to sleep."

"I can't . . ."

"Of course, you can."

"No, really," she protested. "I'm afraid I'll see it all in my dreams."

"Then we'll just have to give you something else to think about." Jonathan leaned down and brushed her lips with his. He meant his kiss to be a light, pleasant, comforting sort of kiss, but Jonathan cursed himself for a fool when his dormant desires sprang to life, and his body began to stir beneath her bottom. He tried to will his erection away, but it refused to be dismissed, and Jonathan groaned at the knowledge that resuming sleep had just become an impossible dream.

India looked up at him. "Are you going to ask me to share your bed?"

"You're already sharing my bed," he said. "Or rather, we're both sharing Mustafa's."

India grimaced at the mention of the eunuch's name.

He smoothed away the grimace with the pad of his thumb, then tenderly kissed the corner of her mouth. "Are you going to . . ." India blushed, faltering for words. "Make yourself my lover?"

"No." Jonathan shook his head. "If I ever become your lover, it will be because we both want it, not because you feel the reaction of my body and think you're obliged to appease it. You belong to yourself now, Lady India, you're not obliged to service any man in order to survive." He made a face at her. "This isn't the first time I've held a woman in my arms and become randy with desire. And God willing, it won't be the last, but I hope I'm enough of a gentleman to assure you that if you'll just close your eyes like a good little lady and go to sleep, it will eventually go away."

"What are you going to do?" she asked before closing her eyes.

"Talk," Jonathan told her. "I'm going to talk you to sleep."

"How?"

"I'm going to tell you a story guaranteed to put you to sleep."

"My nurse used to tell me stories to help me fall asleep," India confided.

"Then pretend I'm your nurse."

"Impossible." India giggled. "My nurse was Indian. She was short with dark hair and eyes. You look nothing like her."

"Then pretend I'm her tall English lover."

India giggled harder.

"Now, go to sleep." Jonathan smiled down at her as she opened one eye to peek at him, then he cleared his throat and began to tell the story.

"Once upon a time there was a little boy of seven who was sent away from London to school in the faraway wilds of . . ."

"Where?"

"Middlesex."

"No, I meant where was the little boy sent to school?"

"The Knightsguild School for Gentlemen."

"The Knightsguild School for Gentleman," she repeated. "It sounds very old-fashioned."

He nodded. "Indeed."

"Is there really a place like that?"

"There is indeed," Jonathan confirmed. "It's a military academy, and it's produced some of the finest soldiers and statesmen this country has ever known. And our little boy desperately wanted to join that august roster of heroes."

"What was his name?"

Jonathan thought for a moment. "Why don't we call him Johnny? Little Johnny Manners . . ."

India fell asleep listening to Jonathan's deep baritone as he related the wonderful adventures of Johnny Manners and his friends as they took on the wicked Mr. Norworthy, headmaster at the Knightsguild School for Gentlemen.

Chapter Eight

India awoke to the sound of a horse snorting somewhere close by. She felt a rush of warm air in her hair and heard the steady cadence of a muffled drumbeat beneath her ear.

She opened her eyes and discovered they were swollen and felt full of sand. She yawned widely, then focused her gaze on the object directly in front of her: a long, flesh-colored object she soon determined was the heavily muscled upper arm of a man.

India realized then that arm she saw belonged to Lord Barclay as did the chest she was using as her pillow and the other arm holding her firmly in place. The muffled drumbeat she heard was the sound of Lord Barclay's heart, and the motion she felt beneath her cheek was the rise and fall of his deep, even breathing as he slept. She lifted her head and attempted to move away, but Lord Barclay tightened his arms around her in response.

She rubbed her swollen eyes with her fists, regretting the vast volume of hot tears she'd shed. But when she'd attempted to apologize for becoming such a watering pot, Lord Barclay had looked her in the eyes and told her that he found no shame in shedding tears—that some of the strongest men he knew had been known to shed buckets of tears on numerous occasions, and then he'd proceeded to talk her to sleep by telling her a story about a boy who was afraid of his own shadow, but who desperately wanted to become a hero. Suddenly she understood that Lord Barclay was little Johnny Manners, the boy who had been sent to the Knightsguild School for Gentlemen at the tender age of seven and had been so sick for home that he'd cried himself to sleep every night.

The horse nickered a second time, demanding recognition from the human beings sharing his quarters.

India turned her head and spied four black hooves and a black nose through the gap in the stall boards. As she watched, the horse lipped at a lock of her hair.

India reached out a tentative hand and patted him on the nose. "Good morning, Fellow," she whispered.

"Good morning."

India blinked in surprise. For a moment, she thought the horse had replied. But the greeting had come from the man she was using as a pillow. "You're awake."

"I've been awake for a while."

"Why didn't you wake me?" she demanded, disturbed by the thought of his being awake while she slept on his chest.

"You needed your sleep," he replied. "I didn't want to disturb you."

India put her hand to her hair and combed it with her fingers as best she could. "I must look a fright."

The air around them grew thick with desire as Jonathan and India gazed at one another.

"You look perfectly lovely." Jonathan spoke the truth. Even with swollen, red eyes, and a red nose, Lady India Burton was the loveliest woman he could ever remember waking up to. And the truth was that he'd spent the better part of the hour while watching her sleep, trying to convince himself that waking up to her every morning would eventually grow old. Unfortunately, he'd failed miserably. He leaned toward her, but India suddenly shied away. Jonathan understood. She was too vulnerable here like this in the bed they'd shared. They were both too vulnerable. He took a deep breath and changed the subject. "I see you've made my borrowed horse's acquaintance," Lord Barclay said.

"He's very friendly," India said. "He made my acquaintance by tugging on my hair."

"No doubt he's hungry as well as curious. If you'll be so kind as to shift your weight a bit, my lady, I'll see to him." Jonathan waited patiently as Lady India pushed herself off his chest, blushing as she moved to the corner of the pallet.

Jonathan sat up, flexed his shoulder muscles, then pushed himself to his feet. He grabbed his shirt off a peg as he left the stall to tend to the horse. It was still quite early. But the village would be stirring with people preparing for their workday.

"Have you anything less revealing to wear?" Jonathan asked India as he bent to check the gelding's leg.

India glanced down at her nearly transparent garments, then peered at him through the stall boards, watching as he fed and watered the horse. "Except for my burnoose, they're all like these," she answered rather wistfully. "I don't have any frocks. Mine were all taken from me, and even if they hadn't been . . ." She glanced down at her bosom. ". . . they'd be terribly out of fashion and much too tight."

Jonathan turned away from the horse and gave her a quizzical look.

"It's been nearly five years," India reminded him. "Fashions change, and so have I."

He bit the inside of his cheek to keep from smiling.

"I do have a smock, and antery, and a caftan to go over my harem clothes to make them less revealing and a black burnoose that veils my face and covers me from head to toe."

"What did you wear to travel in from Turkey?" Jonathan asked.

"I wore the black burnoose over my caftan."

"I suppose that will have to do until we find a dress for you to wear." He smiled at her. "Fellow's leg is fine, and we're going to the village to hire men to help with Mustafa and then on to London. Unless you've any objections?"

India beamed. "Not at all. When do we leave, Lord Barclay?"

"As soon as you're ready," he said. "And my name is Jonathan." He looked at her over the back of the horse. "When two people have given and received kisses and overcome a great many of their demons on a red silk pallet in a stable with only a horse for a witness, I believe it's permissible to address one another by their given names, don't you?"

"A pleasure to make your acquaintance, Jonathan," India said shyly. "And to receive your kisses. My name is India."

"Beautiful, vibrant, exotic India. It suits you."

"Jonathan. God's gift. To those in need." She smiled at him. "Very heroic."

"Just remember," he warned in his rumbling baritone voice, "only my mother calls me Johnny."

"You've a mother?"

"Most people do."

India reddened. "I meant alive."

"Very much alive," he said. "And apart from her ambitions for me and her adoration of the ton and her penchant for committing Debrett's to memory—and for forcing me to do the same—she's a very good mother. And would make a very nice . . ." He'd almost said, *mother-in-law,* but Jonathan caught himself in time and amended it to, "ally."

"I hope I shall have the opportunity to meet her," India murmured.

"If you'll hurry and get dressed while I saddle our noble steed, we can be in London in time for me to make my breakfast meeting and for you to be delivered safely to Lord Davies's house. Then, if you're a good girl, you may get the opportunity to join me and my mother for our weekly nuncheon."

"We're that close to London?"

Jonathan nodded. "The only reason I didn't continue on my journey last night was because I feared the horse might be permanently lame if I didn't stop for the night. But as you can see, he's none the worse for wear for having thrown his shoe."

"It was fate," she said. "You were fated to rescue me."

"That I was," he finally agreed. "And part of that rescue includes delivering you to London . . ."

India took the hint, hurrying out of the stable, down the gravel path, and into the cottage.

Mustafa hurled invectives at her as she entered the back door. He still lay exactly as they'd left him, just as Jonathan had promised. The only difference was that he was awake and furious. Squelching the almost overwhelming desire to kick him, India ignored the angry eunuch, raising her chin a notch higher as she made her way through the kitchen to her bedchamber.

She exited the cottage some ten minutes later carrying the black burnoose over her arm.

Jonathan, properly attired in shirt, waistcoat, cravat, and coat, was leading the gelding from the stable when he glanced at the back door of the cottage. He gasped when he saw India standing there in the early morning light, dressed in sapphire-blue brocade from the ridiculous little hat, worn at an angle and decorated with a king's ransom in precious jewels, to the tips of her blue kid shoes, also decorated with precious gems. There were pear-shaped sapphires in her ears, and he'd bet his title they matched the one affixed to her navel. She sparkled like the constellations in the morning sky. All of her outer garments were embroidered with gold and jewels. Even her buttons were made of precious gems. But the most spectacular piece of the ensemble was an old-fashioned girdle worn over the garment she called a caftan, for it rode low on her hips and was constructed entirely of gold, diamonds, and sapphires.

Jonathan despised the sultan and everything he represented, but he had to admit that the man knew how to dress his women. His body tightened in response. She looked like a queen standing on the gravel path, and Jonathan was struck by how proud of her he was and how much he wanted to have the right to stand by her side.

"I'm sorry," India said, grimacing as she glanced down at her costume, "but this is the only thing suitable for travel. The sultan made me a gift of it when he released me."

No doubt to impress her grandfather and the prince regent, Jonathan thought. And although he couldn't say whether it would impress India's grandfather, the prince regent, who loved beautiful things and was perpetually short of blunt, would be dazzled—as much by the vast wealth she wore as India herself.

She was wise to refuse to wear that into London, for thieves and beggars would set upon her before she reached the city gates.

"The sultan is a fool," Jonathan pronounced. "No man seeing you like this would ever let you go."

Will you? India wanted to ask, suddenly realizing that she felt safe for the first time in years and that Jonathan Manners, eleventh Earl of Barclay, was the reason. "He never saw me wear it. He sent it to the harem the morning I left. Besides . . ." She shrugged her shoulders. "All the ladies in the harem dress this way."

Jonathan laughed. "So much for making a quiet entrance into the village. The good folks of Pymley will turn out like children following the Pied Piper to see this."

"I brought my burnoose." She lifted her arm to indicate the black robe. "But it goes over my head, and I need help putting it on."

He crooked his finger at her.

India moved closer and handed him the robe.

Jonathan dropped it over her head.

It covered her completely. The only things visible were her eyes, and a patch of finely woven black mesh shielded them.

Jonathan didn't know which was worse. Having her dressed like a queen and wearing a fortune in precious gems or having her covered. Either way, they were bound to attract attention. "Is there any way to uncover your face?"

India shook her head. "That's the point. Whenever women go out in public, their faces and their bodies must be covered."

"That may be the way it is in the sultan's realm," Jonathan said, "but this is England, and there's no reason for you to ever cover your face again." He bent to remove a knife concealed in his boot. "Hold your hands against this." He nodded toward the mesh. "While I modify the opening."

India did as he asked, then watched in amazement as he

used his knife to cut out the mesh and widen the opening in order to expose her face and neck.

"There," he pronounced in satisfaction, before lifting her onto the saddle and putting his foot into the stirrup to mount behind her. "Now it looks as if you're wearing a hooded cloak instead of a prison."

Jonathan hired a dray and a team of oxen in Pymley, along with the men needed to work them. He knew the men he hired. He'd worked with them before and knew them to be completely discreet and trustworthy. And to insure that they remained completely discreet and trustworthy, Jonathan paid them handsomely for their services in removing what he had euphemistically referred to as a mound of Turkish rubbish.

Jonathan left Griffin's gelding at the livery to be fitted for new shoes, then hired a gig so that he and India might travel in comfort when they accompanied the group back to Plum Cottage.

They found everything they needed at the village except a dress for India. Pymley was a working village too small to support a seamstress's or a milliner's shop. The dresses the matrons in the village wore were fashioned for work, except for their Sunday dresses that were cut and sewn from fashion plates published in *Godey's Lady's Book* and in London newspapers, but none of the women Jonathan encountered wore the sort of dress India required. Or the sort of dress he wanted to see on her. For that, they needed a lady, and ladies in Pymley were in short supply.

Jonathan knew India was disappointed not to find a dress, but her disappointment paled in comparison to her excitement at riding into the village on horseback and returning to Plum Cottage in an open gig with her face un-covered and turned to the sun.

The journey back to the cottage was brief, and the road, though muddy, was quite passable. Jonathan tried to miti-gate India's disappointment by handing over the reins to the gig and teaching India to drive.

She laughed with delight as the pony sped along far ahead of the dray and the oxen. She laughed all the way to the cottage, and her laughter was contagious. Jonathan laughed more in her presence than he could ever remember doing. As he helped her slow the pony for the turn into the drive leading to Plum Cottage, India turned to him and ex-claimed, "I wish I could drive all the way to London!"

"I see no reason why you can't," Jonathan told her. "So long as you allow me to in the event that we encounter heavy traffic."

"Agreed."

"Then I shall relax and nap while you drive us to Lon-don." He'd do nothing of the kind because, like everything else she did, India drove with a joie de vivre that scared the trousers off him. But he wouldn't dream of ruining her de-light in her new accomplishment by letting on that she was anything but the most capable of drivers.

"Oh, Jonathan!" She released the reins into his capable hands, then flung her arms around his neck and kissed his cheek. "Thank you! Thank you! A thousand times thank you!"

"You'll want to take back some of those thank-yous when your arms feel as if they've been pulled from their sockets tomorrow morning," he warned with a laugh.

"No, I won't."

"Then thank me properly." Jonathan pulled the gig to a stop beside the hitching post near the paddock, secured the ribbons, then turned on the seat and kissed her in earnest.

And India kissed him back. Thanking him most *im*properly for being the man who came to her rescue, for being the man with whom she had fallen in love in the space of a few hours.

They were still kissing when the men from the village arrived with the team of oxen and the dray.

One of the workmen cleared his throat, "Uh-hmm, sir, if you'll just tell us where the mound of Turkish rubbish is, we'll be about our work and leave you to your pleasure."

Jonathan reluctantly ended the kiss, then met India's bemused gaze. "Mound of Turkish rubbish?"

He shrugged his shoulders in a boyish gesture India loved. "It seemed appropriate."

"Most appropriate," she agreed.

"Would you like to wait inside the cottage while I help the men remove it or . . ."

India shook her head. "I wouldn't miss this for all the spice in India."

"Neither would I." Jonathan laughed at the devilish sparkle in her eyes, then removed his coat and waistcoat and rolled up his sleeves. He looked at the workmen. "If you gentlemen will follow me." He led the way to the back door of the cottage, flung it open, and pointed.

Mustafa cursed him vociferously from his position on the floor.

The workmen stared at the enormous eunuch trussed like a Christmas goose on the floor of the cottage. "But, sir," one of them said, "this is a man."

"Only half a man, actually," Jonathan corrected. "And that doesn't change the fact that his presence here is unwanted."

"You were right to hire a team of oxen," the leader of the workmen said. "Moving him while he's trussed up like that is going to take some doing. A team of oxen is the only thing that could move him."

"I'm not suggesting you move him while he's trussed up like a Christmas goose," Jonathan told them. "You're welcome to turn him over and loosen his ties."

The leader of the workmen frowned. "Begging your pardon for asking, sir, but how long has he been trussed up like that?"

"Since shortly before midnight," Jonathan replied.

The workman winced. "He'll be in agony if we loosen his bindings now after spending the night on the floor like that."

"Exactly." Jonathan grinned.

The workman doffed his cap and grinned back at Jonathan. "You've a wicked, mean streak in you, sir. If you don't mind my saying so."

"Not at all," Jonathan replied. "And for future reference, my wicked, mean streak is generally reserved for men who try their damnedest to kill me. And fail."

"Like this mound of Turkish rubbish, sir?"

"Exactly."

"Then we'll be sure to loosen his ties afore we drag him out."

Mustafa screamed in high-pitched agony as Jonathan and the three workmen rolled him onto his side. The blood rushed into his numb limbs as the circulation was partially restored, and Mustafa alternately screamed, cried, and cursed. Jonathan loosened the red silk cord and the brocade sash binding Mustafa's feet and hands to each other, and retied them. He bound Mustafa's hands in front of him this time and retied his feet tightly enough to restrict him but loosely enough to allow the blood to flow.

"Ignore him," India advised as Mustafa continued to curse the workmen in general and Jonathan in particular.

"I don't speak Turkish," Jonathan reminded her, "and

his French is barely intelligible at the moment. What's he saying?"

"He's cursing you," India replied cheerfully from her ringside seat in the gig, "and all your future generations. Mine, too."

One of the workmen crossed himself, but Jonathan looked Mustafa in the eye and replied in French. "At least we'll have future generations, which is more than I can say about you, you mound of sheep dung."

It took them three-quarters of an hour to maneuver Mustafa through the doorway, out into the yard, and onto the dray, but they finally loaded him onto the dray.

Jonathan left the men in the yard and went inside the cottage to write a letter of explanation to the captain of whichever of Lord Davies's ships the men managed to consign the eunuch, along with a letter of safe passage for the men delivering the cargo, and a special letter he composed using a simple version of Bonaparte's cipher. He returned with the sealed letter and a long silk scarf he'd found in Mustafa's room. He tossed the scarf to the leader of the workmen. "Here, Mr. Copley, I suggest you use this to gag him and keep him quiet. And I suggest you use that sail canvas we brought along to cover him—at least until you get him onto one of Lord Davies's ships."

"Aye, sir," Mr. Copley answered.

"I've written a letter of explanation for the ship's captain and signed and sealed it with a mark they'll recognize. And I've written a letter of passage for you and your men to deliver this cargo to the port in Dover. I trust you'll use great caution, for it would be much better for all of us if no one questions the cargo or your right to deliver it."

"That goes without saying, sir."

"Quite right." Jonathan nodded.

"And seeing as how this mound of Turkish rubbish was found *inside* Lord Davies's cottage, I doubt even the magistrate would question your right to remove it, seeing as how you're acting in Lord Davies's stead."

Jonathan nodded, then retrieved his coat and handed Copley a leather coin purse filled with money he kept for emergencies—like this one. "This should cover any *expenses,*" he said.

Copley understood he was to use the coin for expenses and bribes for port authorities, if necessary. "Where do you want the cargo to go?"

"Istanbul," Jonathan answered, "on the longest possible route. And he's to remain confined for the entire voyage and fed like a common sailor."

Copley winced. "Like I said, sir, you've a real wicked mean streak in you."

"Glad to know it's appreciated," Jonathan replied.

"Aye, sir, it is that," Copley replied in an admiring tone of voice.

Jonathan rubbed his hands together. "All right, then, let's get him gagged, secured, and covered."

"Wait!" India scrambled down from the gig as they draped the canvas over Mustafa. "You'll need these to send to the sultan." She reached for Mustafa's right hand and tugged a huge gold ring off one fat finger and a huge emerald off another one and dropped both rings into Jonathan's hand. "The gold one is his seal of office. The other was a gift from the dey of Algiers."

"Anything else?" Jonathan asked.

"These." India reached into the pocket of her caftan and offered him a silk purse filled with the gems she'd taken off Mustafa's clothing while Jonathan had slept.

Jonathan whistled through his teeth when he opened the pouch.

"I'm not a thief," she told him. "But I couldn't take the chance that he might try to purchase his way back."

"I never thought you were," Jonathan assured her. "I'm ashamed I didn't think of it."

"You would have eventually," India offered. "But you were too tired to think clearly last night."

Mr. Copley cleared his throat once again. "We best be on our way, my lord, afore it gets any later."

"Thank you." Jonathan shook hands with each of the men.

"Our pleasure, my lord." They gave him a brief nod and doffed their caps in a sign of respect and appreciation for the job. They'd just earned a month's wages for a day's work.

Chapter Nine

India handled the gig until they reached the outskirts of London. Traffic was light, for it was still quite early for everyone except the street vendors to be about, but Jonathan's prediction was coming true. India was unused to the physical exertion, and Jonathan had taken over the reins when he noticed her arms beginning to tremble from the strain.

But she learned quickly, and her driving had improved considerably with each mile. Before long, she'd be maneuvering her own vehicle for morning jaunts through Hyde Park.

"You've spoiled me," she said, as she handed the reins over to Jonathan.

"How so?"

"I enjoy driving so much, I'll want a pony gig of my own. And I'm never going to stay indoors again." She had shoved the hood of her burnoose off her head during the drive from Pymley and removed her ridiculous little hat, enjoying the breeze in her hair. But she reluctantly donned both the hat and the cloak as they reached the gates of the city.

He laughed. "Then you're going to be a most unbecoming shade of brown, my sweet."

"Not if I wear a bonnet and carry a parasol." She gave a wistful sigh. "Oh, how I'll love wearing a bonnet again! And dresses and a riding habit!"

"If you're willing to compromise your vow a fraction," he offered, remembering her vow not to return to London until she could do so as a young lady, "I'm willing to take you to the most fashionable dressmaker in London *before* I take you to Lord Davies's house and attempt to persuade her to open her shop."

"You can do that?"

"I'm a very good customer," he said. "Or rather, my mother is." He shrugged. "But I pay the bills. I'm sure Madam Racine will be willing to make an early morning exception for me."

"What about your breakfast meeting?"

He was surprised she remembered. "I'm already a day late. A bit longer won't make much difference."

"So long as you think I look respectable and no one sees what's under this burnoose except a dressmaker, I'm willing to compromise."

"You look *entirely* respectable in your black cloak," he declared. "Rather like a young lady in mourning. And I feel rather naughty knowing that I'll be the only man in town who knows what's beneath it."

"In that case," she said, "let's see if we can persuade a dressmaker to open her shop, because I'll be thrilled to be rid of these Turkish trousers! So thrilled I vow I'm going to burn them all!"

"Don't burn all of them," Jonathan suggested gently as they entered the city of London. He urged the pony into a brisk trot, skillfully negotiating the city streets that were all but deserted by anyone except the street vendors and the gentlemen making their way on horseback for their morning rides on Rotten Row.

"Why not?" she demanded. "I'm heartily sick of them!"

"That's understandable." He nodded sympathetically as they made their way around the park to Bond Street in record time. "Although I am certain that you'll look extraordinarily beautiful in a dress, I must confess that I've never seen anyone as lovely as you are in those trousers."

India was stunned. No one had ever told her she looked beautiful in her Turkish trousers. None of the eunuchs, nor any of the ladies of the harem, and certainly not the sultan. The idea that she might look beautiful in the costume they'd forced her to wear, in the costume she hated, had never occurred to her. "Truly?"

"Truly." Jonathan transferred both reins to one hand so he could make the sign of the cross over his heart. "My fondest dream is that I may see you in them again one day."

"Then I shall save them to wear for you on special occasions."

Jonathan pulled the gig to a halt before a beautifully decorated shop window. This wasn't the best place for a lengthy conversation. It was early, and they still ran the risk of being seen, but India was a stranger in London and would be devilishly hard to recognize swathed as she was in an ocean of black muslin. "India . . ."

"I'm not innocent," she said. "I've been trained in myriad ways to please a man—ways I never dreamed existed—"

"India . . ."

"I know I'm ruined because I've spent dozens of nights in the sultan's bed," she confided. "And I've no right to expect marriage to a gentleman who deserves the best, but I want you to know that while I was forced to pleasure the sultan, he was only intimate with me once."

"What?"

"He took my maidenhead because he felt he was obligated to do so. But he never spilled his seed in me again. That honor was reserved for his *kadins*. And although everyone thought I was one of his favorites, I was greatly relieved not to be. So, if you want me as your concubine, I'd be honored to share your bed." She looked up at him to gauge his reaction. "But only if you want me. Rescuing me from Mustafa doesn't obligate you in any way—"

"Obligate?" Jonathan threw back his head and laughed. "My dear sweet love, I was worried that *you* might feel obligated to offer because I rescued you from Mustafa—"

"Oh, no!" she exclaimed. "I offered because I can't imagine life without you. I know it's sudden, but Jonathan . . ."

"India . . ."

"I love you," they said simultaneously.

"What do we do now?" she asked, suddenly nervous.

"I can think of dozens of things," Jonathan said. "And all of them involve you, a bed, those Turkish trousers, and solving the mystery of what keeps that sapphire in your navel."

India beamed at him. "It's—"

Jonathan cut her off by placing a finger against her lips. "Don't tell me," he begged. "I spent a good part of this morning wondering, and I'd like to solve the riddle myself. But not with my concubine. With my wife."

India looked crestfallen. "But, Jonathan, I'm disgraced. Think of your reputation. . . ."

"Hang my reputation!" he exclaimed. "If it doesn't survive my marriage to an honorable young lady, then what good is it anyway? I love you, India, and nothing has made me happier than to learn the sultan was only intimate with you once, but if he'd been intimate with you dozens of times, it would make no difference so long as you survived to marry me."

"Oh, Jonathan!" India flung her arms around his neck and began covering his face with kisses.

Jonathan responded by pulling her onto his lap and kissing her back quite thoroughly in front of Madam Racine's Dressmaking Shop.

An early riser, Madam Racine had been about to go down the street to the coffeehouse for her morning coffee and a cinnamon pastry, when she opened the door and saw a gentleman and a lady kissing. She was astonished to discover that gentleman was none other than the dashingly handsome Earl of Barclay. The lady was a mystery.

Feeling it was her duty to intervene, Madam Racine stepped up to the gig and touched Lord Barclay's shoulder. "Lord Barclay? What are you doing? Here? At this time of morning?"

India buried her face against Jonathan's shirt as he broke the kiss and looked up at woman standing beside the gig. "Ah, Madam Racine, just the lady we've come to see. We need your help."

"How may I be of assistance, my lord?" she asked.

"The young lady is in desperate need of a dress."

Madam Racine gasped. "You don't mean that she is . . ."

"Oh no," he hurried to reassure the dressmaker. "She's fully clothed beneath her cape, but her garments are not the garments of an English lady." He turned the full force of his charm on the seamstress. "Would it be asking too much of you to open your establishment so that we might dress my companion in the manner befitting an English lady?"

The dressmaker glanced down the street at the coffee-house. "I was just about to break my fast with coffee and a pastry."

"I'll make this favor worth your while," Jonathan promised. "And once you and the young lady are safely inside selecting dresses and discussing fashion plates and fabrics, I'll fetch us coffee and an assortment of pastries."

Madam Racine shrugged her shoulders in the classic Gallic gesture. "How can I refuse?"

Two hours later, India was fashionably and properly attired in a sprigged muslin morning dress complete with shawl, gloves, bonnet, stockings, shoes, and the usual assortment of undergarments.

Madam had been so enthralled by India's Turkish costume that she'd agreed to alter two morning gowns she'd completed for another young lady to fit India, after India admired them. She had asked permission to study the cut of India's caftan, declaring it the perfect design for an outer coat to be worn over an afternoon dress or evening gown, and she declared that with slight modifications to the basic design, the caftan would make a darling riding habit. India allowed the dressmaker to study the caftan to her heart's delight and then stood perfectly still while Madam fitted and pinned and basted the morning dresses, an afternoon dress, and an extraordinary pale blue silk evening gown.

They shared coffee and pastries as India and Madam Racine concluded the fabric and pattern selections and Jonathan read the morning paper and nodded his approval of the selections or shook his head to disapprove.

When the dressmaker finished her measuring and the fitting of the gowns she'd promised to make, Jonathan paid for the garments India was wearing and the ones Madam was to make up and send to Lord Davies's address as soon as possible.

"Lord Davies's address?"

"Yes," Jonathan confirmed. "Lady India will be staying there until her grandfather returns and we're wed."

"Wed?" Madam Racine was stunned. She'd been dressing Lord Barclay's mother for years, and she'd listened while Lady Leticia despaired of her son ever submitting to the parson's mousetrap.

Jonathan nodded. "You may wish us happy, madam, for I have asked Lady India to be my wife, and she has honored me by accepting."

Lord Davies rushed into the sitting room of his Park Lane mansion as soon as his butler, Saunders, announced his unexpected callers as Lady India Burton and Lord Jonathan Barclay.

"India, my dear." Lord Davies embraced her. "Thank God you're safe . . . When Captain Marks told me the eunuch refused to leave, I didn't quite know how to manage it."

"You managed it exactly right," India told him. "I cannot thank you enough for sending Lord Barclay to retrieve your parcel."

Lord Davies frowned. "I didn't send Lord Barclay." He nodded at Jonathan. "And I only asked my son-in-law, Lord Grantham, to retrieve you because I couldn't go myself. Not with my wife injured. . . ."

"Be glad that I offered to go in Colin's stead," Jonathan told him. "The eunuch did his best to kill me, despite the fact that I had a key to the cottage."

"What?" Lord Davies was clearly shocked. "I had no idea. We paid the ransom. And Captain Marks explained the significance of the keys. . . ."

"It didn't matter," India told him. "Mustafa's orders came from the sultan, and the sultan considered me his property until my grandfather or an emissary acting in his stead relieved him of his duty."

"Lady India tried to convince the eunuch that I was an emissary sent from His Highness the prince regent and her grandfather."

"And when that failed," India resumed the narration, "Lord Barclay took matters into his own hands."

"Tell me everything," Lord Davies instructed.

"It's a long story," Jonathan warned.

"Then come in and make yourselves comfortable," Lord Davies invited. "And tell me everything."

"By now, Mustafa should be well on his way to your shipping line office in Dover," Jonathan concluded when he and India had related the details of everything that had happened since India had arrived at Plum Cottage. "I don't know where he'll be bound," Jonathan admitted, "but I told the workmen that I wanted him on the longest possible route to Istanbul."

Lord Davies threw back his head and roared with laughter. "That will be by way of Australia. Provided, of course, that your cargo made it to the docks in time. *The Lady of Botany Bay* is scheduled to sail on tomorrow's evening tide."

"They made it," Jonathan told him. "The men I hired are without fault. They've proven themselves on numerous occasions."

"We'll await confirmation from the captain nonetheless," Lord Davies said. "Captain Owen has been with me from the beginning. He's completely trustworthy, and he knows Lady India's grandfather. He'll send word as soon as he receives the cargo." He clapped his hands together and stood up. "In the meantime, we'll see that Lady India is comfortably settled into her room." He walked over to the cord hanging near the door and rang for the butler. "Saunders, please show Lady India to her room. I'm sure she's tired and would like to freshen up," he instructed when the butler appeared.

India rose from her seat and followed the butler up the stairs.

"India," Jonathan called.

India paused on the stair and turned to look at him.

"I'll pick you up for nuncheon with my mother at two."

Lord Davies lifted an eyebrow in query.

"I've asked Lady India to marry me," Jonathan informed the older man. "And she has done me the very great honor of accepting."

Lord Davies looked at Lady India and then back at Lord Barclay. "Isn't this rather sudden?"

"Very sudden," Jonathan replied. "But I'm told that falling in love sometimes happens this way."

"Who told you?" Lord Davies demanded.

"Your son-in-law, Colin."

Lord Davies coughed to cover his laughter. "Is this what you want, Lady India?"

"Very much," she breathed. "For I seem to have fallen head over heels myself. And after spending the last five years confined to a . . ." She blushed. "Confined. I would very much like to begin my new life as Lord Barclay's wife."

"I feel the same way."

"Thank heavens," Lord Davies breathed. "For your grandfather's prayers have been answered."

The shops on Bond Street were doing a brisk business, and tongues were wagging with the news of Lord Barclay's indiscretion by the time Jonathan left Lord Davies's house and returned to his residence at Albany.

He and Lady India Burton had become the talk of the ton in the space of a couple of hours.

Jonathan had just finished his bath and was in the midst of donning fresh linens when two of the three original Free Fellows burst into his apartments uninvited.

"Where the devil have you been?" Colin McElreath, Viscount Grantham, demanded, barging into Jonathan's dressing room and waving his valet away. "You were due back last evening."

"Delivering your father-in-law's parcel." He turned from his shaving mirror and faced them.

"Good God, man! What happened to your neck?" Griffin, Duke of Avon, inquired, leaning closer to get a better look at the collection of cuts. "And where the devil is my horse?"

"Your horse lost a shoe. He's at the stable in Pymley getting new ones," Jonathan answered. "And as you can see, I had a spot of trouble at Plum Cottage. I suffered a few cuts, but I took care of the problem."

Colin glanced at Griffin. "Then the rumors Gillian and Alyssa heard at the milliner's this morning were rubbish."

"That depends upon the rumors," Jonathan replied.

"The rumors that you were kissing a lady in an open gig on Bond Street early this morning," Colin replied.

"I heard the same rumor while riding on the Row this morning," Griffin said. "And at White's this morning, I heard you are engaged to be wed."

"Those aren't rumors," Jonathan answered cheerfully, as he tied his cravat. "I was kissing a lady in an open gig on Bond Street early this morning. And I am engaged."

"Have you lost your senses?" Colin demanded.

"No, my heart."

"Your heart?" Griffin repeated. "May I ask to whom?"

"The parcel."

"I beg your pardon?" Griffin didn't think he'd heard him correctly.

"The parcel Lord Davies wanted delivered. The parcel Colin allowed me to collect in his place. The parcel who turned out to be Lady India Burton, the love of my life. I asked her to marry me this morning."

"You proposed? After knowing her less than a day?" Colin was stunned. "Are you certain about this?"

"You only knew Gillian one day," Jonathan retorted. "And Griffin only knew his duchess one day. Were you certain?"

"He's right," Griff answered with a grin. He looked at Colin, then back at Jonathan. "Lady India Burton," Griff puzzled. "Why does that name ring a bell?"

"Because she was one of the passengers on the HMS *Portsmouth*," Jonathan answered. "And she's spent the past five years in a sultan's harem."

"Good Lord!" Colin exclaimed. "She must be every bit as extraordinary as my father-in-law intimated when he swore me to secrecy, and asked me to collect her."

"She is," Jonathan affirmed. "A most extraordinary woman." He looked at Colin and Griffin, then began to tell them about his betrothed and the extraordinary events that had changed the course of her life and his.

"Your betrothal is going to cause an uproar," Colin warned. "But we'll do everything in our power to ease the way, for we wish you the happiest of marriages."

"I don't know how to thank you," Jonathan began.

"You don't need to thank us. We're your friends. It's the least we can do for you and Lady India and Miss Lockwood." Griffin smiled. "Besides, you're not yet thirty. That means you owe us—"

"Five hundred pounds each," Colin crowed, reminding Jonathan of his Free Fellows League pledge to pay each member five hundred pounds if he married before the age of thirty.

"So I do," Jonathan mused. "So I do. And I'll be delighted to pay it."

"And we'll be delighted to accept it," Colin told him. "So long as you and your countess live happily ever after."

Epilogue

Lady India Burton and Jonathan, eleventh Earl of Barclay, were married two months to the day after her arrival in London so that Lady India's grandfather, Sir Harold Gregory, might arrive in plenty of time to get to know the bride before giving her into the hands of her earl.

Their two months of courtship continued to be the talk of the ton, but no one disputed the fact that they were clearly a couple over the moon for one another. It was just that no one in the ton had ever expected Lord Barclay to marry—especially a young lady with a past.

And what a past! The newspapers were full of the accounts of Lady India's life, and she became an instant heroine when news that her information was helping to secure the releases of other English captives and thwart Bonaparte's plans in the region reached the ears of those who eagerly spread gossip to the members of the ton.

The members of the Free Fellows League and the wives of those who had already blissfully submitted to leg shackles delighted in detailing the stories of Lady India's heroism and in seeing that those marvelously entertaining stories reached the proper ears.

And their plan worked to perfection. Everyone wanted to get a look at the young Englishwoman who had refused to be conquered by the Ottoman Empire, and her wedding day proved the perfect opportunity.

His Highness, the prince regent, attended the ceremony along with four hundred other members of the ton. And he accompanied the happy couple to the wedding breakfast, which was held at Carlton House, where she was formally presented into society as India, Countess of Barclay.

The new countess spent her wedding night dancing with her husband in the moonlight at the Admiralty Ball. She was, of course, the most elegant dancer there. Everyone said so. And India had practiced for nearly a month to make certain of it.

After the Admiralty Ball, India donned her Turkish trousers and spent her honeymoon enticing her husband into solving the riddle of the sapphire in her navel and of discovering dozens of new and exciting ways to make love.

The sapphire, he discovered, was held into place by a thin gold wire that pierced her navel.

And as she lay in Jonathan's arms each night, India said a prayer for Miss Lockwood, thanking her for giving India the dreams that had all come true. Miss Lockwood wouldn't be there to teach them, but India swore that her children would know Miss Lockwood's teachings, and if she ever had a daughter, India intended to name her Dorinda.

Dorinda Louisa Barclay.

Miss Lockwood would like that.

Miss Jenny Alt's
First Kiss

Jacqueline Navin

Chapter One

Genvieve Alt, or Jenny as she was more frequently called, watched her cousin pace before the fireplace on a chilly March afternoon in their London town house in Cavendish Square.

"Why does he have to arrive now? This is going to positively ruin me," the beautiful Cassandra Benedict said. "Mama, you cannot let this happen!"

Her mother, Iris Benedict, who was Jenny's aunt, wrung her hands. "Do not fuss so. He shall be here this very evening, and I'll not have you insult him. He is an earl, after all, and a wealthy man for all his present troubles."

Cassandra flounced into a settee with a crisp rustle of silk and managed to look entrancing even while wearing a pout. Jenny took great pride in her cousin. At eighteen, Cassandra was confident and charismatic. She was the toast of the ton in this, her first London season.

It was Jenny's first season as well, although she was twenty-two years of age. She had not wanted one when she reached her majority. She'd felt shy and awkward, uncomfortable with the thought of being out there, on display, but she could no longer avoid it this year as she had to accompany Cassandra to all her social events. She had made significantly less of an impression on the *beau monde*.

It wasn't that she was so plain. Aunt Iris was kind, and told her that she could be pretty if she wanted. She supposed this was true. Her hair was a lovely shade of honey blond, but as she didn't have a maid, she simply twisted it into a knot every day. And her spectacles were a hindrance, shielding eyes of pale blue rimmed with thick lashes that would have charmed if they weren't hidden. She really only needed her eyeglasses for reading, but as she was *always* reading, it had become a habit to wear them all the time, one she did not alter for the sake of society.

But most of all, she was often overlooked because she did not seek the limelight for herself, for it was Cassandra who should shine. Aunt Iris was very anxious to find her daughter a good match, and Jenny, who loved her aunt and cousin dearly, was equally determined that she would do nothing to detract from Cassandra making a stunning debut.

The result of her cool reception to any man who exhibited an interest in her had been that she was regarded as something of an oddity. She realized this but was at a loss how to right the misunderstanding. Or perhaps she *was* odd. Certainly, her interests in reading and quiet evenings at home were not the typical ones among the circle in which her family traveled. In any event, she was never asked to dance, and no gentleman called upon her.

She was contented, however, to sit with her friends at parties, to play cards and watch the others dance and flirt. Besides, it wasn't as if there had ever been a man who had made her ever *want* to step out of the shadows and draw his interest.

"What is the relation exactly—some second cousin three times removed or some such nonsense?" Cassandra paced, her skirts swishing crisply with each step. "Oh, why is this happening to me? To have a man of his reputation sprung on us now when I am having so much fun!"

Jenny sought to smooth the situation, a duty she regularly performed. "Perhaps if you told us a bit about him, it would ease Cassandra's worry." Jenny spoke gently to Iris. "You've spoken of the matter very little since yesterday, and then only to tell us of his arrival."

"Yes," Cassandra chimed. "Who exactly is he? What does he want here?"

The letter, which had arrived just a few days ago, announcing that the Earl of Hatherleigh was calling upon his distant relations for an extended visit, had sent her aunt to her bed with a migrim and Cassandra into an uproar. The date on the missive was just shy of a fortnight past, but it had been delayed in the post, giving the Benedict household only a day to prepare.

Aunt Iris dabbed at her glistening forehead with a handkerchief. "Yes, yes, how thoughtless of me. I am just so overset. How will I ever manage . . . ? But it is not his fault. Miles . . . well, I suppose he is a good man. I do not know him much anymore. His father was my husband's cousin." She issued a resigned sigh. "When he was a boy my Roger and I saw much of him. He was a *nice* boy. I still think of him as Miles, but I suppose he shall prefer Hatherleigh now that he has inherited the title."

"Why then have I never met him?" Cassandra asked, sinking into a chair.

"He was off at Oxford for many years, dear. And . . . well, he has not been family minded, I suppose."

"If you have not seen him in years, what has him interested in our family now?" Jenny inquired.

Leaning forward, Iris said, "He is set on *finding a wife,* my dears." She paused as if she had just imparted a dreadful secret. "You see, in his letter, he wrote of how he had vowed to his father just before the poor old earl died, to see his duty done before his twenty-fifth birthday. And that is only months away. Poor dear, I can't imagine he's fond of marriage after . . . Well, it's best not to speak of the dead. Let us just say that his first wife was an unfortunate choice."

This upset Cassandra. "He does not have scandal attached to him, does he?"

Iris made a face of disapproval. "He married young, and like so many young men, he married foolishly. She was of loose character and caused him great shame. This time, of course, the woman he marries must be of good family, a woman worthy to sire a future earl. A woman of *society.* This is why he is coming to London."

Jenny was confused. "He is an earl, and wealthy, you said. Surely the *ton* would welcome him."

"Oh, dear, he was shunned by the *ton* when he made such a disastrous marriage, and it made him bitter so that even after the wretched girl died, he continued to associate with the same awful people he became fond of when he was in exile—*the demimonde!*"

Jenny's eyes rounded. The demimonde was the underworld of polite society. They were disreputable and unconventional types—artists, actors, even sought-after Cyprians. They were considered notorious. Nobody of good society ever had anything to do with them—at least not openly.

"He has not been considered good society since," Aunt Iris went on. "He has asked me, as his only relative—and that a thin association, to be sure—to hostess for him and sponsor him to meet eligible women. He has no one else, you see." She puffed up with pride and added, "It really is a compliment. I *am* rather well-connected."

"It is as I feared! All of my beaus will scatter like birds when they hear Hatherleigh is my cousin!" Cassandra cried.

"I don't see why," Jenny said. It wasn't quite a scold, but it was not gentle either.

"Oh, Jenny, you wouldn't understand," Cassandra retorted. "It is not as if you have anything to lose."

Jenny looked away. She was perfectly capable of putting Cassandra in her place for this thoughtless remark. Her habit of not doing so was a conscious decision, not a condition of weakness.

When she'd come to live with her aunt and cousin eight years ago after her parents' death, she had been welcomed by her new family. She was very grateful to them for taking her in, and although Aunt Iris had never made her feel the poor relation, she had been acutely aware of her position as just that.

It had been the fault of her pride, she supposed. She had never wished to be a burden, but rather a help to her aunt and a friend to Cassandra. She had taken the younger girl under her wing, perhaps spoiled her a little, which might account for the lovely girl's tendency to be self-absorbed, at times cruel, but Jenny knew it was not from malice, just thoughtlessness.

She made excuses for her. Cassandra was young, she was vivacious, full of life. It was not good, perhaps, but inevitable that she could be a bit high-strung at times.

"This is terrible." Cassandra wagged her finger at her mother. "His arrival at this time is most inconvenient, Mama—at best. A disaster at worst."

"Pardon me," a deep masculine voice cut in. All heads snapped to the doorway which, Jenny was horrified to see, had been left open. On the threshold was a man, a very tall man. Beside him, Brent, their footman, stood rigidly, his eyes wide with horror.

"Excuse me, madam. But the earl . . ." Brent trailed off, faltering under the tension. "The earl has arrived."

The room fell into thick silence.

The earl stood perfectly still, a mild, lazy expression on his face. When he spoke, his voice was smooth and pleasant. "I fear I am intruding."

He swept the room with a razor-sharp glance. When it momentarily touched Jenny, she flinched.

She could not tell if he were angry or insulted. He seemed calm, guarded. Perhaps even a bit amused. But he made her nervous nonetheless.

"Oh, no! We didn't hear you!" Aunt Iris was flustered, and Jenny vaguely registered the familiar urge to rush to her aid, but she was stricken motionless as well as mute.

"Miles, forgive us. We were not speaking of you. How good it is to see you." Iris rushed on, waving her hands as she smiled a desperate smile. "We have been awaiting you most anxiously. Come in, come in."

He hesitated only a moment, then complied, filling the room with his masculine presence.

He was very broad in the shoulders, lean, well-proportioned. Everything from his shiny shoes and crisply pressed trousers to his black hair combed back off his face and tied into a short queue was perfection.

He paused, focused now on Aunt Iris. He gave a courteous bow. "I am delighted to see you again, cousin," he said with impeccable manners.

"Miles, dear. Er . . . I mean Hatherleigh."

"Miles will do. I detest formalities. Hatherleigh is a place. I am a man."

From Cassandra's direction came a soft, "Oh, my!"

Jenny glanced at her to see that her brow had smoothed and there was a rapt look on her face as she stared. It seemed that Cassandra had ceased being displeased with the earl's sudden appearance.

It was obvious why. He was not only handsome but the epitome of the fashionable lord. His presence was felt as almost a physical thing, a prickling along the flesh.

She should be relieved Cassandra's hysterics were at an end, but she could not relax. There was still the pulsing tension, and her aunt was quite upset.

Iris's voice quavered. "I am afraid we were caught somewhat unawares, I admit. You see, your letter arrived late, and it was only yesterday I learned you were due."

"Then I *am* intruding," he said, a bit startled. But Jenny marveled as how smoothly he accomplished this, polite but uncompromising at the same time. "I should go ahead to my apartments. I've let a suite in St. James. I shall call on you later."

Iris looked desperately at a loss. "Oh, please stay. I-I just rang for tea. Would you join us?"

He thought about this for a moment. "As you will." He clasped his hands behind his back.

"Oh my, I've quite forgotten civility." said Aunt Iris. "This is my daughter and your cousin, Cassandra Benedict."

Cassandra folded into a deep curtsy, turning up her head and offering the prettiest display of fluttered eyelashes Jenny had ever seen her perform. To Jenny's irritation, she noted *Cousin* Miles was not completely immune. The energy around him seemed to intensify as he looked over the feminine offering before him.

Cassandra's beauty was at its best as she was now, with her huge dark eyes shining and a half-smile playing on her lips. Jenny knew she was taking in the stature of the man in front of her: his remarkable good looks, the title, the degree of relation far enough removed for there to be possibilities.

Abruptly Hatherleigh looked up, and his eyes rested on Jenny for the second time. She felt her skin prickle as reaction rolled through her. They were extraordinary eyes, very pale green, like jade. She forced herself not to fidget as he swept a bold, assessing glance from her inexpert coif down to her scuffed but very comfortable shoes. She pushed her glasses into place with nervous fingers.

"And who is this?"

She rose and met his eye, dipping into a brief curtsy. "Genvieve Alt, my lord."

It was difficult to breathe, as if the air had suddenly lost its ability to nourish her. Her heart was pumping swiftly, but she pretended nothing was amiss as she offered a small, courteous nod she hoped appeared cool and unaffected.

"This is my niece, dear Jenny," Aunt Iris murmured. "My sister's child. She lives with us since the passing of her parents."

"Your servant," he said, and bowed slightly. Then he glanced away, dismissing her.

The stirring of her emotions remained. Jenny was glad when he turned away and sat in the chair Iris offered him, yet at the same time she was annoyed with him for taking such little note of her.

"Where is Judith with the tea?" Aunt Iris said. "I could use a cup myself, and Miles, you must be in need of refreshment after your journey." She picked up the bell and instead of tinkling it gently, clanged it hard enough to raise the hairs on the back of Jenny's neck. Jenny reached out and stilled her aunt's hand. Iris looked at her gratefully and made a visible effort to collect herself.

The earl was thoughtful. "I do hope the delay in the letter does not pose any problems in getting my plans under way. I wish to begin attending events as soon as possible." His jaw set slightly, betraying a tension he did not try to hide. "I want to get this over with."

The maid wheeled in the cart. Jenny saw how Aunt Iris's hand shook as she poured out, and the stunned paralysis that had overtaken her at the earl's arrival released her in that moment.

She went to her aunt's side and gently took the teapot, pouring each cup and passing it as she took over the task of making conversation. She began by inquiring as to the earl's journey.

The earl observed her with alert eyes. "It was uneventful, which is what one wishes for in travel."

He seemed then to notice the tension, Iris's stiff smile, Cassandra's expression of awe, and perhaps a touch of the disapproval Jenny was trying very hard not to show.

The corner of his mouth curled slightly. "You are kind to receive me, especially when the circumstances are so strange, Cousin." His smile deepened, and it was kind, not mocking at all. "I trust you were not dismayed to receive a letter from me after all these years."

"It was something of a surprise. A pleasant one, I assure you."

His gaze swept the three of them again. "Somehow I doubt that."

"What Aunt Iris means to say," Jenny interjected, feeling she had to defend her aunt, "is that the delay in the post was the fault of no one. What is important is that you are here, and I know Aunt Iris is very pleased to have it so. And all's well that ends well, correct? Why, she was just telling us how fond she and her husband were of you when you were a boy."

He blinked, and she had the impression he was bringing her into sharper focus. Her heart kicked harder against her ribs. When he glanced back at Iris, Jenny felt released.

"How kind of you. But I am not certain it is deserved. As I recall, I was not very agreeable when you visited."

Aunt Iris erupted with laughter. "Oh, you were naughty, yes, you were. But boys are so. It is what makes them delightful."

"Then you forgive me?" he asked. Jenny saw how his eyes danced. What was this? she wondered as she took a sip of her tea. He'd seemed so severe before, but it appeared he had some mischief in him.

"A prank," he explained, turning to the younger women, reading their questioning gazes. "I placed a few frogs in their room when they came to visit."

They laughed together. "What made you do such a thing?" Jenny asked.

He raised his eyebrows and made a gesture that could have meant anything. "I was put out since I had to take my dinner in the nursery because the adults were having formal dining. It was that way when we had guests, and I grew rather lonely. So . . . I did my best to discourage them from staying too long."

"It gave me a start, but no real harm was done," Iris said, chuckling. "And you were quite sorry afterward."

His bringing up the incident had helped ease the mood, and Iris was beginning to relax. Jenny wondered if he were skilled at charming people or if he'd gotten it right by chance.

"You were very nice about it, I recall. You begged my father not to reprimand me. Do you remember? That made quite an impression on me. As they say, no good deed goes unpunished. I suppose it was remembering this that made me think of you when I had need of a London connection."

"But of course you should come to us," Cassandra said, leaning toward him. "After all, we are *family*."

Jenny knew her cousin so well that at times she could read her thoughts. Cassandra's eyes were dark with excitement. She smiled too much, too intently.

Yes, she thought, *kissing cousins, if you have your way.*

"The relation is a distant one," he reminded her. "Several times removed and all of that."

"But it is a fond one," Cassandra rushed to assure him. "You heard Mama say so."

Jenny thought she must do something. Cassandra was being much too obvious. "Do you have any idea how long you will be staying in London, my lord?" she asked.

She hadn't meant to sound ungracious, as if she were anxious for him to leave. She could have bitten her tongue.

"I am here for the marriage mart, Miss . . . Alt? Yes, Miss Alt. The same as you."

There was no maliciousness in his words, but the implication sent her back poker iron straight. She resented his calling her a husband-hunter.

"I seriously doubt our objects are the same," she said archly.

He reacted to that, sensing a challenge.

"As to my expectations," he continued, "I shall be in Town as long as it takes to find a wife, a vague deadline I find unsatisfactory in the extreme." He narrowed his eyes. "But do not fret; I am certain I can conduct my business swiftly, and be back to my dull life in the country so that you ladies can resume your usual pleasures. I shall be in your way no longer than I have to."

His tone held an edge and his gaze was steady.

Jenny flushed.

"I will make certain you see the best young ladies, Miles," Aunt Iris put in, "just as you require."

"But you must stay as long as you like," Cassandra rushed to add.

"I am in your debt." He flickered a glance at Jenny to see how she reacted to the welcome he was having thrust upon him, as if he expected her to object. There was an undercurrent of amusement in all of his polite words. The thought that he was mocking her rankled.

"Too bad the entire business is not conducted as it is at Tattersall's," she said before she could stop herself. "It would make it so much simpler. One could simply look them all over and strike the deal in one afternoon."

She cursed her temper as soon as she'd spoken. Aunt Iris would be in a faint in a moment.

But he only laughed. "If only finding a wife were as simple as locating a fine piece of horseflesh. But there are similarities. I have heard tell that the offerings at Almack's are displayed not unlike what you describe. Some differences are significant, however. For example, one must dress in evening clothes when making the inspection of the candidates, which is less comfortable."

Cassandra gasped, confused by the jest.

"Not to mention the disadvantage of not one getting a clear view of the candidate's teeth," she replied, taking a delicate sip of her tea. She astonished herself, but his clever rejoinder lit a strange excitement inside her. It was by far the most interesting conversation she could remember, and she could not still her tongue.

"Jenny! What a strange thing to say. Do not mind my cousin, my lord," Cassandra said lightly. "She has a rather odd view of polite society. People remark on it all the time. Why, she only began attending functions this year when I was old enough. She only comes to keep her eye on me."

She looked at Jenny with the same warm regard one might give a beloved spaniel.

"How fortunate you are, then, to have Miss Alt," he said, and his voice and gaze were warm, as if he really thought so.

Jenny felt a rush of embarrassment. Perhaps she had gone too far, made a fool of herself with her rush of temper. "I do not like balls, that is all. There is always such a crush. And I am a terrible dancer, and I . . ."

"Ah," he said, and she knew he was laughing at her again.

The conversation turned to Aunt Iris's plans. He listened intently to the ideas she spouted for his introduction into the London *bon ton*.

Jenny had to admire her aunt. She knew her way in society. Her suggestion to begin subtly, having Hatherleigh accompany them on various outings, such as walks in the park, shopping, going to church this Sunday, was an excellent idea, and the earl was impressed.

He accepted her invitation to stay for dinner, and as the women adjourned upstairs to change, Cassandra strolled beside Jenny, a dreamy look on her face. "He isn't at all what I expected," she said softly.

This disturbed Jenny. As she slipped into a lavender silk gown, she argued with herself, reasoning that there was no cause for alarm. If Cassandra decided that the earl suited her, and the feeling was mutual, why should it distress her?

He was fine catch. No doubt the moment the word was circulated that he was seeking a wife, all the *ton* would be curious. Despite his past, he only needed a chance to make a fine impression to rectify it.

That he assuredly would do. He would show himself to be intelligent, amusing, proud, with enough arrogance to make him interesting. These would not be weighed with as much importance as his fortune—for parents assessing his worth—and his startling good looks to ignite the fantasies of the young women who would, no doubt, vie to catch his eye.

If Cassandra should be the one to do it, Jenny should be pleased. It was what she wanted for her, after all: a good match, a happy one.

When she was dressed, she inspected her reflection in the mirror. She looked so ordinary.

She *liked* looking ordinary. She did.

But tonight it dissatisfied her. On impulse, she removed her spectacles. Touching her hand to her hair, she wondered if she might do something more flattering. Because they had a guest for dinner, she told herself. It was not often Aunt Iris entertained.

No. She could not lie to herself. She didn't want to be invisible tonight.

What was wrong with her? Why could she not be happy for her cousin, for the gleam of delight in her eye or her frequent laughter?

She knew why. She was being selfish. Why had she decided all of a sudden—and at this *most* inopportune time—that she had some strange, disturbing desire for a man to notice her? She had never felt this way before.

Looking again at her image, she felt a weak, sinking sensation in her chest. Selfish . . . and foolish. She replaced her spectacles. What a silly thing, to entertain the slightest idea of interest in a man like the earl. He would never look at a girl like her.

Her feelings were confirmed at dinner. Cassandra was dazzling. She had dressed in a pale peach gown that that made her complexion glow. But perhaps it was the earl's presence that did this. She chattered prettily, laughed, cast her eyes down in such a bemusing way, Jenny was certain no man could resist.

She found his eyes resting on her several times during the course of the meal. His expression was inscrutable. She imagined there was reproach there. Surely, he disapproved of her.

He asked once if she were well, since she was suddenly so quiet. She murmured an excuse and spooned butterscotch pudding into her mouth. It was her favorite dessert, but it might have been gruel for all she tasted it tonight.

As they at last rose to adjourn to the parlor, Cassandra stepped up to Hatherleigh and slipped her hand into the crook of his arm. Jenny felt a stab of pain. It was what she'd feared. Her cousin was enamored of the earl.

What a stupid girl she was to allow it to bother her like this.

"You must excuse me," she said. "I think I will retire. I find myself suddenly very fatigued."

She could only have imagined that the earl seemed disappointed. He bowed and murmured a farewell, adding, "I hope I shall see you on the morrow."

"Tomorrow?"

Cassandra smiled. "The earl shall accompany us tomorrow shopping, Mama just said. Did you not hear her, silly? You will see him then, Jenny."

He was only being polite. He surely was anxious to see Cassandra, not her. "I have other plans," Jenny said quickly.

She could barely stand civilly as the earl studied her, then inclined his head. "I look forward to the next time, then. Good night."

"Good night, Jenny, dear," Cassandra called back happily as they parted ways in the hallway. Cassandra cocked her head to the side so as to best angle a coquettish look up to the earl. "She is sneaking away to read, I'll wager. Oh, well, it is best she runs along to her books. She is such a sweet little mouse, but odd. She prefers solitude to polite company. I will never understand it."

Her laughter tinkled prettily in the air.

The comment left Jenny stinging. Would the earl think her socially backward and odd, as everyone else seemed to? She cringed, thinking he definitely would.

That made her unaccountably sad, a strange reaction, since she was getting what she always wanted: to fade into the background. Yet . . .

Just this once, she would have liked to shine.

Chapter Two

The following day, while Cassandra and Iris were strolling the fashionable shops of London with the handsome Earl of Hatherleigh, Jenny sat by a low fire in the small library, reading. It was her favorite spot, and her favorite pastime. With the curtains drawn against the gloom and the soft spatter of a downpour that had begun a few moments ago, it was cozy. She should have been contented in the quiet house.

She had been completely absorbed by Miss Jane Austin's *Northanger Abbey* since she'd brought it home a few days ago, rushing through the pages to find out what happened next before she caught herself and forced a slower pace so that she could savor every luscious word. Yet today, her mind wandered, and she could not concentrate on the story.

She was doing her best not to think about Cassandra's

giddiness before the earl arrived, about how lovely she looked in her blue dress with her hair caught in a shining cascade of ringlets, or how enchanted the earl must have been when he saw her. Would it dawn on him that he had to look no further than this daughter of a distant cousin if he wished to marry a fine lady of breeding?

Cassandra would charm him, and Jenny told herself vehemently that she hoped she was successful. Was she not always dedicated to Cassandra getting what she wanted?

She sighed, putting her mind to her book again to escape the wayward direction of her thoughts. Cassandra's parting words of last night came back to her.

A mouse, she'd called her. Jenny cringed. It was true that she often preferred her books to the company of others, something her relatives never understood. It was because she always felt she had to play a role with Aunt Iris; the helper, the dutiful ward, always pleasant and aware of her gratitude for a home. But in books, she was free to dream of other lives, other adventures. And romance was so pure, so obviously right (even if the heroine did not know it at first, the reader certainly did).

Jenny would have never admitted it to anyone, but regardless of the liabilities of her age and the unflattering comparison to the beauty of her cousin—which she had encouraged, so she was partly to blame!—she hoped to eventually have a suitor or two. She desired marriage, after all. A life of her own, no longer the poor relation—and children. She very much wanted children.

When she picked up the book again, her mind supplied an image of the kind, patient Henry. It was the earl's face, his smile, and Susan, poor timid creature, took on the aspect of a girl with honey hair and spectacles to hide behind.

She slammed the book shut. This was no good.

"In here, my lord," said Brent, opening the door.

Jenny started. Lord Hatherleigh was entering the room. And he was as surprised to see her as she was him.

"Miss Alt," he said, smiling as if he were pleased to see her.

Her heart fluttered at that smile. She saw that he appeared wet from the rain.

"I was told there was a nice warm fire in here," he said.

"Oh," she uttered, rising to her feet. "Come and sit. I'll have another log put on."

"I can do it." He walked to the fireplace and took a split log out of the pewter pail, placing it on the blaze and stoking it to life. He stayed there, hunched, staring into the fire for a moment.

"Do you have a chill? Would you like a blanket?"

"No. I will be fine." He rose and went to an armchair. "The ladies are changing. You were wise not to go with us. The skies opened up and sent us fleeing home. Here we are, drenched and miserable, and there you are, tidy and peaceful in your chair by the fire."

He leaned forward and peeked at her book. "Miss Austen?"

She covered the book. Some people disapproved of novels, especially ones written by women. She was sure he would make fun of her.

Noticing the gesture, he leaned back and regarded her gravely. "Is it true you prefer the company of books to people?"

"No!" she said, surprised at her own vehemence.

"But I seem to have put you out again. No doubt you were enjoying your solitude. I seem to be intruding upon you all the time, Miss Alt."

He was flustering her. "Not at all. I was just leaving anyway."

She made to rise, but he held out a hand. It was not

delicate, but it was slender, with long, tapered fingers. She did not know why the sight of that hand so near, almost touching her, twisted a faintly pleasant feeling in her stomach.

"Are you running away again?"

"Running away?" She choked on the words. They were far too accurate. "What an extraordinary thing to say. Of course I was not running away." She cautioned herself to stop her heated denials; they sounded as thin as they were. "I was simply going to leave you to relax, here by the fire, to dry off. I am certain you do not wish to be disturbed. Then again, my aunt and Cassandra will be returning soon."

He rose and doffed his coat, spreading it out so that the heat from the fire would dry it. "But I do not wish to be left alone, to the fire, as you say. And your presence does not disturb me in the least."

Having no other choice, Jenny settled back in her chair, putting the book on the table beside her and adjusting her spectacles. "Very well. Well, then." There was an awkward silence. "Did you have a pleasant day on the Town?"

"Quite. We strolled Bond Street, took a turn in the park. I felt rather like a spectacle, I confess. Everyone was very curious. Your aunt had us parading around without the slightest notice of the attention she was garnering, or at least pretending not to. She did an excellent job of it, I must say." He chuckled. "I do believe she came to enjoy herself after a while."

Jenny imagined her aunt had warmed to her task if she had felt the curiosity pointed at them was more envious than gossip-minded. That was a good indication.

"Too bad the rain put you out," she observed.

"Ah, but this is England, and we are used to it, are we not?"

"Yes. The weather is unpredictable." She wanted to groan at such an inane comment. The weather! Her hands were restless. She grasped them together to keep them still.

He had the most intent way of looking at her, as if he were trying to see what lay below the surface. Jenny told herself that this was just her fancy. What could he find to fascinate him about her ordinary appearance? Still, the sensation persisted.

"In the country, it comes swiftly when I am out on the moors or deep in the woods, waylaying me in mud and soggy clothing." He spread his hands out. "So this is nothing new."

"You are very fond of your country home," she observed.

"It is the life for me. It is a much slower pace, with a good deal of solitude and neighbors far enough away to make the occasional get-together an event to anticipate, but not a nuisance with too much frequency. No one to judge you, you see. There is a greater degree of freedom."

"Ah," she observed, "you are a solitary person."

He paused, his eyes glowing that strange shade of green. "At times. I do have friends, however, and I enjoy them very much."

"The demimonde," Jenny said, then regretted her indiscretion.

He only smiled wryly. "Are you a snob, Miss Alt?"

"No, of course not, I simply meant that . . ." *Oh dear.*

"I admit I have enjoyed the company of some who might be considered . . . unconventional. But they are very diverting. Interesting, even fascinating."

Jenny realized this was probably true. One of the chief reasons she was considered such an outsider to the most elite circles was because she found them boring.

"But no one fit to marry," he clarified.

"That is why you are here, after all. To bring a companion home."

"A companion?" His face darkened, the lightness in his
eyes extinguished in a blink. "I am here to find a *wife*. Appalling, isn't it, what a man is reduced to?" His face turned
a bit sour, and he lapsed into silence, his fingers going to a
small rip in the leather arm of his chair. "You hit the mark,
Miss Alt, comparing my present duty to purchasing a horse
at Tattersall's."

Once before, he had offered a glimpse of his reticence.
She longed to ask him about it but did not dare.

She remembered what Aunt Iris had said about his
wife. A disastrous marriage. What had made it so? Did he
love her very much? Is that why this was so difficult, because he missed her?

The thought tugged at her sympathy. "You do not have
to be humiliated," she rushed. "I mean, men of your class
of course seek to make a marriage in the *ton*."

He gave her a strange look. "Yes. There is a reason for
that. A woman of the right breeding knows more what to
expect. I am hoping it is safer." He sighed. "Such morose
conversation. I am to blame. Or perhaps it is the weather. It
has gotten the worst of me, perhaps. Rain in the country is
refreshing. One knows the fields and gardens are being
nourished. Here it only makes for muddy streets and slick
cobbles and puddles to soak one's shoes."

She fell silent, chastising herself for her boldness. Aunt
Iris was always cautioning her about being too forward. It
simply was not in her nature to mince words.

She reflected on his mood. He certainly had been affected by her bringing up the topic of his marriage.

"You are suddenly quiet," he observed. "Last evening,
at dinner, you did not have much to say. Today you de-

clined to accompany us. I find myself wondering, Miss Alt, if you have some dislike of me."

The comment startled her out of her thoughts. "Dislike? Indeed, not. I do not know you at all, my Lord Hatherleigh."

He stretched out his long legs toward the fire. "I thought I made it clear that I prefer my name, my actual name, not my title, to formalities. My name is Miles."

Jenny looked away. "But that would be improper, my lord."

"Why? Are we not related?"

"Only through marriage, and even that is a far connection. I am afraid our relation is not a close enough for convention, as you must already know."

"But we are just the two of us here right now. Surely no one will know."

It was an outrageous thing to say, invoking a feeling of intimacy. The two of them, the cozy fire, the flames reflected in his eyes like tiny imps dancing with mirth.

Yes, he was teasing her, and suddenly she realized what a mistake she had made. She shouldn't be alone with any man, of course, but *him* . . .

"I fear I should not entertain your vanity," she said.

"Do not be afraid, Miss Alt," he cooed with a mocking smile.

"I am afraid, indeed, my lord, of impertinent earls who mistake cruelty for high hilarity."

He was taken aback, unable to speak for a moment before he said, "You think me cruel?"

"You are making sport of me."

"Only because you refuse to say what it is you have against me. You have avoided my company, and I am curious as to why. Have I done something to offend?"

"Besides sweeping into our lives like some great god

from Olympus? But I suppose that is your habit and cannot be helped."

"My goodness, Miss Alt, you are an absolute terror! Those are indeed harsh words. And you have just confirmed what I suspected. I *have* imposed on you. And yet it was you who only yesterday assured me that it was all well. 'All's well that ends well,' you said, and so charmingly that I was forced to believe you."

"You must suspect that my aunt had concerns initially. My cousin is making her debut this year, and your coming is a complication, yes. However, whatever concerns were raised seem to have been put to rest. Thus . . . all's well and such."

"Yes. Cassandra has proven delightful company. I believe she is not sorry for my presence, so it is just as you say."

The sharp stab of jealousy was a physical thing, causing her to inhale sharply. So, he found Cassandra appealing.

That was good. It would make Cassandra so happy.

"But not with you," he persisted. "You still have some concerns?"

"It is just that Aunt Iris . . ." What was she to say? Her aunt's nervous nature had been soothed once the earl arrived. The house was now filled with excitement. Aunt Iris was happy, busy with her new duties, and Cassandra was floating about on a cloud.

"Ah. You are the champion of your fluttering aunt, then?"

"Aunt Iris," she said with a glare, "is not a 'fluttering' anything. She is the sweetest, most wonderful, well-meaning person I've ever met."

He considered her for a moment. "I've affronted your loyalty to your aunt. And you don't hesitate the least to let me know it. I am impressed by your temerity. And you are not impressed by me at all. You are indeed a fascinating study."

"If that is a compliment, I thank you," she said with an air of indifference, but she felt heat flare in her cheeks.

"Why, I get the distinct impression that you do not approve of me."

"It is not up to me to approve of you, my lord."

"I find myself wondering if I should be insulted."

"I think it would be quite impossible to insult you," she observed.

"That is not true. I do have feelings, though you seem to think otherwise. And I am not impervious to others' sensibilities. Though I do admit it was rather high-handed of me to impose myself on your aunt's good nature, she is not worse for it."

"You did not know it would end that way."

"True. I had hoped it would not be an imposition, but I had to take that chance. I am in need, Miss Alt, of something from others, and a man like myself does not like to find himself in that state. I much prefer to fend for myself, and perhaps since I cannot do so in this circumstance, I might have been . . . presumptuous?" He lifted his brows appealingly, as if applying for her pardon.

She wished she could remain stern, but he was charming when he wanted to be. "You would naturally not have a liking for being forced to do what you do not wish."

"Naturally. I am proud to a fault, I've been told."

She chewed her inner cheek, giving him a long, thoughtful look. Even now, his presence did something to her, without any reason or cause. What if he saw, sensed something? Surely a worldly man such as he might guess that he was having a stimulating effect on her.

He spoke with a hint of scold in his tone. "And that is

why I will not apologize, even if you are—as you obviously are—annoyed with me."

"The inability to admit wrong is, as my father used to tell me, a malady of those who have been overindulged."

His jaw grew tighter. She had finally broken his affability. "Folk wisdom. How charming."

"When you are used to getting what you want," she continued, "you don't really care about other people's feelings. I think that is a very unfortunate way to be."

"I see I was correct. You *do* disapprove of me. No doubt you happen to have some handy advice for me. To help me to mend my ways, so to speak."

"Indeed," she said with a toss of her head, "I think you are making sport of me again."

"You make it too enjoyable. Your mind is fascinating, and your wit is quick. I don't think I've ever met anyone quite like you."

"You have turned the tables on me, Lord Hatherleigh. We were discussing you, not me."

"Were we? But I would rather discuss you."

"I would not. There is much I would know of you." She was feeling reckless—was it even a wildness?—she had never before experienced. "I wish to return to the subject of why you find being an earl so disagreeable. You say that is why you prefer to be called by your Christian name."

"All right, I shall tell you. Very simply, I have never found anything of use in it. The one thing I've loved above all else in my life is my freedom. To go where I please, to do what I wish. And I am of a miserable bent to see it cut short for the sake of a duty that gives me no pleasure."

"But you say yourself that your house, your country life, the lands, and the happy existence you have there brings you enjoyment. Surely this is all to do with your being an earl. Would you rather be a shopkeeper?"

His expression told her he was amazed at her boldness.

Why could she not seem to hold her tongue with him? He affected her as no one else did, and she hardly knew herself.

It was thrilling, in a way. Terrifying as well. But still thrilling.

"I have never entertained the possibility. Perhaps I would. A bookshop, for you are fond of books, and therefore you would be a frequent visitor."

"You are not serious."

"No. I am feeling a bit sorry for myself. The rights and privileges of my class are not lost on me. But there are also obligations that cost a price that sometimes feels quite steep."

"You do not wish to be married."

"Oh, Miss Alt, I most emphatically do not."

She spoke carefully, giving each word great thought. "Do not think me unmoved, my lord—"

She hesitated, seeing his look of displeasure at her address of him, then inclined her head. "Miles, then."

"Ah, you do me honor. Then we are friends?"

"If you wish."

"You were saying . . . please go on."

"I do not wish to appear unsympathetic, but no one's life is ideal. We are all of us bound by our duty, though those duties be different. Each of us is confined by our station in life in many different ways."

She thought he was going to shoot back a quick rejoinder, but he paused, peering at her with interest.

"But some of us are better at accepting being confined, Miss Alt," he replied gently. "I am afraid I find it intolerable."

"I am sorry," she said sincerely.

He made a sound, shaking his head. "Oh, Miss Alt, now you show me your kindness. What am I to say to that?"

She blushed, feeling disconcerted.

He leaned forward. "I almost wonder if you yourself do not know something of being trapped. You seem to understand very easily."

He looked at her intently, as if he were searching.

She could not help but pity him. And, yes, she did know something of finding oneself trapped in a life that felt like a role one played for the benefit of others. And duty. Yes, she understood about that, too.

She drew in a quick breath, resisting the pull of such sympathetic thoughts. She had to watch herself. She was vulnerable to him.

"Tell me," he continued in that same persuasive tone. "If you could have the life you dream, what would it be?"

"That is an extraordinary question."

His triumphant look held a challenge she could not refuse. He stayed silent, and she thought about it. "I suppose," she began, wondering if he would be horrified, "that I would like to be a Member of Parliament."

"You joke! And sit in chambers through all those boring speeches?"

"I would not find them boring."

The laugh that escaped him was explosive. "Bravo! It would be a fit pastime for you, for you do love to debate. And *that*, Miss Alt, in case you were wondering, is a most sincere compliment."

"It is good of you, Lord Hatherleigh," she murmured. She felt the hot flush of pleasure.

He grinned. "Indeed it is. You have put me to a most harrowing test."

"You are teasing me again."

"But not meanly."

Cassandra entered, and Jenny noted the brightness of

her eyes as she took in the scene. "What is this? I did not know you were in here, Jenny."

The earl came to his feet. "Miss Alt was keeping me in stimulating company."

Forcing a smile, Cassandra looked at her cousin. "Really? Thank you, Jenny. You missed a wonderful day today." She took the seat close to the earl, and he resumed his. "Did we not have a wonderful time, Miles?"

Cassandra was having no discomfort with the earl's Christian name.

"I was telling Miss Alt that it was quite enjoyable. Until the rain, that is."

"Yes, how dreadful. It spoiled our plan. We were to have tea at a hotel, Jenny. I was positively giddy anticipating everyone's reaction when they saw me walk in with the mysterious Earl of Hatherleigh! But we shall do it some other time, shan't we, Miles?"

"I do hope so." He turned to Jenny. "And I hope we can *all* enjoy such a spectacular outing. Perhaps we can plan it on a day when Miss Alt does not have other plans."

Cassandra's eyes flashed with displeasure. She was not used to having to share any man's attentions.

"Oh, but Jenny is usually so busy," Cassandra said. Her smile, for the sake of the earl, was tight. Her eyes glittered and seemed to give Jenny a warning when they flashed her way.

Jenny felt a rush of panic. Somehow, Cassandra knew.

Chapter Three

Miles arrived at the Benedict house as scheduled, his sense of anticipation keen. He was to accompany the women to church today.

The irony of his being excited to attend Sunday services made him grimace as he rapped on the door. He had not attended them in a very long time, but Iris had determined it was advantageous to do so. He had agreed readily, and not because Iris had proven herself amazingly skilled—and after her first fluster, immensely enthusiastic—in getting his reputation established, but because Miss Jenny Alt was certain to be accompanying them.

She had declined every outing with him so far. But she could not do so today. It was *church,* and she would, as any well-bred girl does on Sunday morning, be accompanying her family.

He was looking forward to seeing her. It annoyed him

sometimes, amused him at others, to remember her pert mannerisms. She had a mobile mouth that expressed her every mood and a tiny upturned nose that flared when she was irritated with him. He had not taken much note of her at first, but the more time he spent in her company, the more alluring she had appeared, until he had concluded her quite pretty in a way that intrigued him.

Cassandra was the beauty, and, yes, he was aware of her interest. She was not terribly subtle about it. It would be rather convenient, he thought, if he chose to make her his bride. She was certainly willing, and well-bred. The family connection was no problem.

But he could not seem to get Jenny out of his brain. It vexed him, because he was not in London to seek emotional entanglements. He'd gone that route, and it had not turned out well.

Cassandra rushed to him as soon as he was shown inside. "Oh, Miles, you are early! I suppose you are eager."

She tapped him on the forearm. He smiled at her. She was a lovely little bit, with perhaps too much energy for him. He'd not yet reached a conclusion on how she would fare in the country. It was not suited to everyone. That had been Marianne's downfall. She'd grown bored. Then she'd grown wild.

"Of course," he said, with a small bow that delighted her. Then he looked for Jenny.

She was not here, and he felt his spirits plummet.

"Miles, dear, do you care for some toast?" Iris said, pointing to a tray upon which lay breakfast items. "On Sundays, we are most informal."

"Mama likes to hurry and get to church early," Cassandra confided with a giggle. "She is afraid of the Reverend Morley."

Iris scowled and checked the mantel clock.

Miles declined the offer of food but poured himself a cup of hot coffee from the tall, silver pot. He paid no attention to it until he took his first sip. Not coffee, but chocolate. He choked down the swallow and placed the cup aside.

Jenny came into the room with a murmured apology for her lateness, and Miles felt a surge of satisfaction. He had been afraid she would somehow escape.

Escape? What an odd thought. Escape what? Him?

She did seem determined to avoid him. It made him crazy trying to imagine why, and even crazier trying to imagine why it mattered so much to him.

Today, she was different; he noticed that immediately. Her hair was not so severe, with a few loose pieces curled around her temples. The new style flattered her.

"Jenny, hurry and have your breakfast," Iris called. She looked at the clock again.

Sending the briefest of hellos his way, she went to the tray. Miles watched her, saw how the blush crept across her cheeks. That tender sign of embarrassment did something to Miles, that tight pulling sensation tightened inside him again.

"Oh, Jenny," Cassandra said, noticing her cousin, "your hair is a mess."

Immediately, Jenny put a hand to the coif. She was nervous, Miles saw. "Nonsense," he said before he could stop himself. "It looks charming."

Jenny ducked her head and poured a cup of chocolate.

"I must warn you, Miles," Iris said, "that Reverend Morley is very exacting. I wish you to be prepared for him and not to take offense if he seems . . . er . . ."

"A prig," Cassandra supplied, then trilled a laugh again. "You must not allow him to bully you."

"I doubt that shall prove problematic," Miles replied dryly.

"Strict," Iris said firmly, with a glare at her daughter. "Miles, dear, remember what we talked about. Parents with eligible daughters will be present. It would put them off if Reverend Morley were not approving."

"We wouldn't wish Reverend Morley not to approve," he replied. He risked a glance at Jenny. She was sipping her chocolate. "I do so detest it when I am met with disapproval."

She ducked her head again. So, she was determined not to confront him. This he found too annoying. He did not appreciate being ignored.

Not by her.

She'd been much in his thoughts. He'd thought about their conversations, how her eyes flashed and her mouth moved when she fought a smile. He had wondered what her scent was like. Every woman had a scent. Would Miss Alt smell of soap and simple rose water, a reflection of her prim exterior, or something spicy to hint at her lively spirit?

He spoke pointedly to her. "Miss Alt, you do not seem overly concerned with promptness. Do you not care for the Reverend Morley's approval?"

Jenny grasped her cup. "The reverend has a right to expect his congregation to be in their pews when services start."

"And yet you were tardy today. Did you not sleep well last night?"

Her back went ramrod straight. "I slept soundly," she replied, not meeting his eye.

"Ah, the sleep of the just. How I envy you."

Just as he'd hoped, she could not resist. "Is your sleep plagued, my lord?"

Cassandra's cold voice cut her off. "Really, Jenny. The earl's sleeping habits are a monstrous crass topic for conversation." She stepped between Jenny and Hatherleigh, cutting off his view. "Miles, pay no attention to her. I told you how ridiculous she was with these forward ideas. It is the folly that comes from reading so much."

"But it was I, Cassandra, who brought up the topic. Surely you are not chastising me?"

She blinked and gave a little laugh. "Oh, no, Miles."

"I like a plainspoken woman, in fact." He managed to don a falsely penitent look. "Although this preference is a recent discovery. I must confess to a perverse enjoyment when being taken to task. It is rather . . . invigorating, I find."

Jenny's hand trembled. He watched her clatter her cup on the saucer. The sound seemed to startle her, and the cup began to tip. She tried to right it and only succeeded in doing worse. It toppled, spilling chocolate down the front of her bodice.

Iris cried out in alarm. "Oh dear, are you all right?"

"I am fine," Jenny stammered. "Thank goodness it wasn't hot. Oh, dear, now we surely shall be late."

"Today of all days." Iris cast a worried look at Hatherleigh. "This will make a terrible first impression. The Reverend Morley abhors tardiness. Do you recall what he did to Amelia Cosgrove last spring, pointing her out to everyone as she took her seat late? I swear, the poor woman's complexion was as red as a ripe cherry for a week."

Brent came to the door. "Madam, the carriage is in front."

"Oh, dear," Iris cried, wringing her hands.

"I shall hurry and change," Jenny assured her and started for the door.

"We shall never make it to our pew before Reverend Morley's procession!" Iris looked apoplectic.

Miles acted quickly. "I suggest then that you and Cassandra go on ahead, and I will bring Jenny right behind, using my carriage. I am certain we can have her put to rights and be under way without too much delay. Have your man send word to have my carriage brought around."

"No!" Cassandra cried, then gathered herself together and spoke more reasonably. "That is quite unnecessary. Jenny will make haste—go on, Jenny. We should all arrive together. Mother, tell him that is a terrible idea."

Jenny didn't move—she did not take orders from Cassandra, Miles was proud to see—and Iris hesitated. "I think we should go, Cassandra. I could make some excuse . . . well, the truth will suffice, and perhaps Reverend Morley will understand if I forewarn him." She waved to her daughter. "Come, hurry, so that we can arrive while he is still out greeting everyone."

"I'll stay as well, then," Cassandra declared. "You go on, Mother. I will be along with Jenny and Miles."

"Do not be ridiculous, Cassandra," Hatherleigh said flatly. "Do you not think it unseemly for your mother to go into church alone and have the whole of her family lagging behind? We will be but a moment."

Cassandra was clearly frustrated. Miles supposed he should be flattered, but an idea occurred to him that made him suspicious of the young girl. Was it her possessiveness that had caused Jenny to keep her distance?

Iris spoke in a firm voice. "I think it best, Cassandra. Please come along."

Leveling a narrow look at her cousin, Cassandra snapped, "Jenny, why do you have to be such a bother? Oh, all right. Try to hurry, will you?" She flounced and followed her mother out of the house.

Jenny looked to Miles, bewildered for a moment. He suppressed the urge to rub his hands together, for he was quite pleased.

He said, "I would like to avoid being dogged by the infamous reverend. Could you make haste?"

As she hurried away, he called after her, "Come directly out to the carrigeway when you are finished. I will be waiting at the door."

It did not take her long to change. She emerged less than a quarter of an hour later in a fresh dress, her hat in her hand.

"Excellent, Miss Alt. Your speed is appreciated." Kicking the fold-out step into place, Miles held out his hand to her. He saw that she hesitated, her eyes wary behind her lenses. He waited, hiking one brow. "We must be under way," he reminded her.

She took his hand with a shrug and allowed him to hand her into the carriage, where she pretended to fuss with her dress while he reclined in the seat across from her. He rapped upon the wall behind him, a signal for the driver to go.

She pushed up her glasses nervously. "I thank you for waiting for me. I am not normally late, not as a rule. But . . . What are you looking at?"

He raised a finger and pointed at her, waving it generally in the region of her head. "You might wish to don your hat."

Quickly, she jammed the hat on her head. As she was about to place in the pin, he shook his head. "Oh, dear. It looks like a sparrow collided with your head."

Adjusting the angle, she asked, "Is this better?"

Leaning forward, he studied her critically. "Not that I'm an expert on these things," he said, and grabbed one side, giving it a neck-jarring yank. "That should do."

She winced. "Well, I suppose that does it for my hair. It is no doubt squashed unmercifully."

"I hope you did not go to so much trouble on my account," he commented.

"I certainly did not."

"But your cousin commented on your appearance. It

is not your habit to take such care, I gathered. I can only assume—"

"Wrongly, I assure you. What conceit."

He smiled, not at all insulted. She *had* changed her appearance because she was to see him today, he was sure of it.

She dismissed the topic with a sniff. "We should be arriving shortly, although there is never any telling. There is sometimes a glut if everyone happens to arrive at the same time." She glanced at him. "Are you nervous?"

"I . . ." He hesitated. "I am not in the habit of attending religious services."

"Afraid you will go up in a puff of smoke?"

He swiveled his head, giving a small nod to acknowledge the quip.

"Cassandra seems to have appointed herself your great friend. She will see to it you are well received. She is quite popular, you know, and well thought of by everyone."

"Yes, indeed, she is impressively well-connected, as I have already seen in this past week. Thanks to her as well as your aunt's diligent work on my behalf, the *ton* seems to have forgotten all about my past." He spoke in a bored tone. "Or as Iris refers to it, 'The tragedy,' " he added with a snort.

"Do you mean your wife?"

"I cannot think you are ignorant of the details."

Jenny flushed. "I do not listen to gossip."

"Yes. I suppose that would be beneath you. Or perhaps you are simply not interested."

"Was it so bad?" she asked, and he was surprised to find her voice gentle, her gaze intent. She was not uninterested, then.

"It was ghastly," he said flatly. He scowled, letting out a long breath. "As most things done in haste are, it was a mistake, ill-fated from the start. I was in a rush to marry her, thus I did not think the thing through."

"Then it was a *grande passion*."

He snorted. *It was lust, plain and simple.* "It was somewhat less than that. My motives, I now see, were not quite as admirable. When the . . . feeling between us died, we found we did not suit at all. She hated the country, hated the life I led. She came to hate me. We had a strange existence in those years. It seemed our goal was to shock and maim the other's pride."

"That is wretched," she said sympathetically, as if she really was sorry.

He looked at her oddly. "I am not a martyr, Miss Alt. I made my bed, as they say, and I was prepared to lie in it. However, since she died and I still have no issue, I must take the plunge again."

"I am sure you will make a better choice."

"I intend to take great pains to do so. Marriage is a contract, an arrangement not unlike any other partnership."

She glanced out the window.

"You do not agree?"

"I am not in a position to say," she answered, "but surely you realize not all marriages result in that sort of situation you experienced."

"I hope not," he replied dryly.

She turned suddenly to face him. "You know, Cassandra has a lovely voice. Has she sung for you?"

The abrupt change of subject disconcerted him for a moment. He decided to follow her lead. "No, she has not."

"You should ask her to. When we are at dinner parties, she is often pressed to showcase her talent. It has won her many admirers, as you might have already noticed."

"I noticed she attracts male admiration."

"Well, of course she is lovely," Jenny said, smiling at him. "But it is not just her beauty that recommends her. She is very accomplished."

"And what of you, Miss Alt? You have no callers, Cassandra tells me. I find that strange, a woman like yourself finding no one to suit. Is it you are not interested in marriage?"

She glanced away. "It is not that."

"Ah."

"What does that mean—'ah?' There is nothing to 'ah' about." Her jaw worked, and he saw she was struggling to remain calm. "Cassandra is very funny. She is a delightful conversationalist. Do you not agree?"

"I do agree." He leaned forward. "But let us not forget the subject of why you have spurned men's attentions."

She swallowed, then gave him her most mutinous look. "Have you not heard, my lord, that I am a bluestocking? You have heard Cassandra say it. Men do not care for my type."

"The devil they don't. So, then, Miss Alt, you mean to tell me that you do not mind being left behind, if only just a little bit?"

It was like watching a storm gather. Her face twitched, that finely wrought nose curled at the nostrils, and her eyes, nearly hidden behind her spectacles, grew narrow.

"Not every woman is bent on capturing a man. I am quite content."

"And brave, to lead a life of independence. Tell me something, then, if you are as brave as you claim. Why do you wear those eyeglasses? Your cousin tells me you only require them in order to read. Certainly you do not rely on them to attend Sunday services."

Touching her fingers to the hinges of her glasses self-consciously, she tried to shrug off his question. "I . . . I like my spectacles."

His lips curled into a dangerous smile. "I think it is because you are hiding."

"That is a preposterous thing to say!"

"Is it? Take them off. I want to get a good look at your eyes."

She pressed back into the squabs, horrified, as if he'd suggested she disrobe. The wayward thought plunged his heart into his stomach, and he realized the idea of Jenny Alt undressed aroused him.

"My lord," she said, cutting out each word with a hard edge, "I have grown used to being dismissed, considered unimportant, and, yes, even odd. But your ridicule is not to be borne."

He felt a moment's hesitation. She seemed dangerously close to tears. If he could see her eyes . . .

He folded his arms in front of him. "Tell me, Jenny, how long have you lived with your aunt?"

"What concern is that of yours? What relevance could it possibly have—?"

"Answer my question, please."

The understated air of command annoyed her, but she couldn't see a way to refuse to tell him. "I came to live with Aunt Iris eight years ago."

"And you were how old at the time?"

She paused before admitting, "Fourteen."

"At the very cusp of womanhood. Cassandra is younger, isn't she? A few years, I think. Four or five? She's very pretty. Was she a pretty child?"

"Yes, of course. She was always very pretty."

"If I were the poor relation—please pardon the term, but I use it only to make a point—I would hardly want to tempt jealousy, not with Cassandra. As the uncontested beauty of the family, she enjoys being the center of attention. Thrives on it, needs it. Am I correct? If I were a homeless cousin, dependent on the family for a home, I might not want to appear to be too much competition, if you understand what I am saying. And you do understand, don't you?"

She stared at him, not moving a muscle. He slipped closer, trying to read what was in her face.

"Miss Alt," he said, "I think you wear your glasses to discourage your cousin's jealousy."

Her scent was light. Flowers and spice. It was clean, refreshing, doing things to the insides of him that were altogether too pleasurable.

"I . . ." She tried to speak, but nothing more came forward.

"Miss Alt," he said again. His voice was softer. He leaned in closer. "I am going to remove your spectacles."

She might have been in shock, or perhaps she wanted him to do it. In any event, she did not protest as he gently slid the eyewear from her face.

His eyes flickered, taking in every feature. He did not think he had ever looked this closely at any woman in his life. It was as if he could study that face for hours and not grow tired of its fascination.

Her eyes were blue, and innocent. She did not blink, and he did not breathe. It occurred to him that he had done something very dangerous here.

"I had guessed they were pretty." He took in a long breath and let it out softly. "Very lovely. You should not hide them."

She did so now, lowering heavily lashed lids.

He was used to women playing coy, but this was not her game. The more she retreated, the more doggedly he pursued, even while he asked himself why. He was not sure, but she was singular, unique, and he could not allow her to slip away.

On impulse, he lowered his head. He wanted to kiss her.

This time, she did not cringe. She did not hide. She remained perfectly still as he lowered his mouth.

He felt the cool brush of her breath against his lips. And just when he was anticipating the soft contact, a blaze of light slammed into the carriage. He sprang back and swung about to see the cheerful face of the driver at the door.

He had not realized they'd stopped!

"I think this will do," the coachman said cheerfully, bending down to unfold the step. "Not too far a walk, but the queue is long today. I don't think you want to wait."

As soon as the step was down, Miles bolted from the carriage. He left Jenny to the coachman. Once she had alighted, she held out her hand to him and stammered, "Please. I need my eyeglasses."

He gave them to her without a word, and she slipped them safely into place.

"Shall we go inside? I think we've managed to make it in time after all." His voice was steady, calm. So different than how he felt.

Cassandra waited for them at the door to the church, just inside the vestibule. Her beautiful milk and roses complexion was mottled with anger.

"The reverend is due to start. I told Mother I would wait a moment longer to show you to our pew. You've made it just in time."

Cassandra slipped her hand into the crook of Miles's elbow, edging Jenny out of the way.

Chapter Four

Coming down the steps of the church, Jenny paused to thank the Reverend Morley for his sermon. He basked in her praise.

She saw Cassandra with Miles and headed in the other direction. Unfortunately, she was so intent on avoiding them that she did not see who was approaching her. But the moment she heard the sound of his voice, her heart sank.

"Miss Genvieve Alt, I must say you do look particularly fine today."

Jenny paused and made herself smile. "It is good to see you as well, Mr. Darlington."

The young gentleman beamed at her. Though his age was a few years older than hers, he was gifted with boyish good looks so that he appeared younger. However, his personality was similarly immature.

"I was looking for you all day. You were late." He

grinned wolfishly as he wagged a finger at her. "You know how the reverend feels about that."

"I was late, yes. Could you excuse me?"

She stepped past him, but Darlington had never been one to take a hint. He was the one man who had refused to be discouraged by her aloofness. Jenny considered this very unfortunate. He had a tendency to drink too much at social affairs and could be loud and very embarrassing with his often unpleasant wit.

For some reason, he had singled her out for a relentless flirtation she had never done anything to encourage. And try as she might, she could not dissuade him. Short of rudeness, which she could not bring herself to employ, he did not seem to take heed of anything she said or did to make it plain that she did not return his interest.

"You know, you amaze me, Miss Alt," he said as he fell into step beside her. "You do know that, do you not?"

"Why is that, Mr. Darlington?"

"Because you do not *flirt*. All the girls flirt, but you do not. Do you know how intriguing that makes you?"

"I would think it makes me unappealing."

"What, do not tell me the rumors are true about you."

She stopped in her tracks. "What?"

He laughed, completely missing her stricken expression. "Come now, you must know what they all say about you."

"No, I do not." She was lying. She was considered strange.

"You, Miss Alt, are a challenge." He puffed out his chest. "You are more discerning, not one to lose your head just because a man makes a bow. You see, I believe I understand you. You are seeking the right man, not just *a* man."

She regarded him with shock. "And do you think you are that man, Mr. Darlington?"

"I think there is more to you than meets the eye," he

said. His voice lowered, and he leaned into her, causing her to back up. "You are not like most girls."

Having had enough of him, she turned on her heel. As she did so, she caught Miles's gaze on her.

It was not the look she was used to seeing on his face. It was dark and accusatory. He'd been watching her.

Aunt Iris motioned for her to come over. Jenny guessed she had some exciting news.

"Lord and Lady Pierpont have invited us over this afternoon!" She clapped her hands together. "I think Lady Pierpont wishes to get a closer look at Miles. This is so thrilling!"

"I am happy for you, but I think I should go home."

"Nonsense, Jenny. Come on, now, into the carriage. Miles has gone to his driver to send him home. He is coming with us."

Miserably, Jenny followed her aunt. She would just have to do a better job at avoiding Miles. Snubbing him as she had was certainly a mistake she would not repeat. It only seemed to incense him.

In the carriage, Aunt Iris was still gloating.

"That went so very well. Very well, indeed. Did you see Lord Iverton come up to us? He said he knew Miles's father—imagine he would remember him after all these years. And he spoke of him so kindly. He was very kind to Miles as well."

Jenny nodded, thinking this must please the earl. He was here for a purpose, after all—a chillingly focused and impersonal matter of marriage. A marriage he didn't want. Jenny felt sorry for the woman who was bartered to this man. For all of his strange allure, he would be cold to a wife he never wanted.

Cassandra had taken the seat across from her mother and spread out so that Jenny had no choice but to sit next to

Aunt Iris. However, when Miles entered the coach, Cassandra slid over and smiled invitingly.

He sat, easing back with a relieved sigh. Catching sight of the three pairs of expectant eyes, he jerked a corner of his mouth up. "It was better than I expected. I think it went rather well."

Iris nearly bounced in her seat. "Oh, indeed, I said the exact same, Miles. Didn't I say the same, children?"

"Oh, Mother, please hush!" Cassandra said waspishly, then freshened her smile before turning toward Miles. "What did you think of our reverend, my lord? Isn't he enough to have a saint yawning himself silly?"

"Now, Cassandra," Iris admonished, "as the reverend himself says, he is about the business of salvation, not diversion."

"He only says that because he is a frightful bore, Mother! Besides, I was inquiring after what *Miles* thought."

He answered, talking more to himself than Cassandra. "I was pleased by today's events. I saw some excellent candidates, expensively dressed. Their carriages were fine, their servants wore expensive livery. Good indications of wealth, for you see, I am determined to have a rich wife to compensate me for this odious business of marriage."

Jenny stared hard out of the window, patently ignoring the sickening pitch of her stomach.

Cassandra cleared her throat. "You should be able to find someone to your liking, someone to meet *all* of your requirements. There is much more to a wife than a dowry."

"Oh, for heaven's sake," Jenny muttered in disgust.

Miles chuckled, seeming pleased as if it had been his intention all along to rile her.

Cassandra laughed, too, as if it were all just a joke, and began to malign with gossip many of the girls who had been present at services. For once, Jenny was glad for her cousin's wagging tongue, for it saved her having to participate in the conversation.

They came to a halt in front of the Mayfair residence of Lord and Lady Pierpont. Miles kicked down the step and alighted, reaching up to hand down the ladies. Iris positioned herself at the door. Cassandra slid into the seat beside Jenny.

She pressed her face close, her eyes wide, her lips curled and trembling, and spoke in a harsh whisper. "You are only making a laughingstock of yourself throwing yourself at Miles like this."

The vehemence of her words left Jenny breathless. Cassandra pulled herself upright, smoothed the lines of her dress and straightened her bonnet, then turned and reached out of the carriage to take Miles's hand.

Jenny was shaken, feeling betrayed. She had done nothing but put her cousin's happiness ahead of her own since she'd come to live with them. With the earl, she had not done a single thing to "throw" herself at Miles, quite the opposite. It was he who seemed determined to pursue her.

A part of her rejoiced, but she knew this was not wise. If Miles's interest was real, she could not repay the kindness of her family by taking the man her cousin most wanted.

Once inside the Pierpont home, she separated herself from the rest after seeing that her best friend, Amy Collins, was also present. She flew to her side, glad to be away from the confusing maelstrom around Miles and Cassandra.

Amy was a pretty, petite redhead with expressive eyes and a wide, infectious smile. "I demand an explanation," she cried, trying to pretend she was angry. "You arrive at church with a dashing man whose appearance sets the entire congregation buzzing so loudly I couldn't hear the sermon—which is a blessing, it is true. Now, give over. Who is he?"

It was difficult to keep her tone cool as she explained about Miles. She didn't tell Amy, however, about their meeting in the library, or the strange interlude in the carriage just that morning. It was difficult to know why she held that information back.

"*He* is the awful earl who commanded your family to take him in?"

"It was not exactly like that, Amy," Jenny replied. "He is not the arrogant beast Cassandra made him out to be."

"Indeed. I thought she hated him," Amy said, pointing to the settee where the beauty sat next to Miles in a circle headed by Lady Pierpont. "She has certainly warmed to him, I can see. And who can blame her?"

They watched with amusement as their hostess poured out expertly as she conducted a subtle interrogation of the earl, all the while seeming to be making only polite conversation. The others hung on every word, while Miles answered in an offhand manner to indicate he didn't have any objection to the examination.

She felt a pang of sympathy for him, and admiration. If he had no taste for the duty he was bound to perform, he did not show it.

"You always see the best in people, but your cousin can be quite determined." Amy had the look of someone who would like to say more. Jenny was glad she didn't. She would not tolerate hearing bad about her family. "She will snare him, make no mistake. Look at the way she is leaning forward. Her bosoms are going to fall into his lap!"

Jenny forced herself to laugh. "Her charms are difficult to ignore. She will marry, whether the earl or another, and then I will be . . ."

She stopped. She'd been about to say "free."

"Then you will marry as well. I do not know why you think you will not."

"Yes, I would like to. If I find the right gentleman." Jenny sighed. "But I am already twenty-two, Amy. Not so young when it comes to making a match."

"Oh, the devil you say! There are plenty of men who like you. Even my brother said his friends often ask about you."

"Amy, you are a dear, but need I remind you I am hardly in demand. Other than last month when Dr. Phillips came when I had a touch of the ague, I haven't had a gentleman caller yet." She had meant it to be a joke, but Amy refused to smile.

"There is Darlington . . ."

"Oh, please."

"*He* likes you."

"He is full of himself and has this romantic notion that he can save me from the terrible rumors circulating about me."

"What nonsense. Oh, Jenny, I don't understand it." Amy stared wistfully into the distance. "There has to be someone for us. Someone who will like the way I smile, for instance, or notice that you have the most beautiful eyes. Someone wonderful for each of us—and smart and sweet and funny and who can make us laugh."

Jenny averted her gaze. Miles had noticed her eyes. He'd said they were *lovely*.

She couldn't have said why, but she didn't tell Amy this either.

"Why do you look so funny?" Amy asked.

Jenny made an excuse and changed the subject, determined to enjoy her afternoon with her friend. But she was aware every moment of Hatherleigh's presence behind her. She even fancied she felt his gaze, as if it were a physical touch tripping lightly along her spine. She scoffed off the notion, quite put out with herself for such flight of fancy. Really, she could usually be depended upon to be sensible and solid at all times.

But she wasn't feeling herself at all of late.

Chapter Five

Miles tried for the fifth time to tie his cravat, still doing a bad job of it. He looked at his fob watch, checking his growing irritation.

He was to fetch the women in three-quarters of an hour to escort them to a ball. He had been pleased Iris had wangled an invitation so quickly to a major event of the *ton*. It was an excellent opportunity to look over the young girls of marriageable age.

Rather like the horse auction at Tattersall's, Jenny had said. An image of Jenny, her cheeks flushed, her eyes snapping, made him smile. The impertinent chit!

The exasperating woman deserved to be throttled. He might have indulged the impulse, except he had an irritating suspicion that if he got her in his arms, it would be quite a different thing that would end up happening.

He wanted to kiss her. He almost had, and his imagination played the scene out in his mind, taunting him with irascible curiosity of what her mouth would feel like, how she would react.

It was a rather remarkable reaction to an insignificant ingenue without a ha'penny to her name. And a tart tongue to boot. He'd never been partial to snappish women, preferring the tractable, worldly types who knew just what he was about and accepted his terms. After his lustful folly with Marianne had brought about such dire consequences, he'd kept his liaisons simple and direct.

Miss Alt might amuse, but he would do best to keep far away from her tonight. He didn't really trust himself, although he wasn't sure why. The idea of a dalliance had, of course, occurred to him, but it was entirely out of the question. One simply couldn't go about despoiling innocent creatures like Miss Alt and still be welcomed in the homes of decent folk.

An affair with a young lady of the *ton* would brand him a rogue and dash all hopes of fulfilling his destiny as Earl of Hatherleigh. That was that.

But, yes, he *was* tempted, never so much than when he saw her that evening, dressed in pale silk, her color high with excitement. She seemed to infuse the room, the carriage, with her presence, setting his teeth on edge. He didn't know what it was about her that made his skin feel too tight for his body.

He focused his attentions on Cassandra. "You are breathtaking," he said to her, taking her hand. "That shade of your gown is the perfect complement to your eyes."

She beamed, exalted at the compliment. He liked that she was so responsive to his attention. What man would not be flattered? She was a beauty. He was toying with the idea of offering for her. He knew she wanted him to, and

Cassandra was lively, very attractive, and brought up in a respectable home. But something kept him from returning her interest.

"Miles, aren't you the cut," Iris said. She was resplendent in purple, glittering jets dangling from her large bosom and sprayed across her skirts. Her hair sported a large peacock feather.

"How privileged I am to be escorting such attractive women," he said. He turned to Jenny, standing with her hands folded. He did not take particular note of women's fashions, but this dress was the epitome of Jenny. The color was soft, and the feminine touches were just right.

She still wore her spectacles, he saw. Like a barrier between her and the world. Until she took them off, he would know she wished to remain hiding.

So be it, he thought with irritation. "If you ladies are ready, we should be under way."

It suited him to give Miss Alt little of his attention. He left her to the coachman and spoke only in the general conversation, never to her directly. It was better this way, he told himself.

He had business to attend to, so he could return home, wife in tow, and escape this brewing discontentment that plagued him since he had set foot in this damnable city.

When they arrived at the posh residence in Belgrave Square, they had to wait in the receiving line. Cassandra demanded all of his attention, pulling him along so as to introduce him to her friends, a tight knot of smug-looking youngsters who clamored together in an exclusionary circle and immediately fell to whispering among themselves.

He glanced back at Jenny and saw her stroll through the room, pausing to exchange pleasantries with those she knew. A few moments later, she left the ballroom.

Cassandra was giggling with her friends. Gentlemen approached, scribbled on her card and bowed, going away to await their turn.

"I best take my dance before you have none left," he said, and he wrote his name on one of the few remaining spots. Handing it back to her, he said, "It seems you will have a busy evening."

Her friends giggled and nudged her with their elbows. One of them said, "She always has a full dance card."

"I am not surprised," he replied.

Cassandra preened.

"Tell me, Miss Benedict, does Miss Alt enjoy dancing?" he inquired. "I saw her leave the ballroom a moment ago."

Cassandra's smile froze in place. Her friends looked scandalized.

"Oh, Jenny hates these affairs. She does not dance."

The giggles started again, as if this was a spectacular joke.

"I do not understand," he said.

"Miss Alt does not like things normal girls do," one of the friends said. The other hissed, "Hush!"

"What Elizabeth means," Cassandra supplied, "is that Jenny does not care to dance."

"She is a bluestocking!" the forward girl said, and this time was jostled quite sharply by her companion. "She doesn't like men."

"Elizabeth," Cassandra purred patiently, as if she was scolding her, but Miles could see she was amused, even pleased, "you mustn't repeat those dreadful rumors about Jenny."

"Well, she is. She never likes any man who shows an interest in her. If one tries to speak to her, he gets the most severe cut. Cassandra, everyone knows it. The only reason anyone is kind to her is because she is your cousin."

Cassandra seemed to grow cross, but there was no true threat to her scowl. "Just because she . . . well, she is just different, that is all. That is no reason to gossip." Turning to Miles, she explained, "Jenny is just not interested in finding a husband, you see. I already mentioned that she has other interests. She likes staying to herself. She is sweet, though, and I love her just the way she is."

Elizabeth murmured an apology, but she did not appear sorry at all. It was all a great game to these types.

Miles wondered why he felt as if he'd just witnessed a clever play. "Enjoy your evening. I will see you at the quadrille, Miss Benedict."

Moving away, he could not stop thinking about what he had heard. How was it that such talk got started?

Jenny was retiring to a fault, but every instinct in him told him that behind her facade was a warm-blooded, fascinating woman filled with love and affection. Could no other man see what was so obvious to him?

Spying Jenny just then, he watched her as she sat with a friend, oblivious to him. She was relaxed, laughing freely and talking rapidly.

He smiled, watching her. There was something inside him that reacted to the sight of her. It was strong, compelling.

He should find Iris, for it was she who would arrange the introductions he sought. It was, after all, the principal reason why he was here. Or it had been when he'd started this whole affair.

When he began to move, however, it was not to seek out his cousin.

Jenny was seated with Amy, sipping punch, when she saw Miles approaching.

"Oh, my . . ." Amy said in a low voice, raising her cup to her lips to hide her smile.

Miles executed a crisp bow. "Miss Alt, are you having a fine time?"

"Indeed, Lord Hatherleigh, I am passing the evening most pleasurably with my friend."

Miles greeted Amy, who appeared as if she were about to swoon.

Turning back to Jenny, he said. "I would like to request the honor of a dance. Might I write my name upon your card?"

She smiled. "But, my lord, I do not have a card. I—"

He produced a blank dance card and held it up for her to see. "How lucky, then, that I have one here." He flipped it over and examined it. "You appear to be available. Would you care to dance now? They are just starting up a promenade I know particularly well."

Her protest was cut off by Amy's exclamation. "Oh, Jenny, do!"

People were watching, making it impossible to refuse without seeming gauche. Jenny knew when she'd been beaten. Rising, she replied, "I would enjoy a promenade, my lord."

He smiled, barely suppressing a look of triumph, and crooked an arm. "Strange. I was told you did not enjoy dancing. Among other things."

"What other things?"

"I am constrained by my honor from repeating them. But I am anxious to prove all the naysayers wrong."

They took their position. "Should you not be spending your time looking over the young ladies?" she asked him. "You are in Town on a matter of marriage."

"Yes, but as you know, it is not a task that holds much

enjoyment for me, so I thought that I would have a little fun before the work of the evening began."

"Fun?" She was surprised.

"With you, Miss Alt. Dancing with you is the most diverting way I can think of to pass the time."

She fell silent, thinking about this. Did he truly like her company so much?

The dance began, and she moved her feet while her mind wrestled with this incredible fact. He *did* seem to always be seeking her out, and as he was neither a fool nor a cad, she could only consider that he was telling the truth.

"You dance quite well," he commented, coming to take her hand. They proceeded down the floor with the other couples. "By the fact that you do not care for the activity, I thought you would be plodding about."

"Really!" she admonished, unable to keep herself from a chuckle. "Do you think me clumsy, then? I do not know why you would entertain such a thought."

"Neither would I. I have yet to find an area where you do not distinguish yourself, Miss Alt."

She blushed. His compliment seemed sincere.

Why was he not with Cassandra? She had imagined he would be dancing in attendance to her all night, ensuring that no other man would take the advantage with her affections.

But he didn't seem at all mindful of her cousin, and she so *liked* dancing with him. People were staring, both at the novelty of the new face, for it was the earl's first appearance at a major assembly, and they might also be shocked to see her on the dance floor. She liked them noticing her. Perhaps even envying her. Instead of the pitying looks she was used to seeing, she saw interest, and smiles that were sly and encouraging.

After the dance, he led her into the refreshment room. She thought he would leave her then, but he did not.

She kept expecting him to announce that it was time to be about the evening's work, but he lingered among the potted palms, where they sipped their punch and talked for a long time. His conversation was clever, and they laughed easily.

She had the card where he had written his name. He reached out and looked at it. No one else had approached her to put their name down.

"I marvel that the men in London are so stupid," he said.

She looked down at his neat printing. It made her happy to see his name there. "It is known I do not dance. It is I, not them, who are to blame. I always decline requests for dances."

"Good heavens, why?"

"I did not have time for such things. It was Cassandra's successful launch into society that was the priority," she said, but the excuse sounded weak. She bowed her head, ashamed to look at him.

"You do not really believe that."

"Perhaps it was an excuse." She met his gaze. "Who would look at me, anyway, when there was Cassandra?"

His gaze was warm, and he smiled, as if to find this a silly question. She considered that it might have sounded as if she were fishing for compliments, and she blushed profusely.

"Miss Alt," he began, then stopped. The beginning strains of a song began to play, and he started. "I believe I have to be going. I lost track of time. We will speak later."

"Thank you for the dance," she said. She held up the cut glass. "And the punch."

He touched her face, brushing his fingertips along her

chin. It was a shocking thing to do out in the open, where who knew who could be watching.

Remembering himself, he dropped his hand. "Thank *you,* Miss Alt, for the dance."

He took his leave with a bow. Bemused by the entire episode, Jenny stood a moment until her sensibilities began to creep back upon her. Without Miles by her side, she felt alone and exposed; certain people were stealing glances at her with speculation in their eyes.

There would be talk, no doubt, about the fact that Miss Jenny Alt's first dance in months had been on the arm of the newly arrived Earl of Hatherleigh. Countless jeers would be tossed over that bit of gossip. No doubt it would be branded a kindness on the earl's part, done out of pity.

She threaded through the crush, seeking the comfort of her friends, and found them at last gathered around a pianoforte in the music room. Amy saw her enter and motioned her over excitedly. Standing beside Amy was Lord James Errol, and he seemed to be smiling a great deal, his eyes watching Amy closely.

It pleased her that Amy might have found a beau. She was attractive and sweet-natured, but did not thrust herself forward as most of the other girls did.

Almost immediately after her arrival, Lord Errol excused himself. Jenny glanced uncomfortably at his retreating back. "I hope I didn't intrude, Amy."

"He knows I wish to speak to you alone. He has just told me something very disturbing that he heard this evening. It concerns you."

Jenny was taken aback. "Me?"

"You see, he has heard terrible things about you being against marriage, that you were a . . . a . . . Oh, Jenny, I hate to say this, but he said he'd heard you had sworn never to marry. What is more, you would cut down any man who dared approach you."

Jenny placed a hand over her thudding heart, taking a long, agonizing moment to assimilate this. "What? But . . . my goodness, I did not realize I had given so bad an impression."

Had this been what Darlington had alluded to the other day after church? She realized it must have been.

"No, don't you dare think that. It is obvious someone has been spreading lies."

"What do you mean?"

"Cassandra, of course."

"Cassandra? Why would she bother to malign me?" Jenny replied. "I've never vied for any attentions with her. Quite the opposite. Oh, here comes Lord Errol! I can't face him, or anyone right now. Please, make my excuses. I'm going to the retiring room."

"I'll come with you," Amy said.

"No, please. I don't want you to. I need to be alone. Stay with Lord Errol, Amy, I think he likes you. I just need to think."

As she began to rush away, a large figure blocked her path. She started, her nerves raw from what she had just heard, and saw it was Lord Darlington standing in front of her.

In his hand, he held a champagne glass, but by the ruddy color in his cheeks and the brightness of his eyes, it was not his first libation of the evening.

"Please, excuse me," she murmured. She was in no mood to handle his clumsy flirtations.

"Did you enjoy your dance?" He spoke bitterly.

That brought her up short.

His lips curled in a gesture that was more sneer than

smile. "I thought you did not dance. At least you never danced with me."

"I think you are not yourself," she said carefully. "Please let me pass."

"Of course, Miss Alt, of course. I would not wish to delay you. It would be such an imposition to prolong our conversation, keep you from other, more interesting matters."

"Lord Darlington, please do not take offense. I . . . I have something on my mind."

"Something? Or someone?" Spite was thick in his voice. "You smell so nice, Miss Alt."

"Please, you are making a scene. Step away."

"Yes, we can't have that, now can we?" He shrugged, but his mouth remained twisted in discontent. "Oh, no, not a scene! Not the proper and oh so very aloof Miss Alt, who spares her precious time for no man." His face changed then, crumpled from anger into grief. "But you have smiles and adoration in your eye for Lord Hatherleigh when you danced with *him*. Why him? Dare I guess he is your lover?"

"You insult me!" Jenny shot back sharply. Her heart was hammering wildly, and she feared she was going to weep. The night had been a rush of mad emotions, from the exhilaration of Miles's attentions to the crush of hearing that her reputation was being blackened by rumor. This was the last straw. "Now remove yourself, or I will call for help."

He stepped away, sullen now, and watched her pass with a glare in his eyes that held a chilling promise.

Chapter Six

Miles was in the middle of a sentence when he saw Jenny rushing through the throng of guests. He watched her take a short hallway to the rear of the house. Pausing outside a door, she glanced around rather furtively and disappeared inside the room.

With a muttered excuse to his companions, he set off after her, not questioning the urge that put him in motion.

He located the door she had used and listened for a moment before opening it. It was a private, informal withdrawing room used for casual company and family evenings, dark and empty this night with only one lamp lit and no fire in the grate. The air was noticeably cooler in here. Jenny stood in the middle of the room. When she heard him click the door shut, she turned.

"What do you want?" she demanded in a voice quite unlike her.

His eyes moved, taking in the shadows. There was no one else here. He had experienced a piercing jealousy at the thought that she might be meeting someone.

Seeing she was alone, his mood eased. "Don't you know girls lose their good reputations when they skulk off to dark rooms?"

She let out a small cry and turned her back to him. To his amazement, she buried her face in her hands and appeared . . . Good God. She appeared to be weeping!

For an uncertain moment, he considered retreat. He detested female hysterics. Marianne had used them like emotional blackmail, and in their early days together, it had been effective in getting him to do whatever she wished. He'd grown immune quickly enough, even disdainful whenever a woman was moved to tears. But he couldn't summon the appropriate amount of distaste for Jenny's distress.

Taking out his handkerchief, he approached her and held it out, keeping his distance. "What did I say?" he asked gruffly.

"M-m-my . . . you said . . . my reputation!"

He pulled her hands away from her face and shoved the handkerchief at her. "I can't hear a word you are saying. What is this about your reputation?"

She raised a mutinous look to him. "I thought you couldn't hear me."

"I could hear you. I can hear you better now, however." She wasn't using the handkerchief, so he took it from her and dabbed the corners of her eyes. "Now tell me what is the matter."

She looked at him with heart-stopping misery. "I thought it was because I was plain. I n-never really wanted to frighten any of them away. It was Cassandra's season, not mine. You see that, don't you?"

None of this made any sense to him, but he said, "Of course."

"How could she be jealous of me? What am I to do now? My aunt and my cousin are the only family I have."

He still wasn't sure what had happened, but he could guess. The words, the look of her, the broken, stammering voice brought on a surge of protective fury. He didn't like it, but he couldn't seem to turn it away.

There was inside him the most undeniable instinct to wrap her in his arms. It was a dangerous idea. However, even as he thought sensible, ordered thoughts about the folly of such a thing, he gave in to it and pulled her close.

She leaned against him, taking his strength, without so much as peep of resistance.

"Hush," he said. He could think of nothing else. It seemed inadequate, and yet it stilled her. He held her like that until she fell quiet. It seemed the right thing to do.

He stroked her hair and murmured, "Don't you see how you outshine her?"

She shook her head, a childlike gesture that made him smile. He was acutely aware that she was not a child.

His thickening blood was clouding his reason. It was dangerous to hold her this way, but he could no more let her go than cut off a limb.

Reaching down, he gently pulled her chin up so he could see her face. Her eyes swam in moist pools of pale blue behind her eyeglasses. Her pert nose was red on the tip, and her mouth was parted slightly.

"These spectacles are no good," he said, and he pinched the middle piece resting on her nose and drew them off. "You remain blind despite them."

There she was. So incredibly lovely, like a flower. Pretty and honest and untainted. She blinked back at him, those gorgeous pools of blue as wide and as deep as any ocean. A man could drown in them. A man could crave it.

Before he could stop himself, he kissed her. It was to be a gentle, quick kiss before he sent her away, a selfish indulgence that had no place in his comforting her but one he could not resist. But he was so hungry for her, and once he tasted her, he couldn't stop.

Tilting her head back, he opened her mouth to him and stroked her tongue with his. He felt her respond, heard her small moan of helplessness, and his gut twisted like a cinched rope. His mind went blank, and heat crawled over his skin.

The madness of wanting took over, and he realized the power of the feelings he had tried unsuccessfully to keep in check. He wanted her with such fierceness that his body shook under the strain. The savage thought warred with protective instincts he had never known he possessed.

Dragging his mouth from hers, he shoved her from him with strength he was surprised he still possessed. "That is quite enough."

Her lips were swollen and red from their kiss, and she appeared dazed. God, he felt like that, too. His body thrummed with life, and he had to step back quickly before his last sensibility, weakening under the desire to hold her again, gave way altogether.

Jenny stared at up at him. Confused, she could only wonder why he looked so hard, even angry. The gentleness of moments ago was gone. She touched her fingers to her throbbing lips. They felt scalding hot.

"I apologize," he said. His tone was crisp. It wounded her after his gentleness. "That was completely uncalled for. I . . . forgot myself."

"You do not think I am cold," she blurted. "You kissed me."

"I kissed you because it is what I have wanted to do since the first day I saw you."

Joy exploded in her breast, eclipsing the confused jumble of emotions that had driven her to seek solitude in this room.

She reached out her hand to him, and his closed over it. It felt large, warm, protective, and powerful. Drawing in a shaking breath, she lifted her gaze.

"Does that frighten you?" he inquired softly.

"Yes," she admitted. "But I am glad, too."

He smiled, then seemed to remember himself. Releasing her hand, he grabbed the hem of his jacket and yanked the smooth fabric into place. "We shall be missed," he said, "if we are gone too long. Let us go before there is trouble."

"Yes." She placed her hand to check her hair.

"Let me go first and see if the way is clear." He slipped out the door, then stepped back in and motioned her to follow.

As they exited, he perused the crowd, apparently satisfied that they had been successful in reentering the party undetected. "Go on. I will not risk damaging your reputation further. Go now. I will speak to you later."

Jenny immediately headed into the card room, where she knew Aunt Iris was sure to be. On her way, she came across Cassandra draped on the arm of one of her suitors.

"Have you seen Miles?" she asked, a hint of accusation in her tone.

"No," Jenny said. It was the first time she had ever lied to her cousin, and she did so without a blink of an eye, to her surprise.

"I wished to dance with him again. I am quite put out with him." She strained to find him in the crowd. "He has been very busy tonight. I saw him out on the dance floor with Missy Hartley and Lady Veronica Swinton. I hope he is not considering either one of them for a wife."

It was meant to be a jest, but the tension in her voice pounded the words flat.

Jenny took her hand to comfort her. "I very much doubt it. Have a good time, Cassandra, and do not worry about that."

"Oh, I will make certain that he makes it up to me," she said with a toss of her head, and she and her partner drifted off.

But during the carriage ride home, Cassandra was not so sublime. "Mama, he only danced with me *once!*"

"But you said he apologized, dear," Aunt Iris noted. "He said he looked for you but could not find you."

"He must not have looked very hard," she said sulkily.

Jenny braced herself, seeing there was a storm brewing. Cassandra was crushed by Miles's indifferent attention.

"Do you think he might have found someone else to amuse him?"

The carriage hit a rut, jostling them all soundly.

"Cassandra, dear, please . . ." Aunt Iris pressed her fingertips to her forehead, her tone conveying her deep dread of Cassandra making a scene.

"He paid me no special attention," Cassandra declared. "None at all!"

She flung herself back into the squabs, her miserable expression sending Aunt Iris into a bout of nervous fluttering. Jenny, who hated to see her aunt like this, vaulted into action.

"Nonsense, Cassandra. He signed your card right off, didn't you tell me so yourself? No doubt he was disappointed to miss a second dance with you, but he does have obligations."

The words were automatic, soothing words that were not exactly lies but rosy suppositions to encourage her cousin away from hysterics. She knew how to assuage the rising temper, but this time, it was difficult to pretend.

"You are making this far worse than it is," she said, soothing the girl, but Cassandra shook her head, refusing to believe it.

As soon as they were home, she told Aunt Iris to go on to bed and that she would see to Cassandra. She ushered her upstairs, leaving strict instructions with a maid to bring fresh water, and when she'd gotten Cassandra undressed, she sat next to her with cool cloths for her face.

"You mustn't get overexcited," she said. She sounded like herself, calm, reasonable, but she wasn't feeling at all normal. She'd always thought of Cassandra first. Tonight she was thinking of herself, how she longed to be alone and reflect upon the fantastic things that had happened tonight.

Cassandra stubbornly refused to be consoled until Jenny said, "What if the earl calls tomorrow? Would you wish him to see you with your eyes all swollen and reddened from sobbing all night long?"

With this enticement, Cassandra managed to get hold of herself. She sniffed, giving Jenny the pathetic look that had always been effective in getting her way. "I cannot help it. I love him, Jenny. I do. I am mad for him. I cannot bear it if he found another."

Jenny froze. The words were like a slap. She hadn't thought it was so serious.

No. It could not be true. Cassandra flirted. She was dramatic and prone to exaggeration. She was like a child with a toy when a new man interested her—she was thrilled for a while, then forgot all about it when a shiny new trinket presented itself. With suitors, she liked the attention, and each new face was a conquest that once won, faded quickly.

She absolutely could not be in love with Miles. Because, Jenny just now realized, *she* was in love with him herself.

Sitting back, she thought about this. The idea was stunning and frightening. What could be a worse disaster than she and her cousin wanting the same man?

"You are very sweet to me," Cassandra said, her hysteria subsiding. "I am sorry I was cruel to you. I was jealous. Silly, isn't it? I do not know what I was thinking, only that I was nearly insane with frustration when he spoke to anyone else."

"This is too much, Cassandra. It is not natural to be so obsessed."

"I know, I know." She looked like a child, her eyes wide and penitent, and Jenny felt a rush of affection. Cassandra was so impulsive that she never saw the predictable consequences.

"You must not treat him like the bucks who trip over themselves for the tiniest favor of your smile. You cannot expect the same puppylike devotion. The earl is a much different sort."

"Yes, you are right, of course. But, Jenny, I am desperate to have some word from him of his feelings. He compliments me and squires me around, yet he speaks no word of his heart. Sometimes I think he is merely being polite, and I couldn't bear that, Jenny."

She began to sob again, then remembered about her swollen face on the morrow and quickly sobered. "I will die if he does not return my feeling. I swear, I cannot bear it if he chooses someone else. I will fling myself from London Bridge."

"Hush now," Jenny hissed, truly angry. "Just talking of that sort of thing will give your mother apoplexy."

"I will. I cannot bear it."

"Do not worry now. It is only one ball. Silly girl, you are getting yourself all in a state over nothing. You will see, he will be here tomorrow, and you will be ashamed of yourself for carrying on so when it is probably nothing."

A combination of firmness and comfort worked best, Jenny had found, but she could not help feeling a cruel person indeed to talk with false encouragement of Miles when she had kissed him tonight.

A harsh shiver rippled over her flesh, remembering the feel of his mouth, his long body rock hard up against hers.

She would never in her life forget that kiss. It had done something to her, woken up some part of her, peeled back her skin to expose tender, pulsing feelings that she never suspected she'd possess.

Why did this have to be the man Cassandra wanted—or *thought* she wanted?

What had she done?

All of her earlier happiness faded. She closed her eyes and drew in one long, shaking breath. She had been wrong to allow the earl's attentions.

It had to end, even if it broke her heart.

Chapter Seven

"Have you gotten your dance card?" Miles asked Jenny at the soiree they were both attending the following week. "I would like first choice."

"I am not dancing tonight."

"At all, or just with me?" he inquired sardonically.

"I do not dance." She tried unsuccessfully to make her voice cold. It only came out choked, sounding unnatural.

"You do, and quite well. Now, what is this? Is it because I kissed you? It is, isn't it?" He practically crowed.

Jenny looked around nervously. Cassandra was not to be seen, for which she was relieved. She was thankful that her cousin had gone off with her friends, as she usually did, but she would come searching out Miles within a short time.

She was determined to end this pointless flirtation now before it created any more problems.

"No. It is not that you . . . that we . . . Oh!" Jenny sighed. "I cannot believe you would bring such a thing up while we are out in public."

Tonight's occasion was a small affair in one of Mayfair's large town houses. The crowd was smaller, and most of the people Jenny knew well. The drawing room had been cleared for dancing. Three musicians played softly, for the night was not yet under way in force, and it was only meant for background music until the festivities began.

"But the only time you allow me to see you *is* in public. I called several times this past week, and you were gainfully occupied otherwise. Or so I was told."

"You . . . we have to stop this."

"What?" he demanded, a mischievous grin on his face.

"You are paying much too much attention to me. It is going to get noticed, and that would be a disaster."

The smile disappeared. His face pursed thoughtfully. "Why?"

"It's simply best if we . . . if this friendship is forgotten."

Nodding sagely, he asked, "Best for whom?"

Jenny glanced down at her hands twisting on her lap. "You know who."

His look was cold. "Come with me."

Taking hold of her arm, he led her through the French doors, which had been left open to admit a cooling breeze.

Outside, the chill in the air raised gooseflesh along Jenny's arms. The flagstone terrace was deserted. The shapes of wrought iron and stone, dark shadows in the twilight, were their only companions.

Miles pulled her gently so that she faced him. "My God, Jenny, when are you going to show some spine? You only think of your aunt and your cousin, what they want. What is it *you* want? To be sure, gratitude is a virtue, but would you really lay aside your entire life, all of your dreams, your own aspirations, for your cousin's pleasure?"

"You do not understand. I am not making some grand sacrifice for her infatuation." She lowered her voice to a whisper. "She is in love with you."

He sighed, and there was sympathy in his eyes. "She fancies herself in love with a new man each month, from Iris's accounting."

"It is different."

"Because I have frustrated her. She loves me, does she? What does she know of me? She is a bright girl, and lovely. She is amusing, I admit, and imbued with a sense of fun that is hard to resist. That is why she attracts so many admirers. But she is also hot-tempered and demanding. I have seen her exhibit behavior that is shockingly self-centered. And, yes, I considered the convenience of taking her as bride when I arrived in London. But in the end, I realized she was too much like my first wife. She is young, merely a girl, and I do not want another girl for a wife, Jenny."

He placed his hands on her shoulders. "I want a woman, a companion, a partner in a pleasant life together, a slow life with simple pursuits and satisfaction as our reward rather than short-lived thrills. Do you think your cousin would enjoy such a life?"

Jenny was confused. His words painted a picture that squeezed her heart. Cassandra would despise such an existence, it was true, but she . . . she thought it was the sweetest, loveliest life she could imagine.

She shook her head, dispelling these thoughts. "You should speak with her."

He agreed. "She must understand I have no intentions toward her. I never did contemplate her as my choice, not seriously. We would never suit."

"Yes, do tell her right away." Jenny was immensely relieved. Cassandra would be furious, and the strain in the next few days would be nearly unbearable, but it was the quickest way to clear Miles out of her blood and get her back to her old self.

"Tell me what right away?" a voice asked, and Jenny whirled to see Cassandra standing in the doorway. She wore a smile, a tight, trembling smile that hinted more of hysteria than pleasantness.

Jenny was acutely aware of the picture they presented. Miles had nearly been holding her, and they were outside, in the darkness, alone.

"Excuse me," Jenny said, and went swiftly into the house. She hoped Miles would take this opportunity to speak to Cassandra. They had to get this painful business behind them, and soon, before things got worse.

Lord Darlington approached her, seeming wary and penitent. "May I offer my apology, Miss Alt, for my behavior at our last meeting. It was inexcusable, but I only can plead my emotions got the better of my sense."

"Thank you, Lord Darlington," she replied coolly. "I accept your apology."

His expression altered, and she could see he was filled with relief. "Then you have made my night. You are most gracious."

Jenny peered impatiently to the open doors. Cassandra or Miles had not yet appeared.

Darlington looked in the direction of her stare. "You are very lovely tonight, Miss Alt. That shade of blue is most becoming."

"Thank you. Would you excuse me?" She moved away from him, not registering the flash of frustration that hardened his boyish features.

He rushed to say, "Miss Alt, if you are dancing this evening, I would be most honored if you would consider me as a partner for one." He tried to smile. "Or two?"

"Thank you," Jenny said. She escaped the uncomfortable situation, giving him no more thought. Her mind was filled with what was happening outside.

When her cousin and the earl appeared a short time later, and Jenny knew immediately that Miles had indeed taken the opportunity to speak frankly to Cassandra. She looked devastated.

It did not take long for Miles to find his way to her side. "I must speak with you," he said.

"Not here."

A country dance was announced, and several couples assembled themselves in the center of the room.

"Dance with me."

"We cannot talk on the dance floor," she protested, but she allowed herself to be pulled along with him.

"I know that, of course." He shot her a smile over his shoulder that knocked the breath from her. "I simply wish to dance with you."

She felt a surge of joy, followed by the sinking feeling of guilt. It would be wrong to flaunt dancing with Miles when her cousin was watching.

"I cannot, Miles," she whispered, planting her feet on the edge of the dance floor and refusing to take another step. What made it all the more difficult was Miles's visible disappointment.

He glanced about to make certain there was no one close to them who might overhear before leaning in to say in a low voice, "Cassandra understood completely. We parted on good terms, Jenny. Now, I wish to dance with you."

"No." Jenny shook her head. She spoke barely above a

whisper. "You do not understand. I saw her face. She was only pretending so as not to embarrass herself."

"You underestimate her. She even agreed to a dance later on. I think I am quite forgiven. And you have overestimated this entire affair."

Jenny wished she could believe him. She had no doubt her cousin had put a great face on her grief, but she resigned herself to another ride home rife with hysterics, and God knew what else.

"Look, see, she is already talking and flirting, as good as new," Miles prompted, nodding his head in the direction of her cousin, who was indeed bestowing one of her "looks" on a group of gentlemen.

Jenny relaxed. It was tempting to think that perhaps she had made too much of the matter. She laughed softly. "I fear I am too used to taking her moods seriously because they always upset Aunt Iris so. Sometimes I forget how transient they are."

"Then, will you?" He cocked an arm, and she slipped her hand in his. Pausing, she glanced at Cassandra.

She was conversing quite intently with a young man. Jenny could not see who it was because his back was to her, but she could see her cousin's face quite clearly. It was animated.

Relief flooded over her. Cassandra was already working her charms on other prospective suitors.

"You are being silly," Miles coaxed.

She allowed him to lead her onto the dance floor. She sighed heavily to rid herself of the built-up tension.

"You know, it has recently occurred to me that I am neglecting my duties," he mentioned, his eyes focused over her head, as if he were distracted. "I have made no progress whatsoever in finding a wife."

They began to move. She said, "Have you not seen anyone you like?"

His mouth jerked as his eyes continued to scrutinize the
people around them. "Oh, yes. Indeed I have."

Jenny ducked her head to hide her reaction. Dare she
hope she might be the one whom he had singled out, or was
he trying to tell her gently, much as he had just done with
Cassandra, that it was not she?

"And are your feelings returned?" she asked with feigned
casualness.

"I do not know." He gave a little shrug. "She is a very difficult woman to read. I am at quite a loss, I must confess."

Her heart was beating. She was afraid to get her hopes
up for fear of desperate disappointment. Was he or was he
not referring to her?

She couldn't be difficult to read—surely he could see
her growing feeling for him in her expression. *She* felt as if
she'd been as transparent as glass.

The dance took them apart. Jenny felt as if she were
floating, her head swirling with doubts and hopes. She noticed when the gentleman to whom Cassandra was speaking turned around. It was Darlington, she saw, and for a
moment the two of them stared at Jenny. She felt a chill,
but it passed, and she was again proceeding through mea-
sured steps opposite Miles.

"What do you think of my dilemma?" he inquired, chin
up and facing forward as they proceeded at a stately pace
through the double line of dancers.

"You should attempt to find out as quickly as possible, I
suppose."

"I intend to do just that." He looked at her then, and a
soft smile appeared on his face, just for an instant, but long
enough for Jenny's heart to leap. *It is me,* she thought sud-

denly. Then her breath caught as his expression froze, and a cold look replaced the smile.

Before she could guess what had caused this change, Jenny felt a hand on her shoulder. She turned to see Darlington in front of her.

In his hand he held a glass of wine. His face was flushed, and his eyes blazed at her.

So many things happened at once. Miles stepped forward, saying, "Sir, you are interrupting our dance," in a cool, dangerous voice that drew a glittering glare from Darlington.

Then Jenny saw Cassandra, her expression cruel and excited as she watched. Others turned, and the dancers, who could not very well perform their steps with Miles and Darlington facing off in the middle of the floor, all stopped, and eventually the music trailed off as well.

"So sorry," Darlington murmured, and threw back the remains of his wine. "And you were enjoying yourself so well. Well, Miss Alt seemed to be liking it, too. I suppose that goes to show she is not a man-hater after all."

He wobbled a bit, turning a grin toward Jenny. "You had us all fooled, I must admit. Why, no one could touch you. You were like *ice*." He protracted a hiss on the last word, slurring it.

"Excuse us," Miles said, grabbing Jenny's hand and starting away.

"There's something wrong with her, you know," Darlington called loudly, drowning out the murmurs that had started up. "She doesn't like men. She's just toying with you because she's jealous of Miss Benedict and she wants to get her back."

Jenny whirled, suddenly infused with rage. She saw Cassandra's visible mortification as Darlington turned to her and lifted his empty glass toward her, as if in salute.

"Aren't you, darling?" Darlington purred as he turned back to Jenny.

Taking a hard step forward, Jenny quite forgot herself until she felt the firm hold of Miles's grip on her wrist. She realized only when Miles had stopped her that she was going to slap the supercilious face mocking her.

Miles acted quickly. He shouldered her out of the way, pushing her behind him in a protective stance. "I have a good mind to call you out."

"Why? How have I insulted her honor?" He leveled a finger at Miles. With a lightning-quick movement, Miles knocked it away.

There were gasps in the crowd. All were silent, everyone watching closely.

Darlington was taken aback. "I don't know why you are put out with me. Everyone knows about Miss Alt." Holding up his hands, he turned to the gawking crowd. "We have all seen with our own eyes Miss Alt's most perverted attitude toward the male sex. She is unnatural, one of those who demonstrates contempt for the institution of marriage and has forsworn a normal life."

Jenny heard someone say, "Oh, my goodness!" and recognized Aunt Iris's voice.

"You—leave us alone!" Jenny exclaimed, panicking for the first time. She felt exposed, and imagined a wave of revulsion in the eyes of those surrounding her.

But Miles spoke then, and his voice was smooth, controlled, giving her a sense of his protection. "You have got it completely wrong, Darlington. You are drunk, and you are rude. Moreover, you are under the mistaken impression that merely because Miss Alt does not care for your attentions, she is unnatural. I can assure you there is nothing amiss with the young lady, and I quite applaud her taste in companions."

Miles took a step forward, his tone lowering to a dangerous pitch. "You are fortunate I do not call you out. So turn around this moment and be about your business before I rethink my generosity."

Darlington scoffed. "Who are you to demand satisfaction on her behalf?"

"We are friends. And we have an understanding." Miles turned to Jenny, and his look portrayed his hope that she would not contradict him.

Jenny saw the situation spinning rapidly out of control but was helpless to stop it. She felt the scalding rush of humiliation.

"What exactly is this *understanding* you claim to have, I ask!" crowed Darlington with a sneer.

"Very simply," Miles retorted smoothly, "marriage."

Chapter Eight

That evening at the Benedict house, Cassandra barely waited until they were inside the door when she confronted Jenny. "How could you do this to me?"

Still unable to believe the chain of events herself, Jenny said in a bemused voice, "I?"

"How could he marry a mouse like you? You are a no-body!"

"Cassandra!" Aunt Iris exclaimed, horrified. "How can you be so hateful?"

Cassandra was already half-gone in hysterics. "She knew I wanted Miles, Mama. She deliberately stole him from me." With her hands balled into fists, she swung back to Jenny. "You waited this whole season to find a way to make me pay for all the men wanting me and not you."

Jenny's head cleared, and suddenly she was filled with rage. "No one wanted me because you told them I was a snob and set against marriage. A man-hater! And it was you who wound Darlington up like a clock and set him loose. I only suppose you hoped to cause so much embarrassment that Miles would avoid associating with me, or perhaps you weren't even thinking that clearly. Perhaps it was just plain spite."

Cassandra's mouth opened to protest, but Jenny cut her off.

"I *saw* you commiserating with him, Cassandra, and I saw the look on your face when he accosted me. You orchestrated that entire scene tonight."

Aunt Iris covered her face. "Oh, Cassandra. What have you done?"

For a moment, Cassandra's expression showed her guilt, then covered it. "How like you to blame someone else. Miles is only marrying out of duty, you know. He doesn't want you." Her face collapsed. "He would eventually have seen I was the best choice. He'll grow to despise you once he realizes what you've done. Just like Marianne. It will be just the same, and you two will be miserable forever!"

She whirled and disappeared through the door.

Jenny was left with the echo of her cousin's last words dying in her ears.

She would be a fool to allow anything Cassandra said in this state to upset her, but there was no avoiding the truth.

Miles *was* marrying her out of pity. The scene Cassandra had engineered had given him no choice but to protect her.

Miles had made one disastrous marriage already.

Miles arrived at the Benedict house, handing the footman his gloves and hat. He was shown into the salon, and as he stood there, awaiting Jenny, he found he was nervous.

Jenny entered shortly after he, dressed in a demure day gown of a dove gray material embroidered with pale ivory filigree. She looked very pretty, even if a bit serious.

"Thank you for coming, Miles," she said. She held her hands clasped together nervously in front of her. "I wished to speak to you about this insane idea of marriage." The laugh she forced sounded like she'd caught sand in her throat.

"Insane idea?"

"I know why you did it, of course, and I appreciate so much that gallant gesture."

His eyebrows hiked. "Do you?"

"But it is impossible, of course. You see that."

"Jenny, what is it you are trying to tell me?"

"I . . . I don't want to marry you." She stopped short, shook her head a little as if to clear it, and drew in a shaking breath. "What I mean is," she amended, "I don't want you to marry me."

"Are those not the same thing?"

She spread her arms wide. "I don't want you to do something you will regret for the rest of your life. So, I'm setting you free."

He tilted his head back and smiled. To Jenny, he seemed relieved. "Ah. I see. Well, that is very good of you."

"Aren't you relieved?" she inquired, puzzled at his nonchalance.

"Immensely." He moved, peeling off his gloves as he took a seat.

Miles felt his body relax as he realized what all of this nonsense had been about. If he hadn't exactly planned to propose marriage a week ago, he wasn't gnashing his teeth over his impetuosity. In fact, he was quite looking forward to it. The idea of claiming her as his stirred something primitive and satisfying.

Maybe he'd intended to have her all along. He hadn't foreseen that, or anything like it, happening when he'd first come to London. But he had to admit he'd certainly had no interest in anyone else, not seriously and not even fleetingly.

He had been so determined that this time, his wife would be a logical choice, a deliberate selection made on consideration of factors having to do with breeding and all manner of things he had no faith in, he'd failed to see what was, in retrospect, ridiculously obvious. He'd wanted Jenny all along.

"I thought a country setting might be best for the ceremony," he said, his voice casual. He pointedly ignored her amazement. "My home is in Sussex, and I believe that will do nicely. It might be best to have the wedding away from the city, in the event talk would linger."

"But, I—"

"Or do you prefer that Reverend Morley perform the ceremony? We can certainly face down the gossips if you are inclined."

"No. I don't like him." She shook her head, bemused. "I don't wish to be married here in London."

"Ah, good. I didn't take to that stuffy church of his myself. Well, then, as soon as we can make the arrangements, we shall set off for Sussex."

"Miles!" She held up her hand.

His lips twitched as he fought a smile. She blinked at him, her eyes wide, and tiny creases of confusion lined her brow. She was absolutely stunning, just like this.

How blind he'd been. He'd never stopped to examine the way Jenny had come to dominate his thoughts, how her favor or disfavor governed his mood, and how enslaved his sense of contentment had become entwined with whether she was happy with him. He'd blundered into passion, never stopping to think.

And damn it if he wasn't a fool for the second time in his life. Desiring a woman past reason was *not* in his plan, but if that was so . . .

Why wasn't he unhappy about the sudden turn of events? For he most assuredly was not.

And he was not going to allow her to get away.

"I don't know why you are doing this," she said.

"How could you not?" He said this as if it were a ridiculous notion. "Poor girl. I am afraid you have quite misunderstood the way of things. Now, do you wish to have a wedding breakfast instead of an afternoon banquet?"

"Stop planning this . . . this . . . absurd . . . thing."

"The correct term is a wedding," he supplied with a grin.

"I am not even certain how it all came about." She sighed. "Miles, why did you tell everyone we were engaged?"

"It seemed logical."

She looked so vulnerable as she turned away. He sighed. Did she really know so little?

Didn't the blasted woman know when a man was in love with her?

She said, "You cannot *want* this."

He stood, going to her and taking her hand in his. "If you wish for me to tell you what I want, then I will happily do so. But you must first take off your spectacles. I am going to kiss you again. And hurry. I am not in a mood to wait."

She looked dismayed. He pulled her up tightly against him and slid her eyeglasses off, holding them while he pressed his lips quickly against hers. He forced himself to make their contact light, merely a touch, for he did not trust himself further than that.

Sighing softly, her eyelids fluttered open, her moist lips parted as if inviting him to indulge more. After a dazed moment, she curved them slightly in a sultry smile that was nearly his undoing, and she said, "Then you do hold me in some affection?"

He frowned, but did not release her. "I seem to be unable to stop kissing you. I would say that indicates a fair amount of affection."

"And you *do* wish to marry me?"

"I find myself quite unaccountably taken by the idea."

"And the fact that I am not an heiress? Or anyone important?"

He felt a wave of embarrassment. "Did I appear so mercenary?"

"You were quite clear that you were in the marriage market to see your duty done. And I recall your having said something about wanting a rich wife to make the trouble worthwhile."

He grimaced. "Not one of my finer moments." A mischievous impulse made him add, "There are other considerations that more than make up for your lack of a fortune. You are a sensible girl, quite bright, which I find I like. I believe we shall suit. And do not think I have not noticed," he added wickedly, "that you are still in possession of all of your teeth."

She laughed. She really was beautiful when she laughed. "Oh," he added, pressing his cheek against her temple, "I neglected to tell you the most important reason of all. I have fallen completely in love with you."

She looked at him, and he had to laugh at her. "You are adorable when you are disconcerted," he informed her. "Does it please you to know you've brought down a man committed to logic and reason, to see him throw all of that away for the passion of the heart?"

"Oh, Miles. I love you, too. I was so afraid . . ."

"Afraid of what?"

"That it could not be. Because of Cassandra. I still worry—"

But he was going to have none of that. "She will recover, and quickly if my mark of her is correct. I hardly think it is the catastrophe you seem to think. It is better she be miserable now for a few days than get what she wanted and be miserable for the rest of her life. I could never make her contented, Jenny, but with you . . . with you, I feel I see a whole new future. Does that sound as droll as I think it does?"

"No. It sounds wonderful."

"And you, do you wish to marry me? After all, you never really accepted me."

"You never really asked," she reminded him with a hint of coquettishness that warmed his blood.

"Then I shall do so, and properly."

On bended knee, he requested the honor of her hand in marriage, and with tears in her eyes, Jenny accepted.

"There," he said, rising to embrace her again. "It is done just as it should be. Now there are no regrets, no questions. Jenny. Why are you still frowning?"

"It is just . . . Aunt Iris . . ."

"She can handle her own daughter. Where did you get the idea that you were indispensable?"

"I never considered myself indispensable," she retorted. But she realized she had been under the impression, perhaps quite false, that Aunt Iris could not survive without her. "Perhaps I did," she admitted. "I think it was my vanity. I was so indebted to Aunt Iris for all she gave me when my parents died that I wanted to give something back. I only wished to help, to show her how much I appreciated her taking me so generously into her home. . . . Oh, Miles, do you really think this will all turn out right? I do not want to hurt anyone."

"Well, Miss Alt, it will hurt me greatly if you do not consent to marriage. The rest will sort itself out, I promise you."

She smiled, and it filled him with a clean wash of pride and happiness.

"Now, one last question," he inquired, releasing her. "French champagne or Italian?"

Epilogue

Jenny balked when she saw the family cathedral, a monstrosity of deeply cut paneling and jewel-toned glass windows depicting some of the more gruesome moments in various saints' lives. Miles changed the arrangements to a smaller church with a cozy feeling, delighting Jenny with his thoughtfulness.

On the morning of the ceremony, she wore a gown of pale blue silk. It was cut smartly in the latest style, with short puff sleeves and a high waist. The skirt fell in soft folds, swishing prettily as she walked. Her new maid—Miles had insisted—piled Jenny's hair in a mass of curls, then wove in a strand of pearls that Miles had presented to her as an engagement gift. As for her spectacles, she changed her mind twenty times, but when the moment came to enter the church, she slipped them off and faced the future without them, determined not to hide any longer.

As she walked up the aisle, she passed faces that smiled at her, most of them belonging to strangers. Miles's obligations to his title had led to a huge guest list. The only people who belonged to her were her family, Amy Collins, and her new fiancé Lord Erroll.

Aunt Iris beamed with happiness even as she dabbed at her eyes. Jenny smiled back at her and felt a catch in her throat.

Beside her, Cassandra smiled weakly. For once, she was subdued, for she had received a hearty comeuppance for the mischief she'd made. Then again, the presence of the man on her other side might have something to do with her mollification. Lord George Pinkney might be a portly fellow of advanced years, but he was not unattractive. He was also wealthy, and he was besotted with Cassandra. And Cassandra was besotted with his being besotted with her. Jenny had no idea if this would be the last and final of her cousin's suitors, but she was happy that she had, if grudgingly, accepted Miles's decision.

She had no ill will toward Cassandra. She had been spoiled, but some of the blame had to go to those who did the spoiling, namely herself. She truly hoped that whomever Cassandra chose for her husband, she would mature in the relationship to find affection and contentment in her marriage. Stranger things had happened. Look at her, for example, a simple "mouse" marrying an earl.

The "intimate wedding breakfast" consisted of all one hundred fifty guests dining for hours on elegant cuisine. A subdued orchestra played softly. And the champagne was French.

That was how she became a countess. Later, in the quiet of the huge bedchamber that was the traditional bastion of the master and mistress of Kinwood House, she became a wife.

"I love you," Miles told her when the door had been closed and bolted and they stood alone in the bedchamber.

Jenny glided into his arms. "I love you," she murmured, turning her face up to be kissed.

His fingers brushed the back of her neck, toying with the neckline of her peignoir.

"I want to make you happy," she said. "I want to make you a good wife."

"I am quite certain that I could not have made a better choice for that," he assured her. "Do you like the house?"

"It is wonderful."

"I want you to love it as much as I do. Country life is much different from the city. I hope you will find it to your liking."

She laid a finger against his lips. "Miles," she whispered, "I am happy. I am the happiest I could ever imagine being. I love it here, and this is my home. I feel it so profoundly."

"Good," he said fervently. He laid his forehead against hers. "That is what I so desperately wanted."

She peered shyly up at him. "Is that all you wanted, for me to like it here?"

His grin deepened, and a delicious shiver passed through her. "I want to make you happy. I want . . . things I did not ever think to imagine would be mine. Ours—ours, Jenny. It makes all the difference, having you by my side. It is an entirely new world."

"For me, too." She slipped her hands around his neck. "We will discover this new world together." She tilted her head and worried her bottom lip with her teeth. "How do you suggest we begin?"

His gaze dipped to the wide gap in her bodice, and his smile disappeared. Dragging his gaze up to meet hers, he smiled again. "One should always begin with a kiss."